ALL THE WAY WITH _____
AN ALTERNATE HISTORY OF 1964

F.C. Schaefer

©2017

Also by F.C. Schaefer

Beating Plowshares into Swords:
An Alternate History of the Vietnam War

Caden is Coming

Big Crimson

Reach me on twitter at @fcsnva

Table of Contents

ALL THE WAY WITH JFK:
AN ALTERNATE HISTORY OF 1964

THE PLAYERS

Ralph Abernathy: clergyman and civil rights activist; close friend of Dr. Martin Luther King.

General Creighton Abrams: commander of the V Corps of the United States Army.

Juan Almaida: commander of the Cuban armed forces; third most powerful man in Castro's government.

Joseph Alsop: syndicated newspaper columnist.

Dean Andrews: practicing attorney in Dallas Texas.

General Alexander Andreyev: commander of all Soviet forces on the island of Cuba.

Manuel Artime: veteran of the Bay of Pigs and leader in the anti-Castro movement.

John Ashbrook: Republican Congressman from Ohio and leader of the Draft Goldwater movement.

Bobby Baker: disgraced former Secretary to the Senate Majority Leader and associate of Lyndon Johnson.

Guy Bannister: former Federal Bureau of Investigation (FBI) agent and private detective; active in anti-Castro groups in New Orleans, Louisiana.

Bentley Braden: Washington lobbyist for the textile industry.

Dorothy Jean Brennan: former Miss Idaho and press representative for the Goldwater campaign.

Leonid Brezhnev: Secretary of the Central Committee of the Communist Party; second most powerful man in the Soviet Union.

Edmund G. "Pat" Brown: Democratic Governor of California.

McGeorge Bundy: National Security Advisor to President John F. Kennedy

Dean Burch: member of Senator Goldwater's staff.

Fidel Castro: leader of the Cuban Revolution of 1959, then Communist dictator of the country.

Raul Castro: brother of Cuban Communist dictator, second most powerful man in the Cuban government.

Murray Chotiner: close aide and long time associate of former Vice President Richard Nixon.

John Compton: civil rights lawyer and member of Senator Humphrey's Capitol Hill staff.

William Harold Cox: United States Federal Judge for the Southern District of Mississippi.

Walter Cronkite: anchor of the CBS Evening News.

Cartha DeLoach: deputy assistant director of the FBI.

David Dellinger: conscientious objector during World War II and longtime peace activist.

Angie Dickenson: Hollywood actress, star of *Rio Bravo*.

Everett Dirksen: Republican Senator from Illinois; Senate Minority Leader.

Anatoly Dobrynin: Soviet Ambassador to the United States.

James O. Eastland: Democratic Senator from Mississippi; Chairman of Senate Judiciary Committee.

Daniel Ellsberg: assistant to the Secretary of Defense and civilian military analyst.

David Ferrie: former airline pilot; worked for anti-Castro groups in New Orleans; associate of Carlos Marcello.

J. William Fulbright: Democratic Senator from Arkansas; Chairman of the Senate Foreign Relations Committee

Sam Giancana: longtime Mafia member and head of the Chicago Outfit.

Barry Goldwater: Republican Senator from Arizona and candidate for President.

Marshall Andrei Grechko: Marshall of the Soviet Union and high-ranking commander of their armed forces.

Ernesto "Che" Guevara: Argentine-born Cuban Revolutionary.

Colonel Alexander Haig: aide to the Secretary of Defense.

Fannie Lou Hamer: Civil Rights activist and member of the Mississippi Freedom Democratic Party.

Wade L. Harbinson: Texas oilman; member of the Draft Goldwater Committee.

Vance Harlow: former FBI agent and private investigator.

William Harvey: Central Intelligence Agency (CIA) station chief in Miami.

Richard Helms: Deputy Director of the CIA.

Herblock (Herbert Block): editorial cartoonist for *The Washington Post*.

Karl Hess: speechwriter for the Goldwater campaign.

James R. "Jimmy" Hoffa: President of the International Brotherhood of Teamsters.

J. Edgar Hoover: Director of the Federal Bureau of Investigation (FBI).

General Hamilton Howze: commander of the 82nd Airborne Division.

Hubert H. Humphrey: Democratic Senator from Minnesota; leader of the fight for the Civil Rights Act.

E. Howard Hunt: CIA officer.

Haroldson Lafayette "H.L." Hunt: Texas oil tycoon and conservative political activist.

Chet Huntley: co-anchor of the NBC Nightly News.

Dr. Mark Jacobsen: German-born NYC physician, known as "Dr. Feelgood."

Lyndon B. Johnson: Vice President of the United States under John F. Kennedy; former Senator from Texas.

Jacqueline Kennedy: wife of John F. Kennedy and First Lady of the United States.

John Fitzgerald Kennedy: 35th President of the United States, elected in 1960.

Robert Francis Kennedy: brother of the President and Attorney General of the United States.

Ayatollah Khomeini: Iranian Muslim religious leader, fierce opponent of the Shah.

Nikita Khrushchev: First Secretary of the Soviet Communist Party and Secretary of the Council of Ministers.

Dr. Martin Luther King: Baptist Minister and founder of the Southern Christian Leadership Council.

Denison Kitchel: Phoenix, Arizona, lawyer and advisor to Barry Goldwater.

Richard Kleindienst: Chairman of the Arizona Republican Party and supporter of Goldwater for President.

Stanley Kubrick: motion picture director of *Dr. Strangelove*.

Edward Lansdale: United States Air Force officer and director of Operation Mongoose.

General Curtis E. LeMay: Chief to Staff of the United States Air Force.

Charles "Lucky" Luciano: American crime boss; considered the father of organized crime.

General Lyman Lemnitzer: Supreme Commander of the North Atlantic Treaty Organization.

Martin Maddox: Colonel, United States Marine Corp and assistant to the President.

Marshall Rodion Malinovsky: Defense Minister of the Soviet Union.

Carlos Marcello: boss of the New Orleans Mafia.

Kevin McCluskey: member of the Re-Elect Kennedy '64 staff.

John McCone: Director of the Central Intelligence Agency (CIA).

Robert McNamara: Secretary of the Defense under President John F. Kennedy.

Anastas Mikoyan: member of the Soviet Central Committee and Politburo; close associate of Khrushchev.

V.M. Molotov: former Soviet Foreign Minister under Joseph Stalin.

Richard M. Nixon: former Vice President of the United States and Republican nominee for President in 1960.

Lawrence O'Brien: Director of Kennedy's 1960 campaign for President.

Kenny O'Donnell: close aide to President John F. Kennedy; member of the "Irish Mafia."

Sam Peckinpah: motion picture director of *Ride the High Country*.

Manual Pinero: head of the Directorate of Cuban Intelligence.

Dave Powers: Special Assistant and Appointments Secretary to President John F. Kennedy; member of the "Irish Mafia."

Frank Ragano: lawyer representing Mafia bosses Carlos Marcello and Santos Trafficante,

Lawrence Rainey: Sheriff of Neshoba County, Mississippi.

Ronald Reagan: Hollywood actor and supporter of Barry Goldwater for President.

Bebe Rebozo: Cuban American businessman and close friend of former Vice President Richard M. Nixon.

Nelson Rockefeller: Governor of New York and candidate for the Republican Presidential nomination.

Ellen Rometsch: German national and hostess at the Quorum Club in Washington D.C.

Walt Rostow: advisor to President Kennedy on foreign policy.

Jack Ruby: manager of the Carousel Club, a Dallas Texas strip joint.

Enrique "Harry" Ruiz-Williams: veteran of the Bay of Pigs and active in effort to overthrow Castro.

William Rusher: Conservative activist and associate of F. Clifton White; early supporter of Goldwater for President.

Dean Rusk: Secretary of State under President John F. Kennedy.

Richard B. Russell: Democratic Senator from Georgia and Chairman of the Senate Armed Services Committee; leader of the opposition to the Civil Rights Act.

Pete Seegar: blacklisted folk singer and political activist.

Vladimir Semichastny: head of the Soviet KGB.

Steve Shadegg: conservative political consultant and public relations director on the Goldwater campaign.

Alexander Shelepin: former head of the Soviet KGB.

Robert Shelton: Imperial Wizard of the United Klans of America.

Sergio Aracha Smith: associate of Guy Bannister and David Ferrie; active in the anti-Castro opposition.

Stephen Smith: brother in law of the President and chairman of the re-election campaign.

Theodore Sorenson: advisor and speechwriter for President John F. Kennedy.

Adlai Stevenson: United States Ambassador to the United Nations.

Jesse Benjamin "J.B." Stoner: founder and Chairman of the National States Rights Party.

Nicolai Suzlov: senior member of the Soviet Politburo.

General Maxwell Taylor: Chairman of the Joint Chiefs of Staff of the United States Armed Forces.

Strom Thurmond: Democratic Senator from South Carolina; staunch opponent of the Civil Rights Act.

Santos Trafficante Jr.: Mafia boss of Miami; owned property in pre-Castro Cuba.

George C. Wallace: Democratic Governor of Alabama and candidate for the 1964 Democratic Presidential nomination.

Jack L. Warner: head of Warner Brothers studio in Hollywood, California.

John Wayne: western movie icon and supporter of Goldwater for President.

General William Westmorland: Commander of American forces in South Vietnam.

F. Clifton "Clif" White: Republican activist and founder of the Draft Goldwater Committee.

Roy Wilkins: head of the National Association for the Advancement of Colored People.

Marshall Georgi Zhukov: commander of Soviet armed forces during World War II.

The following are accounts taken from interviews conducted by author Frank Sheppard for his book, *Kennedy's America: the Untold Story*.

Lt. Colonel Martin Maddox, USMC (I)
Alexandria, Virginia
November 1963 - January 1964

President Kennedy was understandably late for the meeting of the National Security Council in the Oval Office on the evening of November 22nd, 1963, but when he got there, I must say he was remarkably composed for a man who had a bullet miss his head by inches only hours earlier. It was only natural since he was a Navy man who knew what it was like to be under fire, not unlike me, only his action had been in World War II, while mine occurred a few years later in Korea, when a wave of Red Chinese infantry tried to overrun my position in the dead of winter.

The President listened to a series of preliminary reports and then snapped, "What do the Goddamn cables say?" He was referring to the stream of information flowing hourly into the Situation Room from every embassy and overseas military base, all of whom were constantly monitoring our Communist adversaries and anybody else who might be trouble. What the President was really asking was if any of our enemies far and wide had done anything that might tip their hand and expose their involvement in the events during lunch hour in downtown Dallas that day.

That's what was on everyone's mind at the moment.

My job title at the NSC was Advisor for Planning and Intelligence Analysis, which included among other things, the preparation of intelligence briefings for the President and other senior officials. It was what I had been doing ever since the first word of shots being fired at the President reached me at my desk in the Executive Office Building right across from the White House. All afternoon and into the evening had been spent speed reading cables and telegrams from NATO commanders in Europe, Naval posts in the western Pacific and Asia, along with every cruiser steaming in the Caribbean, just out of eyesight of the Castro brothers. I was determined to have a full report on possible enemy activity ready when President Kennedy returned from Texas, but I wasn't finished yet when Air Force One touched down Andrews Air Force Base well ahead of their 7:00 p.m. ETA.

So I took what I had and dashed to the West Wing, where the President had ordered everyone to assemble. I joined my boss at the NSC, McGeorge Bundy, along with the Vice President, Secretary McNamara, the Joint Chiefs, the Director and Deputy Director of the CIA.

There we waited for what seemed like an eternity for the President, who I later learned was spending a few minutes alone with his children in the family quarters - a perfectly understandable delay under the circumstances. When the President came through the door, the only sign that might have betrayed any emotion was some redness of the eyes, otherwise his demeanor was no different than if it were a routine meeting. Not so his younger brother, the Attorney General, who followed the President through the door, he looked as if he was ready to chew someone – anyone - a new asshole at the slightest provocation.

The President asked where things stood from the men whose job it was to give him the answers. The Defense Secretary responded first, followed by General Maxwell Taylor and the rest of the Joint Chiefs, and an Assistant Secretary of State. They gave the President a rundown on the status of our armed forces and the official reaction from our allies in Europe and Asia; there would be a call in the next hour from the British Prime Minister, a statement from De Gaulle in Paris, and probably a meaningless pronouncement from Khrushchev. Secretary Rusk was not there because he was hurrying home from an aborted foreign trip to Japan.

"I want to know where things really stand." I believe these were the President's words at this point. "What do the guys who don't sit on their asses all day have to say?" That is when the President got specific and his attention turned to me.

"What can you tell us, Colonel?" he asked.

Having the full attention of the most powerful men in the government, including the Commander in Chief, is not quite the same as a thousand Chinese riflemen having you in their crosshairs, but it's pretty damn close. And just like on that cold day in Korea, I simply did my job, and proceeded to give them a report of a quiet evening in Europe, a restful night in Asia and the Pacific, and a sleepy afternoon in the Caribbean with the exception of some unusual activity out of Havana.

The last item was read verbatim off a report from a telegram which came in right after 4:00 p.m. from a naval cruiser in the Gulf whose job it was to monitor all activity around the island of Cuba just in case the Russians or their fellow Comrade, Fidel, tried to pull something again.

"What activity? What made it unusual?" This was the first time the Attorney General had spoken. That was his style, always blunt.

"Yes, sir, at least two flights, traveling west to South West, which would put them right on a course to Mexico City; they were confirmed as a DC-3 and a Lockheed small passenger plane respectively. It jibes with the inventory of a Havana to Miami American-owned passenger service confiscated by Castro in January 1960. There is a daily flight from Havana to Mexico City, but never later than noon; this return flight is in the p.m."

Every eye in the room being on me by the time I finished my report.

"Thank you very much, Colonel." I believe that was the President's response before Director McCone and Deputy Director Helms spoke up, saying they would have a report ready in a few hours on any and all activity at the Cuban and Russian embassies in Mexico that day; furthermore they would have surveillance upped on both locations, directions would immediately go out to their station chiefs south of the border. Everybody contributed something except for the Vice President, who stood there the whole time staring at the floor with a real hang dog look on his face. I'd always considered Lyndon Johnson an oily Texas wheeler-dealer, but I couldn't help but feel the man's acute embarrassment over having the President be a guest in his home state and then nearly having his brains blown all over the streets of Dallas by some Communist loser.

There was some more discussion about what might be happening in the Kremlin and Peking, then President Kennedy said, "Well, Gentlemen, this has been a very long day, and I think most of us can't wait to put it behind us, but let me say, as bad as it's been, I'm damn happy to be here now." With that, the President left us for a meeting with Congressional leaders in the Cabinet room.

The Attorney General did not accompany him, as soon as the door was shut behind his brother, he said, "I want all of you to keep one thing in mind at all time in the days ahead, we don't yet know who else was involved with that son of a bitch Oswald, but whoever and wherever they are, we are going to find them. That is your number one priority." The rage in his voice would have made a bulldog piss itself.

The meeting broke up and we filed out of the Oval Office with me heading back to the EOB, where I would have another intelligence report prepared and ready for the President by midnight.

I've often wondered how different my life would have been if hadn't noticed those Cuban planes that day.

As hard as it might be to believe, the mention of Oswald in the Oval Office by the Attorney General was actually the first time I'd heard his name mentioned; I had been so busy reading cables, telegrams and getting reports ready that all I knew about the events in Dallas was what I heard in passing: shots had been fired at Kennedy's limousine as it rode in a motorcade through the downtown, but he was all right. So I missed all the dramatic television footage: of the bullet hitting the tail light of the speeding Lincoln Continental as agents threw themselves on the President and Mrs. Kennedy; a posse of Secret Service and Dallas PD charging into the Book Depository to take down the cornered would-be assassin; seeing Walter Cronkite sigh with relief as he announced that the President was unhurt after the limousine sped to the hospital just in case; the smiling President and First Lady walking out of Parkland Hospital to go to Air Force One; John F. Kennedy, ignoring the Secret Service, walking over to briefly comfort a distraught woman in a crowd of well wishers in the hospital parking lot - it was the front page photo the country saw on most of the major dailies the next day.

I didn't get the real details until I picked up *The Washington Post* the next morning, with its bold headlines: KENNEDY ESCAPES ASSASSIN: SUSPECT SLAIN. A smaller and more ominous headline below proclaimed: HUNT ON FOR CONSPIRATORS. The story that followed told of how a tip had been called into the Dallas Police Department saying there was a sniper on the 6th floor of the Texas Book Depository literally minutes before President Kennedy would have been in the gunman's sights; the secret service got the word with seconds to spare, allowing the driver to hit the gas just in time so that the bullet from Oswald's Italian Army rifle hit a tail light instead of the President.

As for Lee Harvey Oswald, the sniper who was killed on the spot, his ties to a pro Castro group shouted his motive, not to mention his time spent in the Soviet Union. My wife, Betty said my jaw almost hit the floor when I read that Oswald was a former Marine. How could any man who joined the Corp and know what Simper Fi meant possibly be a Goddamn Commie and Presidential assassin? At least that explained where he'd learned what end of the gun fired the round.

But the part of the story which got everyone's attention was the tip phoned into the Dallas PD which saved the President's life; it had come from a pay phone on a street in New Orleans. So far, there were no witnesses who could identify anyone talking on that particular pay phone at that exact time, but it didn't mean one wouldn't be found at any moment, potentially breaking the case wide open.

I went about my duties on the NSC over the next week while the country was riveted on the hunt for Lee Harvey Oswald's accomplices. There was no end of speculation and outright rumor in the press: on Sunday, the *New York Times* ran a story saying there were "sources" claiming Oswald was possibly an officer in the KGB; two days later the Huntley-Brinkley Report led with a story quoting "witnesses" who could place Oswald in Havana two weeks before November 22nd. What was true was that Oswald had been in Mexico City at the end of September and the first of October, and definitely had dealings with the Cuban Embassy there. To everyone, this pointed a big finger at Fidel and company down there 90 miles from Key West.

The main job of the NSC in the week after the assassination attempt was to find the needle in the haystack, a secret meeting behind the Iron Curtin or a movement of troops for no apparent reason which might be a clue pointing to something larger. It proved to be a fruitless quest, everybody, friend and foe, appeared to be on their best behavior. The only exception being South Vietnam, but things had been going to crap there since before Diem had been overthrown by his own military and killed nearly the month before.

My world changed forever on the morning of December 1st, when I got a message to hurry over to Mr. Bundy's office in the West Wing; what I thought would be some routine matter was instantly disabused when I arrived to find, not Mr. Bundy, but the Attorney General himself, Robert F. Kennedy, waiting for me.

He began by reciting my bio: born in Oklahoma, Annapolis Class of 1948, a Bronze Star in Korea, seven overseas postings in less than ten years - one of them to Guantanamo Bay, staff of the Commandant, a year teaching at the Naval Academy, a stint working for Naval Intelligence before joining the NSC, wife and two children. Then he asked me why I joined the Navy?

My answer was succinct: Because I didn't want to spend my life selling nails in a hardware store like my old man, Sir.

That brought the merest of a smile to the Attorney General's face; I knew him by reputation, which could have been summed up in four words: son of a bitch. And I had no problem with it since those same four words could be used to describe a lot of the people I'd had to answer to on the way up the ranks in the United States Marine Corp.

He came right to the point, saying both he and his brother were quite impressed with my work on the NSC, especially the presentation on the evening of the 22nd. That I was able to document the make and model of those planes and their origin on such short notice was better work than the CIA usually turned in - quite impressive. It's what the President respected and needed in times like these - men who could go way above and beyond and function well outside of the lines of the rigid bureaucracy which was the American security apparatus. President Kennedy frequently felt the need to go outside the normal chain of command to get vital information and to get things done, to not do things by the book, a book written by career diplomats and high ranking officers with lots of fruit salad on their chests. The President had listened to those people, and it had gotten him the debacle at the Bay of Pigs. He'd learned his lesson the hard way, and now knew the value of having a few good men in his own corner.

For that reason, the President had been going outside what would normally be considered the proper chain of command to recruit and cultivate assets and sources which could give him access and options Foggy Bottom, the Pentagon and Langley simply were unable and unwilling to give him. He described them as men who were too comfortable working in air conditioning. Many of these assets and sources worked inside the government, wearing proper business suits and uniforms, but there were others who made their living and risked their lives far from the safety of a plush office with a big desk, and a secretary and staff who jumped at their every whim; men with guts and nerve, and most all, the eyes to see what other timid souls either failed or feared to see.

There was a job for me, the Attorney General explained, with a small group he was putting together. Its purpose was to prepare for the inevitable crisis which would arise in the wake of the exposure of the conspiracy behind Dallas. It would be a crisis potentially worse than the one the previous October and to handle it, the President would need men like me who had the right kind of Top Secret clearance and who could be trusted with information to which not even Cabinet officers, the Joint Chiefs or the CIA Director had access.

I instantly grasped the opportunity being afforded me, and the risks as well; success could easily mean the fast track to another star on my shoulder, because with victory comes rewards. But the opposite is equally true, no one prospers in the wake of disaster or defeat when there is the inevitable need for scapegoats as the shit flows downhill. All I needed to remind me of this was a certain Dulles brother and his chief deputy who suddenly had a lot of leisure time after the Bay of Pigs. And working outside the chain of command was the kind of thing that could make you enemies even if you succeed.

But I was a trained warrior and warriors are not ruled by fear and doubt if they want to be worthy of the title; so I said yes to Robert F. Kennedy right then and there, making it clear that if there was a conflict at hand, then I was ready to charge toward the sound of gunfire.

Robert Kennedy did not look particularly impressed with my enthusiastic acceptance, and I quickly learned it was how he usually handled subordinates. He merely thanked me and went on to explain how starting immediately I would be moving to an office in the basement of the White House itself; that I would be working with others possessing the same clearance as myself. They might be of equal rank, but they would report to me because my official title was Deputy Director, which meant I was third in line behind the President and the Attorney General. Much of what we would be dealing with would come in the form of verbal reporting only, while other information might be nothing more than a handwritten note. "You will have to get used to not relying on cables and formal staff reports, but I will make sure you receive copies of everything coming out of the situation room daily, along with briefings from Defense and the CIA. You are going to be our set of independent eyes." It would be my job to take all this raw data and anecdotal information and find the truth hidden below the surface. The truth the enemies of this country desperately want to keep hidden - and make sure the President knew it.

"This assignment might not make you any friends in some of the other branches of the service," the Attorney General warned.

"Not a problem, Sir," was my reply.

It sounded like a real challenge, the kind of thing I'd signed up for on the first day at Annapolis. So that same afternoon, I cleaned out my desk and moved into a small office in the basement of the White House; the space was definitely less, but the proximity to power was so much the greater; that was what counted in Washington D.C.

It was there that I met Colonel Ralph Gillison, thirty years in the Army and the three pack a day Marlboro man who was in charge of a group that consisted of a couple of junior analysts from the Rand Corporation who had consulted with the CIA on the offensive capabilities of the Warsaw Pact; a former car designer from General Motors who'd worked with Harley Earl and had spent five years advising the Defense Department on weapons. All of us would be working solely on the coming crisis arising from Dallas.

This new position came without a standard job description and list of duties written down in black and white; no problem, I just jumped in with both feet when I walked into my new office in the basement and discovered four cardboard boxes filled with papers, some of them handwritten, sitting in the middle of the floor, having been delivered on the Attorney General's order the night before. These boxes came with the request that a report on their contents be ready for the President no later than 2:00 p.m. The first thing I picked up was from Paris Stafford, an old Harvard classmate of the President's who owned a dozen car dealerships, and who did a large amount of business in Europe, some of it on the other side of the Iron Curtain, where there was a small, but lucrative, market for American-made farm equipment. There were other opportunities as well, for it seemed there were members of the Soviet elite who had an appetite for the finer things of American life like Hi-Fi stereos, Coca-Cola, bedroom furniture, Kentucky Bourbon, paperback novels and Playboy magazine - all of which came into the Worker's Paradise by way of crates marked Medical Supplies and shipped from Stafford's warehouse in Atlanta, Georgia. All of this was kept far from Khrushchev's eyes and those of the more orthodox Marxists in the Kremlin, who had no idea how many of their comrades were enjoying the evil fruits of capitalism. The Russian end was handled by Vladimir Roykov, the #2 man to Leonid Brezhnev, a high-ranking member of the Politburo, who was fattening his wallet every time a crate from Stafford off-loaded at the airport in Moscow and passed through customs without being inspected. By the fall of 1963, they were working on a deal by which certain Soviet bigwigs could indulge their passion for high-end Ford and Chevy automobiles while keeping fat old Nikita in the dark about it.

Stafford found a reason to fly to Moscow at least once a month, always meeting Roykov while he was there; and as soon as he got back stateside, a detailed hand written note on what he'd learned while there would be delivered to the President's desk. Most of what was in those notes could be called gossip, but after reading a half dozen of them, it was crystal clear much of it was better than anything the CIA station chief in Moscow reported. Now I had a year's worth of such reports to read over and see if I could find anything in retrospect which might lead back to Oswald.

Gillison's people went to work on Stafford's not always legible notes, and after three hours could not ascertain anything which might point to a Soviet government conspiracy to assassinate the President in Dallas, but I give Colonel Gillison credit for pointing out something no one else in the intelligence services had yet learned: Khrushchev's hold on power in the Kremlin might not be quite so secure. The Colonel drew our attention to how many times during Stafford's visits to Moscow, the Supreme leader was on "vacation" at a spa on the Black Sea according to his best buddy Roykov. And while the cat was away, certain members of the Politburo got together and showed off their latest bourgeoisie acquisitions. "Put all those Red Russian bastards together," he said, Marlboro dangling from his lips, "and they can't help but plot to stick the knife in someone's back, it's in their blood."

I handed the Attorney General the report at 1:00 p.m. sharp (a good hour ahead of deadline) and made sure it highlighted the opinion on Khrushchev's future possible continued employment. This is what got me called into a meeting with President Kennedy later in the afternoon. This time there was only two of us in the Oval Office. "How sure are you about this conclusion, Colonel?" the President asked. "The CIA people in Moscow tell me the exact opposite." He was sitting in a rocking chair; the man suffered from back pain something awful.

"Sir, I am quite confident of my conclusion; so too is Colonel Gillison and the rest of my people. This, of course, is based on the reports Mr. Stafford submitted." Stand firm and hedge your bets at the same time, a technique every middleman has to learn.

The President stroked his chin, looked down at my report in his hand, then said, "This is a bombshell if it is true; if you had to Colonel, would you be able to stand up in a meeting and argue with Director McCone, who would tell you otherwise?"

"Yes I would, Mr. President; I'm not afraid to take fire, even from my own side." That is exactly what I remember myself saying in response to the President.

He tossed my report on his desk and got to his feet, but not without the barest of a wince on his face. "Good enough, Colonel, and good job too. I'll tell the Attorney General to make available to your group everything we keep under lock and key on the Soviets, Cuba Vietnam the Middle East and Europe. My good friend, Paris, is only the tip of the iceberg, because there are many things we need to know that others don't want us to learn. Earn your pay and find something else valuable."

Well, I found out what "tip of the iceberg" meant in the next few days as my group and I were inundated in our offices with boxes filled with folders, many of them containing pages of barely legible handwriting, while others were neatly typed transcripts of telephone conversations where both parties clearly did not know they were being bugged. The source of all this raw intelligence was a motley collection of sources: A Canadian businessman who regularly traveled to Cuba and often had drinks with Che Guevara; a Swedish pharmaceutical salesman who worked out of Hong Kong and did business all over Asia, including Red China; a retired British naval officer (who had met the President when both of them served in the Pacific) who now ran an airline whose territory included West Africa and a good part of Arabia; a Los Angeles construction company owner who made a lots of money under the table selling guns to anyone anywhere on earth; the long, long time mistress of a Greek shipping tycoon who entertained on a regular business major European political leaders; and many others with similar backgrounds. All of them knew the Kennedy family through business with the father, or went to the same schools with the sons or served in the military with them.

The other thing they had in common was that this diverse group could go places and gain the kind of access the CIA could not pull off on their best day. The difference between their intelligence and what Langley and the Pentagon put out was striking. "Salesman and whores," Colonel Gillison observed at one point, "know everything worth knowing."

While me and my group was sifting though barely legible notes and transcripts of telephone conversations, the investigation into the assassination attempt in Dallas continued, but without much success in locating Lee Harvey Oswald's accomplices. Despite my heavy work-load I followed the story in the press, reading every byline in the

Post, and devouring each issue of *Time*, *Newsweek* and *Life*, rereading some stories multiple times. Everyone was focusing on Oswald's past, every night Cronkite and Huntley-Brinkley led their newscasts with videotape of different associates of his being led through a gauntlet of reporters in Dallas to be questioned by the FBI and the Dallas PD, including Marinna, Oswald's Russian wife, who was reportedly kept in an interrogation room for 18 hours straight in an obvious attempt to break her down. Then there were rumors of witnesses to the attempted assassination and friends of Oswald being whisked away to a secure army base somewhere in Texas to keep them safe. There was constant talk of a suspect who was about to spill their guts and break the whole conspiracy wide open at any moment.

During this time I only saw the President a few fleeting times, and then at a distance as he came and went from the White House; the whole First Family spent an extended weekend on Cape Cod for Thanksgiving 1963 - I can only imagine how much the man must have cherished his time with his wife and children after such a close call. I know how he felt: there is a reason our first child was born exactly nine and half months after I got home from Korea. The President adamantly refused to publicly comment on Dallas, Oswald, or the investigation.

"I am most grateful that some people's reach far exceeds their grasp." It was all he said publicly before the reporters, a remark everyone remembers, but it struck me at the time that Oswald was not a poor shot at all, he was a well trained Marine who knew how to hit what he aimed at; the reason John F. Kennedy was still alive was because somebody had snitched on the man who'd pulled the trigger from the sixth floor window. The only sign that things had changed was the doubling of agents on the secret service detail when the President made a public appearance.

On Wednesday, December 11th, I was called over to the West Wing by the Attorney General who wanted to ask me some specific questions concerning a Russian rifle company which supposedly had been helping Communist guerrillas in the Belgian Congo, but had vanished from the fighting in early November. A witness had told one of the President's sources the Russian soldiers had flown west, not east, when they left the Congo. We had a quick and very on point conversation in the hallway outside the Oval Office, one where I was on the receiving end of one of Robert Kennedy's mini-inquisitions, something I learned to take in stride as just coming with the job.

Our exchange ended abruptly when J. Edgar Hoover himself strode down the hall, wearing the darkest business suite I'd ever seen and trailed by a pair of faithful agents, brylcream glistening from their hair and toting briefcases; this myth in the flesh neither looked left nor right nor acknowledged anyone except the Attorney General, who was actually the Director's boss, same as myself, only Hoover greeted our mutual superior with the merest of nods and a polite "Bobby," a greeting I could never possibly imagine any other subordinate giving the Attorney General; then again, what other subordinate was thirty years Robert F. Kennedy's senior and a living legend. The Director's manner was no different than if he had been busting a speakeasy during Prohibition instead of meeting the President.

Only when I was heading back to my office did I realize Hoover's greeting to the Attorney General reeked of barely concealed disdain; an interesting look at office politics on a level far above my pay grade.

It wasn't until the afternoon that I learned the reason for the FBI Director's visit to the Oval Office.

At three o'clock central time a news conference was called in Texas by James Hosty, the FBI agent in charge of the Oswald investigation and Captain Will Fritz of the Dallas PD, where they jointly disclosed the discovery of a rented locker at a bus station within a short walking distance of Dealy Plaza, the contents of said rented locker being a .38 Special, fifteen thousand in cash - mostly dominations of twenty - and a fake passport bearing a photo of Lee Harvey Oswald above the alias of Oliver Howard Lee. What would be known as the smoking gun was the identity of the person who'd rented the locker: Armando Vargas, a Mexican national who was known to the FBI as being in the employ of Cuban Intelligence, who had paid for the locker on Wednesday, November 20th. Vargas's current whereabouts were unknown, but what was known was that Vargas, an associate of his named Hector Bermudez, and a third person of interest, Gilberto Lopez, had crossed the border from Texas into Mexico on Saturday, November 23rd.

Upon hearing this last bit of information, I remembered those two extra planes which flew from Havana to Mexico City on the afternoon of the 22nd of November. Were they to be the means of escape to Cuba for Oswald and the others? All I knew for sure was that all hell was about to break loose.

The three men - Vargas, Bermudez, and Lopez - immediately became the most wanted men on the planet, even though all they were technically wanted for was questioning in the attempted assassination of President Kennedy. Since it was an ongoing investigation, the Administration would have no comment or take any action until the full and thorough investigation by the appropriate branches of law enforcement were concluded. Those were the exact words of the Attorney General to the press.

What was also clear on Wednesday, December 11th, was that the conspiracy to assassinate the President of the United States ran from Dallas to Mexico to Havana.

The next day, the Attorney General came down and spoke to us in the White House basement. "Colonel Maddox," he said, "I think it is now abundantly clear that the Castro government is at war with the United States - that is what those shots in Dallas constituted: an act of war." As of yet, it was not a full out shooting war between opposing armed forces on the field, but hostilities had commenced just the same. It was not a conflict fought all out like World War II, not in the nuclear age, not with Castro cradled in the full embrace of Khrushchev and all the military might of the Soviet Union, but it was still a war America was going to find a way to win nevertheless. Our key to victory would come from intelligence, of knowing what was going on behind the closed doors in Havana and the Kremlin. My group had proven themselves by coming together and accomplishing a lot in a short time, and the President would need us because we were independent. "The Pentagon and State Department are full of career paper pushers who could do the work you are doing, but their priority, no matter what the circumstances, is to cover their own Goddamn asses and make the Agency or the service look good; they did that at the Bay of Pigs, the whole lot of them, and my brother learned his lesson: Don't make the same mistake again. Go outside the chain of command; get your own people who answer only to you."

It made me proud to hear those words of praise from the President's own brother.

Then the Attorney General warned that some of the intelligence we would be dealing with came from ultra-covert operations. "Black bag doesn't even begin to cover it." The what's, why's, and wherefore's of all this could potentially cause quite an embarrassment if it were to become public, not to say giving great aid and comfort to the enemies of this country, a country I have taken an oath to defend against all enemies, foreign and domestic. It should have gone without saying, but my boss was taking the time to remind me: I was an officer in the United States Marine Corp; I would salute, obey orders without question, and as for any personal qualms - flush them down the toilet.

"Sir," I answered Bobby Kennedy, "if you need a Marine to march into Havana and nail Castro's ass, then I am your Marine." For better or for worse, I just made a total commitment.

Things moved fast after that; by order of the President himself, we were to do a critical analysis of our defensive and offensive strategy for the western hemisphere. Why? We'd find out.

Within days we were receiving briefings from the CIA along with reports marked Top Secret; we also had two Generals, Alvin Miller from the Southern Command, and Walter Justin, who had just returned from a year and a half in Brussels, come in and give us detailed looks at the operations and contingency plans for any number of scenarios for if and when hostilities were to break out between the United States and the Soviet Union. Admiral Eugene Thompson, from the Atlantic Fleet, gave us the rundown on how much firepower the Navy had in case of war, and how it would be deployed and used. I can tell you it was heady stuff for me when these men with the gold braid on their dress uniforms - not to mention the medals earned in World War II - sat across an Oak table and answered my questions. I'll tell you there was more than a little glaring and glowering at me, but they had been ordered to be there by the President, so they had to like it or lump it.

"What Class were you at Annapolis, Colonel?" Admiral Thompson asked as he got up to leave.

"Class of 1949, Sir!"

"So I guess you were still in high school when I was watching the Japs surrender on the deck of the Missouri? Missed the whole damn war, didn't you, Colonel? "

"Yes, sir." But I made it to Korea in time to freeze my ass off at the Chosin Reservoir, Sir!"

The Admiral gave me a steely look, and then he returned my salute and left without another word.

"You shouldn't have said that," Colonel Gillison said as soon as Admiral Thompson was out of earshot. "You're on his shit list now for sure."

I couldn't have cared less; I was working for the men who outranked all the Admirals in all of the United States Navy.

The holiday season was spent working on the "critical analysis" of our Operation Plans for the Southern Command and the Atlantic Fleet. Although we hadn't been told why we were doing this work, it did not escape our notice that Cuba, along with the rest of the Caribbean, fell within the area of responsibility for both of those commands.

While this was going inside our basement office, the search was on for the three men - Vargas, Bermudez and Lopez - wanted for questioning in the assassination attempt; the trail led into Mexico, and there it went cold, but much attention was directed at those flights between Mexico City and Havana on November 22nd; that the three men were now in Cuba was a given as far as most Americans were concerned. Meanwhile, the investigations in Texas continued right into 1964 with no new bombshells, while the President and the First Family spent Christmas at Palm Beach in Florida, making no public statements on anything having to do with the events in Dallas or its aftermath. There was a front page photo on every major newspaper showing the President walking on the beach on Christmas day, hand in hand with his two children - a poignant reminder to everyone of what might not have been.

Some miles to the south, in Havana, Castro was not silent in the face of all the accusations directed at him and his dictatorship: "The Yankee Imperialists are liars to their core," he said in a three-hour speech on Christmas Eve of '63. "They fabricate evidence and libel the Revolution, but they are the ones with blood on their hands. They are the ones who plot murder behind closed doors." At the time, we thought it was nothing but bluster.

I would learn different in the first week of 1964, when a call from the Attorney General informed me that my group would be receiving a verbal briefing from an individual the next day, and we had better take good notes, because much of what he had to tell us was of the highest level of confidentiality; that is how it came to be that on January 5th, we were graced with the presence of Harmon Butler, whose official title was assistant to the CIA station chief in Miami. Despite his job title, Butler was quick to imply that his real duties put him far out in the field and in harm's way. My impression of Mr. Butler was that of a real junior James Bond, the kind of guy who thought he could pull off wearing Ray Bans after dark. He didn't help himself when he said it was the first time he'd been inside "the building where they screwed up the Bay of Pigs."

It was from Butler that I learned all about Operation Mongoose and the Agency's secret war against Castro. In lifting the CIA's veil of secrecy, Harmon Butler gave us an account of sabotage, espionage and outright acts of war, all committed in a concerted effort to topple the Castro regime. Butler boasted of the thousands of guns, along with ammo, successfully smuggled into Cuba to help rebel groups and guerrillas. He told of the contaminations of sugar exports bound for Europe and the Soviet Union; the bombings of power plants and copper mines by covert operatives; the counterfeiting of the Cuban peso; the spreading of anti-Castro propaganda from one end of the island to the other, along with a network of spies informing them of everything happening on the island just 90 miles south of Key West. Butler called it counterinsurgency, and it had gone on for three years. Mongoose or JM/WAVE as it was code-named, had employed over 700 Americans and 3,000 Cubans; cost over $50,000,000 a year, and so far had conducted over 2,000 missions, all run out of the Florida CIA station.

"We've been doing the hard work of steadily chopping away at the trunk," Butler said when he was done giving us the rundown of the operation, "and it's only a short matter of time until the tree of Castroism crashes to the ground for the world to see. And all those pinko college professors and professional malcontents who can't love The Beard enough can go fuck themselves." It was said in the tone of a man inordinately proud of his work.

We had not been allowed to tape Mr. Butler, I had made a request to do so and it had been refused by the Attorney General himself on the grounds that only CIA personnel could record other Agency people, so Colonel Gillison and the rest of my group had been busy making notes while Agent Butler spoke. When it was done, I was quite pleased with their work because Butler made a point of not repeating anything, even when politely requested to do so. Another thing he did when he was finished was to make a call from the phone on my desk; when the other line was picked up, Butler said, "I need you to let them know where things stand," and handed me the receiver. The man on the other end of the line was Miami Station Chief William Harvey, Butler's boss, who told me that if I had any doubts as to what his assistant had conveyed to us concerning Operation Mongoose, "I can confirm that every damn word of it is true; can you confirm that every damn word you heard will stay within those four walls?" I answered in the affirmative, and Mr. Harvey thanked me and hung up.

As he was about to take his leave of us, Butler offered his unrequested opinion: "If this operation goes south, it won't be the fault of the men in the field, it'll be because of the cowards in this city, safe behind their desks."

I let his remark pass; I'll put my experience in Korea up against anything this Company man had been through. The next time I saw Harmon Butler, it was years later, and he was on TV sweating through his testimony before Inouye Committee.

Butler's revelations about Operation Mongoose did not impress me; for all their time, trouble and expenditure of treasure, these men running Mongoose had accomplished not much from what I could tell. More than one NSC report from independent sources on the state of affairs in Cuba had come across my desk, and there was little in them to suggested the Cuban people were about to rise up and overthrow the regime anytime soon. After our encounter with Harmon Butler, I decided the people running Mongoose had started believing their own bullshit, always a bad sign.

Because of my opinion as to the worth of Operation Mongoose, I nevertheless had to choose my words well in my next conversation with the Attorney General, who was, after all, running the whole show out of his office in the Justice Department. "Quite impressive," I told him when asked about Butler's revelations, "and it sounds like you've got the right men for the job, Sir."

"I agree, Colonel Maddox," he replied, "and the time is rapidly coming when we will have to integrate our covert operations with our military responses when it comes to Cuba. You will be a big part of it, Colonel, a big part of it."

That is where things stood in the first week of the New Year; my group had just spent a month in preparation for a crisis yet to arrive; it had been a crash course of briefings and the dumping of highly sensitive intelligence in our laps, but things had proceeded at a deliberate pace, without a sense of critical urgency. The events in Dallas had clearly put in motion a chain of events which could lead to a most violent outcome, namely another superpower showdown with the Soviet Union; looking back, I believed it would never come to such an end, reasonable men would find a way to resolve this thing before it came to the worst case scenario. That all the hard work of my group was just an exercise of "just in case."

Yet in the wider world beyond my office in the basement of the White House, there was a real sense of crisis, and had been since November 22nd; how could it not be when there were so many unanswered questions concerning Lee Harvey Oswald and the men in the shadows with whom he had conspired to assassinate the President; all the major news magazines - *Time, Newsweek, Life, Look, US News and World Report* - had cover stories the entire month of December concerning Oswald and the aftermath of his botched crime in Dallas. Everyone was busy trying to tie together the strands of a spider web stretching from Texas down to Mexico and then across the Gulf to Cuba.

Through all of this the Kennedy White House had nothing to say on the investigation, that any response would come only "at a suitable time."

If the White House had decided to take its time responding to the disclosures out of Dallas, others did not feel the need for the same restraint: Senator Fulbright of Arkansas, the Chairman of the Foreign Relations Committee, went on Meet the Press and said that the President had the right to use whatever appropriate action was necessary to remove Castro immediately, and that he was ready to introduce the appropriate legislation in Congress saying as much. Furthermore, he added, "I was for settling this problem militarily back in

October of '62, but other council was listened to, and that was not the course of action taken. Look what it got us."

In his speech on January 16th, announcing his candidacy for the Republican nomination for President, Senator Barry Goldwater said, "It has become apparent to every American that a lawless and murderous dictatorship sits not 90 miles offshore, a Communist dictatorship which has attempted to strike at the heart of America, we must not waste time with meetings to decide what 'proper response' is required, we must strike back at them with the full fury they deserve, and if the boys in the Kremlin don't like it, too damn bad." His audience in the Phoenix auditorium broke into thunderous applause upon hearing these words.

His rival for the nomination, Governor Nelson Rockefeller of New York made a speech in New Hampshire, where he was campaigning to win the state's March primary, stating that Castro needed to be put in the bull's eye as soon as possible, "…and let him see how he likes it."

The columnist Joseph Alsop wrote that the Cuban dictator should be considered nothing more than a common criminal, no different than Al Capone when he ordered the St. Valentine's Day Massacre and should be dealt with accordingly. The *Los Angeles Times* and the *Chicago Tribune* called for a total blockade of Cuba until Castro was forced to flee into exile in the Soviet Union.

There were others who took a more wary approach: The *New York Times* ran an editorial asking if a world crisis more perilous than the showdown with Russia over the missiles in Cuba was in the offing; Herblock drew a cartoon for the *Washington Post* showing a string of firecrackers with the fuse lit - a small bomb was labeled Cuba, while the huge one at the end of the string had Soviet Union on it; the hand holding the match which lit the fuse was simply marked "Dallas." More than a few public commentators were drawing comparison to recent events with the outbreak of World War I by likening the shooting in Texas with what happened in Sarajevo almost 50 years before.

From the situation reports we were seeing, that was the attitude being taken in Havana, where preparations for an invasion had begun in December, including the digging of machine gun nests and the installation of artillery batteries on the beaches. Day and night, the state controlled radio ominously warned the populace how the "slanderous Yankee Imperialists" were plotting to destroy the Revolution with any and every means at their disposal.

The investigation in Texas wasn't completed until the last Tuesday in the month. That's when the FBI, Dallas PD, and the Texas State Attorney General all signed off on the report which was made public on the same day.

I got the gist of it in my basement office when I read one of the first stories to come over the wire a little after 1:00 p.m.; I didn't realize I was holding my breath until halfway down the second page, that's when I read the details about Oswald's trip to Mexico City at the end of the previous September (ostensibly to get a visa), and it hit me exactly how huge a piece of political dynamite this document was going to be. They had interviewed over 125 different men and women, from the guys who picked up the trash on the streets of Big D to Governor Connally himself, including every last person who had come in contact with Lee Harvey Oswald going back to forever. It asserted that Oswald was acting at the behest of operatives of the Cuban Intelligence service when he fired those shots at Kennedy on November 22nd, a fact not only established by the discovery of the incriminating contents of that bus terminal locker, but by the accounts of E. Howard Hunt, the temporary CIA station chief in Mexico City during the fall, and by a Leon Ortiz, an aide to the Ambassador at the Cuban Embassy who had defected in late December. Together, they documented how during the last days of September and the first of October, Oswald had been in the Mexican capital and made contact there with Manual Piniero, the head of Cuba's General Directorate of Intelligence, along with two Mexican nationals in his employ, Armando Vargas and Hector Bermudez, who frequently traveled to the United States to spy on anti-Castro activists under the guise of buyers for a company that serviced and repaired air conditioners south of the border. Men matching their descriptions, but using assumed names, had been sighted in Dallas in the two weeks prior to the assassination attempt; more to the point, these two had crossed into Mexico at Laredo on the morning of November 23[rd,] and from there made their way to the capital and made a brief appearance at the Cuban embassy. They had not been seen since. It was assumed Vargas and Bermudez, along with an associate, Gilberto Lopez, had flown out of Mexico City sometime the next day, when two more unscheduled flights to Havana occurred.

The Oswald in this report was quite the slick character, a former United States Marine and sometime defector to the Soviet Union; a man who publicly espoused pro-Castro sentiments, and then tried to infiltrate at least one of the numerous anti Castro groups while staying in New Orleans. This was corroborated by Guy Bannister, a retired FBI agent and active member of the anti-Castro Cuban Democratic Revolutionary Front and backed up by fellow members David Ferrie, an airline pilot and Sergio Aracha Smith, a former official in the Batista regime, all of whom stated that Oswald had approached them about joining their group. They realized he was a double agent after catching him red handed handing out pro-Castro leaflets on the street. Oswald was promptly told where he and his leaflets could go; apparently when he couldn't cut it as a spy, his Cuban handlers made better use of his skills as a marksman.

There was a hell of a lot of holes in this narrative, like exactly when did Oswald and Cuban Intelligence first get together? Why did he want to get a visa from the Cuban Embassy when he was plotting to kill Kennedy at the same time? How was he planning to get out of Dallas after committing the crime of the century? And who dropped the dime, and ratted out the whole conspiracy just in time to save John F. Kennedy's life?

All questions to which answers would have to wait until the guilty parties were apprehended. That is where the rub came, for the men who could provide those answers were now sitting on a beach in Cuba, sipping on rum and cokes.

The end result of all this was the issuing of Federal and State arrest warrants for Armando Vargas, Hector Bermudez and Gilberto Lopez on suspicion of conspiracy to commit homicide against one John F. Kennedy, President of the United States of America.

By the end of the afternoon, 25 Senators, both Republicans and Democrats, had made public statements calling for an ultimatum to be issued, demanding Castro turn over the three men immediately or face an aerial bombardment which would reduce the Cuban military to a ruin not seen since what was meted out to the Germans and Japanese. Walter Cronkite used the word "crisis" in his opening remarks on The CBS evening network news.

"The shit hits the fan - yet again." That was how Colonel Gillison summed up the day's news. "Get used to it."

There was no reaction from the White House except to say that the President would make a statement the next day. I was ordered to be in the Attorney General's office in the Justice Department in the afternoon. This would be my first time in Robert Kennedy's office; nobody had to tell me another big shoe was about to drop.

Shortly past noon that Wednesday in January, the President - flanked by his brother and Secretary of State Rusk - stood in the press room and before a worldwide audience, and stated that, "The time has come for the Cuban government to come clean; members of its Intelligence Directorate have been caught red-handed conspiring to conduct criminal and terrorist acts on American soil and no amount of blustering and posturing can deny it. The three men, whom arrest warrants were issued for yesterday, are believed to have been given sanctuary on the island, their presence there an indictment of the Castro regime. It shall be the policy of this government to pursue all available avenues in the quest to see justice done. It would be in the interest of Havana to forthrightly end this matter right now." The President refused to answer any questions, neither did the Attorney General and the Secretary of State.

I was prompt and on time to my meeting in Robert Kennedy's office two hours later; there were three others already inside when I arrived. The Attorney General rose from his desk and introduced to me Enrique Ruiz-Williams (who was always referred to as "Harry") and Manuel Artime; the other man, wearing a United States Army officer's uniform, was Lt. Colonel Alexander Haig, an aide to the Secretary of the Army. After the introductions, from which I learned that the two civilian were veterans of the Bay of Pigs debacle, men who had been on the beach and done time in Castro's prisons before being ransomed by the Kennedy Administration. After only a few minutes in the Attorney General's office, I understood that I was in the presence of two of the toughest sons of bitches I was ever likely to meet, and I say this as a Marine Corp officer; Harry Williams was permanently crippled because his body had been riddled with more than 70 pieces of shrapnel, which had smashed his feet, ripped a hole in his neck and another one much too close to his heart, and that was before both he and Artime enjoyed the hospitality of the Beard's prison.

Like I said, I went into this meeting prepared to hear another big shoe drop - that does not begin to describe what I learned from Harry Williams and Manuel Artime; in the words of Robert Kennedy that day "…these gentleman have in their hands the final resolution of the Cuban problem." For 15 minutes, first Williams and then Artime spoke, describing in detail how for the past year and a half, they had been in contact with some of the highest officials in Castro's dictatorship, men who had become quite distressed about the course of events in their homeland and where the Revolution they had dedicated their lives to was headed. In short, these men who considered themselves to be true Cuban patriots were now convinced Fidel and Raul Castro were turning their island into a virtual colony, utterly dependent upon the sufferance of the Soviets, whose ever larger military contingent in the country was coming to resemble an occupying force.

"We fought and bled to give Cuba democracy," Williams explained, referring to the fight against Batista, when both he and Artime had followed Castro, "and there was nothing worse than to see our victory betrayed and handed over to the Communists. Not everyone who felt this way took up arms like me and Manuel; there are those who stayed at Fidel's side because they couldn't bear to leave Cuba. But it doesn't mean they will not act if the time and conditions are right." This meant something coming from men who knew not only the Castro brothers, but Che Guevara as well.

Williams told of a visit he received while in Castro's prison by an old friend and comrade in arms, Commander Juan Almeida, the head of the Cuban armed forces and the third most powerful man in the government; out of this meeting an alliance was formed, one that could now make Almeida the savior of his country, for he was now agreeable to leading a coup against the Castro's regime if the Kennedy brothers could give him the proper cover. Almeida, Williams explained, was one of those men who considered themselves to be true Cuban patriots who had gone from being disillusioned with Castro to genuinely fearful for the future of his country.

"Proper cover," Robert Kennedy said at this point, "is what we are going to give Commander Almeida so that he can stage a coup, depose Castro and resolve the Cuban situation once and for all. Not to mention, hang the bastards responsible for Dallas. And do it all right under the noses of the Soviets."

This is when Colonel Haig explained how the Cuban Coordinating Committee, of which he was a member, had helped reconstitute the Cuban resistance after the Bay of Pigs, establishing and supporting bases in Costa Rica and Nicaragua where exiles had been planning for the day the hated dictator is deposed, and they can return to their homeland to back up a new government dedicated to a free Cuba. A return headed by Harry Williams and Manual Aritme, setting the stage for a final act culminating in their victory in a free election. The CCC had involved Cuban specialists from the State Department and all branches of the armed forces to back up the exiles and create a small army, not big enough to take on the Soviet-backed Cuban military one on one, but capable of being a force in the confusion after Castro was deposed.

Thus the curtain was pulled back even further, revealing to me what had been going on in the shadows, but unlike Harmon Butler and his Operation Mongoose, Colonel Haig and the CCC impressed me as people who knew what they were doing. I'll admit to being more than a little in awe of the length and breadth of the secret war we had been waging against the Communist government in Havana.

Just what my part would be was spelled out by the Attorney General when Colonel Haig was finished: "You are among the privileged few now, Colonel Maddox, the very few who can see the whole picture when it comes to our dealings with Cuba. That puts you in a unique position as we go forward after a lot of arduous hard work and sacrifice by some very brave men; unfortunately, the hardest labor is yet to come, and it will call for even greater courage. Castro will never give up those three men who maneuvered Oswald into that 6th story window from which he nearly blew the back of my brother's head off, and we're going to use that fact to put Fidel in a vise and squeeze for all it is worth. Tighter and tighter until it appears certain we are about to send in the B-52's and level Havana, followed by the 82nd Airborne to mop up and hand his sorry fucking ass over to a group of good Cuban patriots who will promptly stand him in front of a firing squad. Khrushchev will bellow and bluster and make all sorts of threats how if we touch even one little hair on his bearded little friend's head, the big bad Soviet bear will show its claws and bare its fangs, but we will pay them and their threats no attention. That is because Commander Almeida will make his move at the last moment to eliminate Fidel and then install a provisional government, telling his nation how he has acted out of true patriotism when deposing their revolutionary idol, saving them from domination by the Russians while preventing a bloody invasion and an imminent occupation by the colossus of the North. That is the cover we need to give Commander Almeida so he can act on our behalf.

"Your job, Colonel Maddox, will be to get us there, to take all the tools and intelligence at our disposal, and hone them toward the goal of replacing the Castro brothers with a free government, one which will get the Soviets off that island for good. We will need from you a step by step plan which will appear to be taking us to war. But will in fact be the catalyst to finally rid this hemisphere of the of the Communist blight and free an oppressed people. You have just over 60 days to get the job done, as Commander Almeida has let it be known that April 1 is C for Coup Day. This is a chore my brother and I could not entrust to Langley or the Pentagon, despite all the best minds at their disposal, because we have learned the hard way, that if you really want to get something done in this town, you do it with your own people."

These were marching orders if I had ever them; the end purpose of all the briefings and analysis of the past month and a half. The meeting ended, as best as I can remember with Harry Williams shaking my hand and saying he would see to it that I would be received as a hero in a free Cuba. "Before the 4th of July," he said, "Havana by the 4th."

I will admit to leaving the Justice Department building feeling like a Marine who'd just been ordered to take Tarawa from the Japanese, only I had been ordered to take an island the size of Pennsylvania. But it would not come to that; at least if the things went according to the plan I was charged with creating.

Only much later in the day, as I was driving home did the full import of what I was doing hit me: the USA, the Soviets, and Cuba; all of us again hurtling toward a confrontation, and it was my job to thread the needle and make sure our side won without a lot of good men getting killed on a battlefield. At no time in Korea, when all of Chairman Mao's legions were trying to kill me, did my hands shake - not once; but they started to shake right there behind the wheel of my Chevrolet Impala heading south on Rt. 1 on that Thursday in January of 1964.

The next morning I was back in my office in the White House basement, confident in my work and that I had everything to achieve the goal my superiors desired; I say this because it was the day I first heard the name Vance Harlow, the man who would show me the error of my thinking.

Wade L. Harbinson (I)
Owner and President of Harbinson Oil and Drilling
Houston, Texas
November 1963 - April 1964

When I was a child, this was a free country, a place where a man could get as rich as a king through good honest hard work, do as he pleased with what was his own, and God help the thief, or the bum, who got the notion he somehow had a right to what his betters had earned. But that was before Roosevelt and his New Deal socialism, which set the Federal Government to perpetually picking the pockets of every good taxpaying American, starting right with the first buck they ever made.

Like I said, America was once a free country, and there is no damn good reason why it couldn't be one again. All it would take is enough right thinking people to take the right kind of action, and in January of 1964, as far as I was concerned, that meant moving heaven and earth to get Barry M. Goldwater elected President of these United States of America. Not to be too modest, but I was in a position to make it happen since I was willing and able to write the kind of six-figure checks that get things done in politics. That's because my Daddy was a wildcatter like Dad Joiner, one of those who got rich during the Depression when they hit gushers in the East Texas basin; when I was sixteen he put me in charge of a drilling crew of men, some of whom were triple my age, and told them no one would get paid unless I brought in a well in less than a week - made them sign a paper agreeing to such. That's how he operated…and I did bring in a well and the crew got double for the job.

By the early 60's the company my father had started in 1931 was annually ranked in the top ten biggest oil producers in the Lone Star State, that's what I mean by good honest hard work. But in a country where Communist-led labor unions, in league with the Federal government, were threatening to take away the fruits of all that my father had built, a man like me could no longer afford to stay on the sidelines; I had been an admirer of Barry's for years, especially when he would take on some of the weak sisters in the Eisenhower Administration who wanted to cut the budget for the Army, Navy and Air Force - like they didn't know who the hell kept the Russians from taking over. After Kennedy stole the election from Nixon and proved to be worse than FDR at Yalta for selling out free people, it was Barry Goldwater who spoke up and called a spade a spade in the loudest voice. He was my man from the moment he got up at the 1960 Republican convention and said it was time for conservatives to take back the Republican Party after Dick Nixon cut a deal with the welfare loving Nelson Rockefeller to get the nomination without a fight. Where I come from, we are not afraid to put our money where our mouths are; it's why I cut some big checks to the AMA when they needed help fighting Kennedy's Medicare scheme - nothing but socialized medicine by another name.

For that reason, I was among the fortunate few invited to a meeting in Chicago in

December of 1962; there was about fifty or sixty of us at the Essex Motel, like-minded patriots who despised what was happening to our country and determined to do something about it. We were there at the invitation of three of the smartest men I've ever had the privilege to meet: Cliff White, Bill Rusher, and John Ashbrook, young men who had found a cause. We gathered around a big oak table, and after a prayer asking for God's blessing on our enterprise, Cliff White got down to business, telling us this was to be an organization dedicated to the specific goal of nominating Senator Barry Goldwater at the Republican convention.

Then White showed us just how it was going to come to pass with graphs and charts delineating how Goldwater was going to get the 655 delegates needed to capture the prize. It was a real plan, worked out down to the finest detail, showing how dedicated and mobilized legions of Goldwater supporters would - starting at the precinct level - pack meetings and win elections to district and state conventions where delegates to the national conventions would be chosen. Of those 655 votes, 451 of them would come from the South and the West, where Goldwater was adored; that was not counting the 86 votes to be won in the California primary on June 2, where Barry had a good chance of winning. The remaining delegates could easily be picked up in the Midwest and New England where there was a lot of strength for our guy, even if he wasn't the first choice of most Republicans there. When I heard this from Cliff White in that conference room in Chicago, I knew in my gut that for the first time we could do this thing, we could fundamentally change the direction of America. All it would take would be one election.

That, and a lot of money, because to pull this thing off, it was estimated the price would be somewhere north of three million; such was our faith in White, Rusher and Ashbrook, that we raised two hundred thousand right then and there, twenty-five thousand of it from my own pocket. This is the way it should be, good men of property in a common purpose, seeing what needs to be done and taking care of it.

There was one problem, though, our man wasn't sure he wanted to be President, much less run for the job; I think it says something good about the man, that he didn't burn with the desire for power, that he needed to be persuaded to throw his hat into the ring. I was among the many who flew to his office in Phoenix, Arizona early in 1963 to make sure he got the message: millions of his fellow Americans were not only counting on him, but he was their only hope to live in a truly free country again. I had met the Senator a few times earlier in my life when he addressed various businessmen's associations in Houston, but this was the first time we'd ever had a meeting one on one - he actually remembered my name which pleased me no end.

"Wade, there must be a dozen good men who are a hell of a lot more qualified than me to be President," I remember him saying, "you ought to be talking to one of them."

I'd thought he might say something along these lines and was ready with an answer. "Senator, there is absolutely only one man whom millions of Americans are willing to move heaven and earth to put in the White House, and that man is Barry Goldwater. None of those other good men can say the same thing. Frankly, if you don't run, we'll draft you for President."

The Senator laughed at this and said, "Well millions of Americans are frequently wrong; my only intention has been to run for re-election to the Senate next year, but if they're willing to move heaven and earth, the least I can do is think about it." In truth he was already running, having hired some heavy political hitters ostensibly for his Senate re-election campaign.

So we went about our work of getting everything in place to take over the Republican Party in '64, and the Senator edged toward making an announcement early in the new year. It was my job to raise money, even though I refused to take any official title like treasurer; I was on the road a couple days a week over the summer and fall making personal calls on men and women who loved their country and wanted to make a difference; not once did I walk away empty handed. By November, it was a sure thing the Senator would officially throw his hat into the ring come January, in time to run in the New Hampshire primary; Clif White's master plan was well underway, he had no shortage of people willing to pack meetings and file as delegates for Goldwater. We paid no attention to the polls showing the Senator running behind Rockefeller and Nixon for the nomination and losing to Kennedy in the fall. They would all be taken down one at a time.

Then that Cuban stooge, Oswald, took a shot at the President on the streets of Dallas; my reaction was "Thank God," but not for the reason most Americans said those words on that November day: I thanked the Lord we were at least spared the Presidency of Lyndon Johnson, a liar, thief and cheat, not to mention a traitor to everything dear to all proud and true Texans. But the truth is the President's popularity shot up to eighty percent in the Gallup poll after Dallas, and that is one sweetheart of a place to be when you're an incumbent, and it's less than a year before re-election. Seeing those kind of numbers drove home to all of us in the Goldwater effort how this campaign would not be a cake walk, and I won't shade things by saying we didn't feel not a little bit discouraged. Seeing those covers of *Life* and *Newsweek* in the first week of December with Kennedy flashing his toothy triumphant grin on them drove it home.

Then it came out in detail how Castro was behind the whole thing, and I could not for the life of me understand why Kennedy did not call up the Joint Chiefs and order them to start planning to make a landing in Havana. I mean, my God, these Communist sons of bitches have taken a shot at not only you, but your wife as well, and you don't have the guts to draw on the bastards in return. Instead, we got investigations and arrest warrants and prattle about "all available avenues." Those words alone sum up everything wrong with the Eastern Liberal Internationalist world-view, the kind of thinking which has allowed Communism to roll over a third of earth's land surface in less than a lifetime. It made me want to double down and raise the ante in our efforts to defeat every damn one of them.

I was in that Phoenix audience in January when Senator Goldwater made it official, he was running for President, and I was most gratified when he did not mince words when it came to Castro and Cuba, quite the contrast to those weak-kneed liberals in Washington. But I must be honest, what happened when the Senator went up to New Hampshire to take on Rockefeller, and the rest of the Eastern liberal establishment was a debacle for us; the political press took his remarks about Cuba and twisted them, so the Senator ended up looking like a lunatic. I mean saying, "I'd leave Castro to the tender mercies of the United States Marine Corp and get a good night's sleep," or "We have every right to enforce the Monroe Doctrine with the barrel of a gun, and if I were President, it would be a fact made crystal clear to the Soviets," is exactly what Teddy Roosevelt would have said under similar circumstances. I guess recognizing what it means to have some guts is not taught in journalism classes anymore.

When I saw headlines coming out of New Hampshire proclaiming, GOLDWATER TO BOMB CUBA WITHOUT WARNING and ARIZONA SENATOR WOULD ELIMINATE SOCIAL SECURITY, I knew we were in trouble, but there was little we in the Draft Goldwater committee could do, his New Hampshire operation was run by cronies and professionals from Arizona, who kept trying to explain what the Senator "really meant" when they what should have been telling the jackals in the press was that he meant every damn word he spoke. The results were worse than expected, on March 10th, the Senator managed to come in a weak second behind Henry Cabot Lodge, another big Eastern internationalist who had been Nixon's running mate four year before; what made it worse was that Lodge wasn't even an active candidate; he'd spent not one day in the Granite State, the whole time he was on the job in the embassy in South Vietnam, more than a few thousand miles away. The day after the voting, the pundits declared Goldwater's prospects for the nomination virtually nil.

But they didn't reckon with Clif White's planning and the millions of us for whom this was not just a political candidacy, but a holy cause.

And to his credit, the Senator recognized this truth after New Hampshire; I think the defeat there made him realize just how much he wanted this thing after all, not just the Republican Presidential nomination, but the White House as well. Three days after the primary drubbing, he issued marching orders and merged the campaigns; no longer would the official campaign be run solely by the old hands from Arizona, but those of us in the Draft Committee came aboard in an official way, brought into the room and made a part of all decisions. Clif White was made Director of Operations, a nice title which let him share power with Dean Burch, the official campaign manager, and because I had proved to be such a success at raising money, the title of Deputy Director of Operations was created for me so as not to compete with the hack they had has Treasurer. We all never became one big happy family, in truth, some of those Arizona guys hate the ground we walk on to this very day, but we were all united in the purpose of electing Barry Goldwater President.

Our main opponent for the nomination was the luckless Tom Dewey's successor as Governor of New York, Nelson Rockefeller, a multi-millionaire who would turn the Republican Party into a hand maiden with the Northern Democrats on welfare and Negro equality. Rockefeller would be easy work; the man had already shot himself in the foot by divorcing his wife of thirty years and then marrying one of his secretaries, who'd left her husband and given up custody of her own children. The good Governor was an out and out womanizer - no other word for it - and all we had to do was point out his personal history to convince Republicans of what a disaster the man would be in a general election.

It was Kennedy we were already thinking about back in March right after having our asses kicked in New Hampshire, and nobody was kidding themselves as to what a bitch of a chore it would be to defeat him in November. Yet everyone at the March 15th meeting was absolutely sure that in the end, we were going to take him down on the issues, that when the hard working, over taxed and Communist-hating real Americans saw and heard our candidate, there would be no choice.

It was what we told ourselves, but I for one thought it might be necessary to find an edge.

The Kennedys, with their fine clothes and high style, might have fooled a lot of Americans, but I most certainly was not one of them. I took one gander at the old man, Joe Kennedy, who'd made a fortune bootlegging during Prohibition among other things, and knew the apple didn't fall far from the tree; if there were any edge to be found against the Kennedy clan, I would have to shake the tree. My Daddy always said where there was money, there was at least a secret or two; the Kennedys had plenty of money…

It comes down to having to fight fire with fire, and when you go after big money, you go get bigger money. So I made a few calls and got in contact with a man whom I had known for a quarter of a century, but had not seen in the flesh since about 1954: a fellow Texan named Howard Hughes. There are few men I admire as much as my late Daddy, but Howard is one of them; he's a man who understands completely what a buck can do for you. After catching up on some old friends and commiserating on the sorry condition of our beloved country, I explained to him the purpose of my call; I had a proposition to make, one only a certain type of individual would be able to take me up on. Said proposition being his: in return for derogatory and extremely damaging information about the President of the United States, I was willing to pay the sum of one-half million dollars. It would go without saying, but I would be sure to reiterate that this information must come with fully documented proof, the kind which would hold up not only in a court of law, but in the court of public opinion. It must be unimpeachable. So much so, that the minute John F. Kennedy was to concede defeat on the evening of November 3rd, I would sweeten the deal with another half million.

What I needed from Howard was a name of someone with the connections to pull this thing off, while at the same time, affording me and the Goldwater campaign the right amount of insulation from any and all acts which might cross certain legal and ethical lines, and bring the wrong kind of attention from either the vultures in the press or the proper legal authorities. There are those who might blanch at my actions, but I saw it as nothing more than doing my due diligence as a member of the Goldwater for President campaign; those Kennedys were known for playing rough themselves and turnabout is always fair play.

"Wade, I applaud you for doing this," was Howard's reply when I explained the purpose of my call, "and there is nothing I'd like more than seeing that son of a bitch who's ruining this country get tossed out on his ass, I mean he's proposing laws that would mix the races - disgusting. But old Joe taught those boys well; it won't be easy getting anything on them; for some reason, they inspire a lot of loyalty. And they do know how to buy silence."

I pressed my case, telling Howard it was our duty to the country to leave no stone unturned; my reasoning must have worked because he told me to sit tight while he made some inquiries and then he'd call me back. My friend and fellow Texan proved to be true to his word when my phone rang at three the next morning and he gave me a name.

That was how I ended up in a back room of the Carousel Club in Dallas Texas, sitting across a table from a man named Vance Harlow.

Lt. Colonel Martin Maddox (II)
February - March 1964

With a deadline of April 1st staring us in the face, the days after I got my marching orders from the Attorney General are a blur in my memory as my group went about the business of planning for a war that would never be fought down in our office in the basement of the White House. My people rose to the occasion after the briefing I gave them, instantly grasping the challenge and wading into a mountain of reports and operational plans to create a situation where a coup inside Cuba could successfully be pulled off with absolutely minimal risk to the United States.

We grasped right away how two things needed to happen at once, each parallel to the other, but heading toward vastly different outcomes: the first was a diplomatic effort to resolve the crisis by using third parties to negotiate with Castro while the second would be a steady military buildup in the Southeast and in the international waters around Cuba. The diplomacy was in the hands of the President, but the logistics of military planning and the application of force to achieve the desired goal were our bread and butter and we put in back to back dawn till dusk days getting a plan ready for immediate implementation. We took Operations Plan 316, which would have been used if the invasion had gone forward in October of '62, as our master mold to construct a new plan to bring about a different result. 316 called for a full-bore invasion of the island with 120,000 US troops following an extensive aerial bombing campaign designed to soften up the Cuban defenses; this is what the Cuban people had to believe they were being spared from when Commander Almeida staged his last minute coup.

A detailed presentation had to ready for the President on the first Monday in February.

It was around 10:00 a.m. on Saturday when there was a call to my desk. "Colonel Maddox, you will be getting another call in about an hour," said the now familiar voice of the Attorney General. "It will be from a man identifying himself as Vance Harlow; I strongly recommend you listen to everything he has to say, because he has information which you will find extremely valuable, not to mention critical, to the job you have been given by the President. Again, I strongly recommend you pay good attention to what Mr. Harlow has to say, and I don't have to remind you that all these matters fall under the umbrella of the highest security clearance."

My answer to this was a simple affirmative; when the Attorney General asks you do something, you do it, so when the call came exactly one hour and five minutes later, I listened intently, even though I had no idea who this man named Vance Harlow was or why his words might be valuable to me. What I did not expect was a request to meet him for a drink promptly at 1:00 p.m. at O'Donnell's, a well-known sea food restaurant on E Street.

The man who stood up from a back table and greeted me when I got there may have been my senior by decade or so, he had a thick thatch of brown hair with only traces of gray at the temples; he gave me a firm handshake and said, "Colonel Maddox, any man who was at the Chosin Reservoir has already earned my respect." He clearly knew who I was, my first impression of Vance Harlow was that he wore a dark suite the same way I wore my uniform.

I declined his offer to buy me a drink once we'd sat down, saying I was on duty, instead ordering a cup of coffee while he had a whiskey sour. I got right to the point, saying I was told he had information valuable to my work.

"First off, Colonel" was Vance Harlow's reply, "you must be asking yourself who I am and why I'm someone Bobby Kennedy himself would vouch for. For starters, I was born in Shreveport, Louisiana the year we declared war on the Kaiser, I joined the FBI a year before the Japs bombed Pearl Harbor; worked for Mr. Hoover for fifteen years, including three of them as the agent in charge of the Miami field office. I received four commendations for bravery during my years with the FBI, including one for the time a bullet barely missed my right lung after kicking down a bank robber's door; I didn't miss the space between his eyes. Upon leaving that position, I worked as an investigator for the McClellan Committee, specifically during their inquiry into the Teamsters Union and the activities of its President, Mr. James Hoffa. I believe you have heard of him?"

I answered with a yes, everyone had heard of the notorious Jimmy Hoffa, but if Harlow had worked for the McClellan Committee, then he was acquainted with the President and his brother.

"My work there led to three racketeering convictions, along with a dozen perjury charges. After that stint, I went into business for myself, becoming a private investigator; over the years, my clients have included the Ford Motor Company, MGM, Warner Brothers and Chase Manhattan Bank among others; the management of The Sands and Stardust casinos in Las Vegas dial my number regularly."

He paused at this point, presumably to let his resume sink in and properly impress me; it did, although I hoped it did not show.

After gulping down the last of his drink, Harlow asked me where I was parked, and I told him my car was at a garage two blocks away. "Good, let's go back there, what I've got to tell you will require privacy." I drank down a half cup of black coffee and followed him out the door, passing a room full of tourists enjoying their shrimp and crab meat lunches.

"Why couldn't we have just met in the garage in the first place if that's how it was going to be?" It was the obvious question I asked as soon as we were outside.

"Daily routine: I have a glass of Canadian Club first thing in the morning and early afternoon; my breakfast and lunch every day since I left the Bureau."

He then made a point of asking me my favorite baseball team and we talked about the Dodgers chances in the upcoming season all the way back to the garage; it was an obvious attempt to divert the conversation until we were in a place private enough to satisfy Harlow. I was glad to comply; can't say I wasn't more than a little intrigued by this whole situation with its 007 overtones.

"I left out the names of some of my better clients," Harlow said as soon as he was settled into the passenger seat of my Impala, "for reasons which are understandable, because you do not blurt them out where any Tom, Dick, and Liz might hear you talking about who cut you a paycheck and what you did to earn it.

Sometimes Uncle Sam needs people who are not on the government payroll to handle matters most delicate or dirty; to go through doors a good Company man or G-Man could never knock on in the first place. To sit down with some people who are not model citizens, but whose interests and those of the government coincide and convince them to work for the mutual benefit of all. It's called recruiting 'assets.' Do you understand what I'm saying, Colonel Maddox? Because if you are uncomfortable with the direction of this conversation, I will thank you for your time and go my own way, but if I leave now, you will be passing on a chance to have a direct pipeline to the General in command of all Soviet armed forces on the island of Cuba; I think that might come in handy when you consider what's in store come April Fool's Day."

I grasped that he did free-lance work for the CIA and the Bureau, but his knowing about the planned coup shocked me, it was the ultimate confidential secret of the United States Government.

"I didn't come here to waste my time, Mr. Harlow."

And that was how I learned the American government and the Mafia had made common cause in the war to rid us of Fidel Castro. There has been a lot of speculation and outright lies over the years of how deep the involvement between organized crime and Feds went, so here is what I learned from Vance Harlow on

a cold February afternoon in 1964: he had been retained by the Central Intelligence Agency in the summer of 1960 to make contact with Johnny Rosselli, a known member of the Mafia who operated in Las Vegas and Los Angeles, through this Rosselli character a sit down meeting was arranged in Miami with Carlos Marcello, Sam Giancana, and Santos Trafficante Jr., the bosses of New Orleans, the Chicago Outfit, and South Florida respectively.

"I actually did most of my talking through Trafficante's lawyer, Frank Ragano; those crafty sons of bitches were damn careful not to say anything which might incriminate them. You don't rise to the top in their business by being stupid or careless. It was mostly the lawyer and me doing the talking while those two bastard's contribution to the conversation simply consisted of a lot of nodding and shrugging."

A deal was struck at that meeting in the summer of 1960 whereby the good gentlemen of the La Cosa Nostra would aid the Agency in killing Castro and in return they would get back all their lucrative casinos and hotels in Havana confiscated by the Revolution. Thus a trio of Mafia bosses became "assets" of the American government.

The high cards the Mafia Kingpins were holding were a small army of loyal associates still on the island, former croupiers, front desk men, bouncers and cooks, even prostitutes, all eager to get rid of Castro and go back to their old well-paying jobs for the Mob. They proved quite helpful to Operation Mongoose in aiding everything from gunrunning to assassination squads.

"A year ago," Harlow said, "two Cuban patrol boats were sunk in Havana harbor, that wouldn't have happened if the amigo refueling the boats didn't use to chauffeur arriving VIP's from the airport to the Tropicana in a shiny black limo before the Communists took over and put him out of work."

I asked an obvious question. "Why the hell can't the combined forces of the CIA and the Mafia kill one man?"

"Because those Goddamn Cubans can't keep their mouths shut," Harlow answered. "The whole exile community is riddled with Castro's spies; he knew the Bay of Pigs was coming on account of his double agents inside the exile camps in Nicaragua and Costa Rica told him. Cuban Intelligence has got scores of spies on the streets of Miami right now, listening for anything of interest. You better be careful who you tell about what's going down come April 1st."

I took that opportunity to ask Harlow how he knew about C-Day.

"I was told by the same man who told you," was his reply.

Then Harlow elaborated on something he's said earlier. "The commander of all Soviet forces on the island is General Alexander Andreyev, a tough son of a bitch who was with the Red Army when it captured Berlin in 1945. He arrived in Havana on New Year's Day and has been making his headquarters at the Capri Hotel, an establishment whose former owner was an American company whose chief stockholders were Marcello, Trafficante and Giancana. The cooks and maids who used to jump at the beck and call for Trafficante's manager now do so for General Andreyev and his staff. They're quite loyal to their old well-paying employers. So imagine this, Colonel Maddox, imagine what would happen if, on the night of the coup, a personal message from the American government could be hand delivered right to General Andreyev? That might save a lot of lives, American and Soviet, and not just in Cuba either. Secure communication with the enemy in the field; that is what I am putting on the table Colonel."

This was a lot to take in, to say the least. "It's certainly something to consider."

"You don't have to make up your mind right today, but I know things have got to be finalized soon because you got to get a lot of ducks in a row, so to speak, if you want Castro's head on a platter come April 1st." He then gave me a number, saying I should call him when I decided his help was needed. "Just tell them you want to talk to our mutual friend in Miami; they'll contact me within an hour and I'll call you back, we'll take it from there."

Harlow offered me his hand, and I shook it, but not before a last question. "Why? You were a G-Man, why would men like Trafficante and Marcello trust you?"

"They don't, but I have a reputation for loyalty to whoever is paying me and keeping my mouth shut. I do a job, and unlike you, Colonel, I am no longer bound by any oath. In these situations, that matters." And then he opened the passenger door and was gone.

Was I shocked at the revelation that my government and organized criminals were working together to overthrow and murder the leader of a foreign nation, even if said leader was a Communist dictator? Would anybody have been shocked if it came out that Al Capone had helped FDR and Churchill try to knock off Hitler during WWII?

That Harlow apparently had the trust of the Attorney General said a lot; I was a Colonel working out of an office in the basement of the White House. Who was I to question anybody?

It took us until late Sunday night to get it finished, but the plan was ready when I stepped into Oval Office on Monday morning. It was designated Operations Plan 365, and the papers I handed to the President across his desk was the first typed up copy. It was just the President and myself; a quite intimidating enough situation.

The President thanked me and immediately began perusing the report. After a few minutes, President Kennedy stood up stiffly and then proceeded to give me a point by point analysis of Op Plan 365, which called for a six week very public buildup of military forces in Florida and the Caribbean in clear preparation for an invasion of the island of Cuba; something that would not happen because Castro would be overthrown before it became necessary.

"You've got a problem right here," the President began, "with the number of units from the 101st and 82nd Airborne you intend to mobilize. By my count it only comes to 75,000 men, and there is no way anyone would believe we're preparing to mount a credible invasion with those numbers. We could only do it with a bare minimum of a hundred thousand, and honestly I wouldn't sign the orders if it didn't include at least a commitment of a force greater than 120,000. Castro's spies in Florida, and certainly the KGB man in Havana, can count, Colonel. They will know a bluff when they see one, and Goddamnit, America can't appear to be bluffing. Revise it and add an armored division and as many Marine units as you think you'll need."

I answered him with an affirmative.

"Same thing with the number of light bomber wings," the President continued, "we'd have to take out their radar and anti-aircraft batteries before the B-52's could roll in and hit the big targets, you're a little short on the A-4's needed to do the job."

"Yes, sir."

"Your projected deployments from the Atlantic Fleet are adequate, but we're going to have a problem if Khrushchev decides to intervene at the last minute, and I wouldn't put it past the old son of a bitch. We will be violating agreements made only a year and a half ago; he'll be in a red hot fury when Castro goes down. Dobrynin was in this office two days ago and I got him to get that stone faced bastard Gromyko to fly over next week because we've got to make it look like we're giving diplomacy a chance. They don't know it's just window dressing."

"Yes sir, they will never know."

The President frowned. "But here's the one thing which might make me want to shit can this whole operation: there are already thousands of Soviet military personnel on the island and it is entirely possible that at some point after the coup, it will become necessary to introduce some American forces into the country. It could be some of Castro's diehards prove to be a real problem and maybe they are a job for the Green Berets. That could lead to a direct confrontation with Soviet troops on the island; I don't want to see any Russian blood spilled during this operation. Secretary Rusk, Ambassador Stevenson and General Taylor will give me valid warnings about what the Soviets will do in Europe and the risk of stretching our forces too thin. This is no small concern, Colonel Maddox, there are no missiles in Cuba this time, but there are nuclear weapons in some other bad neighborhoods where we don't want a fight to break out."

I had to think fast as I listened to the one man who had the authority to pull the plug on a sure career-making assignment. That's when I managed to remember a pertinent piece of information. Without mentioning the names of Vance Harlow or any Mafia kingpin, I told the President there were CIA "assets" capable of contacting the Soviet commander in Cuba, if possible we could reach him at a critical moment, maybe with an appropriate message from the President himself that would minimize the possibility of bloodshed. It was worth putting out there.

"Any Russian officer who'd even consider receiving a communication from the American President would end up in front of a firing squad faster than the time it would take him to read a communication from me. Then again, those troops in Cuba are going to be cut off from Moscow and totally dependent on the US Navy to allow a ship through if they ever want to get back to the Motherland; it might be worth a try. Work up a plan and run it by the Attorney General." I think my little impromptu scheme of contacting General Andreyev appealed to the President's love of cloak and dagger style operations; whatever, Operation 365 was still alive.

"And I want you to expand this plan, what you've given me will only cover things up to C-Day, but the situation may be dicey after April the 1st even under the best of circumstances. It may well be days, if not weeks, before the Provisional Government has complete control of the island, and I want to plan for the worst case.

There was one immediate problem which came to mind if even limited American forces were to go in post-coup: "Sir, what will be our policy if any ranking member of Castro's government or even one of the Castro brothers themselves were to be captured by American military personal?"

The President fixed me with a particularly steely look, and believe me, you did not want to be on the receiving end of an expression like that from John F. Kennedy. "They are not our concern, Colonel Maddox, and what happens is not on our heads." What I took from this was that the fate of the Cuban leadership had already been decided: the Beard and his brother Raul would not survive General Almeida's coup and the blood would strictly be on Cuban hands

The President's secretary, Mrs. Lincoln, called from her outer office to let him know that his next appointment was there, I believe it was a group of Senators from the Armed Services Committee, because she mentioned the name of Senator Russell of Georgia who was the Chairman. Our meeting was over and I told President Kennedy the changes he wanted were as good as done, a revised version of Operation 365 would be ready within 24 hours. He said that was good. Time was of the essence and April 1st would come quick.

"Yes, sir, unless Castro decides to turn those three over to us; in which case, we'll just file this plan away with all the other contingencies that were never needed."

I will never forget the President's reply. "Colonel Maddox, there is absolutely no chance of that; absolutely no chance."

Only later, after much water under the bridge, would I come to see the President's final words to me at that meeting on the first Monday in February of 1964 in a different light.

The final version of Operation 365 was handed to the Attorney General two days later; he read it over and took it to his brother, the next thing I knew I was scheduled to make a full presentation to the National Security Council at 1:00 p.m. in the Cabinet room on February 7th. Remembering what the President had said, I went in there prepared for tough questions and hard criticism. I was not disappointed, and despite being forewarned about the Secretary of State and the UN Ambassador, they were far from the only ones expressing sharp skepticism as to merits of 365, to say nothing of its outcome. Everyone in the room - except for the Vice President, who sat with his chin against his chest the whole time - voiced some doubt that General Almeida could actually pull off a coup against Castro, especially Ambassador Stevenson, which didn't surprise me, the man was known to be the squishiest of liberals, but the Defense Secretary, Mr. McNamara, was almost as bad, specifically saying a coup by a heretofore loyal Cuban General was a thin twig on which to rest the solution of America's thorniest foreign policy problem.

By far the biggest sticking point was the Soviet Union and what their reaction would be to losing their foothold in the Western Hemisphere. Secretary of State Rusk was adamant on this point, explaining it was not just West Berlin or West Germany at risk, but all of Western Europe could be put in peril. General Maxwell Taylor, the head of the Joint Chiefs, was worried about Asia, more to the point, the Korean Peninsula and Southeast Asia, two opportunities for the Russians to make a lot of trouble if they so choose. The only ones who could be considered whole-heartedly in favor of the plan were the Attorney General, along with John McCone at the CIA and McGeorge Bundy, the head of the NSC and my old boss, said this could well be our last chance to resolve the Cuban problem.

Throughout the meeting, I did my best to inform on each point of the plan and answer every question thrown in my direction. My toughest moment came when Secretary Rusk asked what would happen if the Soviet military forces already on the island intervened on Castro's behalf. There was a contingency plan, I replied, one which could greatly mitigate the possibility of Soviet intervention. This prompted the CIA Director and General Taylor to start grilling me on specifics.

They were cut off by the President himself, who said he had faith that the Soviets in Cuba could be handled, "The risks of this plan are great and cannot be dismissed lightly, but the events in Dallas prove beyond a shadow of a doubt that there is no living with this government in Cuba. This is not a personal matter with me, even though I'm the one the shots were aimed at; the American people know who the guilty parties are concerning Dallas and they expect justice. Prepare the necessary orders. I'll put my signature on them; we will go forward from here."

The meeting ended with a stern warning from the Attorney General about leaks. "That's how they found out about the Bay of Pigs ahead of time, and we damn well don't want a repeat of that again."

I walked out to the meeting with a true sense of triumph; I went back to my basement office and heartily shook Ralph Gillison's hand. I made a short speech to the rest of my group, telling them how proud I was of all their hard work and how the pay-off would come soon when all of us would gather in a free Havana.

I thought the tough part was done.

I was never more wrong about anything in my life.

Operation 365 officially got underway the next day when the President signed orders directing units from the 101st Airborne to deploy from their home at Fort Campbell, Kentucky to staging areas in Florida. The same day two destroyers from the Atlantic Fleet, that had been patrolling in the eastern Mediterranean, turned around and headed due west for the Caribbean, ostensibly to take part in "exercises." On the same day Gromyko was scheduled to touch down at Washington National, the appointment of General Creighton Abrams to the Southern Command was announced; Abrams, who had been deputy to the Army Chief of Staff, and who had seen plenty of action with Patton in Europe, was a born battlefield commander, the kind of guy you called on when it looked like the shit was about to hit the fan. All things which received due coverage in the press and were sure to get noticed in Havana.

And they were picked up on in the American press: SHOWDOWN LOOMING WITH CUBA was the headline in the *New York Times* on February 10th; the following story detailed the military deployments to Florida. A cover story in Newsweek asked the question: Diplomacy or War? An important pundit, Joseph Alsop, wrote that nothing short of unconditional surrender by Castro would be an acceptable resolution of the crisis. An editorial in the *Chicago Tribune* called for an immediate ultimatum to Cuba demanding the handing over of the three Intelligence officers, if not, then invade. The *Los Angeles Times* stated we should just hit Castro with everything we had right away. There were a few dissenting voices on the far left, to whom Castro was a hero, mostly among intellectual elites like the faculty at Harvard, who sponsored a "peace" gathering.

We paid no attention to such noise in the basement of the White House, what we did pay attention to was Andrei Gromyko's arrival in Washington on February 13th, for a two-hour meeting in the Oval Office with the President. Gromyko was one stone-faced bastard, never letting on what he was thinking; less than two years earlier he had sat in the same room and denied there were missiles in Cuba.

This time it was John Kennedy who was holding cards he wasn't showing.

The Soviet Foreign Minister sat there and listened as the President prevailed upon him to pressure their fellow Communist to turn over the three suspects in the assassination attempt and come clean about its complicity in the crime. Over and over he made this point so no one would ever say that the President did not go the extra mile for a peaceful resolution.

Gromyko told the President the Soviet government expected the United States to abide by all agreements made concerning Cuba - period. If the United States wanted to take the matter to the United Nations, all well and good, it was none of Moscow's concern - otherwise hands off.

The meeting in the Oval Office solved nothing, but to the world, it appeared as if President Kennedy was searching for a peaceful solution. But as the days ticked by, more of Operation Plan 365 went into effect: General Hamilton Howze, whose father had charged up San Juan Hill with Teddy Roosevelt, was given command of the 101st Airborne the day after Gromyko left Washington; Howze had previously been in charge of the 82nd and would have been the senior officer in command on the ground if we'd gone into Cuba in October of '62. Now it appeared as if he would be given a second chance and to those watching in Havana, there was now another combat ready officer added to the Southern Command. By the 25th of February, there were twice the number of destroyers and cruisers in the Caribbean as had been the first of the month; more would arrive by the first day of March. By then at least three more fighter wings had moved to bases in Texas and Florida. Day by day, the unmistakable military buildup proceeded.

None of this escaped notice in Havana, between New Year's 1964 and early March, Fidel Castro gave a score of interviews to the European press where he often rambled for an hour or more, all of them filled with vitriolic denouncements of "Yankee Imperialism," and pronouncements on how the Revolution were not the ones with "blood on their hands." Even before the first of the year, the entire country was on a state of high alert; by late winter, the number of mounted artillery and machine gun emplacements on the beaches had doubled, same with anti-aircraft batteries stretching from one end of the island to the other. I couldn't look at these developments and not believe things were coming together just fine.

My contacts with the Attorney General consisted of daily phone calls and in-person meetings at least four times a week in his office in the Justice Department. I have worked for many demanding superiors in my career, but none more so than Robert Kennedy, a man who was on the job 24 hours a day. Over the course of February and March his attention to the implementation of Op Plan 365 grew to a near obsession. No detail was too small it couldn't be run through my office in the basement: the number of B-52's at Barksdale AFB; how many extra fighter wings from the West Coast could be accommodated at bases in Florida; how many of our destroyers and cruisers were being dispatched to Cuban waters; the battle worthiness of the Marine Brigades en route to the staging areas. I'm proud to say he got a satisfactory answer to his every question. Robert Kennedy was a man who thrived on challenge and truly enjoyed doing the dirty work for his brother. There are many pictures of the President and Robert Kennedy during those years, in many of them, the President has a radiant smile on his face, few, if any, show the same for Robert Kennedy.

On the morning of March 8th, I got a call from the Attorney General concerning the CIA "assets" and the possibility of using them to make contact with the Russian commander in Cuba. I included it as an option when we reworked Op Plan 365 by request of the President. The possible high loss of life from the Soviet contingent was still a problem, the Attorney General said, one that had to be solved. He was asking me to exercise the option to make contact with General Andreyev. I told him to consider it done, hung up and called the Florida number Vance Harlow had given me and left a message for him to call me back right away.

True to his word, Harlow called me back exactly fifty-three minutes later. "Colonel Maddox, where the hell have you been?" he said by way of a greeting, "Been expecting your call for at least two weeks. What can I do for you?"

I explained to him that we needed the "assets" he'd told me about at our previous meeting to arrange for a message to be delivered to General Andreyev on the night of March 31st. This was top secret information being discussed on an open line, but time was of the essence, and it couldn't be helped.

"Let me get on it," was Harlow's reply and he hung up.

I thought that was it; the deal was done, and the "assets" and the CIA would simply take it from there; I said as much when Robert Kennedy called me late in the afternoon, and I was able to tell him what he wanted to hear. Driving home late in the evening, I was a happy man, satisfied with a good day's work done, but when the phone on the wall in the kitchen rang as I was eating a late dinner, the muscles in my back tensed; some inner radar told me I wouldn't like what I was about to hear.

It was Harlow - I never learned how he got my home phone number - saying it was imperative I meet him in the parking lot of the Tastee Freeze across from the main gate at

Keesler Air Force base in Biloxi, Mississippi at 3:00 p.m. the next day. "Sorry about this, Colonel," Harlow said, "but there's been a last-minute knot in the plan and I need you here to get it untied. And be sure to bring a civilian suit and tie with you. Also use military transportation only, don't want your name on any commercial passenger lists." The man didn't apologize for the inconvenience, and I didn't ask him any questions; if the mission required me to be in Biloxi by the next afternoon and avoid the airlines, then that is what I would do.

I told Harlow I'd be there, hung up the phone, told Betty an urgent matter demanded I hit the road and then went upstairs to pack.

An early a.m. military transport to Warner Robins in Georgia was my ride to Keesler after pulling rank to get a seat; the main gate was right on the Gulf, Harlow was waiting for me. I changed out of my uniform into a civilian suit inside the Tastee Freeze bathroom and then we off, heading west in a rented black Ford Fairlane.

"Some people know an opportunity when they see one," Harlow said as we drove down Highway 90. "And the really smart sons of bitches know when they got you over a barrel and when they can drive a hard bargain. If you want this deal bad enough, then you are going to have to agree with the terms, shake the hands and seal the deal yourself. This is too important for a middle man like me to finalize, it has to be someone who walks into the White House every day. That's you, Colonel; you still want to do this?"

I knew my mission and I was a good marine. That was my answer.

"Good enough, Colonel, consider whatever message you want to send to General Andreyev at the Havana Capri as good as done."

We drove along the Mississippi Gulf coast into Louisiana and then across Lake Ponchatrain and into the suburbs of New Orleans, passing the time talking about the season's prospects for the Yankees and the Dodgers and our mutual hope that Jim Brown would keep setting records as a running back in football for years to come.

Only when we were in New Orleans proper did Harlow talk business again. "You're here because I'm working for hire and they're not going to simply take my word for anything, and they don't trust the Agency because they're not the ones who can throw their asses in the Federal pen for the rest of their lives. You have an office in the White House and talk to Bobby Kennedy on a daily basis, as far as they are concerned, it's the same as talking to the President himself. You and I know that's not the case, but sometimes it's all about perception. It should go without saying, but I'll say it anyway, nothing about this trip and nothing said on this trip will ever appear in any official report. Any references to matters discussed and agreed to must be done through the use of distinct euphemisms, such as 'our mutual friends' and 'independent associates' and if need be, 'assets,' but absolutely nothing specific - it's for the protection of all concerned."

A few minutes later Harlow steered the car into the parking lot of a roadside motel; it was the kind of place where tourists of moderate means and looking for a good deal would stay. The tall sign next to the office with the obligatory carport proclaimed it the Town and Country Motel and Restaurant.

"I've done my part, Colonel," Harlow said as he eased the car into a parking space. "Now you need to go in there and do your part: go to the front desk and ask for Mr. Bannister, he will take you to the 'assets,' you will listen to what they have to say, and when they are done, hands will be shaken, and then you come over to restaurant and get me, and we'll be on our way. That's all you have to do, any questions or concerns?"

I asked Harlow why he was not coming inside with me. "My job by was to get you here, and these people don't like to have too many witnesses in the room when they conduct business."

It wasn't the same as charging a Red Chinese machine gun nest in Korea, but walking into the lobby of the Town and Country Motel and Restaurant was putting it on the line just the same. The lobby appeared busy for late in the day; there were a number of men sitting around, Latin in appearance and a few of them well dressed, all looking bored as if they were waiting for a taxi to come. The desk clerk nodded when I asked for Mr. Bannister and then slipped to the back. I could feel every eye in the lobby on me as I waited. Clearly this was a place where strangers were watched; the desk clerk returned after a few minutes, with him was another man, older than me, but wearing a dark suit similar to mine. He introduced himself as Guy Bannister, and after confirming that I was Colonel Martin Maddox, he led me back to the manager's office.

There, behind the desk, sat a bulldog of a man, who upon first meeting, instantly gave you the impression you were on his bad side, if for no other reason than there was no good side to him. There was another man sitting on a couch who had a high receding hairline; he might have been the manager of a clothing store. Neither one of them stood when we entered, nor offered their hands when introductions were made by Bannister.

And that is how I met Carlos Marcello and Santos Trafficante, the "assets" who were in a position to do the United States government a big favor, and who expected a big favor in return. There were two other men in the room as well, I recognized Frank Ragano's name as Trafficante's lawyer, while the other's name, David Ferrie, was familiar, only later would I remember where I'd first heard it. Bannister, Ragano and Ferrie, remained standing after I was beckoned to a seat, it was clear by their body language who was in charge. They did the talking, while Marcello and Trafficante sat and occasionally nodded as terms and conditions for a deal was laid out, if anything needed to be clarified with the bosses, it was done in hushed whispers.

The bottom line was this: the employees at the Capri hotel in Havana, formerly the property of Marcello, Trafficante, and their many associates, and who were still receiving stipends from their former bosses, would lend their valuable assistance to the United States government in an attempt to contact one of the hotel's present guests, General Alexander Andreyev, commander of all Soviet forces in Cuba. In this way, these mobsters were helping to mitigate the loss of life, both American and Soviet, when, due to recent events, the imminent American invasion occurred. For their patriotic service, the United States government would make sure Marcello, Trafficante, and their many associates got back all the property stolen from them by Fidel Castro, property which included not only the Capri, but the Tropicana nightclub, the Havana Hilton, and a sugar plantation near Camagüey, which Marcello insisted be included on the list; all to be returned once the island was liberated from the Communists by the US military. Not only that, but the United States Justice Department and all of its many branches would cease all of its myriad investigations and prosecutions of Mr. Marcello, Mr. Trafficante, their families, friends, business partners and associates immediately upon the freeing of Cuba from the vile Communist tyrant presently oppressing the island.

That was it in a nutshell.

When these terms were agreed to at last, and Marcello and Trafficante had nodded their assent, everyone stood and the two mobsters walked to the middle of the room, where Marcello thrust his hand forward. "You tell that Goddamn Bobby he gonna be able to slip a message to those fuckin' Russian bastards just fine, just fine," he said as I pumped his hand. "We got our own private line to de island, we know more than those CIA Boy Scouts. And when all dis is over, and Castro is in hell, we all gonna get together in Havana, have a high old time and drink mojitos. Let the bygones be bygone." There was the merest of a smile as he spoke, with absolutely no mirth in it.

Then it was Trafficante's turn to shake my hand. "Bobby will leash his dogs, and all stolen property will be returned," he said as he leaned in close. "Everyone gets what they want; everyone go home happy. You understand?"

"Yes, sir, I do understand completely." Mr. Trafficante very much liked being referred to as "Sir and it was true, I completely understood, but not in the way they thought. This whole Devil's deal was predicated on an American invasion of Cuba, and Commander Almeida's coup would make such a possibility a moot point. Marcello and Trafficante would make good on their half of the deal on the eve of the coup, while we would never have to come through on our part because all those lucrative properties in Havana would never be ours to hand over. We were coming out of this thing a winner all the way around…or so I thought at the time.

Marcello insisted we have a glass of J.T.S. Brown to celebrate everybody getting what they wanted and he refused to let us leave without dinner at the Town and Country's restaurant on the house. That is where I found Harlow when my business was done, enjoying a drink. I wanted to leave right away, but he insisted I sit and enjoy Marcello's hospitality - the man would be insulted if I didn't. So I sat there and dined among the oblivious tourists and watched the TV above the bar; Walter Cronkite was giving the news and even though the sound was muted, I was able to follow the stories on the latest fruitless negotiations with Castro to extradite the three conspirators; images of President Kennedy and the Beard making speeches suddenly gave way to tape of the Beatles, whose recording sales were breaking all records. As well I knew, my twelve-year old daughter had cried for days when we refused to buy their album for her, but that age is just too young to be exposed to rock and roll so much; but the story on the British invasion made me realize how this thing had taken me far from home.

Harlow got back to business once we were back on the road. "What you have to keep in mind, Colonel, is plausible denial; there's no record of this meeting, and there will be no record of the meeting you will have with the Attorney General tomorrow when you brief him on what has transpired today. I've already told you to pick your words carefully, but I am sure he will have no trouble getting the picture, Bobby has always been perceptive."

I got back to DC the same way I'd come, not getting home until almost sunrise; after a shower and a shave I was in the office of the Attorney General. "I guess some old sons of bitches are going to piss themselves good when they don't get their casinos and whorehouses back. Some things are just too damn bad." That was the comment I remember most from our meeting of March 10th; he was on the phone to his brother as I was leaving.

The plan arrived at was this, two CIA teams would be deployed into Cuba on the eve of the coup and make contact with General Andreyev at the Capri in the early hours of April 1st. Andreyev would be told that the situation of the Soviet contingent in Cuba was about to become untenable, and that the American government did wish see them lose their lives for a lost cause. The United States would guarantee the safe conduct of a Russian transport to Cuba for the purpose of evacuating Andreyev and his men; a secure radio frequency by which he could make contact with Guantanamo Bay would be given him. This offer was only good if Andreyev kept his men out of Cuban internal affairs.

I was feeling quite satisfied with my job at this point, even the "negotiations" with the Mafia Kingpins; I was working to rid the Western Hemisphere of the Communist menace and free an enslaved people, a noble goal which I defended then and still defend today. While the invasion planning was underway, efforts to resolve the crisis diplomatically continued without success; the Swedish Ambassador to Havana tried to negotiate the extradition of the three suspects to a third party country; the President of Mexico offered to have the three tried in his country; the Secretary General of the UN made three futile trips to Cuba, hoping to leave with Vargas, Bermudez and Lopez each time. It all got nowhere as Castro was making daily speeches and pronouncements denouncing the United States. "I may die, but I will never be put in chains by the Yankees," he proclaimed. It was music to our ears as a belligerent Castro played right into our hands.

The military buildup in the Southeast hardly escaped the notice of the press, which was also part of the game plan. For weeks on end, there were front pages stories in every daily paper on military options being weighed by the Kennedy Administration, movements of troops and ships duly noted. It gave the impression something big was about to happen.

On March 19th, Secretary of State Rusk called a press conference and announced that all of the diplomatic efforts had come to naught; the Castro government had consistently refused even to discuss the possibility of turning over the three men to any third party. Henceforth, the Secretary said, the United States government would no longer be a party to any proposed diplomatic solution. It now considered the Cuban regime to be an outlaw nation. One whose members were guilty of criminal acts perpetrated on American soil, so therefore, the Cuban government had three weeks to resolve the current crisis to the satisfaction of the American government or face "dire consequences."

It was an ultimatum pure and simple, one designed to bring the utmost pressure to bear on Castro and give Commander Almeida the justification and cover for his coup. The term "dire consequences" was just vague enough to give us some room to maneuver; two days later the *New York Times* had a headline story on plans to mine Cuban harbors and ground all air traffic commencing on April the 9th, the day the ultimatum expired. There were similar stories in other papers and magazines filled with speculation on what was likely to happen in a little less than two weeks.

I attended the Oval Office meeting on March 23rd where the plan for C-Day was discussed and debated; my job was to brief the NSC on the status of Op Plan 365 and what the endgame might be. It began with a rundown of C-Day, a little more than a week away at that point, and by all reports, things were proceeding according to the plan. On April 1st, Commander Almeida and a loyal cadre of officers would seize control of the necessary government buildings in Havana, along with the state-controlled radio in the early hours before dawn. Fidel and Raul Castro would be "isolated" so as not to rally the faithful while Almeida would go on the radio and announce the formation of a provisional government - an act justified after Fidel Castro turned their beloved homeland into a colony of the Soviet Union, so much so that he had invited an invasion by the United States, bringing death to hundreds of thousands of Cubans while trading one foreign master for another. Thus Almeida's actions would be framed as an act of true Cuban patriotism. It was estimated that Almeida would need ten days to three weeks to establish firm control over the island, as there was sure to be die-hard resistance from hard core Communists; small units of American Special Forces would be inserted into the country to help subdue the resistance and help protect against an attack on Guantanamo. In preparation, Commander Almeida's wife and children had discreetly left for Europe, a signal he was truly committed to the coup, while a large sum of money had been deposited in a Bahamian bank for him to draw on once he had assumed power in Havana.

There were already a dozen CIA teams on the island and the six more slated to go in just before the coup. Harry Williams and Manual Artime were already in Nicaragua where they would join a force of nearly 500 exiles who would sail for Cuba the night of the coup. Both men were slated for high positions in Almeida's provisional government.

What most of the meeting was spent on was the possible reaction of the Soviet Union to the coup, an action they would most certainly blame on the United States. President

Kennedy was adamant on this point, "It profits us nothing," he said, "to rid ourselves of Castro only to end up with a bigger problem in Europe or Asia; West Berlin, the Dardanelles, what's to keep Khrushchev from going for one of them if we grab Cuba."

Secretary Rusk and Director McCone argued that as long as there were no American boots on the ground in Cuba and Almeida was not seen as a puppet, Khrushchev had no case. Secretary McNamara and the Joint Chiefs countered that there was no way the Kremlin would not see Almeida as a tool of America and not respond in some way. Secretary Rusk answered that Almeida was a legitimate hero of the Revolution, someone who fought at Castro's side against Batista; unlike the Miami exiles, his credentials as a patriot in the eyes of the Cuban people were beyond reproach.

The Attorney General took exception to this, perhaps because he thought the Secretary's remarks were a dig at Harry Williams and Manual Artime. He pointed out that there was no intelligence indicating the Soviets were preparing a military response to an American move on Cuba; nothing from the CIA station chiefs in West Germany or Moscow, nothing untoward to report from any "unofficial" channels – he was referring to Vladimir Roykov. As far as anyone knew, Khrushchev himself was still on a long vacation in the Crimea. Furthermore, the Attorney General asserted, during the Missile Crisis, the Soviets did not put their military forces on high alert anywhere, even as the United States was preparing to launch the biggest invasion since Normandy. There was no reason to believe they would do any different now.

This was when the President spoke up. "We're walking a fine line here gentlemen," he said. "Any stumble and things could spin out of control, and God only knows what might happen, all I know is that it would be a shit storm, with no telling how many lives, American and otherwise, being lost. But recent events have proven there is no making peace with Castro, though many have said otherwise, and as long as he remains in power, he will be an obstacle to finding any path to peace with the Soviets. And that is the greater good which must be served here, the survival of the human race in the nuclear age. We simply cannot afford to indulge strutting tin pot tyrants anymore and allow the lives of hundreds of millions be hostage to their whims and conspiracies. Whatever the risk there might be in going forward with this plan for a coup, it is nothing compared to the risk of simply going on as before." John F. Kennedy had made up his mind.

The meeting ended with me giving a report on the expected status of our forces on the last day of the month, which would be on the eve of Almeida's coup, when there would be nearly 100,000 men ready for battle, including units from the 101st and 82nd Airborne, along with an additional division of Marines; I made a point of mentioning the extra fighter wings the President had requested along with the extra destroyers and cruisers from the Atlantic Fleet, which would put a solid ring of steel around Cuba by C-Day.

"That ought to convince them we're coming and we mean business," was Robert F. Kennedy's comment when I was done. The meeting ended on that note of triumph: this time there would be no defeat and humiliation like the Bay of Pigs and a last minute deal like the Missile Crisis. This time there would be nothing short of victory.

We would not have been so exuberant if we had only known what was going on half a world away behind the walls of the Kremlin, for our intelligence was dead wrong when it came to the complacency of the Soviets - it was a false face indeed.

It was true Nikita Khrushchev was at his dacha at Pitsunda, but it was no vacation, for he was confined to his house and under guard by the KGB, all power having been stripped from him except in name. On March 10th, the Soviet Premier had been handed a report from the head KGB officer inside the embassy in Washington stating unequivocally that the United States was preparing to invade Cuba within 30 days; the report noted troop movements, the positioning of the Atlantic Fleet, and the stationing of extra fighter wings in the Southeast and Caribbean - their spies had been awfully busy. Khrushchev immediately called a meeting of the Politburo where he went into a tirade, denouncing the personal betrayal by John F. Kennedy after the man had agreed not to invade Cuba in return for Khrushchev's agreement to pull the missiles out. "If he thinks a few gunshots fired at him by outlaws in the Wild West have nullified his pledge to keep his hands off Cuba and its revolution, then he will have to be taught different." Khrushchev then pointed his finger at the Defense Minister, Marshall Radion Malinovsky and ordered him to begin preparations to send the 9th Rifle Division, one of the crack units of the Red Army, to Cuba so that if Kennedy dared to invade "he would find the bravest men in the Soviet Union waiting for him on the beaches, standing side by side with their Cuban brothers in defense of the socialist revolution." And he wanted them there as soon as possible.

Marshall Malinovsky saluted like a good soldier, but as soon as Khrushchev was out of the room, voiced his concerns to other members of the Politburo, chief among them being the fact that he would be sending the best men in the Red Army on a virtual suicide mission which would ultimately accomplish little or nothing – once hostilities commenced, there was no way to support or reinforce a Soviet division in Cuba, the distance was simply too great. They would fight bravely and then be killed or taken prisoner by the Americans, and the prospect of Soviet POWs in American hands was an intolerable sight to imagine for a Russian commander. If sending the 9th to Cuba was a bluff, then it was one surely to be called, Malinsovsky complained.

The Marshall's words fell upon receptive ears, for some among Khrushchev's right-hand men had been actively plotting for some time to oust him from power. In another failure of US intelligence, the fact that by early 1964, Nikita Khrushchev was an aging and ailing leader, with a cadre of younger men behind him and ready to shove him aside at the first opportunity had completely escaped notice. One such man was Leonid Brezhnev, who had actually been working on a plan to blow up Khrushchev's plane, but upon hearing Malinovsky's complaint, realized he could rally his fellow members of the Politburo behind a grand scheme to seize power for themselves and deal a blow to the West at the same time.

Brezhnev approached Nicolai Suzlov, a fellow Politburo member who wielded much power behind the scenes and enlisted him in the plot; Suzlov was a real Communist hard-liner and a true Stalinist at heart, and the thought of landing a knockout punch against the West after years of Khrushchev and his seeming accommodation to US Presidents had a lot of appeal. If Cuba were to be lost, then the Western Imperialists would be made to pay a heavy price somewhere else, but first, they had to gain the authority to make it so. To do so, they enlisted Alexander Shelepin and Vladimir Semichastny, the former and present head of the KGB; with these two signed on, the success of the plot was guaranteed, providing they moved quickly enough. On the night of March 12th, a detachment of security officers surrounded Khrushchev's dacha in Moscow and informed him that he had been "temporarily" relieved of his official duties by a secret vote; the reason he was not sacked altogether was that the plotters did not want tip off their counterparts in Washington that there was a change in Moscow and possibly ruining the opportunity the Cuban invasion was availing them. According to reports, the old Bolshevik greeted this development with an outburst of true fury, cursing and spitting at the KGB officer who ordered him to pack his bags so he could leave the capital for a "holiday" in Pitsunda. The old man refused, relenting only when a pistol was drawn and pointed at his wife's head; Khrushchev must have had real guts, from all accounts he then stepped between the KGB man and his wife so that the pistol was pointed at his forehead and said he had never stooped so low as to treat a woman is such a way.

The next day there was a brief item in Pravda and on Soviet radio announcing the Premier's "holiday," otherwise, life in the Russian capital appeared perfectly normal, with none of the Kennedy's back-channel intelligence sources the wiser. We were utterly in the dark on one of the biggest power shifts behind the Iron Curtain since Stalin's death, and it was likely that while we were meeting in the Oval Office on March 23rd, making plans for the liberation of Cuba, there was a similar meeting in the bowels of the Kremlin, where very different plans were being made to best exploit the loss of Cuba to the Western Imperialists.

The last days of March were filled with reports and briefings as the final pieces of Op Plan 365 fell into place: daily General Abrams sent cables from HQ at Southern Command, giving us updates on troop readiness and the movement of units; the goal was to have 25,000 paratroopers from the 82nd and 101st ready to drop into Cuba by the first week of April. Nearly 200 naval landing craft were loaded onto transports at Norfolk - a picture of one of them being hoisted by crane graced the front pages of the *Washington Star* and the *Richmond Times-Dispatch* on March 26th. The same day, a number of destroyers and cruisers began patrolling right up to the Cuban territorial limits; all these things gave the world the clear impression we were ready to go into Cuba as soon as the ultimatum expired on the ninth day of April.

Only a few knew that the real go date was the first day of the month; preparations were well underway as March ran out. Teams of CIA infiltrators were landed on secluded beaches, something that had become increasingly perilous as Cuban gunboats stepped up their patrols. The operatives tasked with making contact with General Andreyev made it onto the island under cover of being Mexican importers, accompanying them was one of Trafficante's enforcers from the Batista days; he knew everyone in Havana still connected to the Mafia. It would prove to be a most dangerous mission. In the Nicaraguan exile camps, Williams and Artime were telling their compatriots they would be taking part in a gunrunning operation on the night of March 30th, what they didn't tell was that the trip would be one way. At the White House, everyone was sweating bullets that somehow Castro would be tipped off to Almeida's coup ahead of time; as far as we knew, the conspiracy was confined to a small group of officers loyal to the Commander, but there was always the possibility that one of them would lose their nerve at the last minute. The island had become one big prison under Communist rule and pulling off something like this was enormously risky.

It really caught our attention when, four days prior to C-Day, Castro had another one of his interminable press conferences where he gave a detailed recounting of Operation Mongoose's Keystone Cops attempts to assassinate him, backed up with confessions by those unlucky enough to fall into the hands of Castro's police. The American government has shown its true face when it sends gangsters and murderers to shed my blood. "They dare to slander the Revolution with accusations of murder and think it an excuse to wage war against the Cuban people; I spit their lies back in their faces." This got no attention in the United States, mainly because there were no members of the American press present, but it made the front pages in France, Italy and West Germany, where there was a lot of public skepticism that Castro was behind the events in Dallas - many newspapers there were openly speculating how it was a conspiracy of right-wingers and segregationists who wanted Kennedy dead.

There were still efforts being made to reach a diplomatic solution: envoys from Canada, Sweden, and Norway flew to Havana and then Washington in vain attempts to get one side or the other to soften their stances. A group of college professors from Berkley got to Cuba through Mexico and declared their solidarity with Castro, but no one paid them any attention here, from Gallup to Harris, in every poll taken, the American people overwhelmingly backed the President's ultimatum to Castro.

There were standing orders for the week running up to C-Day that everyone in the White House was to carry one like normal, do nothing which would tip off the ever watchful press that something might be up. So after putting in a fourteen hour day, I went home where I sat at the kitchen table and made calls into the wee hours, checking in with the Situation Room as a steady stream of cables and communiqués rolled in from the Southern Command and the Atlantic Fleet.

My home rang at three in the morning on the eve of C-Day, it was the officer on duty in the Situation Room with a report from the captain of the destroyer *Lawrence* saying the boat delivering Williams and Artime to the island had been captured by the Cuban navy. I rushed to my basement office and spent three frantic hours trying to confirm the report; in the end, it proved to be erroneous after I got the CIA station chief in Managua to break radio silence with the ship tasked with delivering the exiles to Cuba. The mission had gone off without a hitch; the two men were safely on the island; turns out the captain of the *Lawrence* had witnessed a fishing boat filled with fleeing Cubans being captured by Castro's navy. I'll admit to having a few nervous moments there, contemplating Williams and Atrime being tortured under Fidel's personal direction. I'm sure neither of them would have told them anything, but there was enough information on their boat to have blown the whole operation and forced the President to pull the plug at the last moment. Later in the day, the Attorney General came down to my office and put me through a pretty icy interrogation about the event which might have gotten C-Day scrubbed; both of the Kennedy brothers detested failure. If I learned anything during my time in the White House, I learned that much.

I would like to take this opportunity to say there was no premature celebration of Castro's fall in the Oval Office, with the champagne flowing, on the night before Almeida's coup where a number of the NSC staff got quite drunk. I know that differs greatly with what Seymour Hersh wrote in his book on the Kennedy Administration, but it's what I remember, and Hersh never bothered to interview me.

Those last hours before things were supposed to pop in Cuba were spent in the White House watching the clock, whatever was going to happen was out of our hands; I wasn't the only one in town doing the same thing, from the Pentagon to Langley, men like myself were waiting to get the word from far to the South. I would spend much time later in my life making it up to my wife and children for all the days I wasn't there for them.

Everyone began Wednesday, April 1st, 1964 with great expectations; I was in the Situation Room before dawn, even though no one thought we'd hear anything from Cuba for hours. The coup was set to begin in the predawn hours when troops loyal to Almeida would surround key buildings in Havana, the most important of them being the Directorate of Intelligence, on the pretext that canopies had been sighted in the night sky to the west of the city, which surely meant the American invasion had commenced.

In Washington it was to be business as usual on the surface, only more so as to give the impression the actions in Cuba were totally spontaneous and had come as a total surprise to the American government; President Kennedy boarded Air Force One at Andrews just after 9:00 a.m. for a flight to Cincinnati, Ohio for an afternoon speech to the convention of the American Medical Association, followed by an appearance at a Democratic campaign rally, he was not expected to be back in the White House until early evening, when, if all went well, he would make a brief statement welcoming the turn of events in Cuba. The Attorney General would be at the Justice Department all morning in a lengthy meeting with the Federal Prosecutors who were pursuing a perjury indictment against Teamsters President, Jimmy Hoffa. As I said, it was business as usual and designed as a defense against the inevitable accusations of complicity in C-Day.

The signal we were all waiting for was to come by way of Radio Havana, the official voice of the Revolution, when Almeida was to take to the airwaves and announce the overthrow of Castro and the assumption of authority by the army to forestall a foreign invasion. Naval cruisers just outside the territorial limit were listening intently for anything which might indicate the coup's time was at hand, and not only them, but listening posts inside Guantanamo Bay were tuned in as well. At 9:40 a.m., Radio Havana's Spanish-speaking announcer began reading a translated copy of a North Korean government propaganda screed; he read no more than a few lines on the cruelty of the American occupiers and their puppets in Seoul before a loud exclamation was uttered by somebody in the studio and then nothing…dead air. Minutes went by, then an hour, then another, then two more. One of the CIA infiltration teams in Havana broke radio silence to report gunfire in the city, most of it around the harbor area and the national capital building.

By now we were starting to sweat because that old saying about no news being good news is really just horseshit. It was just before noon when the Secretary of Defense called an impromptu meeting of the NSC council in the Executive Office Building to come up with a plan or plans to deal with an unknown and fluid situation in Cuba. "We don't know something until we do," Ralph Gillison told me as I left the basement office, "and you know what happens when we assume." If he was trying to buck up my spirits, he failed, because as I walked from the White House to the EOB, my worst fears enveloped me: the coup had utterly fallen apart and we were looking at the mother of all foreign policy disasters; in my head I could envision our sworn enemies behind the Iron Curtain and in Asia laughing at John F. Kennedy.

It was a hateful prospect, but then we got word that Commander Almeida was speaking on the radio at last, announcing that he had taken control of the government in the name of the Cuban people in order to spare them invasion and occupation by the United States. He did so because Fidel Castro and his brother had pursued a course so reckless as to provoke such an attack, no doubt at the behest of a foreign power to which Fidel had mortgaged the future of their homeland.

Those words were music to my ears, although to remember them now is bittersweet. We all breathed a sigh of relief; the President was notified in Cincinnati, where he was between events. A debate immediately broke out over how long we should wait before recognizing Almeida's provisional government; at the same time a statement was being prepared for the President to give that evening at Andrews AFB when arrived back from his Midwest trip, one which said he "welcomed this turn of events in Cuba." The Attorney General arrived at the EOB around two o'clock; for once he looked happy and made a point to go around the room and personally congratulate everyone on a job well done. "Colonel Maddox, you've been a rock through all of this," he said when it was my turn, "an absolute rock."

If ever there had been a moment to pop the champagne corks, this was the one, and it went by incredibly fast, for at five minutes past the four o'clock hour on that Wednesday afternoon we received word from the Situation Room that Fidel Castro had just spoken to the Cuban people by way of Radio Rebele, a station set up by the rebels when they were fighting Batista. The Beard was not only alive, he was in a fighting mood on this day: "Brothers and sisters, the Revolution has been betrayed by a nest of imperialist vipers clutched close to its heart; the streets of our cities, the lanes and fields of our countryside, the valleys of the mountains must run red with the blood of traitors before they can deliver our homeland to their imperialist masters. We must kill them all if necessary or Cuba shall again be put in chains."

I had to admit, the Beard's call to arms beat Almeida's justification for the coup against him; the minute I heard Castro's words, my heart sank as all our hard work was apparently slipping away. Then I remembered what I'd learned the hard way in Korea: an enemy may beat you and defeat you, but only you can give up…and I wasn't about to give up yet. Castro's resurrection had the expected effect on everyone else in the room, especially the Attorney General, who - although he did his best to hide it - looked absolutely crestfallen at the news. "We have to get planes in the air, Sir," I remember saying to Robert Kennedy, "we need reconnaissance because we have no idea what's happening on the island and we have to learn fast, the President is going to have to make decisions, and he's going to need the right intelligence." My words had some effect, two minutes later, Secretary McNamara was on the phone, issuing orders for two immediate surveillance flights over Cuba and within the hour, a pair of U-2's took off from a base in Orlando.

At the same time, phones were ringing, and reporters were scrambling in every newsroom across the country and at the networks in New York, a huge story had just broken, the biggest since the attempted assassination in Dallas the past November, a story which had also seemingly come out of nowhere in the middle of a weekday afternoon.

Everyone was scrambling to answer one question? What the hell was going on in Cuba?

"So here we are again." Those were President Kennedy's words in the Oval Office to his National Security Council that evening, less than an hour after Air Force One had touched down at Andrews, returning from the trip to Cincinnati under circumstances much less triumphant than originally hoped. And by "again." he meant his third Cuban crisis. His voice was calm and even, but he must have been feeling the same crushing disappointment the rest of us were experiencing at the possibility Castro might have wriggled off the hook one more time. The first thing he asked for was an assessment of the situation on the island, and I'm glad to say I was able to give him a detailed report on what was happening right up to the hour. Commander Almeida's forces appeared to be in control of most of Havana, having caught Castro's loyalist by surprise there, units loyal to the Commander appeared to have established perimeters of control around Santiago and Cienfuegos. Aerial reconnaissance showed troop movements from one end of the country to the other, whether to rally to the rebel cause or back Castro, it was impossible to tell. Castro and Almeida had been back on the radio right after sundown, both claiming to have the upper hand and exhorting their supporters to show no mercy to the other side. The disposition of Russian forces in Cuba was not known; so far, Soviet state radio had yet to comment on the day's events. One CIA infiltration team was reporting constant gunfire could be heard in Havana, where a total curfew had been announced.

In short, the situation in Cuba was in flux, while a civil war was rapidly engulfing the country. That was the situation at 9:00 p.m. on C-Day.

"It's is a hell of a long way from where we wanted this thing to be, a Goddamn hell of a long way," the President said when I was done, "but be that as it may, the question is: what do we do next?" On this matter, the room seemed almost of one mind: Secretaries Rusk and McNamara felt the President had all the justification he needed to officially intervene against Castro since he was officially implicated in what happened in Dallas; General Taylor said his people at Southern Command and the Atlantic Fleet were ready to move at a moment's notice; Director McCone raised the possibility of mining the harbors and ports as a means of cutting off Castro from his ally, the Soviet Union; McGeorge Bundy and Adlai Stevenson cautioned against any military moves at the moment, Almeida might yet pull it out.

Then the Attorney General spoke up. "Almeida's ace card is that he appears to have no strings on him, any aggressive move by us now will make him look like another Batista in waiting."

When they were done, the President weighed in. "What my brother says is true, if we go in there tomorrow, Castro becomes a victim of the Colossus of the North, an instant martyr, and Almeida instantly becomes a pawn of the Yankee Imperialists. It doesn't matter if it can be justified by drawing a direct line between Dallas and Cuban Intelligence; Castro has to go by the hand of his own people. For that reason, we are going to stay our hand for the moment, but that doesn't mean we can't give Almeida covert help, there's a lot of good people fighting down there, some of them personal friends of ours.

"Then there is the matter of the Soviet troops…I mean we tried to send General Andreyev a message which would allow us to open up a line of communication to him, but we don't know for sure if he got it. The fact remains that if we start bombing tomorrow, Soviet soldiers will be in the crosshairs and that will be taken as an act of war by Moscow, making it a hell of a risk."

The meeting broke up with plans to reconvene in the morning and reassess the situation. The President would wait to make a decision, but events would rapidly begin making decisions for him.

The first reports of refugees fleeing Cuba came in around noon the next day when two dozen fishing boats arrived at Key West, later in the afternoon a cramped motorboat came ashore at Miami Beach, soon followed by a hundred more. This turned into thousands as desperate Cubans began taking advantage of the turmoil on the island by grabbing anything that would float and taking to the sea. A flyover of the Florida strait at midday, Friday, April the 3rd showed the water dotted with anything from inner tubes tied together to yachts; all of them filled to overflowing and heading for the United States.

At the same time, there was a reverse flotilla heading south, as thousands of members of the exile community in Miami took up arms and began sailing back to liberate their homeland. On the CBS newscast that same Friday, Bob Scheiffer interviewed a garage mechanic from South Florida who was preparing to sail back to Cuba in a motor launch, armed with nothing more than a .22 rifle. There were thousands more like him.

Overnight, this became a political issue for the Kennedy administration: Governor Rockefeller said the United States needed to go into Cuba if only to stop the influx of refugees; Senator Goldwater echoed his comments, adding that Castro's Communism alone had justified military action for the past three years; in a Senate speech, Senator James Eastland of Mississippi decried the hundreds of Communist spies slipping into the country under the guise of being refugees and that all of them needed to be put behind barbed wire in detention camps.

On Saturday the Florida National Guard was activated to deal with the refugee crisis while two brigades of military police were hustled from the west coast to Miami in an effort to get on top of the situation. Those fleeing Cuba proved to be an invaluable source of intelligence as what was happening down there; many of them were deserting soldiers from Castro's army who suddenly didn't know whose orders to obey and were desperately afraid of ending up in front of a firing squad. The job of interrogating anyone who held an official title in Cuba was given to the CIA with the promise of asylum, a thousand dollars, and a new suit if they provided worthwhile information. From one of them, we learned how one of Almeida's supposedly loyal officers had lost his nerve and gotten drunk the night of the coup and then spilled his guts to the head of Cuban Intelligence. The upshot of this was that Castro was saved from an ambush while coming back from visiting one of his mistresses outside of Havana in the early evening by a matter of minutes. It says something about Castro that with his country on the verge of invasion, he still found time to slip between the sheets with one of his concubines. By then Almeida's men were on the move, taking over strategic positions in Havana; Castro fled to the countryside where he was able to make a radio address later in the day, rallying his forces.

The typewriters in the basement were going day and night during this time as my group processed all the incoming intelligence for reports to the President and the NSC; Ralph Gillison had real talent as a proofreader, and a master of grammar - he made me look good when I had to stand before the President and give him the lowdown. There was heavy fighting in the streets of Santa Clara, Santiago and other cities with no clear picture of who was winning. It was appeared Soviet forces were aiding Castro's supporters - there were eyewitness accounts of Russian soldiers in uniform mowing down a squad of Almeida's troops on the outskirts of Havana. Every Cuban arriving in Florida told stories of armed Castro loyalists dragging anyone suspected of sympathizing with Almeida or spying for America into the streets and getting a bullet in the back of their heads; same for Almeida's men, who were doing the same to anyone they even remotely suspected might take up arms for Castro.

"Who's on top now," President Kennedy would ask me when I'd brief him, "our son of a bitch or their son of a bitch." For most of the next week, there was no clear intelligence as to which son of a bitch was winning; daily we went over the recordings of Castro and Almeida's radio speeches in which both claimed they were about to crush the other as all good Cuban patriots were rallying to them. Nothing was heard from General Andreyev or the CIA team sent to make contact with him; same for Williams and Artime, after going ashore the night before C-Day, they hadn't been heard from since.

On Sunday, April 5th, the fighting in Cuba took a decisive turn as forces loyal to Castro pushed into Havana and began taking the streets from Almeida's men; many of whom threw down their guns and begged for mercy, while others took to the sea as the flow of refugees to Florida went from a stream to a torrent. It was becoming more obvious by the hour: military intervention was inevitable. It was a truly hateful prospect, but that is where this show was heading five days after C-Day. If John F. Kennedy wanted to avoid another Bay of Pigs times ten, he would likely have to act within 36 hours. At a briefing later in the day, he grilled me about the Russians: How many might be killed if American troops went in? What were their orders if we invaded? "If our GI's are killing Red Army troops in Cuba," he asked on Monday morning, "what's to keep it from spreading to Europe and Asia?" No one had a good answer for him.

Two minutes after getting back to my office after that gloomy Monday briefing, I got a call from Richard Helms over at CIA with some news he thought we at the White House might find interesting: it seemed a KGB officer assigned to the staff of General Alexander Andreyev was at that same moment sitting in a room inside the Miami CIA station, sipping a glass of vodka and spilling his guts. The KGB man, Major Fyodor Firsenko, who having become separated from the rest of the Soviet detachment in Havana, had decided to jump aboard an aging prop plane with some of his compatriots in the Cuban secret police and fly to Florida, taking their chances with the United States rather than trust the tender mercies of Almeida's rebels and the good citizens of Havana, many of whom had family and friends who'd had an unpleasant encounter with their ilk.

Several hours later I had a report from Miami in hand on the first interrogation of the Major, and as I read it, something clicked, and the seed of a plan started to form.

Major Firsenko was one hell of a coward and a font of information, not the least of it being the location of General Andreyev after he had abandoned the Capri when the situation in Havana became untenable for the Soviets. It seems the General had retreated to a bunker beneath the villa of the rural Blanco sugar plantation near Camagüey, a safe distance from the capital and was commanding the Soviet contingent from there; it was doubtful he was in contact with Moscow since the Soviet embassy in Havana was surrounded by Almeida's troops.

It was Firsenko's mention of a sugar plantation in Camaguey that caught my attention; Carlos Marcello made mention of just such a place when we were talking terms back at the Town and Country Motel and Restaurant, for some reason he wanted that property returned to him. I called Helms back and asked for everything the Agency had on this place; a manila envelope was on my desk two hours later. Inside were some twenty pages of documents. I consider Helms a true patriot despite what a later court said.

The documents told the history of Blanco plantation, which before being appropriated by the Revolution in 1960, had been owned by the LaSeur Distillery of New Orleans, which had purchased the property from the Albany Fruit Company of New York in 1950. In truth, the place had been the country home of one Charles "Lucky" Luciano, the most successful bootlegger and pimp in American history. The imprisoned Luciano had been deported to Italy after World War II as a payoff for the Mob's help during the war in keeping the New York waterfront safe from Nazi sabotage. But Charlie Lucky had no intention of running his American criminal empire from Naples, and for years had crossed the Atlantic incognito and would conduct business from rustic Cuba, close enough to home, but still far enough from the watchful eye of American law enforcement. Eventually, the Federal Bureau of Narcotics forced the Italian government to crack down on Luciano, who was now running the world's largest drug smuggling operation, and he was kept on a short leash in Naples for the rest of his life.

But Luciano's tropical home away home remained behind in Camaguey, on paper the ownership might have changed, but the same people still had the title. And it seemed something else remained behind from the days Lucky ran the show: a private telephone line located in an office on the ground floor of the main house, (not unlike the newly installed "Hot Line" between Washington and Moscow) put in at great expense for Luciano's personal use, running to the United States, so that he could secretly talk directly to his partners in crime in the country from which he was forever exiled. According to the CIA report, this private telephone line had never been tapped nor had a trace run on it, even though it used the same undersea cable owned by ITT. The kicker to all of this: the owner of the LaSeur Distillery of New Orleans was none other than Carlos Marcello, and some of the Mob's old Cuban hands had been using Luciano's private line to keep the Mafia kingpins informed of happenings on the island - info passed on to the Agency.

This made me stop for a moment and ponder just who got the best end of this deal with the Devil.

But I now had a plan and had to act fast.

I picked up the phone on my desk, called the White House switchboard and requested they connect me with the Town and Country Motel and Restaurant outside of New Orleans, Louisiana. I identified myself to the front desk clerk who picked up on the other end and said it was imperative that I talk to Mr. Marcello immediately; when told that Mr. Marcello was not available, I left my name, number and a message for him to return my call as soon as possible, and said it would be worth it to his employer. While waiting for the phone to ring, I seriously questioned the wisdom of what I was doing, how maybe I should have called the Agency or the FBI and let them handle it, but that would have taken time, which we did not have if a Cuban invasion was imminent. I thought about calling Vance Harlow to arrange things, but as a free agent, he would have wanted to be compensated, another wrinkle which would have cost us precious time. And if Luciano's "Hot Line" had never been tapped, then there was a reason why, and in going through the law enforcement bureaucracies, I would surely run up against it.

No, time was running out fast on that Monday afternoon for the President to salvage the situation in Cuba, and if a major stumbling block could be removed by a simple telephone call to a Mafia Kingpin in Louisiana, then so be it, and let the consequences come what may.

The return call I was waiting for came seventy-three minutes later. It was not Marcello, but Frank Ragano on the line. I told him what I knew about Blanco plantation, its former owners and the existence of a secret telephone line to the states. Then I told him what I needed from Marcello. "I am sure the President and his brother will be most grateful if Mr. Marcello could render them aide which would prove most helpful in resolving a national crisis, most grateful indeed." That was how I ended my request, wanting to be careful not to promise anything specific in return for the American end of Luciano's "hot line."

When I had finished, the lawyer told me to hold on for a minute, then I could hear him talking to someone else in the room, presumably his boss; this went on for several minutes and the discussion got quite intense at times, though they were careful not to speak loud enough to be overheard by me. At last the lawyer came back on and said that one deal had already been negotiated, contact with the Russian Commander in exchange for the return of confiscated property, if my side desired any further service of his clients, Ragano said, I would have to met their price.

I put Ragano on hold and used another line in my office to track down Robert Kennedy, who happened to be in the Oval Office with the President. It took me a good ten minutes to explain to him the existence of Luciano's "hot line," its potential value in reaching General Andreyev and the delicate situation I was in with a certain party in Louisiana. There I was, with a Mafia Kingpin on one line and the Attorney General on the other, and myself in the middle.

Robert Kennedy must have consulted with his brother briefly; then he came back on the line and told me to agree to whatever the other party asked for, only tell him it would not be honored until Cuba was free, this being an incentive to ensure his honest cooperation. "And good work, Colonel," he said before hanging up, "my brother and I appreciate what you're doing."

Once back on the line with Ragano, I explained what I needed from his client and then asked what the price would be for his cooperation. That is when Marcello himself, who must have been listening in on an extension, came on the line, loud and clear, "I want a Goddamn pardon from John F. Kennedy hisself, nothing less," he said, "for all crimes committed, and ah do mean for all crimes - all crimes!" I informed the man that such a document would be forthcoming only when operations in Cuba were successfully completed, that being a condition required by the Attorney General himself and not subject to negotiation. There was silence on the other end save for Marcello's heavy breathing, and I was sure the man was going to tell me to go perform an unnatural act on myself. But after a long minute he said, "Fair enough, I'm not one to look de gift horse in de mouth; go to the penthouse in the Mirabeau Hotel in Miami, inside dere's an office with a great big desk; there you'll find the telephone you want. Charlie Lucky was going to run to whole damn show with dat one phone, and if you'd evah met him, you'd know he'd have done it." Then he gave me the number. "Maybe your Russian general will pick up when you call, maybe he won't, but no maybes 'bout it, I gave you what you asked for, and I want that pardon signed and delivered the day Santos and me and the boys get our Cuban property back. Make no mistake 'bout it, Marine Colonel Maddox, make no mistake 'bout it."

And with that I concluded my business with Carlos Marcello of New Orleans, Louisiana; an hour later I was in the Oval Office describing my plan to the President and the Attorney General; it was simple, the President would call General Andreyev directly in Cuba an offer him a truce.

President Kennedy was more than a little dubious about this scheme of mine, but if a single phone call might - and it was a big might - save lives and mitigate a potential confrontation with the Soviets, then he was more than willing to try it. The man loved to take risks and I think the whole thing appealed to his love of going outside the chain of command. Most to the NSC were doubtful of the success of my plan, fearful it would compromise a military operation before the first shot was fired. Secretary Rusk made the point that even if he'd had the opportunity, Roosevelt wouldn't have spoken directly to Field Marshall Rommel on the fifth of June, 1944. "He would have if he thought it would shorten the war and save lives," the President countered, "and FDR certainly would have done it if he thought it would have driven a wedge between Hitler and his top General." He went on to say that our fight was not with the Russians in Cuba, it was worth a try.

The matter was settled; within an hour, a team composed of CIA agents and Army Intelligence officers descended on the Mirabeau Hotel in Miami, finding the telephone right where Marcello said it would be. By 4:00 a.m. Tuesday morning, the necessary patches had been put in, allowing the President to pick up a phone in the Oval Office and speak directly to Blanco plantation in Cuba. Major Firsenko was brought to the penthouse because it was believed the Soviets would be more disposed to stay on the line if they first heard the voice of a fellow comrade. The Major cooperation was assured when he was reminded that he could easily be delivered to the Soviet embassy the next day, where he could explain to the KGB why he should not be considered a traitor and a deserter. The man was given a shot of rum, so his hands would not shake when he held the receiver.

There was no way to be sure General Andreyev would be at the plantation outside Camaguey when the call was made, but U2 reconnaissance photos taken that day showed a heavy concentration of Soviet troops in the area, so maybe the odds were in our favor.

The entire NSC was in the Oval Office when the number was dialed and Lucky Luciano's private line to Cuba was opened. It rang, once, twice, three times and while it did so, my anxiety was excruciating as I was convinced the whole plan was about to fail and I had made my superior look like a fool. But on the fourth ring, it was answered by a voice which spoke Spanish with a heavy Russian accent. So far so good, Firsenko did his job, getting three Soviet officers on the line, each one of higher rank, until at last, he was speaking to General Alexander Andreyev himself, who sounded as if he'd been up all night in a smoke filled room pounding down shots of vodka. He demanded to know why he was talking to an officer who'd been reportedly killed in action on the streets of Havana. This is when the whole plan could have gone south, because Firsenko now had to reveal his location and true circumstances.

To his great and everlasting credit, Andreyev stayed on the line, an act which instantly made him a traitor in the eyes of his superiors. The General asked Major Firsenko to explain how a KGB officer came to be in Florida while the United States was preparing to attack Cuba, his duty post. Firsenko was all but sobbing as he explained to the General how he came to be in his present situation. There must have been something in his tone that convinced Andreyev to keep listening, for we later learned that the Soviet command in Cuba had been cut off from any communication with Moscow since C-Day and were without orders on how to proceed in the face of a civil war and an imminent American invasion. The General had no knowledge of the recent events in the Kremlin, but he did know that his men were expendable as far as his superiors were concerned; knowledge which must have focused his thinking because he still listened when Firsenko handed the phone off to a CIA Soviet expert who spoke fluent Russian.

The CIA expert set things up for the President to come on the line, assuring Andreyev that no record of this communication would be kept (not exactly true) and that no one in the American government would ever disclose to anyone in the Soviet government that these conversations had ever taken place. "If you are saying no one in America will remember that we talked," the General said, "and no one will ever find out in Moscow, then there is no harm in me listening to what you have to say."

This is when President Kennedy came on the line, and using the CIA expert as a translator, said he was speaking as Commander in Chief the American military to the Commander of all Soviet forces on the island of Cuba, and that first and foremost, they were not enemies. There was a legitimate quarrel between the government of the United States and Fidel Castro, but not one between America and General Andreyev or his command. The President said he fully appreciated the position of the General and his men, who were simply being good soldiers in a dangerous place. Soon orders would be issued which could bring the good soldiers at the President's command into conflict with the good soldiers of Andreyev's command, with the result being a lot of good men being killed. It did not have to be that way, for the President was willing to make the following offer: if the General would pull all Soviet forces back to within five miles of the city of Camaguey in the next 48 hours, the area would then be treated as neutral territory. Andreyev had the solemn promise of the Commander in Chief of the United States that all Russian forces therein would not be molested in any way, they would not be bombed from the air or fired upon from the ground; there would be no surrender request or command to disarm. They would be treated as equals and fellow soldiers; at the first opportunity, they would be allowed to leave Cuba and return home without hindrance. So swore John F. Kennedy, President of the United States.

The President ended by reminding Andreyev that as young men, both of them had gone to war against the same enemy; that both of them had seen too many other young men like themselves die far from home, never to see their loved ones again, never to have families or know the love of their children. Now, so many years later, with both of them holding positions of great authority, did they not have a sacred obligation to the dead to try and prevent any more good men from sharing the same fate.

General Andreyev's response was to say that he had heard the President's words and they were true, "though it was a shame their conversation had never occurred." He told the President he had no such fine words of his own to speak, and besides, he was a man who believed actions said more anyway. The General asked the President to do him the courtesy of staying close to his phone over the next day or so and then hung up, but not before telling Major Firsenko he hoped to see him soon, and then he could tell him all about how he came to be in America.

I don't think President Kennedy had a finer hour than the one in which he talked General Alexander Andreyev into pulling all forty thousand Soviet troops out of the fight in Cuba. Later, on Tuesday afternoon, aerial reconnaissance photos of Camaguey showed a greater concentration of Soviet troops there, photos on Tuesday afternoon showed an even bigger concentration. Andreyev was doing as the President requested; in the early hours of Wednesday morning, the phone in the penthouse at the Mirabeau Hotel rang, it was Andreyev. "Please thank the President for his kind words and consideration for my men," he told the CIA translator who picked up, "and tell him I have done my part, now I expect him to do the same."

Thus the biggest roadblock to an invasion of Cuba was removed.

On Wednesday morning I received my marching orders from the Attorney General, Op Plan 365 was now a working blueprint for a military operation, one that would go forward in a matter of days It had been designed to be a bluff, but that bluff had been called, and folding was not a viable option.

The President scheduled a meeting with the JCS that afternoon as soon as he returned from the funeral for General Douglas MacArthur, who had passed away on Sunday; MacArthur was a personal hero of mine, and we sure could have used a man of his abilities on this day. At the meeting, the plan was gone over and approved; Theodore Sorenson was tasked with writing a speech announcing the start of military operations in Cuba. At noon on Thursday, I briefed the NSC on what came to be known as Operation Cuba Libre. The only major concern raised at this meeting was the Soviet Union and what its potential reaction would be once American bombs started falling. Director McCone mentioned reports of unusual troop movements or naval vessels being rerouted, while Khrushchev remained on vacation at Pitsunda, having been there throughout the crisis. There was plenty of blustering in the Soviet press over Cuba, with Pravda running daily denunciations of the "American Imperialists" who were responsible for all of Castro's woes. TASS carried stories of "atrocities" and "war crimes" committed by American puppets against the Cuban people. They all agreed that, other than talk, all was quiet on the Soviet front.

We were wrong.

"This is the toughest part of this Goddamn job," the President said after he signed the orders. "If anybody ever puts up a monument to me years down the road, I hope it's not for what I've done today."

I do remember what the Attorney General said to me as we were leaving the Oval Office. "If he hadn't dropped dead two years ago at a Naples airport, I would've given Lucky Luciano a full pardon and welcomed him home; his secret phone line was the ace we needed to cash out Castro."

The decision to go into to Cuba had come not a moment too soon; forces loyal to Castro retook the National Assembly building in Havana from Almeida's men on Thursday; the Commander himself had not been heard on the radio since Tuesday. The refugee arriving in Florida that week told stories of round the clock firing squads, as neighbor turned on neighbor and pointed the finger at any and all suspected "traitors to the

Revolution," while in Miami, thousands of exiles demonstrated and demanded Kennedy intervene. The *Huntley-Brinkley Report* on Tuesday led with a huge demonstration in Miami where speaker after speaker demanded that Kennedy go in now; one sobbing woman who spoke was the wife of a naturalized Cuban-American who'd earned two Purple Hearts in Korea, killed near Mariel two days before.

Late on Thursday night, the phone rang in my basement office. It was Vance Harlow. "You boys do realize you're going to be expected to come through on all those deals you made, you won't be able to use the coup as an excuse to get out of returning some valuable property - not to mention a pardon for all crimes committed. This one is on you Colonel; hope you don't regret it your deal with our friend in Louisiana."

I told him petty deals were the last thing I on my mind at the moment.

"You call them petty deals, Colonel?" he replied before hanging up. "Well, petty deals are what it's all about, you'll see."

I remained in my office all night, monitoring communications from the Southern Command so I would have a report ready for the President at 9:00 a.m.; I stepped outside to watch the sun come up on a gorgeous Friday morning, at the same time, a squadron of jets took off from McDill AFB in Florida, and entered Cuban air space minutes later.

John Compton (I)
Washington D.C./Atlanta, Georgia
November 1963 - April 1964

If there was one thing for sure, it was that John F. Kennedy's domestic agenda was dead in the water as of November 1963. I had taken a job on Capitol Hill earlier in the year to help get the Civil Rights Act passed and after Dr. King's march on Washington at the end of the summer, not to mention Bull Conner's shenanigans in Birmingham, there was real momentum as public opinion turned in favor of racial equality and the need for federal action to achieve it.

But we had been woefully naïve when it came to the southern bloc in Congress, the grandsons of the of the men who'd taken up arms for the Confederacy were determined to fight on without a hint of compromise, much less surrender. While the Civil Rights Act, which would have put a bullet through the head of Jim Crow, passed the House Judiciary Committee easily, it was promptly bottled up in the Rules Committee whose chairman, Howard Smith of Virginia, was a man who'd dedicated every day his eighty years on this earth to reversing Appomattox. It had to pass the Rules Committee before the full House would take a vote, and hell would freeze over before Judge Smith let that happen.

I still consider myself a good son of Georgia, but like a lot of men of my generation, I didn't grow up enduring the depression and then going off to fight in World War II only to come home and aspire to be Herbert Hoover or Andrew Mellon. The GI Bill was my ticket to a law degree and by the time I passed the bar I had developed the firm conviction that it was not right for me to have risked my life fighting Fascism abroad and then turn around and tolerate a police dictatorship for citizens of a darker complexion right here in America. So I became a rarest of species, a white Southerner who was willing to go into the courts of old Dixie and defend the victims of Jim Crow.

Although I never joined either organization formally, both the ACLU and the NAACP called on my services regularly to defend clients in criminal court whose plight they championed. I was most proud of having saved the life of Aaron Graham, a Jackson, Mississippi delta farmer railroaded for the murder of a white man who attempted on his own to forcibly take one of Graham's mules as payment for a debt. The facts clearly pointed to self-defense. I was told point blank to my face by the local Sheriff that if I saved Graham from the electric chair, he'd hunt me down and put a bullet between my eyes; well, Graham got life in Parchman prison, which might well have been worse than the chair, and I've yet to see Sheriff Bennett Wilson.

But this kind of work was merely putting a band-aid on a gaping knife wound, something I realized after a few years; if things were going to change, it would mean electing men willing to make it happen. That's why I signed up with the Hubert Humphrey campaign in 1960, taking on any job they gave me. Humphrey had been a tireless warrior for civil rights since the '48 Democratic convention, and the one man in America who I felt would really make a difference.

Thus I became one of the poor souls who went up against the Kennedy juggernaut in the West Virginia primary. I suppose I should have been happy that a fellow WWII vet was emerging as the frontrunner for the nomination, but the way old Papa Joe Kennedy spread the dough around in the valleys and hollows of West Virginia to sew up the state for his little boy, while a good man like Humphrey, whose father had been a druggist, got plowed under, left a really bad taste in my mouth. So much so, I seriously considered voting for Nixon in the fall, which wouldn't have been a stretch since I'd voted for Eisenhower twice; if I hadn't been swayed by Kennedy's phone call to Mrs. Martin Luther King when her husband was jailed in Georgia, I really might have voted for the Vice President.

Out of gratitude for my help in his campaign, Senator Humphrey offered to help get me appointed a Federal prosecutor back in Georgia, I was tempted to take the job, but I was no fan of Robert Kennedy, the man behind the smearing of Senator Humphrey as a "draft dodger" during the West Virginia primary. Instead, I went back to Georgia and resumed my practice, only now I was bringing suites against school districts to force them to desegregate.

Then in the summer of '63, I got a call from the Senator with a different job offer; President Kennedy had just sent a civil rights bill up to the hill, and Humphrey was going to lead the fight for it in the Senate once it got there. "Johnny," the Senator said from the other end of the line, "this is going to be one tough battle, and I'm going to need a man like you - a man who knows the southern justice system backwards and forwards - to help me get the job done. Your country needs you; I need you."

I couldn't say no and was put on Humphrey's congressional staff, where my courtroom experience would be put to good use lobbying Congressman who might be sitting on the fence. "You're a professional man, Johnny, and most members of Congress fool themselves into thinking they're the same - they'll listen to you." It's not boasting when I say I made a difference in a lot of cases. The President's bill sailed through the House Judiciary committee in early November, before hitting the Rules Committee, where Howard Smith stood ready to turn it back like a Confederate sentry.

Then on November 22nd, that bastard Oswald shot at JFK in Dallas and things got worse. The Civil Rights Act had been a story below the fold before Dallas; it disappeared completely from print afterward. The confrontation with Cuba consumed all of Congress's attention, as the country forgot about marches, protests, police dogs and church bombings. Christmas Day 1963 was the most depressing of my life, and I include the one in 1944 spent manning a machine gun in a forward position in the Philippines.

Our opponents in Congress made the most of the crisis, in the words of Senator Strom Thurmond, the old Dixiecrat demagogue himself, "In this hour of crisis, when foreign enemies have struck at the heart of our democracy right here on our sacred home soil, it is not the time to debate a piece of legislation championed by the kind of people who fired the bullets in Dallas. This so-called Civil Rights Act will tear this great nation apart in an hour of great peril; to even consider it on the floor of this body in any way is to give aid and comfort to those who wish us the greatest harm. If the President will not withdraw it, then we here in Congress must kill it forthwith."

I am sad to say a lot of good men on Capitol Hill who were not in the same corner as Ole Strom began expressing similar sentiments, not because they were secret hard core segregationists - although many of their constituents were - but because they were cowards. We saw it happening and was galled by it, they had battled the Old South and its strangle-hold on the Senate and House for more than a decade with nothing to show for it but weak legislation borne of bitter compromise, and now it looked as if they wouldn't even achieve so much as a symbolic victory.

It was a bitter blow to Dr. King and the good men and women in the Southern Christian Leadership Council who had taken the blows in places like Birmingham only to see it slip away because America took its eye off the ball.

I was especially bitter at Bobby Kennedy's Justice Department for abandoning the fight after November of '63. I guess vengeance against Castro took precedence. There were meetings at the White House where the President told Senator Humphrey that the Civil Rights Act remained among his highest priorities, bur Congress had to do its part. The Attorney General told the Senator the same thing in a meeting just before New Year's. Roy Wilkins, the head of the NAACP, saw the President and his brother the same week and got the same message; Dr. King himself, journeyed up from Georgia the last week of January hoping to speak to the President, but all he got was fifteen minutes with the Attorney General where the good Reverend made a forceful plea that the moment had come to strike at Jim Crow and it could not be allowed to pass. Bobby Kennedy listened and agreed with Dr. King, but also pointed out that it was Congress who had the ball and that was where his attention should go.

Two hours after his meeting with the Attorney General, King and his associates were in Senator Humphrey's office, and they were not happy. "Politicians often mistake rhetoric for action," Dr. King told us. "And seldom do they understand while they prattle inside these marble halls, there are good people dying trying to achieve their basic rights as American citizens." Dr. King then gave us a detailed account of arrests, beatings and four murders committed in the South against peaceful protesters since the beginning of the year. It was clear the man was not impressed with our efforts, and I did not blame him. Ralph Abernathy voiced the opinion that President Kennedy wanted to have it both ways; get the credit for sending a Civil Rights Bill to Congress, but just as happy to not have it pass in a Presidential election year so southern Democrats wouldn't desert his re-election campaign in the fall.

It was at this low point after King returned to Georgia that Senator Humphrey decided to go to the office of his old Senate colleague, the Vice President, to get some advice - and that's the operative word, "advice."

Despite how some historians portray it, this was not an act of desperation and Senator Humphrey did not go on his hands and knees seeking help from Lyndon Johnson. No, on the last Thursday in January, Senator Humphrey had a half hour meeting with Johnson in the Vice President's office. The next morning, it was the Vice President who came over to the Senator's office, and he came not with "advice," as Humphrey requested, but with a plan, one he said guaranteed us success in breaking the logjam keeping the Civil Rights Act from getting passed.

This was the first time I had seen the Vice President up close and in person; I had glimpsed him passing in the halls or presiding over the Senate, the one duty given to the Vice President by the Constitution, and one that Johnson seldom bothered to fulfill.

The man I saw sitting at Senator Humphrey's desk looked older and heavier than the one I remembered from the '60 campaign. And if the rumors were true, we wouldn't be seeing much of Johnson in '64. There was no love lost between LBJ and Bobby Kennedy and that disdain extended to the tight circle around the President, the men who would run his re-election campaign. What the President's real intentions were concerning the Vice President he would not say, beyond reiterating that there were no plans to change the Democratic ticket in 1964. Which wasn't saying much; maybe it was a bad fit from the start as Johnson, the Senate Majority Leader during the Eisenhower years, looked painfully out of place among all those New Frontiersmen. That was before the Bobby Baker scandal broke, and though Johnson was not directly tied to his former aide's illegal actions, the two men had been joined at the hip during the Vice President's days in the Senate and when Congressional investigators had shown a light on how Baker made his money, it illuminated Johnson's dealings as well. There was a particularly juicy story concerning an insurance policy kickback in the form of a nine-hundred dollar Magnavox TV which made for unflattering comparisons with the crony scandals under Truman. Then there were investigative stories in *Life* magazine where they looked at how Johnson had become such a wealthy man on a Congressman's salary, or more to the point, how Lady Bird had grown rich by investing in industries with heavy government regulation, starting with a pair of Texas radio stations.

All of this was embarrassing to the Vice President, to say the least; others would call it criminal. But Johnson's troubles were driven out of the news by the events in Dallas. Those shots fired at JFK might have been one lucky break for Johnson, indeed *Life* was going to put him on the cover that week, but instead there was a photo of the President's limo speeding to the hospital on the cover with Kennedy's Close Call in big block letters above it. The Johnson story was inside, but it's not why anyone bought the magazine.

But Johnson's lucky break hadn't stopped the trickle of rumors he would be dropped in '64, if anything, they'd increased during the winter while most of the capital was obsessed with the assassination attempt and a trail leading from Dallas to Havana. The JFK reelection committee was still hard at work behind closed doors, it was headed by the President's brother in law, Stephen Smith, but everyone knew Bobby Kennedy really ran the show, and no crisis, no matter how grave, could ever distract the Kennedys from politics. You didn't need a PHD to figure out where most of the dump Johnson rumors originated.

So it was a man staring at political oblivion who sat in Hubert Humphrey's office that January day, but if it was true, we wouldn't have known it by the performance we witnessed when Lyndon Johnson immediately went into a detailed account of how the Kennedy Administration had ignored his good advice and not cleared the legislative decks before sending the Civil Rights Act up to Congress - now all of Kennedy's agenda, which included an across the board tax cut and a bill to provide health insurance for the elderly, were being held up by the Southern block as potential hostages against civil rights. "If they had only listened to me, we wouldn't be up this particular shit creek right now, all they had to do was get those other bills disposed of and then go for Civil Rights, but all the smart boys around the President in the White House knew better than a man who'd spent most of his adult life on Capitol Hill."

After he'd made the case that everyone should always listen to Lyndon Johnson all the time, the Vice President said, "It would pass the House in a heartbeat if it could only get to the floor for a vote, but old Judge Smith's got it locked up tighter than a hen's ass in his Rules Committee and he's never going to let that happen. If it ever gets to the Senate, Jim Eastland is going to drown it like a litter of barn kittens in his Judiciary Committee. And if by some miracle it gets voted out of Judiciary, then Dick Russell and Strom Thurmond will make sure the damn thing is filibustered till hell freezes over."

The answer to these problems he went on to say was to break them down and tackle each one at a time, all the while keeping a steady pressure on Congress to get this thing passed even if there was a major foreign crisis happening at the same time; there was no other way, Johnson explained except to push right on through and make the showdown with Castro work in our favor. "While all the country's eyes are on Cuba and what we're going to do to those bastards behind Dallas, we're going pull off a legislative coup right here under the capitol dome. There are some in this town who would compare me to a cut dog, well a cut dog still has a tongue and can bark, and he still has teeth to bite with; all I need is a telephone. "

The first order of business was the House, and that meant moving the immovable Judge Smith and the only way to do it was by using a discharge petition - a resolution to discharge the control of the Act from the Rules Committee and bring it to the floor of the House for a vote. It required the signatures of a full majority of the House members, which meant the magic number needed was 218. Democrats had a majority of 257 out of 435, but getting to the necessary majority was complicated since 90 of them were from the South outright with others from Border States where the cause of racial equality had few supporters. This meant we could count on only 160 Democrats at best, the rest would have to come from Republicans, many of whom had sympathy for our cause, but far more of whom felt deference toward powerful committee chairman no matter how odious their politics or how out of touch they were with modern America.

The Vice President was undaunted by these hard facts and proceeded to use Senator Humphrey's phone for the next hour to make calls to various members of the House and the Senate. When he was done, Johnson assured us we'd have more than half the votes we'd need within 24 hours and then left. He proved to be true to his word as we had most of the Democrats needed by the end of the next day; over the next two weeks, Johnson returned to the Senator's office, working the phone and making lists of those committed to our side. It was the House Republicans he was working on now, and we would need at least 50 of them to sign the discharge petition. How we came by them is a story that's never been told.

This much can be said, on or about the first day of February of 1964, I was given a list by the Vice President with the names of five Republican Congressman on it and told that I was to make an appointment with each one. "Johnny boy," Johnson said with his hand squeezing my shoulder and his face leaning in close, "This is a job for a good lawyer who knows how to say the wrong thing in the right way; I can't do it, neither can Hubert or John McCormack, but you can." Then he went down the list, name by name, and told me what to convey to each Congressman.

I had to call some offices multiple times before a face to face meeting was guaranteed between the men on the list and myself, they were all busy men, and I was a nobody on the staff of Senator Humphrey; the reason given for the meeting was for a brief opportunity to lobby the Representative on behalf of the Civil Rights Act and if any refused, William McCulloch, the ranking Republican on the House Judiciary Committee and a big supporter of the Civil Rights Act would call them and request they to meet with me as a favor; I want to say Congressman McCulloch did not know what I was going to say in such meetings or the business transacted, he was doing it because the Vice President of the United States told him it was all nothing more than routine lobbying for a cause we all believed in.

Thusly I paid a visit to the offices of five Republican Congressman and told them in delicate, and carefully legal language, that they were in a position to render drastic and unique aid to the cause for racial equality in these United States, firstly they were to sign the proper resolution to discharge the Civil Rights Act from the Rules Committee, and secondly, they were to get commitments from at least ten other members of their Republican caucus to sign the same discharge petition in writing and deliver them to Congressman McCulloch's office. None of these Congressmen had expressed any public willingness to vote for the Civil Rights Act before my meeting with them and all of them to a man politely and firmly declined my request when first asked. Most gave what to them were valid reasons for not giving their support: the legislation was too great an expansion of Federal power; they really didn't like the part of the bill concerning "public accommodations," that it might violate property rights; that it would be handing Kennedy a big victory in Congress in an election year; a majority of their constituents didn't believe in telling Southerners how to live.

I heard them out and then told them that if they could find a way to render "drastic and unique aid" to the cause of equality, then there might be a way for them to receive "drastic and unique aid" in return. And then depending on to whom I was speaking, I explained what that last part could entail. A California Congressman, who was the silent partner in an Orange County construction company in which he'd invested his life savings, and which was now facing bankruptcy, could possibly receive a low-interest loan from a Fort Worth, Texas bank; the Army Corp of Engineers could reverse themselves on a recently killed big project and drain a hundred acres of Mississippi bottom land, greatly benefiting Continental Agriculture, one of the largest employers in a Missouri Congressman's district; First American Bank of Springfield, Illinois would be allowed to merge with Union Trust of Fort Wayne, Indiana, something which required SEC and Treasury department approval as it was a transaction that ran afoul of much regulation and red tape and would be to the great financial gain of Union Trust's largest stockholder, the brother of an Indiana Congressman; a trash company owned by the wife of a Nevada Congressman could double its business if it was to get the contracts to haul the garbage from a half dozen military installations in Southern California and Arizona.

The operative word I used there was "could" and never once did I use any language which might be construed as the proffering of a bribe or a quid pro quo…at least not in a court of law. If I felt any guilt about my actions, I just remembered the common good I was serving; the statute of limitations has long since expired, and most of the parties involved are long dead. Anyway my work paid off, by the end of February, we had nearly 50 Republicans committed to sign the discharge petition. Word evidently got around, I was contacted by at least three other Republicans, and to my surprise, two Democrats from Georgia and Arkansas, all offering to round up names for the discharge petition for the right price; I discussed it with the Vice President and he said not to push my luck and politely tell them no thank you. In the end, all it took was the mere threat of discharge petition being filed to get Judge Smith to strike his colors and admit defeat. He promptly allowed the bill to come up in the Rules Committee and then be sent on to the House for debate.

The day after this happened, front page stories appeared in both the Washington Post and the Star detailing how Vice President Johnson, a man whose political fortunes could charitably be described as waning only a month before, had diligently been working behind the scenes to resurrect the Civil Rights Act and free it from the death grip of the Rules Committee. The story painted the Vice President as the hero who arrived at the last moment to save the hapless liberals from themselves. I was none too happy with the way Senator Humphrey was made to look so feckless that he had to beg his old Senate mentor to save the day.

It was a hard pill to swallow and when I told Senator Humphrey call a press conference and tell his side of the story, he simply dismissed me with, "Johnny, that's just the price of having Lyndon on your side, he gets the job done, but he has to get all the glory."

I was not the only one who was less than happy with the story. There was a late night meeting between the Kennedy brothers, where Bobby reportedly blew a gasket over the way LBJ had made an end run around them on the issue of civil rights, something which had been the bailiwick of Robert Kennedy's Department of Justice; he raged about the way Johnson had obligated them to Republicans in Congress and exposed them to extreme political risk. "The son of a bitch could get us all impeached and kicked out of office," Bobby was later quoted as shouting at his brother. "He was buying Goddamn votes, which means you were buying Goddamn votes." The President let this go on for awhile before he told his Attorney General, "Bobby, we got our hands full, and Lyndon got the damn bill moving again, it's a victory and I'm not going to turn around and snatch defeat from its jaws."

Bobby Kennedy didn't like it, but LBJ was officially put in charge of the effort to get the Civil Rights Act passed the next day. I think Johnson's actions really impressed JFK, a man who valued success no matter how it was achieved. Just to keep on top of things, Lawrence O'Brien and his staff were brought in to "assist" the Vice President.

Late in the evening of this same day, the phone rang in my Arlington, Virginia, apartment; I had been dozing, but came wide awake when the voice on the other end identified themselves as the White House operator and that I was to stand by. There was a click and a familiar voice with a Massachusetts accent came on the line. "Mr. Compton," the President of the United States said, "I understand you are the man to talk to when it's time to make a deal, and I hear you have been making them all over the capitol building. I would be pleased if you would enlighten me as to what you discussed with certain gentlemen of the House Republican caucus."

I don't remember exact words of my stammered response to the President of the United States, only that I told him what he wanted to know. "Sounds reasonable enough," he said when I was done, "I knew men who sold their votes far cheaper when I was in Congress." The President thanked me for what I had done; he was sure the country would be better off in the long run. "But in the future, Mr. Compton, please do not go into anyone's office on Capitol Hill with any kind of similar offer without letting Mr. O'Brien know about it first. And I would consider it a great courtesy if you make no mention of this phone call, or that you and I have discussed these matters, to anyone. Thank you and good night." Then he hung up.

I will note that no recording of this call has ever turned up and as we all know, JFK taped himself thoroughly when it was in his own best interests.

A lot of heavy hitters came to Washington to lobby the full House when the Civil Rights Act came up for a full vote, the AFL-CIO, the National Council of Churches, and every major organization dedicated to advancing equal rights starting with NAACP. Dr. King himself stayed away, fearing he'd become too much of a lightning rod. All the hard work paid off as the House passed the Civil Rights Act on March 26, 1964, by a vote of 265-160, not an overwhelming margin as a number of northern Democrats and mid-western Republicans got cold feet at the last moment after putting their fingers to the political winds. It didn't help when Harry Belafonte and some other activists held a rally on the Capital steps on the eve of the vote declaring their solidarity with the people of Cuba and all of "history's victims of colonialism and militarism." Didn't these fools remember Joe McCarthy?

And despite the good publicity Lyndon Johnson received for his efforts on behalf of the Civil Rights Act, it did not stop talk of him being replaced on the ticket. Days after the vote in the House, a transcript of testimony to Senate investigators by an insurance agent who'd been shaken down by the Vice President's associates during the sale of a policy to Johnson was leaked to a number of reporters and columnists. Again, the crisis with Cuba softened the impact of the story, but it was damaging enough, and everyone knew the source of the leak had to be Bobby Kennedy.

Nevertheless, the Act had cleared the House, but our victory was a classic case of going from the frying pan into the fire; on the day the Civil Rights Act was introduced in the Senate, a move by Senator Mansfield to use parliamentary procedure to keep it from the clutches of James Eastland and his Judiciary Committee failed because not enough Republicans would back him.

"This so-called Civil Rights Act is as dead as day old road kill," the Mississippi Senator said to a group of reporters in his Senate office on the day the bill came to his committee.

"Looks like we have got our work cut out for us," said the Vice President minutes later to a group of us in Senator Humphrey's office.

Lt. Colonel Martin Maddox (III)
April - May 1964

"This is a fight not of our making, no American wanted this, but our hand was forced and we have no choice but to intervene in order to rescue a suffering people." It is the line most people remember from the speech President Kennedy gave to the nation on Friday, April 10th, 1964, announcing our military intervention in Cuba. He would take some heat for those words in the years ahead.

By the time the President spoke on Friday afternoon, over two dozen sorties had been flown over Cuba, most of them hitting anti-aircraft batteries and coastal artillery positions trained on potential landing sites. For the first couple of days, the fighters concentrated on targets around Havana, Mariel and Santiago, softening up the areas where the troops would be going in; although not all the targets were purely of military value - it took multiple tries before Radio Rebele (from which Castro was attempting to rally the Cuban people against "Yankee aggression") was knocked off the air on Saturday. On the third day, the B-52's began saturation bombings on military positions and transportation hubs in central Cuba. That was also the day we took our first casualty, Air Force Major Glenn Farris of Cleveland, Ohio, who's RF-101 was shot down over Havana while on a reconnaissance mission.

I took great satisfaction at the way Op Plan 365 had gone from a bluff to a fully functional operation. I lived in my basement office during those early days of Cuba Libre preparing briefings for the President, who was always asking pertinent and somewhat skeptical questions when I was done. "Castro will attempt to go to ground and fight it out," was his comment after one of my more optimistic talks.

The bombing campaign itself spawned contention behind the closed doors of the White House and the Pentagon right from the start, one which would eventually go public. The Chief of Staff for the Air Force was still General Curtis LeMay, a man not in the good graces of the Kennedy brothers to say the least, for it had been LeMay who had argued most vociferously (and some would say rudely) against the President's plan to quarantine Cuba in October of '62. The General had invoked Munich to the President's face in arguing that Kennedy immediately take out the missile sites in an operation the President had likened to Pearl Harbor in reverse, which was not the best way to approach this President...to put it mildly.

I delivered the Oval Office briefing on Sunday, April 12th, with LeMay and the rest of the Joint Chiefs in attendance, where the plans for ground operations on Cuba were discussed. General LeMay sat quietly through my positive report on the success of the air campaign so far, and the number of targets taken out, but when I mentioned the concentration of Russian forces at Camaguey and the need for this area to remain off limits, LeMay spoke up. "Cuba is a theater of war where Americans are engaged," he said to the

President, "and those Russian personnel are enemy combatants and should be treated as such. It makes no sense to allow the enemy a safe haven on their home ground." The General was not privy to the information we had, and the President did his best to explain the arrangement reached with Andreyev. LeMay would have none of it. "The only thing the President should have done when he was on the line with this Russian General was demanded his total surrender," LeMay said to me with the sharpest glare I've ever received from a superior officer in my entire career. "We have him outnumbered ten thousand to one; those Russians would be nothing but a grease spot within an hour if I could just give the order." At this point the President reminded the General of the obvious, that the Kremlin had a say in this and Russian casualties were sure to provoke a military response from them in Europe or elsewhere; so far the only thing coming out of Moscow were fierce denunciations of American aggression which killed no one, but that could change.

"Khrushchev hasn't mobilized one single soldier since the first bomb fell on Havana, there's nothing he can do, and he knows it. There are tons of munitions, artillery and ordinance there with those Russian personnel in Camaguey and it will all be handed over to the Cubans as soon as the first American GI hit's the beach. A lot of good boys are going to die when we go into Cuba; some them could be saved if I'm allowed to act right now." That was how LeMay laid it out, but the President would not budge, and no bombs would fall on Camaguey. There are many differing versions of the exchange between President Kennedy and the General on the second Sunday in April, and I'll put my hand to God that is how it happened. Curtis LeMay was the man who reduced Tokyo and Yokohama to ashes and built the Strategic Air Command, and I would never dare cal him a liar, just certain other historians and hacks.

In truth, most of the meeting between the President and the Joint Chiefs concerned coordination in the landing of ground forces on the island in accordance with Op Plan 365, and on this matter I am proud to say there was little in the way of dissension, the only real back and forth was over timing as General Taylor wanted the bombing to continue for a week to thoroughly degrade the Cuban military before our boys went up against them. But the President was wary of letting it go that long for a couple of reasons, not the least of which was the flow of refugees fleeing the fighting and flooding into Florida by the day - they were rapidly becoming a political matter as camps to house them were being built all over the southern part of the state.

Then there was the internal situation on the island; during the first week of April, the CIA station in Miami had taken advantage of the turmoil and aggressively landed a number of covert intelligence teams on the beaches and from them we had learned that the opposition to Castro was being decimated on the ground, if we did not act soon, there would be nobody left alive to form a provisional government. In other words, there were a lot of brave patriots counting on us now to come to their rescue, and if we didn't move soon, there would be no one left alive when we finally got there.

For these reasons, President Kennedy pushed the Chiefs to have the air campaign concluded by Wednesday with the invasion to follow immediately. General Taylor proposed doubling up on the bombing runs and insisted on an extra day in which to fully hit all the targets; the President agreed to this and before the meeting adjourned, he signed the orders for General Abrams to commence ground operations no later than midnight Thursday, the 17th of April.

Within hours, Army units and Marine Brigades began loading aboard transports in Miami, Charleston, Savannah, and Norfolk, while paratroopers from the 101st Airborne began preparations at Fort Benning to be dropped in country prior to the first landings.

No one made note that the 17th was the third anniversary of the Bay of Pigs.

It was not part of my concern at the White House, but I could not help but be aware of how the new Cuban crisis was being perceived among our allies abroad and among the American people at home. While at the house to catch a shower and change into a fresh uniform, I caught a *Huntley-Brinkley Report* feature on a march in Paris where nearly a hundred thousand people took to the streets to protest American "aggression" against Cuba, I remember thinking those people needed to be reminded of just who saved them from Nazi Germany's "aggression" not that long ago. It didn't help that General De Gaulle's public support for our policy was less than ringing, privately he was even more dismissive of "America's inability to stay out of trouble." or so I was told. Nor did we get much support from Great Britain, which I know was a big disappointment for the President, but the Tory government there had been brought to its knees by the Profumo scandal the year before, and it was clinging to power by its finger nails, which left no political capitol for rallying the British public in support of a war against a Communist tyrant. As Britain saw it, Castro and Dallas was solely an American problem; they just wanted to be left alone so they could listen to their Beatles records.

South America was much worse; Communists and leftists staged demonstrations which escalated into riots from Caracas to Buenos Aries, all of them bloody with loss of life; the State Department feared the Cuban crisis might result in multiple countries in Latin America going Red before the end of the year.

"Jesus Christ," the President supposedly said when he'd finished reading this depressing forecast, "I might as well start packing my bags right now because this will elect Goldwater in a landslide."

At the time, I was most disappointed at the sniping which occurred right here in America; a bunch of students at the university in Berkley, California actually held signs saying "Viva Fidel" at a rally protesting the bombing campaign, while others carried posters with Che Guevara's face on them. That rally was probably the first time the President was compared to Hitler. On the other hand, there was the Senator from South Carolina who wanted all the Cuban refugees to be herded into barbed-wire compounds and then shipped off to Central America before the "Communist vermin among them had a chance to infect the rest of the country."

As preparations went forward for the ground invasion, I found the President to be tough questioner during my briefings, constantly questioning the sources of intelligence as to their veracity, and to the faith they had in what they were saying, pointing out the hazards of proceeding through the fog of war. "Most of what we know about Waterloo today," he said at the end of one of my more positive reports, "was completely unknown to Napoleon and Wellington on the day of battle; same can be said of Grant and Lee at The Wilderness and Spotsylvania Court House."

The Attorney General was at most of these briefings; his main concern was the whereabouts of the Castro brothers, Commander Almeida along with Williams and Artime. He clearly wanted to salvage something after the disappointment of C-Day. At one point, he expressed hope that both Fidel and Raul Castro would end up in unmarked graves. When I cautioned him that we might be making Socialist martyrs out of the pair, he replied, "I can live with it."

The opening of ground operations in Cuba called for paratrooper units from the 101st Airborne to size the harbor at Mariel in the predawn hours of April 17th; there was a high degree of fear that one or more of the C-130's would be shot down before the men could make the jump, but that part of the operation went off flawlessly, and every plane got back to base without incident.

Not so the docks at Mariel, where as the first soldiers to come ashore on Cuban soil immediately came under sustained sniper fire. The first American to die in country was Cpl. Douglas Dixon of Burlington, Vermont, killed when a Kalashnikov round severed an artery in his leg, causing him to bleed out right there on the pier. I was in the room when the President called Dixon's parents the next day.

There was a fierce firefight at Mariel while the sun rose as the 101st went about securing the docks, in the end, it would take six and half hours to clear the buildings overlooking the port and secure its approach at a cost of twenty seven more paratroopers killed and twice that many wounded - in the end more than a hundred purple hearts would be awarded for action on April 17th alone. Mariel was the Cuban port closest to the United States, and it had a natural harbor, making the ideal point to launch ground operations; General Howze himself stepped ashore at noon on the first day and took command; the picture of him on the docks at Mariel was on every front page the next day. It was a reassuring sight to most Americans - the General confidently issuing orders on enemy soil, but I think it gave a false impression that taking Cuba would be easy.

But there would be no denying our success on the first day: by evening, units of the 1st Armored Division would start coming through Mariel, while at the other end of the island, a full Army division began off loading at Guantanamo Bay and heading in country with their first destination being the port city of Santiago de Cuba. The timeframe was to complete full ground operations and end all organized opposition within three weeks, and on that day I certainly believed we would meet our goal. To his credit, President Kennedy did not share my optimism. "The hardest part is in front of us," he reminded me more than once in those early days.

Yet the first days in Cuba really was the story of one success after another; despite tough initial opposition, Mariel was taken, and troops and material began pouring in through the port; Army units reached the outskirts of Santiago within 24 hours, taking little hostile fire along the way, a Marine Brigade easily secured Tarara beach east of Havana, a point from which an advance on the capital could be attempted. We were taking casualties, but in numbers far less than any of our worse case scenarios; there were some members of the NSC were openly speculating about having military operations completed by the first of May, after which, hopefully, a short occupation would begin. The evening news showed video tapes of happy Cuban civilians greeting American soldiers shouting "Kennedy *Si!*," reinforcing the image of us as liberators.

On the third day of the invasion, while I was at home taking a shower and grabbing a quick nap, the White House received news that the forward advance of American troops had run into heavy opposition on the main highway outside of Havana and on the outskirts of Santiago, suffering three hundred casualties in two hours; later in the evening, two surface to surface missiles hit the Marine beachhead at Tarara. By the fourth day, every ground unit in the island was engaged in combat with Cuban regulars; Castro had been holding back.

It had gone from "Kennedy *Si!*" to "Die Yankee Pig" within a day, dashing any and all hopes of an easy victory by the first of May. This prompted a tense meeting in which Robert Kennedy asked very pointed questions as to why Cuban defenses were still so effective after days of aerial bombing; many thought he was speaking for his brother who didn't want to appear petty by having the Commander in Chief criticize his officers to their faces while their men were under fire. President Kennedy promptly approved a request by Secretary McNamara to send General Abrams units from the 1st Infantry Division, "The Big Red One," stationed at Fort Riley, Kansas; in a matter of hours these men received orders to prepare to deploy to Cuba. The next week consisted of brutal house to house fighting all the way into Havana; one of my best friends in the Corp would later tell me of a harrowing encounter with a half dozen T-54 Soviet tanks in which my fellow Marines stood their ground and took them out one by one. We were giving as good as we were taking.

President Kennedy grasped quicker than anyone that the fight in Cuba had turned into a slog; I also want to say that at no time during these days was a withdrawal ever discussed, much less mentioned. I do not know who Seymour Hersh's sources were for his account stating that such a thing was debated by the NSC in the White House on April 23rd of 1964, but whoever it is, they are out and out liars.

In the meeting on April 29th, I cautiously predicted May 15 as the earliest possible date when all organized resistance in Cuba might end; the 1st Armored and the Marines had reached Havana and were preparing to occupy the city. The President's comment, "I'll be happy if it's done by Memorial Day." He also mentioned how Ambassador Dobrynin had requested another meeting later in the day, no doubt to deliver another protest note over Cuba.

"What's to protest," General Taylor commented, "we haven't dropped one bomb anywhere near Camaguey, all of his Russians are safe and sound. We've kept our word, and they've kept theirs."

But Dobrynin's meeting with the President had nothing to do with another "protest" note; instead, the Soviet Ambassador delivered a message of a different kind, one from the Soviet government demanding an immediate cease-fire in Cuba and a pledge to end to all military operations within 24 hours. Dobrynin punctuated this ultimatum by announcing that he had been instructed by his government not to leave the White House without a yes or no answer from the American President. John Kennedy rejected the Soviet demand on the spot without equivocation and politely showed Dobrynin out; the Ambassador was simply following the instructions he'd received from Andrei Gromyko in Moscow, in no way was he aware of the developments behind the closed doors of the Kremlin.

In the language of diplomacy, ultimatums mean war; everyone instantly grasped that we were about to hear the sound of the Russian Bear dropping the other shoe. And everyone scrambled to figure out where it would land. An attack on West Berlin was the most likely move for the Soviets to make, or in the worst case scenario, an all-out invasion of West Germany, sometime in the next 48 hours. But Director McCone countered that there was absolutely no intelligence indicating any unusual activity in Moscow or troop movements behind the Iron Curtain. The Soviet plans for war with NATO were well known by both the CIA and the Pentagon, and there were no signs of the mobilization necessary to put them into effect.

The only unusual thing noted was the continued absence of Khrushchev from Moscow, as far as anyone knew he was still on vacation in the Crimea, same as he had been for a month. Now his long disappearance from public view took on a decidedly ominous overtone. "Gentlemen," the President said at the end of another long Oval Office meeting, "it appears the ball is in the Soviet court." He promptly issued orders putting all American forces in Europe on the highest state of alert short of war, same for the Strategic Air Command.

It was simply not possible for the Soviets to launch a successful assault on NATO without some kind of prior preparation; a war machine like the Warsaw Pact just couldn't go from zero to all-out offensive warfare in a day. It was Ralph Gillison who woke me up to the obvious reality when he said, "They're going to hit us somewhere else and leave Europe alone for right now."

I could have kicked myself for not seeing it sooner, and promptly got on the phone, requesting every cable from every CIA station in the Middle East and the rest of Asia; anything and anyone who might have put something in an intelligence report which would tip us as to what the Soviets were planning - a troop movement or a MIG flyover which would have allowed the President to order an adequate response in time. But all I and my group did was flail and accomplish nothing.

That I was seeing through a glass darkly was the problem. We'd known nothing of the coup to oust Khrushchev, even the President's back channel informant, Vladimir Roykov, had not caught wind of it, he'd been going about his business of providing cases of Coca-Cola for members of the Politburo along with the latest issue of Playboy none the wiser.

But in the preceding weeks, as meetings in Washington planned for the liberation of Cuba, similar gatherings were happening inside the Kremlin as the secret cabal running the Soviet Union were making their own plans to exploit the situation. They looked at the inevitable loss of the socialist paradise in the Caribbean as a great potential triumph if things went right.

The first instinct of the hardliners, led by Nicolai Suzlov, was to go for the obvious: not only move on West Berlin, but West Germany as well and deal NATO a fatal blow in one lighting fast massive attack. It would all be over in a matter of days while the United States was tied down in Cuba and unable to organize an effective response. Defense Minister Malinovsky argued for an attack on Turkey, where the United States had placed missiles aimed at the Motherland not long before; the big prize here would be control of the Dardanelles and the Bosporus, the straits between the Mediterranean and the Black seas, an objective of Russian governments all the way back to Peter the Great.

Though both plans invited a nuclear response from the Americans as soon as the military situation went against them, Suzlov brushed these concerns aside, declaring that Kennedy was like all Americans, he would lack the nerve and never give the orders go nuclear; America had not suffered during World War II like the Russian people, all they cared about was making money and living a soft life. At different times it appeared as if an attack on West Germany or an assault on Turkey would carry the day, only to be shot down by Brezhnev and Gromyko, who would make the point that if Kennedy hesitated to use the nuclear option, he would surely be overthrown by his own Generals in the same way they pushed Khrushchev aside and bombers loaded with nuclear payloads would be on their way into the Soviet Union with little or no warning.

It was just too great a risk to take.

Fortunately, there was one objective which was completely outside of NATO's nuclear umbrella and right on the Soviet Union's southern perimeter: Iran. The conquest of Persia had been a dream of the Tsars and now was the time to make it happen, Brezhnev argued. The Shah was an American puppet who was allowing his territory to used by the

CIA to spy on Soviet territory, already at least three secret listening installations had been built in the northern end of the country, and new construction had commenced in the last few weeks, possibly an air field from which spy planes impervious to Soviet radar could be launched into the country. Far worse, the American might be planning to build secret missile sites the northern mountains, a reverse of what Khrushchev had attempted to accomplish in Cuba in the fall of 1962. The rewards for conquering Iran, while not as great as what might be obtained by forcibly reuniting Germany and defeating NATO, were still quite tangible and held the promise of paying off big time for the Soviet Union in the decade ahead. Foremost among these rewards were Iran's oilfields sitting atop some of the world's largest reserves of crude; control of them would give the Soviet Union virtually a free supply of oil as far into future as could be seen and a valuable commodity to sell on the world market. Furthermore, the occupation of Iran would put Soviet guns on the Straits of Hormuz, giving them control of the Persian Gulf and the ability to choke off oil exports from Iraq, Kuwait, and Saudi Arabia. This fact alone would give the Soviet Union tremendous influence in the Arab world and surely lead to the recruiting of more client states like Nasser's Egypt. It was not inconceivable that in ten year's time, the entire Middle East, stretching from Pakistan to Morocco, could become a second Soviet bloc like Eastern Europe.

It was this scheme which carried the day in the Kremlin; plans were quickly drawn up and the invasion of Iran proceeded to the implementation stage within 48 hours.

I will say this much, the Kremlin did a masterful job during March and April of 1964 at not showing their cards; they must have known our primary attention would have been on Europe and Berlin, so they were able to go about making preparations for military action in their far southern military districts. At some point, Khrushchev was brought back from Pitsunda and put under house arrest in his official dacha in Moscow - it seemed the men who'd usurped him still had use for their former leader. He was handed a speech and told to make a recording of it, said speech being an address to the Soviet people and the world announcing the invasion of Iran and defending it as a justified response to "lawless American provocation and aggression." The Premier read over the copy and exploded in rage, observing that his erstwhile comrades on the Politburo had "shit for brains" or whatever the Russian equivalent of that phrase might be and how their plan to invade Iran was potentially as colossal a blunder as Hitler's decision to attack in the East on June 22, 1941.

The old Bolshevik's protests fell on deaf ears, and when KGB head Vladimir Semichastny reminded him that the continued good health of Nina Khrushchev depended upon his cooperation, Nikita reluctantly complied.

So while Washington's attention was wholly focused on Cuba, the Kremlin, with great stealth, made its own plans. It would be one of the greatest intelligence failures in American history.

Teheran is eight and a half hours ahead of Washington, so it was late at night when the first hazy reports from our embassy there reached us concerning possible explosions at the airport; I was still busy reading cables and intelligence reports trying to discern the Russian's strategy, but in the moment, I knew I was hearing the sound of the other shoe hitting the floor.

In the predawn darkness, units of the 103rd Guards Airborne Division parachuted in and took control of the terminal buildings and tower in less than thirty minutes; they fired less than a dozen shots, all of them fatal to the Iranian police officers summarily executed on the spot. By sunrise on April 30th, the Russians had complete control of the airport in Teheran, by noon, military transports were landing one after the other, unloading the rest of the crack troops of not only the 103^{rd,} but the 7th Guards Division as well; by late afternoon, all the key government buildings in the Iranian capitol were in their hands, while important bridges and intersections were seized and the American and British embassies surrounded. As this was happening, the 73rd Rifle Division and the 4th Tank Army crossed the border and began making their way south through the mountains, opening a way for the rest of the Red Army. Soviet bombers came in over the Caspian Sea and began air strikes on other Iranian cities. The Iranian government was decapitated, fourteen of the Shah's generals were killed outright on the first day, while most of the rest were captured; the casualty rate among the ruling council was even greater, a third of them killed on the first day, a third captured, and the rest disappearing into the sea of refugees fleeing the city. As for the Shah himself, he and his family drove in a limo to a secluded airfield and flew out of the country on a private jet; he landed in Paris as the Russians were mopping up back in Teheran.

Not much of this was known in the West at the time as our best intelligence assets were lost with the capture of Teheran; while the CIA teams in the country there to gather information on the Soviets, were promptly rounded up by the KGB. The Agency's station chief in Beirut was able to smuggle in some agents by driving in through Syria and Jordan, then slipping by boat across the Persian Gulf, but what intelligence they provided was of limited value.

Khrushchev's speech was broadcast on the morning of the attack, to the entire world it appeared as if the Soviet leader had caught the West napping; the invasion was justified as a preemptive move against the United States to keep them from using Iran as a base from which to launch offensive actions against the Motherland. We felt the sting of an apparent Soviet triumph most keenly, and the inclination was to hit back immediately; on the first day of the invasion, the Pentagon issued orders diverting warships from the Atlantic and Pacific to the Indian ocean, while an extra fighter wing was moved to Turkey. NATO went all out to pivot from defending against an attack from the Warsaw Pact to offensive operations in the Middle East. Unlike Cuba, our European allies had large investments in Iran, both the British and French were adamant the Russian aggression not be allowed to stand. But a successful military operation in that part of the world would take weeks, if not months of logistical planning and troop movements to pull off, it was hard for us professional warriors to admit that while we were in up to our waists in Cuba, we were in no position to get in up to our necks in Iran. Nevertheless, the Joint Chiefs came to the President two days after the Soviet invasion and presented him with a plan for a bombing campaign and the insertion of NATO forces - primarily American - into southern Iran in order to prevent the Soviets from capturing the Persian Gulf ports; the plan stated that there was a small risk the Soviets would use battlefield nukes as part of a response.

President Kennedy heard listened to his military commanders and then gave them his answer. "Gentlemen," the President said when we were done, "this is a serious crisis, but it is not Armageddon. Think of how much direr the circumstances would be if the Soviets had made a move in Europe; if that were the case, I have no doubt we would be seriously talking about the nuclear option at this very moment. Iran is a big country - over 70 million people - and when you look at the big picture, the Soviets have taken only a small portion of it. I think they have bitten off more than they can chew. We are right in the middle of a military operation in Cuba and the one being proposed in Iran carries serious risks, not the least of which is the risk of unintended consequences once a shooting war develops between American and Russian forces. I believe we should hold our fire for the time being and I am willing to take the risk in doing so."

The President went on to make the point that Americans and Russians were not killing each other anywhere in the world at the moment, and the situation required them to do whatever it took to keep it that way across Europe and Asia. There was a line that had not been crossed yet, even though General Howze was reporting how the Soviets at Camaguey were giving arms to Castro's resistance.

I must admit to not being in total agreement with the President's thinking; the British and French foreign ministers were floating the idea of mining the Iranian ports on the Persian Gulf and the Gulf of Oman before the Soviet forces took control of them while their navies established an intimidating presence there. I thought such a plan was the least we could do. But the President did not agree, he really believed the best course of action was to hold our fire for the time being; many in the Pentagon and Langley were quite unhappy, there was talk behind closed doors of mass resignations, that General Taylor had to talk some of his best officers out of it, something I did not learn about until later.

As I've said, I am a good Marine and I know my duty, and looking back, I will gladly concede that John F. Kennedy knew what he was talking about when he said the Soviets had bitten off more than they could chew. Only days after he spoke those words an advancing Soviet rifle brigade was ambushed outside the holy Muslim city of Qom by a homegrown Iranian militia, twenty thousand strong, made up of volunteers and surviving units of the Iranian military; they decimated the Soviet brigade so bad that only a hundred survivors escaped, the wounded left behind were shot where they lay by the Iranians, many of whom were armed with nothing more than 19th Century British long guns. We didn't learn of this Soviet defeat until a month later.

I will admit to being wrong, we absolutely should not have jumped into a war in the Middle East in the days after the Soviet invasion, it would have fatally tied our hands at the wrong time; others were watching these developments from Peking, the Korean Peninsula and the jungle of Southeast Asia and were making their own plans, plans which would be acted upon with stunning swiftness soon enough.

Wade L. Harbinson (II)
March - May 1964

I must admit to being quite impressed with Mr. Vance Harlow upon our first meeting, after spending no more than five minutes with him in the back room of the Carousel Club in Dallas, it was clear to me he was the kind of man who got things done. We were there in that low-rent strip joint at his insistence, telling me during our first phone conversation, when I loosely explained my proposal for him, that we needed to meet face to face in a place where the owner and the employees could be counted on to have total discretion.

My proposal was simple, I was going to elect Barry Goldwater President and was willing to pay good money for him to get the dirt on the Kennedys and bring it to me - providing said dirt could be documented and would hold up in the court of public opinion.

Mr. Harlow asked me how much good money I was willing to pay and I told him a figure in the low six figures. "Damn you Texans are tight," was Harlow's reply, "you want to buy the Presidency, not a shopping center in downtown Houston. It can't be done for less than a half million, if you don't want to pony up then get on the phone to some of your Big Oil buddies, they hate Kennedy like poison." He went on to explain how this was not an amateur operation I was asking to be done. What Harlow was willing to do was make the right phone calls to the right people who would be willing to do whatever it took to bring me the kind of information I desired. It would cost me a cool one hundred thousand just for him to make those calls, and the people picking up on the other end of the line were not angels or choirboys, not by a long shot. They would be taking big risks and possibly breaking confidences and trusts, and they would not be willing to do such unless there was the certainty of being well compensated. There was no reason to continue our discussion if I wasn't willing to meet the price.

In for a penny, in for a pound, without hesitation I told Harlow the money would be there, I guaranteed it, so he'd better start making those calls.

"I like doing business with people who know what they want and are willing to open their wallets to get it." That was Harlow's comment as we shook hands in the back room of the Carousel Club; he stayed for the show, I did not.

I had no knowledge of the people Harlow would be talking with, nor did I want to know, this is how business is done when one wants to find an edge. I had no doubt the little bastard Bobby Kennedy would be using whatever means necessary to document every incident of Senator Goldwater jaywalking and I had no guilt for what I was doing.

If it put Goldwater in the White House, thus saving the United States of America, then it would be worth it all.

Let me also add, at no time in any of my conversations with Vance Harlow did we discuss committing any criminal acts, nor did we discuss monetary compensation as an inducement for either Harlow or any third party to commit any criminal act, nor a monetary reward for anyone who might commit a criminal act as a result of any conversation I might have had with one Vance Harlow.

My Daddy might have raised a fool for a son, but it wasn't this son.

In the following weeks, the Goldwater campaign rolled ahead amidst a continuing national crisis as the Kennedy Administration made a hash out of the confrontation with Cuba, they'd wasted months trying to negotiate with that wretched Communist murderer who'd snuck agents across the Rio Grande to commit an act of war on American soil. Then this courageous General Almeida stood up to free his people, and Kennedy sits on his ass when the 82nd Airborne should have landed in Havana to support these brave rebels the next day.

It was enough to make me puke.

And it was enough to make a lot of good Americans puke as well. On the second Sunday in April, Senator Goldwater made it plain where he stood in an appearance on Meet the Press when asked by Robert Novak on how his policy in Cuba would differ from the President's. "If I were in the White House now," he said with conviction, "instead of the current incumbent, Juan Almeida would be in charge in Havana and Fidel Castro would be facing a Cuban firing squad; and there would be no desperate refugees washing up on the beaches in Florida because the full force of all three branches of the American military would have been standing behind General Almeida on Day One."

It was the kind of talk that couldn't be matched by Ambassador Lodge and Governor Rockefeller, both of whom would not criticize the President once the fighting in Cuba began. It was a fatal move for their campaigns as Republicans began flocking to the Goldwater banner in even greater numbers. Two days after the Meet the Press appearance, the Senator flew to California and in a speech in San Diego laid into Kennedy:

"I reject the notion that we must always be mindful of what the men in the Kremlin will think and do when conducting *our* American foreign policy; instead, let them always be mindful of what the men in Washington are thinking and doing when *they* plot their crimes. It's not that way now with our present Administration, but it will be when I'm elected, so help me God." The crowd went wild when Barry spoke those words.

GOLDWATER WOULD CONFRONT SOVIETS was the headline in the *New York Times* as the eastern elites reacted with horror at the notion America was about to elect this bellicose blowhard President. Barry was taking off the gloves, and millions loved it, we had twice the number expected show up at district conventions in Tennessee; the same thing happened at a dozen state conventions during April and May, allowing us to amass more than half the total needed to secure the nomination on the first ballot.

Clif White's plan was coming together and the success brought a level of harmony to the inner circle of the campaign, the Arizona Mafia - Dean Burch and Richard Kleindienst - and the true believers like Clif White, Bill Rusher and I managed to put aside our differences and work together for a common goal. It became a well-oiled machine, although I never forgot that if we'd listened to Burch and company, Barry Goldwater would have gone down in flaming defeat. I will give them credit for hiring a former Miss Idaho to handle the press briefings; it never hurts to have pretty gal out front in any operation.

The other thing which brought so many to our cause was Kennedy's so-called Civil Rights Act passing the House - this really put the fear of God into our brethren below the Mason-Dixon line and they knew where Barry stood; he'd made it clear for years that he didn't think it any of his business what the good people of Alabama and Mississippi did inside the confines of their sovereign states. The Democratic Party used to stand on the same principle, but I'm sorry to say it was now taking orders from that charlatan, Martin Luther King. During the second World War, I had the privilege of serving with some fine Negroes, brave men who didn't turn rabbit at the sound of enemy gunfire, and this Communist witch doctor King could not so much as stand in their shadow.

Then the Russians went into Iran and the Civil Rights Act was forgotten in the wake of another Kennedy disaster. In the days after the attack on Iran, my phone rang off the hook as millions of Americans, convinced that the Third World War was breaking out, donated more than a half-million dollars in an effort to make their country come out on the winning side. But the one call I didn't get during this time was from Vance Harlow, but I wasn't concerned, things like what I wanted done took time and had to be done right. Kennedy still led in the polls and many Americans still fell for his huckster's charms; which is why I was willing to wait and pay for whatever it took to put him down once and for all.

All things come to he who waits. That was another thing my Daddy used to say.

Lt. Colonel Martin Maddox (IV)
May - June 1964

    I was an absentee father during the month of May 1964, as I slept in the basement office most nights, only going home to take a shower and change uniforms; I spent many years making it up to Betty and the kids. The President put in some long hours too, but all he had to do was leave the West Wing and go up to the family quarters.

    There were reports on an ever changing battlefront coming in every hour from Cuba and Iran. Havana was still held by Castro loyalists two weeks after the first American troops landed on the island, reinforcements from the 1st Infantry Division were making a difference as Santiago was finally secured as we began to make a push eastward; Castro's army was still in the fight and well-armed as those AK-47's took their toll - 3,000 dead by the third week and 5,000 wounded. It was sobering to see those flag-draped coffins come home and the coverage of the funerals at Arlington, although the stories of coffins coming home to a small town in Kansas or a neighborhood in Queens where whole communities showed up to support a grieving family were the saddest. The President insisted on looking at the KIA list every day; it's a testament to his skills as a Commander in Chief that the sorrow he must have felt in private never appeared in public.

    Getting any kind of good intelligence out of Iran was a problem at first, the British had better luck getting operatives into the country, and they had a lot of native sources in the Middle East to draw upon. The Teheran airport had Red Army troop transports landing every hour, while mechanized divisions opened the roads in the north for the heavy armor which would give them a big advantage in the open country in the south. The Red Army's occupation of the country would be complete by the third week of May, or so the Pentagon estimated. On the 6th, there was another meeting with the Joint Chiefs where they again made another push for an extended air campaign against Soviet military targets and supply lines in Iran using long-range bombers based in the Mediterranean and the western Pacific.

    While the President heard them out, he calmly declined to sign on yet again. "If we go down this route, we'll not only be taking resources from NATO that will be badly needed if there is a sudden crisis in Europe or elsewhere, but a counterattack might be exactly what the Kremlin wants, then we'll be involved in two major military operations at the same time, while they're tied up in only one, which for them can be won through the simple application of overwhelming numbers. And it would leave a Goddamn million Red Army infantrymen free to make a move against NATO, which might just be their objective all along."

    The President concluded by saying we needed to wrap up Cuba as fast as possible so our hands would be free to deal more effectively with greater challenges. To their credit, the Chiefs saluted and followed orders, even General LeMay, who frowned but said nothing. The President would be vindicated, and soon, though that outcome was far from clear during those days in early May.

We were way beyond Op Plan 365 by this point; I cannot say we were making it up as we went along; it was more like finishing up what had already been put in motion. The flow of men and materiel into the Southern Command continued at an ever greater volume, with heavy emphasis on armor. Whatever was needed to get the job done and done soon was our mission. Two days after the May 6th meeting with the Joint Chiefs, the big push to take Havana got underway, and the preliminary estimates put it at six days minimum to secure the city. But that didn't take into account General Abrams's history with Patton and the lessons he learned fighting the Germans; relying heavily on tanks and personnel carriers, he was able to get the 1st Armored Division into the center of the city a little more than thirty-six hours after the attack commenced, even though they had to plow through massive barricades made up of overturned Chevys and Fords and city buses erected by bitter end defenders. The capture of the National Assembly building was a big morale booster at the White House, that along with the securing the Havana airport by the Marines.

On the same day, a report reached my desk stating how a former waiter at the Capri Hotel, who'd just reached Miami by way of a crowded rowboat, was telling interrogators Castro had established a command post in the basement of the hotel. When I showed this to the Attorney General, he was quite adamant that the Capri be bombed immediately. I had my doubts as to the veracity of this intelligence, we had knowledge of a number of Castro's hidden bunkers command posts in the city, all of them in more secure sites than a hotel on the waterfront; my hunch was that the Beard had hightailed it into the countryside because that was how he'd beaten Batista. The Capri was leveled by bombers before the end of the day anyway, which underscored a mission objective not written down in black and white and not spoken about openly - Fidel Castro was not to be taken alive. There were three CIA teams on the island tasked with making sure this goal was achieved as quickly as possible. I thought about the deal struck with Marcello and Trafficante and concluded, too damn bad.

The fall of Havana was a moment of supreme satisfaction for all of us in the White House, the picture of American GI's standing on the city's famous seawall on the front page of the *New York Times* May 10th edition made even the Attorney General smile, even though he was a realist like the rest of us and knew there was a lot of fighting left to do along with a lot of loose ends to be tied off.

One of those loose ends was taken care of the next day when a call from General Abrams himself informing the President of the capture of a wounded Fidel Castro in a Havana suburb, the apprehension accomplished by a squad of American Infantrymen after an intense house to house firefight. Castro had been wounded in a bombing attack two days before and was discovered in the back room of a house, attended by two nurses. A piece of shrapnel had ripped a hole in his right thigh, and he was lying unconscious on a cot after being injected with morphine. The aide who swore to put a bullet through the Maximum

Leader's head rather than let him fall into the hands of the Yankee Imperialists simply could not do it when the time came, he broke down and wept uncontrollably as Castro was put on a stretcher and loaded onto the back of a Jeep for a trip to the nearest field hospital.

"This is not how it was Goddamn well supposed to have happened," the Attorney General snarled when he got the report on Castro's capture. "The bastard was never supposed to be taken alive. NEVER! Those sons of bitches should have been told to finish Castro off then and there. Nobody would have asked any questions; we'd made sure of it." It was then pointed out to the Attorney General that it was illegal to directly order an American soldier to commit cold-blooded murder. That did not ease his disposition in the slightest.

There were still an estimated 50,000 well-armed Castro loyalists in the field despite Fidel's capture, a figure that would later be revealed to be laughably low. Then there was the matter of a post Communist government; the plans for C-Day were now utterly moot, for when the 1st Armored reached the center of Havana, they learned the sad fate of Juan Almeida; this brave man had been shot in the back by officers he thought were loyal to him in a desperate attempt to save their own necks, not unlike the German conspirators who turned on Von Stauffenberg after the plot to kill Hitler failed. And those brave patriots, Harry Williams and Manual Artime, hadn't made it either, both went down fighting in a sugar cane field two days after walking off that beach into the countryside, betrayed by a man they'd trusted who turned out to be one of Castro's spies. I am told that both the President and his brother wiped away tears when informed of the circumstances of their friend's deaths.

We'd put all of our eggs in General Almeida's basket and were now left in charge with no one to take the lead. The best we could do in the wake of events was to set up a military administration to try and get the electricity back on and take care of basic needs, but to the rest of the world, we looked exactly like military occupiers, which in truth we were.

Then there was the problem of the Russians at Camaguey, they had kept up their end of the bargain and stayed out of the actual fighting; the only Soviets taken prisoner were a few stragglers who appeared to have gone native after enjoying the company of the local females, along with a squad of KGB agents attempting to pass among the population, who were turned in by a civilian who'd once been one of Batista's policemen.

More than one ranking officer over at the Pentagon wanted to demand surrender from Andreyev or at the least, the laying down of his soldier's arms. President Kennedy would have none of it. "I told Andreyev that Camaguey would be treated as neutral territory," he firmly reiterated at one Oval Office meeting, "and that no surrender would be required of him if he did as I requested. He has lived up to this end of our agreement. I can do no less."

If only it could have been so simple, but there are always complications, and as the days of May 1964 passed, the complications in Cuba multiplied. The story surrounding the Soviet fallback to Camaguey began leaking out to the press, the original sources being officers in the Pentagon and Southern Command who were not happy with the situation and the deal that had been struck between our side and the Soviets. SOVIET MILITARY OUT OF FIGHT IN CUBA was the headline for a story in the *Washington Star* on May 7th, its sources being frontline Army officers and men. The networks did similar stories that evening, with all of their correspondents in Cuba making mention of Camaguey for the first time. The next day Walter Cronkite, reporting from Cuba, and citing local informants and sources in Washington, said that an apparent "truce" was in effect around the Soviet "zone" because of express orders not to bomb the area or approach it from the ground. The enterprising Cronkite was somehow able to get through the lines and get an interview with a Soviet officer who confirmed as much - it was the lead story on the May 10th broadcast of the *CBS Evening News*. Within 24 hours there were stories in the *Los Angeles Times* and the *New York Post* asserting that Camaguey had become a safe haven for members of Castro's government, among them Raul Castro himself and Manual Piniero. The story firmly implied that the three men named as Oswald's co-conspirators could be found there as well.

Equally troubling in the story were charges that the Russian military on the island had been freely sharing arms and ammo with Cuban forces as they were killing and wounding American GIs. It hardly painted the picture of a truce.

Overnight, Camaguey became a problem, so much so that an NSC meeting was called on the morning of the 11th of May to deal with it. "This thing is being made to look like something it's not," Secretary McNamara said first thing. "It's being made to look as if we're going easy on the Soviets down there while they have been backing Castro in every way except to shed their own blood. They'd all be dead or prisoners now if we had not reached out to them and they need to appreciate that." It was a pretty fair picture of how it was playing out in the press and on the campaign trail, which though it was seldom mentioned, was always a consideration with the politicians in the room. General Taylor said the only acceptable solution was some kind of formal acquiescence by Andreyev to American authority on the island, Mr. Bundy and Secretary Rusk agreed with him.

"That would be suicide for Andreyev," the President said, "he's already done enough to warrant a firing squad back home; if he so much as mentions surrender, it's not only his death but probably exile to a Siberian work camp for all the men in his command."

The President had a point; Stalin had not dealt kindly with any of the returning Red Army POW's who'd had the misfortune of being captured by the Germans in WWII.

"This is going to be untenable very soon," the Attorney General said. "We have to formalize the relationship with the Russians down there as soon as possible, but it has to be on our terms and they have to agree."

I believe it was the President who first came up with the term "armistice" which is a truce by any other name, but one which implies cessation of hostilities among equals. "We treat Andreyev as if he is the true power on the island," the President said, "as if he is the

Kremlin itself. That should take care of any problems with his pride." It was agreed that General Abrams would request a face to face meeting with Andreyev to discuss terms, among them being a list of Cuban nationals they might be harboring. My group was tasked with coming up with a list of points for Abrams to bring up at the meeting. "Getting those Russian bastards out of there," Ralph Gillison observed, "is going to be one damn hard nut to crack."

Later, President Kennedy would be faulted for not using Luciano's "hot line" to negotiate directly with General Andreyev, but it was decided that having Andreyev meet with a fellow commander in the field was the way to go; then there was the political risk to the President, who could be charged with selling out American interests while American boys were dying on a battlefield. There would later be harsh questions and criticism that the President did not try hard enough to open a dialogue with Moscow during these tense days as both countries plunged deeper into troubled waters. My answer would be that there needed to be someone on the other end willing to pick up on the other end of the line; from mid-March on, every request to talk to Chairman Khrushchev directly had been rebuffed for reasons which became clear later on. As I have noted, there were a number of meetings with Ambassador Dobrynin, but he was a much out of the loop as to what was happening in Moscow as we were.

The work on the armistice terms would prove to be the last chore we would do on the Cuban operation for some time, for while all our focus had been on the island, others had been watching every move we'd made and biding their time. And they were not just eyeballing Washington, but Moscow as well. In Peking, Hanoi, Pyongyang, events had been monitored, moves had been noted, debates had been waged and decisions made. If the Americans and the Russians were going to bog themselves down in foreign conflicts in an effort to spite the other, then an opportunity was at hand, one they could not afford to let pass.

But it was not only men of power watching things unfold, for there were men and women in Eastern Europe, trapped for nearly 20 years behind the Iron Curtain who watched and waited as well for just the slightest lifting the Soviet boot heel. These people were listening to Radio Free Europe and hoping against hope they might be like the Cubans and also be freed from a tyrannical system. And in the rumors drifting back from the fighting in Iran and the reports heard on illicit foreign radio broadcasts, they believed they heard a chink being hammered into the Soviet armor.

What happened over the second half of May would seem like the falling of dominos, one crisis tumbling into another, and looking back afterward, it would all seem inevitable. Not so at the time, and really not so at all.

The first crisis would come from Southeast Asia, where the nasty bush war between the South Vietnamese and the Communist Viet Cong guerrillas had been raging for years, with the latter getting the full support from the Communist government in the North. The

South had really been on the ropes since an army coup had deposed and then executed President Diem the previous November. Diem had been losing the support of his own people and was suspected by a lot of men in the Administration of secretly going behind our backs to make a deal with the Communists after America sent a lot of aide, money and advisors to his country to prop him up - so I thought it was no great loss when the ingrate went down on November 2nd of '63. And for a few weeks, South Vietnam was a big story; it looked as if it would be the next big test of our resolve to stop the spread of Communism in Asia.

Then came the events in Dallas and South Vietnam disappeared from the front pages and the evening newscasts. It also ceased to be anything close to a priority for the Administration as the assassination conspiracy investigation led back Havana and the ensuing confrontation with Castro. Still, the brush war in the countryside of Vietnam simmered and spewed; more than once during the winter, there were reports of intense fighting in the Central Highlands of South Vietnam which got the attention of the Pentagon and the State Department for a day or so before some development elsewhere, almost always Cuba, grabbed the spotlight.

Vietnam came back into focus on May 16th when General William Westmorland, the newly installed commander of the American mission in South Vietnam, sent an urgent cable to the Pentagon informing them that not only had the Viet Cong captured two provincial capitals in the critical Central Highlands, but they had also wiped out a large contingent of the South Vietnamese Army just outside of Saigon. Not only that, but there were a number of details concerning these defeats which were especially ominous, not the least of them being the latest version of the Type 56 variant of the AK47 the Viet Cong irregulars were armed with, along with the short range surface to surface missiles they used as well. Somebody was sending their best arms and ammo to Ho Chi Minh. Equally bad was the report from the Highlands that Russian advisors were spotted on the ground, aiding the Viet Cong in battle; if true, this was a serious escalation; it could also mean Moscow was fishing in more troubled waters than just Iran.

In tandem with Westmorland's message was one from Ambassador Lodge, stating that the junta in Saigon which had replaced Diem was in disarray and on the verge of collapse, completely unable to mount an effective defense of the country. In unusually blunt words, Lodge said that if the present circumstances did not change, the whole country would likely be past the point of saving within 30 days.

An emergency meeting was called by the President on May 17th in response to these developments. John Kennedy was not a happy man at the prospect of yet another foreign policy crisis; his frown grew even more pronounced when Walt Rostow, an assistant to the NSC director, made an impassioned talk on the strategic importance of Southeast Asia as it fit into the Cold War and as a roadblock to Communist expansion. Rostow urged the President to immediately bomb the port of Haiphong to prevent the Soviets and the

Chinese from resupplying Hanoi, while sending at least an infantry combat brigade to take on a combat role until the South Vietnamese Army could get back on its feet.

"I wasn't aware they were ever on their feet to begin with," was the President's comeback to Rostow.

What was unspoken at this meeting was the immense political liability the President would face if another Asian nation fell to the Communists the same way China did under Truman in 1949. That memory must have been on the minds of Secretaries Rusk and McNamara and General Taylor when they concurred with Rostow's reasoning.

President Kennedy mentioned that such actions might require Congressional authorization, which would take too long. The Attorney General interjected that any action taken in South Vietnam could fall under the resolution passed by both Houses of Congress in February approving military action against Cuba, since the new problems in Southeast Asia were simply an expansion of an already ongoing crisis.

"That's a real stretch there, Bobby," the President said, "a real stretch indeed."

In the end, President Kennedy didn't have much choice, the Soviets were expected to reach the Persian Gulf by the end of the month, completing their conquest of Iran; there was no way he could sit by and allow another Communist triumph over an ally. He signed the orders for the bombing of the port of Haiphong and the deployment of a Marine infantry brigade to South Vietnam before the day was over. In the early hours of the next morning, he stood in the White House press room and made the announcement, during which he referenced his own inaugural. "I said we would have to 'bear any burden' and I was talking about times such as these when our foreign enemies test our resolve; whether it will be found wanting in South Vietnam is entirely up to us."

On May 20th, the day General Abrams finally met face to face with General Andreyev at a sugar refinery outside of Camaguey, reports began flooding in from the Korean peninsula alerting us that North Korean military units were massing just above the DMZ. It seemed Kim Il Sung was emulating his fellow Asian Communist, Ho Chi Minh, and getting in on the act while the United States and the Soviet Union were otherwise engaged. I can't possibly describe my own reaction to the news from Korea; I couldn't get the faces of the good men I had seen die in the cold and snow there, out of my mind.

The North Korean mobilization made it clear that our other enemies and rivals had been busy while our attention had been focused on Castro and Cuba.

The bad news coming from Korea required an immediate response, this time there would be no emergency meetings of the NSC, instead Secretaries Rusk and McNamara, along with the Joint Chiefs gathered in the Cabinet Room with the President to lay out a course of action. I was in the basement looking over the latest cables from Cuba and not present, although I heard an account almost immediately afterward and I trust its accuracy over some other versions which turned up in memoirs many years later.

The stark reality of the situation was laid out for the President: the plan in place called for the 60,000 American troops stationed in South Korea to hold off the combined might of the People's Republic until reinforcements from Japan and the United States could arrive and turn the tide. But that plan was now defunct because most of those reserves were now in Cuba, while the others would be needed in Europe if the very real threat of open warfare between NATO and the Warsaw Pact became a reality. In short: America could simply not afford to commit the necessary reinforcements to Korea; we were rapidly getting ourselves into more wars than we had resources to fight them.

This was when a remarkable thing occurred; John F. Kennedy and Curtis LeMay put aside their considerable differences and found a way to work together. The General had been in the dog house ever since the Missile Crisis and his outspoken opinions during this latest emergency had not endeared him to the Administration any better, but on this day he took the floor in the Cabinet Room and calmly and in detail, laid out a plan to stop the North Koreans in their tracks before it even began; if they struck first and held the initiative, there would be no stopping them.

The Air Force Chief of Staff's plan called for the use of virtually every strategic long-range bomber in the Pacific in an extensive aerial campaign against the North Koreans that in firepower would rival anything he'd thrown against the Japanese in 1945. The General did not mince words, boldly stating his plan was designed not only to destroy every possible target of military value between the 38h Parallel and the Yalu, but was also calculated to inflict the maximum casualties to break enemy morale. It was total war at its most ruthless; the kind of thing a warrior like LeMay did better than anyone else.

"Mr. President," General LeMay reportedly said, "when I'm done with them, the only thing the North Koreans will have left to throw at us will be rocks and sticks."

"I know what you are proposing to do," President Kennedy said as he signed off on LeMay's plan, "will seem barbaric and cruel to some, but they will come to understand in time." When it was brought to the President's attention that some of our bombs were certain to fall on Russian and Chinese military personal, he said our hand had been forced, and it could not be helped now. The orders the President signed authorized the Chief of Staff of the Air Force to make use of every fighter and bomber based not only in the Pacific, but west of the Mississippi if he deemed them needed. LeMay got everything he wanted.

The scrambling began the instant the doors of the Cabinet room opened; orders went out as the American Air Force turned on a dime. In a matter of hours, a minimum of 200 fighters and bombers, along with at least 30,000 active duty personnel were ready to go to Japan, Okinawa, and the Philippines. It proved to be a very long Saturday of a Memorial Day weekend; LeMay was on the phone from his office in the Pentagon round the clock, pushing everyone to the limits to get the job done. We all heard about the officer in charge of the docks in San Diego who didn't get a tanker filled with jet fuel seaborne fast enough to suit LeMay, the man literally pissed his pants when he got a call from the Air Force

Chief asking to explain why he was a half hour off schedule. Everyone was under the gun because the North Koreans could have launched their attack at any moment.

President Kennedy would later say the day he made the decision on North Korea was the worst of his presidency. At a few minutes after 7:00 p.m. he went on the air live from the White House, announcing that the "forces of aggression" were once again preparing to launch an attack on a "staunch ally," and that "our resolve will not falter; we will not shrink from our duty; we will pay the price that must be paid for a people to remain free. This is the debt we owe to those who fell from Inchon to the Chosin Reservoir to Pork Chop Hill." It was already Sunday morning in Korea, and the bombs began falling just after sunrise.

I have been asked from time to time by historians about my feelings over what has come to be known as," "Napalm Sunday," the first day of the air campaign where the 5th People's Army was incinerated by the United States Air Force just north of the 38th Parallel. "I'm fine with it," is always my answer even when they show me pictures of burned corpses heaped in mounds. They say the smell of a hundred thousand burning North Korean infantrymen was truly horrendous when the breeze changed and it blew south over the American lines causing a lot of our guys to vomit. When I'm challenged further about the morality of what happened, I recall my experiences in the first war on the Korean peninsula, and my first hand encounters with the North's cruelty, and then I point out how a protracted conflict there would have killed far more people than the short, brutal air war we waged in 1964. I had a heated argument over the morality of it with my daughter when she was in college more than a decade later. I have no patience with certain college professors and authors like Noam Chomsky who make comparisons between the United States of the 60's and Nazi Germany of the 40's. It is one of the reasons why I often speak at our institutions of higher learning to make sure the record is kept straight. I do it for free.

There would be 150 sorties in the first three days, and 27 planes were shot down with most of the crews killed upon impact, but it stopped Pyongyang cold in its tracks and saved the Republic of South Korea. Once this became clear, the big worry was the Soviet and Chinese reaction; for that reason alone, the readiness of all America forces worldwide was raised to DEFCON 3 on May 25th and all military reservists were notified that they could be called back to active duty if necessary.

If we had known for sure what was happening behind the closed doors in the Kremlin, the President might well have raised the readiness level even higher.

The Soviets had routed the Shah's military and occupied the northern half of the country in record time, but when they began pushing south to the Persian Gulf, their hastily thrown together plan ran into serious trouble because Malinovsky had rushed into battle with too few troops to get the job done. They should have paused and consolidated their gains, but the plan required them to reach the Gulf before the West could mount a countermeasure. Thus they had to beat a clock of their own making

By the time the Soviet's 68th Mechanized Division began its advance south on or around May 15th, it was facing an opposition force of a hundred thousand and growing by the day. Some of these irregulars were made up of units of the Shah's army and air force, but many of them were simply civilians determined to resist being subjugated to the rule of "Godless infidels." Whatever their motivation, they inflicted massive casualties upon the Soviets right from the beginning. When the Soviets responded with bombing campaign far more savage than anything we did in Cuba, Vietnam or Korea, the Iranian will to fight grew even stronger. On the day we launched our preemptive strike on North Korea, the Soviet commander in Teheran sent a message to Marshall Malinovsky stating that he would need another 200,000 troops immediately and acknowledging that the goal of reaching the Persian Gulf by the target date was not going to happen. The General was relieved of his command and packed off to Siberia the next day, but his replacement could do no better. Soviet warships had already passed through the Straits of Hormuz, but there would be no Red Army to greet them at the Iranian ports.

Washington breathed a palpable sigh of relief when first reports of the Soviet setbacks in Iran came in; many were already resigned to a Russian occupation of the country. These reports detailed the scope of the active resistance to the Soviet attack and how it had become a holy cause in the Arab world as young men from as far away as North Africa found their way to Saudi Arabia and Iraq before slipping across the border or the open waters of the Gulf to join the fight. To our detriment, we did not pay enough attention to the emerging leadership of the Iranian opposition with its call for all Moslems to stand up to the foreign invaders no matter who they might be; it was in one of these reports that I first heard then name of the Ayatollah Khomeini mentioned.

I am more than willing to concede that we should have given him and his cause more attention. What we had absolutely no intelligence on was the Kremlin and who was in charge there; only a few surmised what the real truth and I'm glad to say one of them was Ralph Gillison.

"They got Old Nikita locked in some room behind the walls of the Kremlin," he said at one point when another report on what might be happening in Moscow came to the White House. "Locked up tight and only brought out when they need a show."

"What makes you say that?" I asked him. "When you get kicked out over there, you're lucky if you end up in some one-room shack far east of the Urals with only a pot to piss in."

"Old Nikita knows how to talk the talk, but also he knows how to keep his horns reigned in just enough so no one gets fatally gored. He showed as much back in October a year ago; this chicken shit stuff in Iran reeks of something done after a palace coup." Colonel Ralph Gillison should have been head of the CIA. If he had, a lot of problems would never have come to pass.

What became the final crisis of that long month of May in the year of 1964 began completely out of sight of the rest of the world in a military district in Poland where units of the Polish People's Army were fulfilling their part as a cog in the Warsaw Pact. Despite being locked up tight behind the Iron Curtain and having the Communist Party line rammed down their throats daily, the good people of Poland knew full well what was happening in the rest of the world, thanks not only to Radio Free Europe and illegal radio reception of the BBC, but also to a whispering grapevine with deep roots which ran the length and breadth of the Soviet military machine, stretching from Iran to every command in Eastern Europe where the Red Army was stationed.

During the last week of May, a rumor raced through units of the Polish Army stationed outside of Warsaw that they were about to be deployed to Iran and put under Soviet commanders who would push them out front in the advance to the Persian Gulf - in other words, they would be cannon fodder, dying on the front lines in place of Russian infantrymen. Overnight the word spread through the ranks, and a consensus was reached among the lower ranks that no matter what, they would not leave their barracks and get on any trains, even if it meant disobeying a direct order from a superior officer. In any Communist country, this is rank treason, the kind that earns you a firing squad, not a court martial.

Naturally, the Polish high command did not react well to even the hint of mutiny in the ranks and the suspected units were ordered confined to their quarters and their officers were arrested. By then word that Polish sons were about to be sent to die in a Russian war had spread to the civilian population, and they rallied behind their soldiers by blocking the road in front of army camps and the railway stations - there were rumblings from some of the steel mills that the workers would walk out if any move were made to compel the Polish Army to fight in Russia's war. The Catholic Church gave their blessing to a movement that had overnight become resurgence of Polish national pride.

Gasoline was thrown on this fire when a new rumor swept through the ranks that since the loyalty of the Polish Army was suspect, divisions of the East German Army were preparing to move into Poland to massacre a Polish rifle company as an example to the others. If there is one thing that enrages every Pole no matter what their political leanings, it is the thought of German troops crossing their borders, natural since memories of the second World War are still quite fresh and searing in that part of the world. It did not help when the leader of Poland, Wladyslaw Gomulka and the head of East Germany, Walter Ulbricht, had issued statements of fulsome support for the Soviet invasion of Iran on the day after it was launched; statements which received a lot of attention in the state-run press.

On the first day of June, thousands of Polish shipyard workers in Gdansk threatened to walk off their jobs and fight for their country if the Germans dared to cross their border again. Behind the Kremlin walls, this news provoked a furious reaction, for there was one thing all the factions in the Politburo agreed upon: territory taken in the Great Patriotic War at the cost of much Russian blood would never be given up, and no dissension in the ranks of the captive nations would be tolerated. Their fears were that Poland, or any of the other Eastern European nations might want to emulate the Cuban people and be freed of Communist rule. On that same first day of June when Polish shipyard workers stood up, orders went out raising the alert status for the entire Warsaw Pact. The great fear in the Kremlin was that NATO would take advantage of any crisis behind the Iron Curtain and exploit it to launch a preemptive strike.

Because of two decades of hard work by the CIA and the British MI5, our intelligence out of Poland was very good; I dare say we knew of a few developments before Moscow learned of them.

What we did not know was what was happening inside the Kremlin, where cracks had appeared in the unity of the junta as soon as it was clear that the Iranian adventure was not going according to plan. According to later accounts, there were some quite heated meetings among members of the Politburo, where fingers were pointed, and at one point, blows were exchanged before the two parties were pulled apart. But no one had an easy fix; it was too late to turn around in Iran and the only course they could see ahead was to send in more troops. Then overnight, an insurrection broke out in Poland and suddenly these bureaucrats and Communist party hacks were staring into the apocalypse. It was Suzlov, the hardest of the hardliners, who carried the day this time, demanding the Warsaw Pact begin mobilizing in case of a full out attack from the West. "Now would be the time for the Americans to do it," he is recorded as saying in notes taken at the meeting. "They have the taste of blood in their mouths."

The war hawks, led by Shelepin, and Semichastny had determined that an even greater show of force was an absolute necessity if the they were to ultimately prevail. This meant a deliberate mobilization of the Warsaw Pact as a means of intimidation, first of NATO, lest they come to believe they could exploit a situation behind the Iron Curtain at the Soviet Union's expense, and second, the situation itself - the mutinous soldiers in Poland or anywhere else in Eastern Europe who might subscribe to the heretic notion that Moscow didn't call all the shots in that part of the world. To ice the cake, orders were sent out to reduce every city in Iran not in Russian hands to rubble, and when it was done, bomb them again just make the rubble dance. A cable was sent to the Soviet ambassador to Poland, making sure he knew to impress upon the country's leadership that any and all mutineers among its armed forces should get the extreme penalty once this crisis was passed so anyone in the future would think long and hard before challenging Soviet authority.

In the early hours of June 5th, cables began pouring in from NATO's Supreme Commander, General Lyman Limnitzer, detailing a sudden frenzy of Warsaw Pact activity - infantry and mechanized units were being moved into forward positions, as extra fighter wings arrived in East Germany and Czechoslovakia.

A full meeting of the NSC was called at 2 p.m. in the Cabinet Room, one attended by the entire Joint Chiefs of Staff as well. For a half hour John F. Kennedy sat and listened as first the Secretary of Defense, then the CIA Director, Mr. Bundy and finally General Taylor, outlined the extent of the apparent mobilization behind the Iron Curtain and what our options were in the face of an imminent Soviet attack.

They painted a bleak outlook if the Warsaw Pact scored the first blow with their massive numbers of men, airplanes and tanks. "We have the capability of stopping them," Secretary McNamara told the President, "but not before we lose most of West Germany."

Mr. Bundy stated that once the Warsaw Pact had seized the initiative, it was fifty/fifty at best they could be stopped short of the English Channel.

That is unless we went to the nuclear option, the only thing guaranteed to halt the Soviets, the kicker being it guaranteed an equally harsh response. Everyone in the room knew it.

That is, almost everyone. "You have to strike first, Mr. President," General LeMay said, speaking up only after the point was made how the odds overwhelmingly favored the Soviets if they landed the first blow. "You absolutely cannot allow the Russians to make the first strike; we can do to them what we did to the North Koreans." He went on to summarize how a massive and sustained air attack upon the Warsaw Pact's offensive capabilities could fatally cripple any planned offensive against Western Europe before it got started.

I must say it was masterful in the way he rattled off the number of bombers he had at his command and the amount of firepower they could deliver with devastating effect. "In East Germany alone," LeMay said at one point, "we can drop in two days the equivalent of all the conventional bombs that fell on Japan in the last six months of the war." When it was brought up how this might provoke to Soviets to go to nuclear, the General dismissed this possibility with, "I see little chance of it happening."

Mr. Rostow spoke up almost immediately after the General and said LeMay's plan might be our only viable option; he was seconded in this opinion by General Earle Wheeler, the Chief of Staff of the Army. Secretary McNamara said a full mobilization of NATO could begin as soon as the British, the French and the Germans were notified, something which would take no more than an hour. This was one of the few meetings where the Vice President spoke; Lyndon Johnson reminded everyone of the sacrifices made by thousands of American boys in two World Wars to preserve freedom in Europe and that the American public would never forgive this administration if it allowed that freedom to perish on its watch.

The final decision was in the President's hands. "I am not totally convinced," he said when everyone else was finished, although later accounts, including more than one memoir, would leave out the word "totally." The President went on to state that since our forces were already at DEFON 3, it was not necessary to order a full mobilization of NATO at that point. Therefore this meeting of the NSC was adjourned for twenty-four hours unless events dictated otherwise.

And with that, John F. Kennedy pushed himself up from his chair, and with his back ramrod straight, strode through the door, leaving shocked and silent room behind him.

"What the hell just happened?" General LeMay was heard to snort.

I beat a hasty retreat to my basement office, where I informed Ralph Gillison what had just occurred. "Something's up," was his comment, "something big, you know how much Kennedy likes to do things outside of channels."

Not ten minutes later the phone rang at my desk. It was the Attorney General. "Colonel Maddox," he said, "my brother believes that if we're seriously talking about launching a Super Pearl Harbor attack against the Soviet Union, then this situation has gotten about as far out of control as it had better go. He intends to talk face to face with Khrushchev or whoever is calling the shots in Moscow and intends to do it in the next few days. You and I are going to make it happen, be in my office in the Justice Department building in half an hour."

Lyndon Johnson spoke the truth when he said we truly had our work cut out for us trying to get the Civil Rights Act through the Senate. We would somehow need to get 61 votes to invoke closure and cut off the inevitable filibuster by Southern Democrats. This is where it became a numbers game, for there was a minimum of 24 votes from the Old Confederacy and border states against the Act, reducing the Democratic votes in favor to between 40 and 45, which meant the rest of the Yea votes would have to come from the Republican caucus, filled with ultra-conservative men from Mid-Western and Rocky Mountain states, men who had very few black constituents and who thought Paul Harvey spoke the honest truth daily.

Cuba exploded just when the fight in the Senate began, and that story drove the cause of equal right off the front pages and the nightly newscasts right at the time when we really needed public support.

Nevertheless, three days after the coup in Cuba, our broad coalition met for the first time to hash out a strategy to defeat our segregationist opponents who were willing to fight us night and day, now and forever. Everything was different now, not like in January when Senator Humphrey had asked his old friend, the Vice President, to come by his office for some "advice." It was all out in the open, with Johnson in charge, although Larry O'Brien was in the room as the President's representative; he had a reputation as being a pro, unlike some of the other hacks in the White House; more importantly, O'Brien was a Jack Kennedy man, not one of Bobby's boys. This would prove to be an important difference down the road.

A truth known to everyone, but unspoken by all, was that we were well into a Presidential election year and despite the good press for his efforts to get the Civil Rights Act through the House, there were still many in the Kennedy camp damned and determined to dump Lyndon Johnson from the ticket at the August convention. Unknown to anybody outside the circle, earlier in the week, there had been a meeting of the President's closest aides involved in the campaign - the President and O'Brien were absent - where Bobby Kennedy talked openly about replacing Johnson with either Senators Henry Jackson, Stuart Symington, and even Senator Humphrey himself. I include this information as it shows just where things stood at this point in '64.

At the meeting, Senator Humphrey and most of the other liberal Democrats were still on a high after their victory in the House; the Vice President quickly brought them back down to earth. "We are in a Presidential election year," he told us, "and the winds of public opinion can change faster than in a hurricane." To prove his point, he described what he was hearing from many Republican members of the Senate. "They are getting calls and telegrams from the good people back home who always turn out and support them in election after election - small town bankers and lawyers, home builders, the man who owns the biggest grain silo in the county - and they are listening to Goldwater when he says this bill will trample all over their rights to property and free association. These are the people who take that little sign in their favorite diner - the one that says they got the right to refuse service to anyone - very seriously. And they don't like the idea of some Fed from Washington in a suit and tie coming in there and telling them to take it down. They don't like it one damn bit, and old Barry has painted quite the picture of what will happen if this evil legislation becomes the law of the land. As they see it, this country is going toe to toe with the Communists in Cuba, so why pass a law championed by Martin Luther King, a man they consider to be a Red sympathizer. Goldwater is drawing huge crowds, and at this point, is gaining more adherents by the day and overcoming them will be no easy chore."

The Vice President's words woke everyone up the tough job ahead, and we went out of the meeting with no illusions. The first hurdle for the Act to clear in the Senate was James Eastland's Judiciary Committee. Only the day before, the Mississippi Senator had spoken these words in an interview with the Associated Press: "Never in my career have I seen a more blatantly unconstitutional piece of legislation than this so-called Civil Rights Act, the authors of our sacred Constitution must be spinning in their graves at the thought of such a thing becoming law."

NO MIRACLE IN THE SENATE was the title of an April 7th Evans and Novak column in which they related how the supporters of the Act would be unable to repeat in the Senate their success in the House; and not just because it was trapped in the Judiciary committee, but because three Republican Senators likely to vote yea were backtracking after hearing from their agitated constituents over the Easter break.

My heart sank when I read the column. I wondered how we would look Dr. King and all those who marched with him in the face and tell them - after all the beatings, bombings and fire hoses - they would just have to try harder next time.

The thought filled me with dread.

It was the state my mind was in on the third Friday in April when I received a call from Senator Humphrey first thing in the morning, telling me to be in the Vice President's Senate office no later than half-past three in the afternoon, my services would be needed then. I remember this distinctly because my plans had been for me to fly back to Atlanta in the early afternoon to spend some time with my family - my father was then in the midst of what would turn out to be a losing battle with congestive heart failure. When I tried to beg off, the Senator simply said, "Johnny, we need you today like we've never needed you before. Do this for me and go spend the next week in Georgia; I'll buy your ticket both ways."

I couldn't turn the Senator down after hearing him put it that way; I actually arrived at the Vice President's office even earlier than requested, Johnson was there early as well, which was something of a surprise as this was the day we began bombing Cuba and I would have thought the Vice President would have been at a meeting in the White House. When I asked Johnson a question about the ongoing military operations, "All I know is, we're going to kick the shit out that bastard Castro," was his reply. Soon after, Senator Humphrey arrived, and right behind him followed Mike Mansfield, the Democratic Majority Leader and Johnson's successor in that post.

"Johnny," the Vice President said as soon as the other two were there, "we need you to do a real service for your country today, we need you make the rest of us look like we are going way, way out on a long limb to make a very risky offer to an old and dear friend." LBJ, who stood a half foot taller than me, leaned in close as he said this until his nose was no more than an inch from my own.

Senator Humphrey elaborated, "I know you've heard of 'good cop, bad cop.' Johnny, well we need you to be 'bad liberal' this afternoon." He then asked me how much I charged an hour for my legal services. This confused me; I told him it was normally $25.00 per hour. "Good enough," said Senator Humphrey, who promptly pulled out his checkbook and wrote me out a check for $100.00. "You are on retainer for the next four hours," he said while pushing the check into my hand.

"Let me ask you this, Johnny Compton," the Vice President said before I could protest, "you've spent more than a little time toiling in the unique Southern justice system, so tell me your honest opinion of Federal Judge William Harold Cox of the Fifth District of Mississippi?"

Though I'd never had the privilege of appearing in Cox's court, I was well aware of his reputation as a Judge who often expressed his segregationist views from the bench and referred to Negro defendants as "niggers" on a regular basis. It was a true stain on John F. Kennedy's legacy when he appointed this man to the Federal court early in his administration as a courtesy to Senator Eastland, who recommended his old law school room mate to fill a judicial vacancy.

I told them exactly what I thought of Judge Cox and did not mince words. When I was done, the Vice President said, "Pretty good, but you are going to be asked to repeat that opinion in a few minutes in front of our guest. When you do, please be sure to punch it up with a few more adjectives if you please."

That is when the guest arrived, Senator Eastland himself; this surprised me not in the least after my opinion of Judge Cox had been broached. I considered the Senator's record and publicly stated views and wondered how a simple sit down could possibly change things.

I had seen the jowly Mississippi Senator up close more than once, and he'd always reminded me of an ante-bellum plantation owner, the kind of man who sat on the verandah while his overseer cracked the bullwhip. That's probably unfair, but I had no doubt he was the kind of demagogue who was holding back the 20th century single-handedly.

Yet the greeting he received from the Vice President and Senators Humphrey and

Mansfield forcefully brought home to me that no matter what their political differences, these men were colleagues and members of the world's most exclusive club where respect was always given and received; and more than that, these men were friends with much in common. After I was formally introduced to the Senator as a member of Senator Humphrey's staff, drinks were poured, followed by a brief discussion of the situation in Cuba (the big story of the day), before the talk turned to farming, specifically the dry conditions on LBJ's Texas ranch and Eastland's delta cotton plantation, with Senator Humphrey commiserating and promising legislation to aid suffering farmers nationally was sure to sail through the Senate by Memorial Day no matter what the international situation might be, everyone wanted to be the farmer's friend in an election year. Senator Mansfield, a man not known to waste words, spoke up about tough times among the cattle ranchers in his home state of Montana.

I sat to the side and observed; it was just four old friends shooting the shit in the afternoon over drinks. I don't really remember who brought up the subject of the Civil Rights Act, most likely the Vice President, but I distinctly remember Senator Eastland saying "Lyndon, I know you understand better than anyone what the good people of Mississippi sent me here to do, and there is no way I can allow this totally unconstitutional piece of legislation to advance one inch in the Senate. As far as I'm concerned, that is as far as it going to go."

The other three men countered with the argument that the very least the bill deserved was a vote up or down, yea nor nay, on the Senate floor, it was what the people of the United States wanted. "Once this thing gets to the floor," the Vice President said at one point, "you and Dick and Strom get to offer all the amendments you want, filibuster until Christmas comes and do whatever the hell you want to defeat the bill, but this issue deserves a straight up and down vote on the record."

"No one's asking you to vote against your principles, Jim," Senator Humphrey added. "All we are asking is for you to allow it to come to a vote in the Judiciary Committee."

"It's not my concern what the people of the United States want," the Mississippian countered, "my concern is what the people in my home state want, and they want no part of this damn thing."

I wanted to speak up and tell Eastland there were a lot of people in his home state who desperately wanted a part of this damn thing, but they were black, which meant they didn't count to him. But I knew my place in this room was not to lecture United States Senators, so I kept silent.

Though what I heard next made me want to stand up and shout "Hell no!"

"What would the good people of Mississippi think if you passed up a chance to put a native son on the Supreme Court?" Those were Vice President Johnson's exact words. He was dangling the nomination of William Harold Cox to the Supreme Court of the United States before the one man in the country who most desired such a thing. It can't be overstated how much the Warren Court was despised below the Mason-Dixon Line and how much the Deep South felt it was being persecuted by an unelected body with no members who represented their views. I knew many a fellow white Southerner who'd never forgiven the *Brown* decision and strongly believed that if a true man of the old Confederacy - someone who'd fight tooth and nail for Jim Crow - had been on the Supreme Court, none of this civil rights nonsense would have come about.

It was Senator Humphrey who put it in plain words, "All we want is a vote on the Civil Rights Act in the Judiciary Committee, allow it, and you can put any name you want at the top of the list the next time there is a vacancy on the Supreme Court. You can put forth the name of your good and dear friend and native son of Mississippi, Federal Judge William Harold Cox and the President will send his name up here for confirmation. All you have to do is schedule a vote in the Judiciary Committee, nothing more."

Everyone knew there were enough votes in the committee to send the Civil Rights Act to the floor, so Eastland knew what they were asking of him.

To his credit, Senator Eastland didn't take this outrageous offer at face value. He simply laughed and asked what all "those Northern liberals and part time Communists" who were hell bent on stirring up the good Negroes of Mississippi and the rest of the region would think of such a thing.

That was when Senator Humphrey turned to me and said, "Johnny here is one of those whom you would consider a full-time Communist - he's taken money from both the NAACP and the ACLU to represent Negroes in the courts of Mississippi. So Johnny, what do you think of Judge Cox?"

They told me not to mince words, and I did as requested.

I told them in no uncertain terms how I felt Judge Cox's well-stated views on segregation, Jim Crow and race in general rendered him manifestly unfit to sit on any bench anytime, anywhere in America, much less the Supreme Court. More than that, not only did I consider Judge Cox unfit for his job, I sincerely believed him to be a public disgrace, not only to every decent citizen of the Fifth Federal District, but to every American of good will.

Senator Eastland's heretofore jovial expression soured considerably as he listened while I spoke; a Southern gentleman does not sit idly by while good and faithful friend's reputations were impugned. Before he could rise to Judge Cox's defense, the Vice President said, "We know damn well what the liberal wing of the party will say if we do this thing; don't take it too personal what Johnny just said, he's just repeating what hundreds of thousands would think. But we wanted him here to say that to your face, and in front of us, so you'd know we were damn serious about this offer."

Eastland asked Humphrey and Mansfield if they were backing this Cox offer as well; Humphrey said he would never vote to confirm a man like Judge Cox, but he solemnly promised not to advise the President against nominating him. Senator Mansfield made the same commitment.

After a moment of silence, Eastland sat his drink down and said, "Hope you understand, Lyndon, I've got hear Jack Kennedy's own words, he's got to tell me himself if he's going to name Judge Cox if I ask him."

The Vice President's answer was to pick up the phone on his desk and dial. After going through the White House operator, LBJ exclaimed, "Larry, Senator Eastland is right here, and he has something he wants to ask the President."

I hadn't even wondered where Lawrence O'Brien was during all these negotiations when he was the President's man on Capitol Hill in these matters, but he had been at the White House all this time, lining up the President on his end. That John F. Kennedy would take the time to make a deal which could actually get the Civil Rights Act passed on the same day we went into Cuba raised his estimation a thousand degrees in my book.

The President came on the line, and the phone was passed to Eastland, who put it to Kennedy straight, Cox for a vote in the Judiciary Committee. I was too far away to hear JFK's words on the other end, but there was no mistaking the smile on the Eastland's face when he was done. "Thank you very much, Mr. President," he said. "I think we all see eye to eye and there's no reason for anybody to be unhappy." Then he passed the phone back to the Vice President to conclude the call.

At no time, did anybody verbally agree to a quid pro quo, but when Senator James Eastland left the Vice President's office, none of us had any doubt of the outcome. Ten days later, a motion was made and carried in the Senate Judiciary Committee to bring the Civil Rights Act to a vote; Senator Eastland was not there that day, he'd had to hurry back to Sunflower County, Mississippi to tend to "urgent business" on his cotton plantation. No matter, he was there three days later, when the full committee voted, and the Act passed by one vote; Eastland voted "nay" and stayed true to the good people who'd sent him to Washington.

It had been the Vice President's idea to have Senator Humphrey put me on retainer for the duration of the meeting with Eastland; it was their way of ensuring silence about what went on the room through attorney/client privilege. They needn't have bothered; I wouldn't have talked then anyway, even though I was horrified at the thought of Judge Cox on the Court. I can talk about it now because I tore up the check the next day; so technically, Senator Humphrey never hired me as an attorney.

Thus the Civil Rights Act went from the Judiciary Committee to the floor, and if there was any celebration on our side, it was muted, we had merely overcome a hurdle, not crossed a finish line. Our hope was to begin floor debate before the Memorial Day recess, but the Southern block proved formidable and used the uncertainty on the international stage to get postponed until they came back in the summer. Their point was made the day the Soviets invaded Iran. The day after we started bombing North Korea, Senator Thurmond repeated his admonishment that this was no time to take up such a sensitive and divisive issue. What was more troubling was how Senator Everett Dirksen, the Republican Minority Leader and a man we very much needed on our side, echoed the same sentiments.

I still to this day think we should have pushed and got the Act before the Senate in May of '64; still bitterly regret not doing so.

Lt. Colonel Martin Maddox (V)
June 1964

On the evening of June 5th, 1964, the Attorney General and I, accompanied by a pair of United States Federal Marshalls went to one of Georgetown's finer French restaurants, not to eat dinner, but to wait for a regular Friday night customer, Sergei Ivanov, whose official title was Special Attaché to the Soviet Ambassador, but in reality, he was Colonel Sergei Ivanov, the highest ranking KGB official in the country and a man whose secret cables were read by members of the Politburo daily. Traditionally the top KGB man in any country is the Kremlin's true eyes and ears, while the diplomats are nothing more than ventriloquist dummies.

We arrived early as per our plan, worked out in the Bobby Kennedy's office earlier in the day. The two of us retired to a storeroom in the back while the pair of Marshalls took a seat right next to Ivanov's regular table in the corner. I was not in uniform, as per the Attorney General's request, such attire might have attracted attention and stayed in the minds of other diners.

The Kenney brothers were going outside of channels once again on the day when the President and the NSC had seriously discussed a first strike against the Warsaw Pact.

The Attorney General and I passed the time waiting by discussing the Red Sox's poor prospects for that year; I'd begun to fear we had picked the one Friday night that Ivanov would be a no show when one of the Marshalls appeared and informed us he was just being seated. I followed the Marshall back to the dining room and took great satisfaction at the look of surprise on the KGB Colonel's face when I sat down across from him and introduced myself, flashing my driver's license at the same time just to prove I had put one over on a top agent of the world's most secretive organization. Robert Kennedy assured me Ivanov would know who I was since, "they make it their business to know the names of everyone on the NSC staff, your service records, school, marital status and number of children." I didn't like it much that a KGB officer would know my wife's name, but couldn't do much about it either.

Ivanov, a tall, almost cadaverous man with a thin mustache, looked at my license and then asked in heavily accented English why a member of the NSC would interrupt his dinner. I politely asked if he would not mind accompanying me to a back room where a gentleman wanted to have a brief word with him; afterward he would be free to return and enjoy the fine meal he must have been looking forward to all day.

I had a suspicion he might not go for it, figuring it might be a ruse to kidnap a top enemy agent and pump him for he was worth with the world situation being what it was at the time. It was a fear for nothing, for less than a minute later the head of the KGB in the United States was shaking hands with the President's brother in a back room whose shelves were packed with flour and cooking oil, while air smelt faintly of vinegar.

I stepped outside as part of the plan; Robert Kennedy intentionally didn't want anyone listening in on this conversation; I believe so that no American could later contradict his version of what was said for the historical record.

Why was it necessary for me to be there? "You're an insider," Robert Kennedy explained earlier, "I couldn't send a Marshall, nor a CIA or FBI man, Ivanov would never have gone with any of them, but you work under the same roof as the President, and Ivanov knows it."

Despite what some "historians" have alleged, I believe Robert Kennedy when he says he gave Ivanov a message from his brother proposing a face to face meeting between the President and Chairman Khrushchev as soon as it could be arranged in a place of mutual agreement. Ivanov, it must be emphasized, had absolutely no authority to negotiate anything; he was merely an expedient conduit to the Kremlin. Ivanov played his part to perfection, listening politely to the Attorney General, making few comments, then shaking Robert Kennedy's hand before returning to the Soviet Embassy only 45 minutes after leaving for what he must have thought would be a leisurely evening of fine dining. By the time we walked through the doors of the West Wing at 8:30 p.m., an urgent cable was already on its way to Moscow.

"This is one hell of a roll of the dice," John F. Kennedy said after his brother reported on his meeting with Ivanov. The President boldly predicted we would get a positive response from the Kremlin in no more than 24 hours.

Only much later did President Kennedy learn how close he came to being made to look the fool.

A complete account of the meeting between Ivanov and Robert F. Kennedy was in the hands of KGB Chief Semichastny by midnight Washington time, which was just after sunrise in Moscow on a Saturday morning. All later accounts agree on what happened next, telephone calls were made and the major movers among the secret junta running the Soviet Union (Brezhnev, Suzlov, Shelepin) were made aware that the American President was requesting a face to face meeting with the man who the rest of the world thought was still in charge of the world's second super-power, Nikita Khrushchev; a man who had been under house arrest for nearly 3 months. The Soviet Junta in the early spring of '64 had somehow run the largest empire in history from the shadows and had not been found out, no small accomplishment.

Now in the first week of June, their bluff was being called and their run of luck was all but played out. Upon hearing of Kennedy's request for a summit, the immediate consensus was for a full meeting of the Politburo to discuss the matter; one was set for 11:00 a.m. local time. That perhaps was the only thing these men agreed upon, for in the days and weeks since seizing power, many of the alliances of convenience had frayed to the point of pulling apart. When they gathered around a conference table at the appointed hour inside the Kremlin, the hardliners, led by Suzlov, made it plain that they wanted to reject

Kennedy's request out of hand. "The Americans have lost their nerve," Suzlov asserted, "they posture like a bully, but have no stomach for a real fight against a real foe. It's a fear we must exploit here and now for our own advantage. Let's not jump at their first offer. Instead we hold out before going to the negotiating table, let them become even more fearful, so that in a week or so, they will come hat in hand, willing to sign anything that assures them a precious peace. We must instruct Dobrynin to go to the White House this day and tell Kennedy we are not interested in any talks."

The hard line Communist's words swayed the room and might have carried the day if others had not already been making plans. Leonid Brezhnev, the original instigator of the palace coup against Khrushchev, had for weeks believed the Soviet position was unsustainable: the Red Army was taking tremendous casualties in Iran despite an intense bombing campaign and the unrest in Eastern Europe was threatening to bubble to the surface at any time. The one thing the Soviets feared above all else was the loss of control among their European satellites. Though he was in the minority, Brezhnev had found one potentially powerful ally in the Defense Minister Malinovsky, who was being quietly made the scapegoat for the failures in Iran in whispered conversations by other junta members. Marshall Malinovsky had gotten wind to this talk, probably from Brezhnev himself, and was infuriated at being blamed for simply following the wishes of his fellow conspirators; it should be said that Malinovsky was looking at an inglorious exile to Siberia at best for his supposed incompetence, far worse if his former allies were not in a merciful mood.

By all later accounts, the Kremlin meeting of junta had droned on for about an hour before Brezhnev and a few others excused themselves from the deliberations, promising to return momentarily. No sooner were they gone before the door to the conference room was kicked open, and a squad of Soviet paratroopers entered the room, Kalishnakovs in hand. There was a brief argument, followed by a few seconds of gunfire, which left a half dozen men dead, Shelepin and Semichastny among them, but not Suzlov, who was taken into custody. When Leonid Brezhnev re-entered the room a few minutes later, he was the undisputed leader of the junta and for the moment, the most powerful man in the Soviet Union.

Brezhnev did not waste any time, accompanied by a group of loyalists, which included the ultimate survivor, Andrei Gromyko, but also Khrushchev's longtime friend, Anastas Mikoyan, he went to the dacha where the Chairman had been held under house arrest for so many weeks and offered the old man a deal whereby his imprisonment would end, and he would resume his public role as leader of the Soviet Union, albeit under the strict supervision of the surviving members of the junta. Khrushchev reportedly told his old comrade to go to hell; he wanted nothing more than to wash his hands of the whole thing and simply retire. Besides, he proclaimed, he was an old man and tired, his days of usefulness were at an end. Brezhnev appealed to his patriotism, saying that in the present crisis, his country needed him.

"You want me come and clean up the mess you have made," Khrushchev declared, "I have too much pride that I would foul my hands with another man's shit." It was a stinging rebuke, but the old man did not stick to his guns, for his friend Mikoyan appealed to that very pride, saying that if his career ended there and then, history would record that for all his hard work and sacrifice on behalf of the Soviet Union and its people, he had simply been kicked aside in the end by men lesser than himself.

At 5:00 p.m. Moscow time on that June Saturday, Nikita Khrushchev road back through the gates of the Kremlin and strode into his office; two hours later, Sergei Ivanov received a cable from the Chairman himself, ordering him to immediately inform the American Attorney General that the Soviet leader was prepared to meet with President Kennedy in New Delhi, India in five day's time to discuss the world situation.

I got the word from the Attorney General just after 3:00 p.m., Washington time, informing me that they'd just heard back from Ivanov and the summit was on; the President went on TV that evening and informed the country that he would meet with Khrushchev in an emergency summit in New Delhi, India, commencing on the morning of Wednesday, June 10th.

Almost immediately there was trepidation among the NSC over having the summit in New Delhi, the Soviets choice of location. CIA Director McCone and the Secretary Rusk were adamant that the Nehru government had never been a friend of the United States, and for all their proclamations of neutrality between East and West in the Cold War, the Indians had always tilted to the Soviets when the chips were down. Prime Minister Nehru had from the beginning of the crisis been in touch almost daily with Washington and Moscow offering himself as a mediator, and the Soviets had simply taken their old buddy up on it; in truth, the Indian Prime Minister was in poor health, and when he died suddenly the day after the summit ended, it was said that he would have passed weeks earlier if not for his determination to mediate an end to the crisis. McCone and Rusk wanted to move the summit to Zurich in Switzerland, but the President would have none of it, saying preparations were already under way and the matter settled.

By this point in time, everyone was exhausted after putting in a week upon week of twenty hour days, and it had been my hope that my services would not be required in New Delhi, but it was not to be, I was tasked with preparing briefing papers for the President to take into the meetings with the Soviets. It also meant that I rode over on a crowded Air Force One, which except for a brief stopover in Paris, spent eight hours in the air. I was struck by how utterly relaxed the President was during this trip over, despite hours of intense meetings in the back of the plane going over the points they needed to make with Khrushchev, not to mention the stakes at play when he got to New Delhi, President Kennedy spent a lot of time just sitting around talking sports, mostly with his staff, or telling anecdotes from foreign visits. When he talked about his trip to Ireland and the enthusiastic greeting he received in his ancestral homeland, his eyes really lit up, and you could hear the joy in his voice. The man clearly took great pleasure in his job - most days.

For some reason, the conversation turned to current music and President Kennedy expressed his bafflement at the popularity of The Beatles, telling us he couldn't understand the youth of America's passion for a quartet of young British men of questionable sexual orientation, only the President put it in much cruder terms, stating that no matter what, he'd always be a Sinatra man.

We arrived in New Delhi early on the day before the summit was scheduled to begin; no sooner had the President was settled in at the American embassy to catch up on some much-needed sleep, a whole new problem arose. It seemed that in their capacity as hosts of the summit, the Indian government had not just invited the leaders of the United States and the Soviet Union to attend, but had also extended a blanket invitation to all nations with a grievance to send a representative. In all the rush to get to the meeting with the Soviet leaders, this fact had been overlooked. Now we were greeted with the news that Chinese Premier Chou En Lai had arrived by plane only an hour after Air Force One had touched down to represent the North Koreans and the North Vietnamese.

The presence of the #2 man in Red China at the summit put most of the President's men in a panic; since 1949, as far as the USA was concerned, the only legitimate leader of China was Chaing Kai-chek, currently enjoying his exile on Taiwan. So adamant were we in this, that in 1954, then-Secretary of State John Foster Dulles had reportedly refused to shake Chou's hand during the Geneva conference that settled the partition of Indo-China. Then there were the Chinese troops Mao and Chou had sent to aid their fellow Communists during the Korean War; I'd had the pleasure of meeting a few of them personally in 1951. Any Democratic President who so much as thought about acknowledging the existence of Red China was opening himself to charges of appeasement, especially in an election year.

Behind the scenes, Secretary Rusk was most insistent that the President not be in the same room with Chou, if necessary, he should be prepared to simply get on Air Force One and leave rather than give any recognition to the Communist government in Peking. Some of the others, like my old boss, McGeorge Bundy, advised the President to simply ignore Chou and his presence at the summit. A tired John F. Kennedy listened to all this and then called his brother in Washington, who told him it was too great a risk in an election year to acknowledge Chou, he would be handing the Republicans an issue to run against him; just let it wait until the second term.

As soon as he concluded the call to his brother, the President then called in Secretary Rusk and instructed him to call the Indian Foreign Minister and request that he serve as an intermediary between the American delegation and the Chinese Premier - this was asking something of the Indians because of the short war they'd fought with Red China in the fall of '62 over some piece of territory in the Himalayas, but as President Kennedy pointed out, the Indians had taken it upon themselves to host the summit, so it was the least they could do under the circumstances. To their credit, our hosts readily agreed, settling the matter for the moment and allowing the summit to proceed.

While the President was able to sleep off some of his considerable jet lag in a nice bed inside the embassy, I was up all night preparing reports on the situation in Cuba among many other things for the President to take into his first meeting with the Soviets in the morning. As of the first week of June, we had over 125,000 combatants engaged in pacifying the island; organized resistance was supposed to have ended two weeks before, but units of Castro's forces refused to give up and even though our casualty rate was down dramatically from the first week of the invasion, we were still losing at a minimum a half dozen men a day down there. As of the 10th of June, there was no real governing authority in Cuba other than General Abrams; Castro himself was being held under guard in the Guantanamo Bay hospital, his brother Raul had reportedly sought sanctuary with Andreyev while Che Guevara had escaped back to Argentina.

All of this was in the report I handed the President in the morning as he left the embassy for the site of the summit, an old 300 room British colonial era hotel called The Burnham. It was a massive building, a relic from the days of the Raj and perfect to host a superpower summit. The sessions between the Soviets and us were to be held in the main dining room, an ornate area with a high chandelier dangling from the ceiling over the long tables where the delegations were to sit. John F. Kennedy made sure he was there a good 45 minutes ahead of schedule, and though he had been complaining of back pain earlier, he made it a point to jump from the back seat of limo when the car pulled up in front of the Burnham, vigorously shaking the hand of the Indian Foreign Minister for all the news cameras to record.

The self-assured public image the President was projecting was helped immeasurably when the Soviet delegation turned out to be late; there was much speculation as to the condition of Nikita Khrushchev after seemingly being AWOL throughout most of the crisis. The Soviet leader we observed enter the Burnham was noticeably heavier and moving slower as he ambled through the same doors the President walked through earlier. The biggest contrast between the American President and the Soviet Chairman was the entourage who followed close on Khrushchev's heels. At this time, we had no knowledge whatsoever of the recent events behind the walls of the Kremlin, but something appeared different here, as Brezhnev, Kosigyn, Mikoyan and Gromyko, among others, shadowed their supreme leader. Our Kremlin experts had pages of notes ready by the end of the day.

Though Khrushchev appeared older and slower at first, his old aggressiveness came back the minute he walked into the hotel, again becoming the man who'd greeted President Kennedy at Vienna in their first summit almost three years to the day in 1961. He marched across the lobby with his hand thrust forward for the President to grasp, and then with his finger jabbing the air, made it clear through an interpreter, that as far as the Soviet Union was concerned the Americans were solely responsible for the tense circumstances which had made the summit necessary. Despite all the nastiness inside the Kremlin, Khrushchev and the rest of the gang put on the tough guy act when confronting their enemies from the West. When the President finally got a word in, he suggested "it took two to tango," and Khrushchev shot back that they were most certainly not there to dance.

What I saw and heard inside the conference room pretty much jibes with the official version and what historians have written since.

Khrushchev came out swinging with his opening remarks, accusing the American government, and especially John F. Kennedy by name, of lying, scheming, breaking their word and committing military aggression against a peace loving nation whose only crime was to be part of the world-wide socialist revolution. Nothing short of an immediate American withdrawal from Cuba and the complete restoration of the Castro regime would make things right; he also warned that those who had planned and participated in said aggression should be tried for war crimes. There he was talking about me.

"The Cuban people must have justice," Khrushchev demanded. "This crime cannot be allowed to stand." He then linked the invasion of Cuba to an American plot to thwart the tide of history which was leading toward the inevitable victory of socialism and the liberation of all victims of capitalist imperialism; the worker's paradise of the Soviet Union, along their socialist brothers in North Korea, had every right to defend itself in any way it deemed necessary against such aggression.

"Strike at us," Khrushchev stated at the end of the opening remarks, "and we will strike back in kind, it is our right." It was a performance worthy of the Soviet dictator in his prime, back when he was banging his shoe in the U.N. and despite whatever misgivings he might have had in private, the man gave a full-throttled defense of everything the junta had done while he was under house arrest.

There has been much criticism of the President because he did not respond in kind or rebut Khrushchev point by point when his turn came; nor did he mention the assassination attempt in Dallas and the trail of evidence leading back to Havana. He only briefly mentioned the invasion of Iran, saying the people of that country might have something to say about crimes against humanity. Instead he brought up the increased tensions between NATO and the Warsaw Pact, the situation on the Korean peninsula and in South Vietnam, making it clear that their job at this summit was to deescalate the tensions and restore stability to the world.

"The greatest crime against humanity, Mr. Chairman," the President said as he summed up, "would be for us to leave this summit with nothing accomplished; to simply sit here and trade accusations and recriminations. It is a tragedy for all those who have died up until today, but starting tomorrow, those who perish will be because of a criminal act, and we will be the guilty parties."

I was sitting in the back of the room behind the President while he was speaking and through it all, his tone was one of calm and reason. To have thrown a documented list of Soviet atrocities in Iran back in Khrushchev's face would have accomplished nothing.

The morning session went on in the same vein for two hours, with Khrushchev pounding his fist and making accusations, and the President countering that done was done, and the only thing to be settled was how they went forward. "I think we've cleared the air enough," the President commented when the morning session broke up. As soon as the President left the conference room, he asked for a pen and paper and dashed off a note on the back of an aide's briefcase, folding it double and giving it to the Indian Foreign Minister to hand deliver to Khrushchev. This is what I witnessed, with no knowledge of the note's contents, but having no reason to doubt the President's assertion that he was merely informing the Soviet leader that he was welcome to send a naval transport to Havana and evacuate Andreyev's troops.

Twenty minutes later, I was witness to the Foreign Minister's return with a note from Khrushchev for the President; this prompted a quick huddle among the President, the Secretary of State and Mr. Bundy. A minute later those three men slipped quietly from the room, moving so deftly as not to be noticed. It was not until the President returned three-quarters of an hour later did we learn of the private meeting he'd just had with Khrushchev in the hotel's floral garden. Of course it was not truly a one on one as the Soviet leader was accompanied by Brezhnev and Gromyko, who discreetly stood by and let Khrushchev tell the President that if he proposed a reasonable date to have all American troops out of Cuba at the next session, he would be willing to reciprocate in kind on Iran. The Soviet leader offered his hand, and they shook on the deal.

And just like that, the breakthrough was accomplished.

When the sessions resumed, the President threw out the proposal of a one-year deadline for both countries to have all their troops out of Cuba and Iran respectively; Khrushchev gave a blustering response, but, good as his word, did not reject the idea of a withdrawal date out of hand. I noticed that while old Nikita was haranguing, the President was furiously writing on a legal pad which he quickly passed to Secretary Rusk; once it was the turn of the American side to respond, the Secretary put on his glasses and calmly read off a five-point plan to ease the immediate tensions between the United States and the Soviet Union, which included a ten-month deadline to get all foreign troops out of Cuba and Iran along with the immediate standing down of all American and Soviet armed forces worldwide.

Again, Khrushchev snarled and growled and got the withdrawal date changed to nine months, then after another forty minutes or so of the pretense of haggling, agreed to the President's five points. It took another hour to get everything typed up and ready for signature.

I was in the room through all of it, though sitting off to the side, and what I've just recounted is what I've told various historians in the years since. There were no "secret" or "side" deals made, and I've disputed anyone who has said otherwise since that day. D'nesh D'Sousa and I really got into it when we jointly appeared on the "O'Reilly Factor" just last year after he'd written some screed purportedly exposing President Kennedy as a sellout who let pass a chance to win the Cold War right there in New Delhi.

On that day, the Soviets had fifteen divisions bogged down in Iran, facing a furious homegrown opposition growing stronger by the day, while in Eastern Europe, fear among local military units that they would be sent to the slaughter house in the Mid East had reached such a proportion that open defiance of the Soviets was growing by the hour - Polish, Hungarian and Czech infantry battalions had come together and voted to obey only orders issued in defense of their homelands. The Kremlin junta had truly made a hash of things, but the full impact was yet to be known.

While the President and Khrushchev were settling things in the main dining hall, the Indian Foreign Minister had been in the ballroom across the lobby talking with Chou En Lai; the Chinese leader had proposed a complete American withdrawal from the Korean peninsula and Indo-China, positions which would greatly benefit North Korea and North Vietnam whom he claimed to represent. But everyone knew Chou was there to further the interests of Peking, whatever they might be. At the end of Kennedy and Khrushchev's final session, the Indian Foreign Minister reported that negotiations with Chou were at an impasse and he was refusing even to consider a proposal for a simple cease fire the Indians had put on the table.

This is what happened when the President learned of this development; with a translator in tow, he stepped around to the Soviet side of the table and engaged Khrushchev in conversation - they were quickly joined by Brezhnev and Gromyko. They spoke for fifteen minutes with old Nikita vigorously nodding his head several times, with another hardy handshake when they were done. Then the President spoke briefly with Secretary Rusk and Mr. Bundy before striding to the lobby and entering the ballroom where the meetings with Chou were going on.

What happened next made was on the front page of every newspaper around the world the next day: John F. Kennedy shaking hands with an obviously surprised Chou En Lai. The meeting between them lasted barely a half hour, just long enough for the President to get Chou to agree to a de-escalation in Korea and Indo-China, an agreement which ultimately proved to be utterly worthless, but a line of communication had been established. I've always believed the President's assertion that the decision to meet with Chou was a spur of the moment one.

The only thing left to do was a final signing of the agreement between Kennedy and Khrushchev, where Chou joined them - the only time all three leaders were together. The smiling President stood between the rather glum looking Communist leaders, an image that told the world the crisis, which had gripped it for weeks, was over.

Back at the American embassy, orders were issued for all our military forces worldwide to begin standing down; this applied to four squadrons of B-52's in Europe who were all fueled up with crews ready to fly into Iran to hit forward Soviet positions.

On the trip home on Air Force One, the President sat down and explained to us his thinking and reasons for what he did and had accomplished the day before.

"I knew going in the best I could get done would be the small stuff," he said. "To simply get us and the Soviets off the path we were on; the path toward a fatal confrontation as bad as the one over the missiles in Cuba if not worse." That is why he had kept the discussions in the area of stand-downs and de-escalations. "I knew they were all things the Soviets could live with in the end."

There were several times when he mentioned the deteriorating Soviet position in Iran. "If I had gone for anything that called for them to even acknowledge the possibility of defeat, the summit would have failed. It's why I had no choice but to link Cuba and Iran in some kind of withdrawal deal; you can't turn a huge military machine around on a dime, giving us anything more than a six-month deadline is a win and a chance to put our guy in Cuba and keep another Castro out." The problem with exploiting the situation in Eastern Europe was that it amounted to playing with fire. "The Soviets aren't going to let their satellites go and provoking a fight there is a sure way to a nuclear showdown."

On Khrushchev himself, the President said he was clearly not the man he'd met in Vienna three years before. "The man who walked into that summit was almost a shell of his old self, he could put on a good front and talk the talk, but something's happened, and he's clearly not in total control anymore." Yet at the end of their negotiations, when the President had come around to the Soviet side of the table, he saw the old fire again. "I told Khrushchev I wanted us to get together right after the election in November - no time to waste waiting till the second term. Told him we absolutely had to talk about limiting and ultimately eliminating nuclear weapons and making concrete progress toward reducing the tensions between us, to have something like what the French call détente. It's time to talk about where we can cooperate and make the world a better place. And you should have seen how Khrushchev's eyes really lit up when I said this. He grasped instantly what I was saying and was on board. I threw out mid-November in Stockholm for our next summit and Khrushchev ordered Gromyko to get to work right away on it."

On the meeting with Chou, President Kennedy had this to say, "There is just no Goddamn good reason why we shouldn't be negotiating with the Chinese face to face - they represent nearly a fourth of humanity and keeping them in isolation is just untenable in the long run. I couldn't let Chou hang up this summit; I had to get some kind of agreement to lower the tensions in Korea and Vietnam and thought it was well worth the political risk to go in there and shake his hand. I'll catch political hell from Henry Luce and the rest of the old China Lobby for this, and an election year is the worst time possible to make a public gesture to the Red Chinese, but that's the way things worked out." He pointed out that Khrushchev wouldn't even talk to Chou when he had the chance. "This is something we must exploit to our advantage," the President emphasized, "in the years ahead."

I was later told that General LeMay was quite unhappy about ordering his bombers stand down when they were fueled up and ready to take off for Iran, but in public he was silent.

I got off Air Force One with the worst case of jet lag I've ever experienced; I went home and slept for nine hours straight, then had my first home-cooked meal in two months. When I got back to the office, my main concern was getting Andreyev's Russian troops out of Cuba, a problem which wasn't solving itself.

I believe I was reading over a situation report from Abrams's staff when the phone on my desk rang. "I guess congratulations are in order, Colonel, you and Kennedy seem to have gotten a pretty good deal from the Russians over there in New Delhi." I instantly recognized Vance Harlow's voice. With no idea why he was calling, I thanked the man for his kind words. "Don't thank me yet, Colonel, at least not until you hear why I'm calling this morning. In case you haven't been keeping up with the news, this is a Presidential election year, and there are some big shots with a lot of money to waste who've let it be known they're paying top dollar for any and all dirt on Jack Kennedy and his administration. I just want to let you know there are some pictures circulating of you taking advantage of the hospitality at Carlos Marcello's Town and Country Motel from back when you and I made our little visit there in March. It could be a big problem if it ever saw the light of day. I like you, Colonel, and feel like I owed you a call."

Wade L. Harbinson (III)
June - July 1964

There were those who were impressed with the way John F. Kennedy handled Khrushchev, I was not one of them, nor was I alone, the Goldwater campaign set a record in fundraising in the week after that sham of a summit in India, where JFK let one sworn enemy off the hook for what it had done to the people of Iran, and then threw his arms around an equally devious foe, the Red Chinese. Not only did we get a great infusion of cash after Kennedy played patty cake with the Communists, but there were also record numbers of people enlisting in the cause and signing up to volunteer for Senator Goldwater, so in some small way JFK did us a favor.

On the day Kennedy flew back from his Indian love fest with our Communist enemies, I finally received a call from Vance Harlow at last, saying he wanted to meet with me again in Dallas at the Carousel Club. At the time, I was quite impressed with his professionalism, how he was careful to never discuss any aspect of our business on the phone. He was later to tell me he had complete confidence in the discretion of the owner.

I met with Harlow there on the afternoon of June 19th in the same back room where we'd met months earlier. My expectations for this meeting were high, summer was here, and the conventions were not far off, it was getting close to the time when it would be necessary to bring out the big artillery, and I was hoping to get the political equivalent of the A-Bomb from Mr. Harlow.

"Let me ask you this, Mr. Harbinson," he said after I shook his hand took a seat opposite Harlow, "are you absolutely sure you want to go through with this proposal? You sure you want to go down this road?"

I had no doubt whatsoever, I told him, that you have to take risks if you want to get anywhere in life, and big rewards - like electing a great man President - require the taking of very big risks.

Harlow was pleased with hearing this. He then went on to tell me he had made some discreet inquires of the kinds of individuals who would - for a price - deliver what I wanted. These inquiries had produced promising preliminary results, but it would take time, and furthermore, these people were no rubes, they knew how to drive a hard bargain. And in the unfortunate nature of these things, I had tipped my hand by offering a million dollars up front. The bottom line: I needed to be prepared to fork over more green to get what I wanted.

I'm used to dealing with people who know how to drive a hard bargain, but if I was going to dig deeper into my pockets, then I wanted some idea of what I was paying for; all dirt is not the same, some of it will yield a fine field of corn, while another plot will get you nothing but thistles. I explained as much to Harlow, saying I was willing to pay more, but only for the former, not the latter.

Harlow was silent for a moment, clearly weighing his words carefully lest he reveal too much too soon, the sign of a good negotiator. "Okay Wade, this is what you can get for your money," he said at last, "I have seen documented proof that the Kennedy brothers are conspiring with known members of the Mafia to further their mutual interests. I have also talked to individuals who claim they can get their hands on a 'secret medical file' on the President which will reveal a whole host of ailments John Kennedy has kept hidden from the American public. Then there is the allegation of a woman who says she regularly visited the White House to have sexual relations with the President of the United States. I've seen no proof of the latter two, but if I can get my hands on it, and if it proves to be true, I think it would be most worth the while."

A secret medical history; the Kennedy brothers in bed with organized crime; the President revealing himself to be an immoral degenerate; as far as I was concerned this was better than any Christmas morning And if all three could be proven to be true beyond the shadow of a doubt, then they would be well worth any price. I made it clear to Harlow that I would get the money to compensate any and all who could get the proof of John Kennedy's unfitness for office. "When you want to bring down the big game, you got to load for bear," is how I put it.

"Good enough," Harlow replied, "but let me remind you that these individuals I'm doing business with are not good patriots like you, Wade. They're in it only for the money and expect to be well compensated for the risk of crossing the men who can call J. Edgar Hoover any hour of the day and night.

I had no illusions as to the character of the people Harlow was dealing with, and I more than appreciated the risks involved, but with success within reach, it was not the time to go weak in the knees. I affirmed my commitment to Vance Harlow to see this through.

"Good enough," Harlow said, "but it will likely be well into the fall campaign before anyone delivers."

That was fine with me.

I flew home from Dallas more convinced than ever of the rightness of my actions and if they bent the rules of propriety to the breaking point, then so be it. An abomination of a Civil Rights Bill was actually being considered in the Senate, while the President of the United States kissed the ass of the dictator of the Soviet Union and extended his hand to the Communist Chinese - desperate times required desperate measures. No, the times required real and true Americans to fight back against the vipers in our midst, to sever their heads before they destroyed the hard work of nearly two hundred years.

"Senator," I said to Barry Goldwater when I saw him two days after my meeting with Harlow, "you might want to pick out the drapes for the Oval Office right now."

"Wade you're putting the cart before the horse," the Senator replied, "there's a campaign to be waged, and I know Jack Kennedy very well, it's not going to be easy."

I so wanted to tell the Senator he didn't know Jack Kennedy nearly as well as he thought, but he would learn soon learn otherwise.

Kevin McCluskey (I)
Re-elect Kennedy '64
March - July 1964

There was one thing everybody knew from the beginning, Bobby Kennedy was running his brother's re-election campaign, even if Steve Smith was "officially" in charge. And the one thing the Kennedy family valued above all else was loyalty; that's how I got my job with them. My family on my father's side was true Massachusetts Irish - my great grandfather from County Cork came over to Boston in 1848, but it was my old man who opened the door for me. He'd enlisted in the Marines the week after Pearl Harbor and saw his action in Pacific, and when a fellow Irish American veteran first ran for office in the Bay State, he was among the first to sign up for Jack Kennedy. As the owner of a chain of dry cleaners stretching all the way up to Bangor, Maine, my father was in a position to raise some big bucks for John F. Kennedy in both his Senate races in the 50's. One of my first political memories was taking Kennedy posters around to people in our neighborhood when I was in the 7th grade. What I'm saying is my Dad was an original Kennedy man who'd always been there when they needed him and had always come through; the kind of person JFK and Bobby never forgot.

Not that I hadn't already proven my bona fides as a Kennedy warrior in 1960 when I took off a semester from Brown to work in the trenches for the campaign. I spent the months of September and October going door to door for Kennedy-Johnson in the Italian neighborhoods of Paderson and Bayonne, New Jersey. I got the job because, as the head of the Kennedy campaign in the Garden State put it, I was a "little wop." The slur didn't bother me, that's because I got my looks from my Sicilian mother, the jet black hair and olive skin, but at five feet eight inches, I've always been touchy about my height - played a lot of football in high school to compensate. My younger brother, Eddie, took after our father with his red hair and fair complexion, but as far as I know, nobody ever called him a "Mick."

It was our common Catholic heritage that made my family fierce Kennedy partisans from the beginning; both my parents were not shy about letting my brother and I know how our grandparents and great-grandparents had not been welcomed to America with open arms. My father was proud he'd made a success of himself in Boston, a city where'd they'd once hung out "No Irish need apply" signs. But for me it was also something generational, for John F. Kennedy was a break with the past, with a country where everyone waited their turn, respected their "betters," and never dared rock the boat. So many of my parents' generation would have been just as happy to have lived out their lives like the Cleavers and the Nelsons on TV, but JFK promised to get this country moving again, to not just manage the status quo, but to meet challenges like the Cold War head on.

That was why I was such a Kennedy partisan going into 1964, plus I knew a good opportunity when I saw one, the contacts I could make in the Kennedy campaign would open a lot of doors for me if I played my cards right. All it took was a few calls from my father to Lawrence O'Brien and Kenny O'Donnell to get an interview - a formality - since all the Irish Mafia knew Sean McCluskey. Without a formal title or salary, I was told to fly to Oklahoma and interview prospective candidates to head the re-election effort in the Sooner State and come back with a recommendation in two days.

The President had little chance of carrying Oklahoma, especially against Goldwater, but I was more than happy to take on a job for which I had no qualification; I booked a flight to Oklahoma City, did exactly as I was told and was back in DC 36 hours later to recommend the owner of the largest Ford dealership in the state for the job as Chairman. My criterion for picking the man: he was a Navy veteran of the Pacific and his enthusiasm for Kennedy was palpable.

Steve Smith heard my report on Oklahoma, listened to my recommendation, thanked me for my hard work and showed me the door. More than a little puzzled, I went back to hotel room, not sure what had just happened or what to do next. Then the phone rang, and I was amazed to find myself talking to Robert F. Kennedy himself, the Attorney General and JFK's brother. He didn't waste words but said he was impressed since the man I'd recommended in Oklahoma was exactly who he would have picked if it had been his call. Therefore I had the job as special assistant to Kennedy '64 campaign, a fancy title which meant little, for my real duties would be trouble shooting for the campaign - going around the country and getting on top of problems at the ground level - like some local Democratic office holder who was putting his own interests before that of the reelection campaign - before they got on the front pages of the papers and caused an embarrassment or a distraction to the President. It paid $150.00 a week plus expenses.

The next day, Oswald took a shot at Kennedy in Dallas.

I was shopping for a new suit and saw the news breaking on a display TV in a Sears window in downtown Washington; when I got to the campaign headquarters, all anyone knew was that the President's limousine had rushed to a Dallas hospital. There were rumors saying the President and the First Lady were dead while the Vice President was wounded. The tears were flowing, first out of fear and grief, then out of relief when the news came that JFK and the First Lady had walked out of the hospital and spoke to reporters.

Dallas changed everything, for within days, all the country could talk about was who was behind the attempt to murder the President. Nobody thought Oswald could have acted alone, the tip to the police proved as much; it was just a matter of finding his accomplices. That it would be Castro came as no surprise, the guns and money found in the Dallas bus depot locker closed the case. "We need to get those Communist sons of bitches once and for all," were my father's words at Christmas dinner that year. My brother Eddie urged caution and was shouted down for his trouble.

After Dallas, the country was facing an ongoing foreign policy crisis, not just with Cuba, but potentially with the Soviet Union and it drove the campaign off the front pages; and for us, it meant a campaign without an active candidate as it was made clear to us by Steve Smith that as long there was the possibility of American boys dying on a battlefield, the President would not be making any partisan political appearances

We naively thought the country would rally around the President in a crisis.

I spent the winter of 1964 on the road touching base with the reelection effort in more than 20 states. The marching orders we'd received was to start building the well-oiled machine needed for in the fall - get back the people who'd been with us in '60 and bring in newcomers and win by a landslide in November.

I was determined to do my job well; there were plenty of stories about more than one advance man who lost his gig because he did a lousy job for one of the President's surrogates who were barnstorming the primary states in his place. Somewhere along the line, I got the reputation as a guy you didn't want to cross; it got back to me that I'd been called a "little know-it-all son of a bitch" by the state chairman in Ohio after a contentious meeting in Cincinnati.

New Hampshire voted on March 12th, and Kennedy took 90% of the vote; no big surprise there, but when I flew into Madison, Wisconsin the next day, I quickly discovered that the smooth running JFK re-election campaign was about to hit a speed bump in a state that went to polls on April 7th.

I hadn't been in town an hour before two members of the state central committee were in my hotel room with news I found hard to believe: John F. Kennedy was facing a close race in their state on primary day from Alabama Governor George Wallace. It seemed that a genuine grass roots movement for Wallace had sprung up overnight, spearheaded by a right wing couple who had accomplished all the work needed overnight to get the Alabama Governor's name on the ballot along with a full slate of delegates filed to compete with the President's. Wisconsin's primary was "open," which meant Republicans were free to vote in the Democratic race, something that was a real possibility since none of the Republican candidates had bothered to run there.

Why was Wallace doing so well? It seemed that while most of the press had been concentrating on the crisis in Cuba, a lot of working class voters had been following the debate over the Civil Rights Act in Congress and they didn't like what they were hearing about this bill. Union workers in auto plants would lose their seniority if the company were forced by the Federal government to hire blacks; homeowners who'd spent 20 years paying off mortgages would see their home values plummet when the Feds forced their neighbors to sell to blacks; qualified whites wouldn't get good jobs because the Feds would make the boss hire shiftless Negroes. These were the sentiments being expressed by many good Democrats according to the Wisconsin state party chairman.

When I expressed some doubts, I was told, "If you think Wallace can't win here, you should remember this is the state that elected Joe McCarthy to the Senate twice."

I could hardly believe what I was hearing; the President was getting high marks in the polls for his handling of the crisis in Cuba, and the numbers were even higher among Democrats. Nobody had been paying attention in January when the segregationist Wallace, who had tangled with Bobby Kennedy's Justice Department, had announced he would challenge the President in the primaries.

To see if things were really as bad as they were being portrayed, I went to a Wallace appearance the next day at a VFW hall in Milwaukee. If I wasn't convinced Kennedy had a problem before going inside, I was more than persuaded by the time I left. The room was packed like sardines, at least a crowd of 700, and when the bantam-sized Wallace first took the stage he looked distinctly uncomfortable in front of this distinctly northern crowd. But something electric happened when the MC, a Marine veteran and bar owner, began his introduction by ordering the few Negroes in the crowd to leave and then excoriated them by recounting how they beat up old ladies, raped white women, refused to work and lived on relief. He ended this with an emphatic, "I didn't survive months of hell on Iwo Jima to come home to this!"

The crowd went wild when they heard this and when Wallace finally spoke, he clearly realized he was among the like-minded. His message was simple and direct: the Federal government in Washington wanted to take away your freedom and if it could force the people of Alabama to integrate against their will, then what could they do to the good people of Wisconsin. "It's time for the pointy-headed bureaucrats in Washington to get the message," he said at one point, "we want them to leave our homes, our jobs, our schools, our farms, our businesses alone. They belong to us, not them." Then he added, "I wish the President cared as much about the freedom of the citizens of Alabama and Wisconsin as he does about the freedom of a bunch of foreigners in Cuba." The crush of admirers was so great it took Wallace more than an hour to get out of the hall.

Back in my hotel room, I placed a call to Steve Smith and did my best to convince him we had a potential problem in Wisconsin. My words fell on deaf ears; there was no way the President could be having a hard time against a two-bit demagogue. The problem that all this was happening at the same time the ultimatum to Castro was coming due and neither the President nor the Attorney General had any time for political matters - or so I thought. For the next two weeks, we watched as Wallace drew large and enthusiastic crowds across the state while the President's supporters were relying on the power of an incumbent to rally the faithful.

I was back in Washington one week to the day before the voting in Wisconsin when the phone in the Arlington, Virginia apartment I was subletting rang; it was Robert Kennedy, and he wanted to know what the hell was going on in Wisconsin, the latest newspaper poll in the state had it a dead heat between Wallace and the President. I gave Bobby Kennedy a rundown of all I had seen, along with a detailed description of the

Wallace rally. "There's no damn way that little son of a bitch is winning Wisconsin over my brother," Kennedy said and thanked me for being honest and giving him the low down. I want to point out this conversation occurred on the day there was an attempt to overthrow Castro when as far as the country knew, the entire Kennedy White House was focused on Cuba.

Whatever, but somebody lit a fire under the Kennedy effort in the final week before the primary vote, overnight Kennedy campaign signs began dotting yards, while billboards touting the President went up on every major highway. The national Presidents for the UAW and the Meatpackers came in to personally fire up the rank and file who were very susceptible to Wallace's fiery rhetoric. To ice the cake, Senator Hubert Humphrey, from next door in Minnesota and a beloved figure to many liberals in Wisconsin, took time out from getting the Civil Rights Act through Congress to make a series of speeches on the weekend before the vote.

When the returns came in on the 7th of April, the President won with over 60%, but Wallace came in with a solid third of the vote; it would have been a big story if the invasion of Cuba had not been imminent on Wednesday morning. PRESIDENT WINS WISCONSIN; WALLACE IN SECOND PLACE was a below the fold story in the *New York Times*.

Two days after Wisconsin went to the polls there was a meeting in Washington attended by all the old hands from the '60 campaign, along with newcomers like me. Given the situation in Cuba, neither the President nor the Attorney General was in attendance, but it was chaired by Lawrence O'Brien, a first among equals when it came to politics in the Administration.

Many of the participants have written their memoirs in the years since - O'Brien's being the best and most honest in my opinion - and they have downplayed the threat Wallace was now posing to the President in upcoming primaries, especially in Indiana and Maryland. No one was in a state of panic, but it was made clear that we were going to the mat with Wallace from here on out; to call on Union leaders to twist arms for the President; touch base with every single volunteer from '60 in those states and get them on board again; make sure every Democratic office holder gets off their asses and out working for the President; stage events from one end of each state to the other with Presidential surrogates; get lists of Wallace supporters, especially financial ones and find out if they did any business with the government in any way. "Maybe it's a bar owner in Indianapolis who's writing Wallace a check," someone used as an example, "well, he has to get a liquor license from the state. Make sure Governor Welsh knows who he is and what he ought to do about it."

At one point in the meeting, I made a pitch to have the Vice President come out on the campaign trail and speak for the President; after all, he was up for re-election too and he'd gotten some recent good publicity over his efforts to get the Civil Rights Act through

Congress. This was met with stony silence from the Irish Mafia, later I broached the idea to Dave Powers, an old friend of my father's, and learned that Bobby Kennedy was damned and determined to get Johnson replaced on the ticket. Powers added that while the President had not made a decision, "Bobby can't stand old Rufus Cornpone, never has and never will; he'll use that Baker stuff to dump him, but it's pure hate, pure and simple." Rufus Cornpone was the nickname the inner circle had given Johnson, and though I was a solid Kennedy man, I felt bad for the Vice President.

So we had our marching orders to make sure there were no awkward headlines coming out of Indiana and Maryland, the two states where Wallace was taking on Kennedy next. The Democratic rank and file in the Hoosier state, which voted first on May 5th, was mobilized for the President in a big way that did not escape the notice of the political press core: INSURGENT WALLACE FORCES KENNEDY TO PICK UP PACE was the headline of a story in the *Los Angeles Times* on May 1st. The Alabama Governor was drawing huge crowds in both states, hitting the Civil Rights Act at every event and playing to the fears of middle-class white voters by making the case over and over that any gain by a black man meant a loss for a white. "They talk a lot about the so-called civil rights of Negroes," he said at a rally in Evanston a week before the primary, "but they never mention your property rights; they don't talk about how some pointy headed bureaucrat in Washington is going to force your neighbor to sell his home to a *Negro*."

I'll never forget what the head of a steelworker's local in Gary, Indiana, told me three days before the primary vote, "I fought in WWII, I love John F. Kennedy, but I'm marking Wallace's name on the ballot and sending JFK the message he can't take us for granted."

The primary fights in Indiana and Maryland enlightened me to something that had been going on away from the attention of the networks and the big daily papers while they focused on events in Cuba, Iran and the Soviet Union, how the struggle for racial equality in America had turned into to a pitched battle: in Cleveland, Ohio, a white mob had beaten up blacks protesting employment discrimination; a high school in Tennessee facing a court order to integrate had been dynamited over the Easter school break; black protesters in San Francisco had joined hands vowing to block the entrances to the city's largest supermarket chain until the company's management met with them and agreed to promote blacks to management positions - the store's owner called the police and a violent melee resulted; a black man had taken a seat at a table in a white's only restaurant and bar in Baltimore, the establishment's owner promptly attacked him with a tire iron and cracked his skull, an act which set off three days of demonstrations and violent encounters with the police; the Committee for Racial Equality arranged to have several hundred pounds of garbage dumped on the ramps to the Brooklyn Bridge just before morning rush hour to protest "the system;" eight black churches were set afire by arson, six were in the deep South, but one was in Kansas, and the other was all the way out in California; footage of Malcolm X was repeatedly shown on the TV news calling for blacks to arm themselves and form "rifle clubs" for self-protection. All of this happened between the middle of March and late April, just as the Presidential contest was getting into high gear and the Civil Rights Act was making progress in Congress.

To punctuate all these developments, I caught a snatch of a speech by Goldwater on the *CBS Evening News* where he said, "As your President, I will work tirelessly to protect law and order, and I pledge full cooperation with Federal, State, and local law enforcement to defend the families, the homes and the jobs of every honest and hard-working American." He was speaking to an overflow crowd at an arena in Oklahoma City on the weekend of the state Republican convention; the similarity between what he was saying and Wallace's message was striking.

This boded potential trouble in the fall for the President, but first, the re-nomination had to be locked up. True to form, the Kennedy machine kicked into high gear, first in Indiana and then in Maryland. They changed the tone of the campaign; both primary fights coincided with the invasion of Cuba and overnight every speaker for the President began appealing to the voter's patriotism, telling them it was their duty as good Democrats to stand behind the President in this moment of crisis.

"Jack Kennedy is fighting for you; he needs you to fight for him." That line was repeated by every pro-Kennedy speaker at every rally and gathering across the Hoosier state. Still, when the returns came on the night of May 5th, Wallace polled 37% of the vote against the President, a good showing against an incumbent. Indiana had been a state with a big KKK presence for much of the 20th Century, so it could have been worse, or so I told myself.

Maryland had rural areas with much in common with Alabama, plus Baltimore had been the sight of recent strife between blacks and whites, things which made the state fertile ground for Wallace's message. So word went out to every Democratic office holder in the state that if anyone of them so much as thought about voting for Wallace, they could kiss their public careers goodbye. Not only that, but everyone was expected to have a Kennedy sign in their yard and to bring at least ten other voters to the polls on Election Day. Word also got around that certain lucrative federal projects, like money to upgrade the port facilities in Baltimore, might suddenly become scarce if Maryland embarrassed the President. I also know for a fact that Wallace's biggest financial backer in the state, an Eastern shore poultry farmer, was told he could expect visits daily from FDA inspectors at his three Cambridge processing plants unless he stopped writing checks to Wallace for President and stroked one for Kennedy '64.

Still, Wallace drew large and enthusiastic crowds wherever he went; his speeches were a litany of the evils of the Civil Rights Act and its proponents. "When I am your President," he said in a speech at Laurel the Friday before the primary vote, "there won't be any more of this nonsense about marching and protesting and whining and complaining; the only people who I'll listen to will be the good Americans with jobs who don't have time to march around waving some sign saying, 'Gimme or else.' And if any civil rights protestor sits down in front of my car, it'll be his last time."

It was potent language, and in the end, it got Wallace 43% of Maryland's vote, his best state; it might have gotten a lot of press if not for the President raising the readiness of NATO in anticipation of some other move by the Soviets. That was the headline in every paper the day after the primary, so we got off lucky in that respect, but there were those picking up on a trend: "THE WHITE BACKLASH HAS OFFICIALLY ARRIVED" was the title of a three-page story in *Time* magazine's next issue.

Wallace went on to compete in the California where he didn't stand a chance in the June 2nd primary; Governor Pat Brown was a fellow Catholic, a huge Kennedy supporter, and a hell of a politician who wasn't about to get caught napping. Yet the Alabama Governor won nearly 40% of the vote when California Democrats went to the polls, with his biggest totals coming from suburban Orange County. Again, we caught a break of a sort because the crisis with the Soviets was coming to a head and the summit in New Delhi was only days away, so the Democratic results in California were not big news.

The Wallace insurgency was for me, ultimately the backdrop for a real turning point in my career and my life as well. It was during the week before the California primary, and I was in Los Angeles basically killing time since Governor Brown had things well in hand, when the phone rang in my hotel room, and to my absolute shock, discovered Bobby Kennedy himself on the other end of the line. "Mr. McCluskey," he said, "you've proved yourself quite capable in the last few months, the kind of young man who knows how to get things done and how to be loyal; those are things my brother and I value highly, and your contribution to the campaign hasn't gone unnoticed." This was quite a compliment coming from the #2 man in the administration. After my swollen head had deflated to normal size, I was told of an urgent task in need of attention. That I would take on the job was not a question; instructions were given, certain details were elaborated upon when requested, I profusely thanked the Attorney General for the opportunity and then he hung up.

In short, what I did next was to take a rental car up to the Holmby Hills section of L.A. to the home of one of the top men in the William Morris Agency, a man whom I later learned represented one of RCA's biggest recording stars and the top box office star of the 1950's; a man who knew everybody who was anybody at every studio. This person, whom I will not call by name, handed me a satchel filled with fifty thousand dollars in cash, which I did not take my eyes off of for the next eight hours as I left the City of Angels and flew back to Washington D.C. where I handed the satchel to Dave Powers, who was waiting for me at 4:30 a.m. in Steve Smith's office at the Kennedy '64 national headquarters on Pennsylvania Avenue. He told me, "In this business, you've got to be prepared because you never know what you'll find on the front page of tomorrow's paper." Mr. Powers took the satchel from me and put in a closet. When he opened the door, I got a glimpse of the closet's contents: at least a dozen more satchels and briefcases inside, and I had no doubt in my mind what was inside them.

That was my introduction to campaign finance; I was about to learn much more; much more indeed.

Dorothy Jean Brennan (I)
Goldwater for President
January - June 1964

They say I got my job on account of my pretty face, I don't deny it, I was Miss Idaho, 1960, after all, but they never seem to mention the degree in journalism I got from Bosie University the following year, third in my class. I had dreams of being just like Jean Arthur in *Mr. Smith Goes to Washington*, the plucky reporter who always got the story, but life is not like the movies, there just wasn't many jobs for a woman reporter unless she wanted to start out writing obituaries or advice to the lovelorn, but I was raised by my parents to use my talents and abilities to always find a way to make a difference in this world.

That's how I got into politics, a field where there were almost no opportunities for a woman unless she was a secretary or a candidate's wife. Though I grew up on my father's ranch in southern Idaho, my mother's family had roots in Arizona all the way back to the days of Spanish rule, and my uncle had gone to work in one of the Goldwater family department stores during the depression when he lost his salesman's job. He'd risen to a manager's position and knew the Senator personally, he was the one who called me in the fall of '63 and tipped me to an open position in the Goldwater for President campaign; at the time I was working a file clerk for the Los Angeles Times, the only job in anything close to journalism I could get. Uncle Jack said it might be good experience, something which would look nice on a resume in the future.

It was an easy choice to make, more so since my family had always been active in the Republican Party - I joined the Young Republicans at USC, something which came in handy when I applied with the campaign. Even though I was in grade school at the time, I can well remember how crushed my father had been when Thomas Dewey lost to Truman; my father detested the New Deal and thought the whole thing was a criminal waste of the taxpayer's money. Surprisingly, he didn't care all that much for Eisenhower, mainly because he wouldn't even attempt to repeal Social Security and had gone all the way to Europe to meet with Khrushchev during his first term. "No damn good can ever come from talking with the Communists; Roosevelt proved that at Yalta; the only thing which they understand is actions, not words." As for John F. Kennedy, he was Irish, Catholic and from the East, it didn't matter what his politics were, he already had three strikes against him as far as my family was concerned.

It was with great enthusiasm that I applied for a job with the Goldwater campaign; I flew out to Phoenix for an interview with Dennison Kitchel, the man putting together the nuts and bolts Goldwater '64. It proved to be a mere formality as my Uncle Jack knew Mr. Kitchel; I was hired as an assistant to the press secretary.

That meant I spent a lot of time typing, but it also gave me the opportunity to travel around the country with the candidate, a man whom I met on my second day on the job.

What immediately impressed me was how utterly down to earth and unpretentious Barry Goldwater was, the man you saw in public was the man you saw in private, which also meant he didn't make much of an effort to clean up his language in front of ladies, but you got used to the "hells" and damns" pretty fast. It all seems tame compared to the way people talk now. You couldn't be around this man anytime without becoming passionate about electing him President.

It was a conviction that everyone in the campaign shared: Senator Goldwater was the only man who could turn this country around after decades of socialists and internationalists running things. This faith sustained us through the first rocky days of the campaign in the winter of '64 as the Senator tried to rally support for the New Hampshire primary and caught hell from the press for daring to suggest Kennedy's response to the assassination attempt was weak. All the polls showed him trailing the other contenders - Rockefeller, Lodge, Scranton, and Nixon - while losing to the President by double digits. It got so bad in the last weeks in New Hampshire that the regular spokesman for the campaign just came out and refused to go do the daily briefings which were part of the political rituals. "They're all a bunch of pro-Communist liberals," he said, "and I'm not going to take any more of their disrespectful questions." I believe it was Steve Shadegg, a man who had helped in the Goldwater campaigns in Arizona, who suggested that I go out there and brief them, because, after all, I was a former beauty queen and knew how to handle myself in front of a crowd.

I was terrified the first time I stood before the political press core in Manchester, New Hampshire, but what Mr. Shadegg said was true, my experience on the pageant runway came back to me, and I pulled it off. Then I pulled it off the next day and the day after, and soon the job was mine permanently. Before long I was writing up the press briefings myself, condensing what the Senator said that day into a few short lines, which was usually that Castro and his Communist Cuba should receive no mercy; that the Federal government taxed too much and wasted too much. The press was determined to portray the Senator as a warmonger and hard-hearted, but I would give them my best smile and repeat the truth over and over, whether they understood it or not. I think I earned some grudging admiration for my efforts; Mary McGrory, a reporter for the Washington Star and part of the liberal Kennedy-worshipping Washington press, would always compliment me on a job well done at the end of each briefing.

We took on the chin in New Hampshire, losing to Lodge in the state's primary on the 10th of March. It was even tougher to read the analysis of the results the next day in the papers: all of which said Senator Goldwater's campaign was as good as dead; it just hadn't fallen into its inevitable grave yet. I was part of the March 15th meeting in Phoenix where everyone got together and hashed thing out. That was the meeting where the two sides of the Goldwater campaign - the old Arizona people and the new guys who'd gotten the Draft Goldwater movement off the ground - came together. I think the galvanizing words came from Clif White, who told us, "I don't care how much money Rockefeller and Lodge have right now, what they don't have is a group of people like us, people who love their man and will do anything to put him in the White House."

Everyone came out of that meeting with their marching orders; first the nomination and then the election - win them both. I formally put in charge of dealing with the press. It was a real point of pride to me that my work was one of the few things both sides agreed on as having gone well in the campaign so far.

Those days in March proved to be the rock bottom for Goldwater's fight for the nomination; with a united effort, things started coming together. The campaign stayed on point and our people turned out by the hundreds and some cases, by the thousands, from the Carolinas to the Mississippi Delta to the plains of Kansas to the heart of Texas to the Rocky Mountain States; they showed up early and stayed late, and they won and they won and they won.

This did not happen just because Clif White had a plan or Dennison Kitchel and Dean Burch knew how to run an organization. It happened because a man, Barry Goldwater, found his voice at the right moment and got people to listen to him.

When I say moment, I'm talking about those days and weeks after Lodge beat us in New Hampshire, when the Kennedys were issuing "ultimatums" and treating an act of war on American soil as if it were an offense in traffic court. There was no doubt Oswald had been in the pay of the Cubans after all that incriminating evidence was discovered in the Dallas bus terminal, yet months later, the boys in the White House were prattling about negotiations because doing the right thing and defending America might upset Moscow. No other Republican candidate for the Republican nomination dared call out the Kennedy brothers for their timidity in the face of criminal aggression.

But not Senator Goldwater; there have been stories of how his inner circle sat him down and explained how he needed to take an even harder line on Cuba and the Soviets than the one he'd already staked out. Nothing could be further from the truth, nobody ever had to set Barry Goldwater down and tell him what to think or what to tell anybody. Not that he would have listened if anyone had dared try. No, the Senator himself was disgusted at the administration's course of action toward Cuba and simply told the truth as he saw it, and the crowds responded. "We're going to have to go in and get rid of Castro," he told us the day the ultimatum to Cuba was announced, "there's no way around it and I don't know why Jack just won't get off his ass and do the job." That was the sentiment he expressed over and over and his best speechwriter, Karl Hess, worked into his remarks.

The thing that really did it for the Senator and for the rest of the true conservatives in America came when General Almeida rose up and tried to overthrow the Communist tyrant and Kennedy did nothing. "It is utterly intolerable...intolerable...that our President sits on his hands while good Cuban patriots are dying to free their island," the Senator thundered to an open air noon crowd in Kansas City on the fifth day of April, "while looking over their shoulders to make sure they're not doing something which might get Khrushchev's nose out of joint. " The crowd went wild when they heard this, and it was the same at the next event and the one after that one. He stayed true even after Kennedy finally sent in American troops to finally oust Castro, lamenting all the good and brave men, like General Almeida, who were lost because America drug its feet.

As the events of that spring unfolded, we were ever more convinced Barry Goldwater was the only man who could turn America around; when the Soviet Union trampled over the people of Iran, when North Korea prepared to resume its aggression, when the Red Chinese sought to fan the flames of war; when the North Vietnamese took advantage of our weakness in Indo-China and tried to overrun the South, Barry Goldwater was the lone voice who stood up and said we had to hit back and hit back hard.

As the crowds grew larger, so did the number of volunteers for the campaign; the same can be said for donations, as money poured in as winter gave way to spring '64.

I've read many accounts of the Goldwater campaign by outsiders - Theodore White's *The Making of the President* book being the worst offender among them - which state how we were "desperate" and "flailing," midway through the nomination battle and that the Senator "stumbled" upon the issues that ultimately worked in his favor.

Again, nothing could be further from the truth. Millions of Americans flocked the Goldwater banner because of what they saw happening in the country and then heard the Senator's words.

I'll offer these examples:

After Kitty Genovese was knifed to death in New York while her neighbors ignored her pleas for help, Senator Goldwater said in a speech in Concord, New Hampshire: "When I am your President, I will make the individual safety of every single American my priority, not only safety in their homes, but in the streets of our great cities as well. And to the predatory criminal who preys upon the innocent, there will be swift and true justice." When was the last time anyone heard Kennedy say anything about the criminals who were treated better than their victims by the courts?

On April 15th, when millions of Americans were scurrying to the Post Office to mail off their tax returns to the IRS, Senator Goldwater had this to say at a noontime speech in Kansas City: "It's time we stopped confiscating the hard-earned wages of good Americans and then giving the money to bums on relief. It's time for the bums to get jobs and start paying their way like the rest of us." When did Kennedy ever talk about those who loafed on the taxpayer's dime?

When the so-called Civil Rights Act passed the House of Representatives and Communist inspired protesters took to the streets to coerce its passage, Senator Goldwater stood up in Indianapolis and proclaimed: "There are those hell bent on increasing the power of the Federal Government to that of a dictatorship, one which could potentially rival Stalin's Russia. An American dictatorship which tramples upon the individual state's right to conduct their own affairs; the right of the independent businessman to run his enterprise as he knows best; the right of each individual American to own and keep his property as he sees fit." When was the last time anyone heard Kennedy say anything about state's or property rights?

Before the month of March was out, we could feel the momentum turning in our direction as the majority of the states began gathering in conventions to select their delegate slates to the national convention; in one two week period, we took the majority in South Carolina, Tennessee, Kansas and Nevada. Then Goldwater easily won primaries in Indiana, Nebraska, and Texas. The Senator took a decisive lead in the delegate count, while the Lodge campaign withered away and the Rockefeller effort was all but given the Last Rites by the pundits. By the first of May we had more than half what was needed to obtain a first ballot victory.

The final weeks of the primary campaign was overshadowed by developments in Europe and Iran and the ensuing confrontation with the Soviet Union; Senator Goldwater made no secret of where he stood: he called for the US Air Force to go in and decimate the Soviet divisions in Iran while putting NATO on full alert as preemptive measure. At the same time, he dared Governor Rockefeller to tow the same line, when the Governor came out for bombing Iran; we hit him hard for being a "Me Too Republican" and reminded the voters they should vote for the man who'd been right from the beginning. We ran into a speed bump in the Oregon primary on May 15th when Rockefeller upset us there, but we were still picking up delegates from state conventions and our total only grew higher.

The final primary fight was in California on June 2nd, and because the state party had the "unit" rule, which the candidate who won the most votes on election day got all the votes of state's delegation, even if he won by only a single vote; if Rockefeller had been able to win there he could've halted the Goldwater momentum. The primary fight in the Golden State occurred against the back drop of ratcheting tensions in Europe, and stories of restless Poles and other Eastern Europeans increasingly straining against the chains of the Soviets and it became an issue in the race. After an appearance in Sacramento, Governor Rockefeller made an offhand remark to the press that "This is not the proper time and we should refrain from fishing in troubled waters."

The Senator responded the next day in San Diego by asking, "And I would like the Governor to tell us when is the 'proper' time to come to the aid of an enslaved people?" We hit Rockefeller hard for that remark, but there was also plenty of fire turned on the Kennedy Administration, who could not wait to sit down with the Communists and sell out more free people. The anxiety among Republicans over the world situation and Kennedy's handling of it played right into our hands, California handed the Senator a victory over the Governor of New York by a margin of 55% to 45%, settling the battle for the nomination right there. Richard Nixon, who'd been positioning himself to be the compromise choice at the convention, publicly endorsed Goldwater the day after the California primary and

Governor Scranton of Pennsylvania, another eastern liberal who'd been making noises about getting into the race to stop Goldwater, announced he would not be tossing his hat into the ring after all.

Our celebration at achieving total victory was short-lived, there was a convention in July to plan and fall campaign to be waged.

There was a full bore meeting of all the top men in the campaign in Phoenix on June 16th, the day after Kennedy met with Chou En Lai in New Delhi and sold out Chaing Kai Chek and Taiwan, one of our oldest and most loyal allies in Asia. I remember how agitated Senator Goldwater was over this news and how everyone thought it would boomerang against Kennedy to our advantage. I remember there was a lot of back and forth over who would take what position in the fall campaign, Clif White clearly thought he'd earned the right to run the whole show, but everyone knew the Senator was more comfortable with men like Dean Burch, Dennison Kitchel, and Dick Kleindenst. There was also some contention over who would be the director of finance for the fall effort; I remember this clearly because one of the fiercest claimants for the job was Wade L. Harbinson, a Texas oil tycoon, who'd been allied with the White camp.

There had been little contact between me and Mr. Harbinson so far in the campaign, and the few times we'd met, he'd always called me "Little Lady" or "Sweetie" in the way I guess all big rich oil men do down in Texas, but not the way gentlemen do in the rest of the country. I mention Mr. Harbinson here since it was my supposed close proximity to him that got me into the worst fix of my life; it started when a well dressed man approached me after a press briefing in New Orleans and told me I needed to give a message to Wade Harbinson right away. "Tell Harbinson not to pay anything to that son of a bitch, Harlow," he said, "tell him those exact words. I'll give him exactly what he wants for a hell of a cheaper price than what Harlow's asking. What I got can bury the whole damn Kennedy crew, tell him that; tell him to call me at this number." He then pushed a folded note ripped from a legal pad into my right hand. "Tell him to call it; I'll make it worth his while." Then he was gone.

And just like that, this former beauty queen got caught up in a conspiracy hell bent on destroying American politics as we had come to know it.

John Compton (III)

June - July 1964

All my life I'd heard how timing is everything, I never really knew what it meant until June of the year 1964, and the lesson was a hard one. On the first day of the month, we held a meeting in the Vice President's office on the final push to get the Civil Rights Act through the Senate and hopefully on Kennedy's desk by the 4th of July. We were free of Jim Eastland's Judiciary Committee, and all we needed to do now was defeat the expected Southern filibuster, to achieve that, we would need at a minimum 20 Republican Senators to vote for closure and shut the Southerners down. The key to getting those Republican Senators was Minority Leader Everett Dirksen, a man who in the past had enjoyed a cordial relationship with Lyndon Johnson. It was agreed that he would work in lining up support from Dirksen and the fellow members of his caucus, while Senator Humphrey would be chief floor manager and head counter for the debate on the floor; never mind that the Senate had invoked closure only once since 1927. We felt history was on our side as Americans from all walks of life couldn't help but be thoroughly disgusted by the Bull Conner like tactics of the Old South and were through with the police dictatorship that was required to keep Jim Crow in place.

I should have been paying better attention to what was going on in the wider world. While we had taken advantage of the ongoing foreign policy crisis to move the stalled Civil Rights Act from the House to the floor of the Senate, we had been blinded to the fear and suspicion engendered among average Americans to the inevitable consequences which would come from the Act being enacted into law. This fear and suspicion had been capitalized on by more than one politician in the winter and early spring when the Presidential nomination process got underway. George Wallace had done much better than simply make a showing when he challenged Kennedy in Wisconsin, Indiana, Maryland and even California by championing racial hatred and resentment; and that was just in the Democratic Party.

Somewhere between the snows of New Hampshire in late winter to the sunny skies of California in late spring, Barry Goldwater found a way to tap into the roiling fears and paranoia of many Republicans in the year of 1964 as certain lines began showing up in his stump speech. "To the Communist, negotiation is just another tactic, to him, there is no such thing as good faith." According to Goldwater, Washington was in thrall to a gaggle on nitwit socialists who were determined to trample on the God-given Constitutional rights of the American people. "Washington has no business telling you who to associate with; to whom you can sell your house; who your employer can hire." That law and order trumped justice and equality. "Criminals and malcontents do not own the streets your tax dollars paid for."

Goldwater beat Rockefeller decisively in the California primary on the first Tuesday in June, and with it secured the nomination while repudiating Republican Party's stand on equal rights for blacks going back to Lincoln. Goldwater himself was on record saying he personally disapproved of segregation, but also believed he had no right to tell the good people of Mississippi how to run their state.

It also put many a Republican Senator on the spot when it came to taking a vote on the Civil Rights Act; did they want to stay true to Lincoln or undercut their Presidential candidate, who just might have a winning issue against a heretofore popular incumbent? A lot of us naively thought it would be the former.

The first sign of possible trouble came when Senator Dirksen appeared on Meet the Press on June 6th; when asked where he stood on the Civil Rights Act, he promptly replied, "I have grave reservations about several provisions in this piece of legislation; specifically Title II, which deals with public accommodations, I, and many of my fellow Republican Senators, worry that this provision goes too far, that it unconstitutionally encroaches on the rights of millions of small businessmen, while at the same time giving far too much power to the Federal Government." Title II of the Civil Rights Act outlawed discrimination based on race in any and all public accommodations engaged in interstate commerce; its passage would be the bullet to the head of Jim Crow.

At the time, I wrote Dirksen's remarks off as a negotiating ploy, he was simply staking out a hard line position from which to bargain concessions; Dirksen himself was florid and theatrical in manner and used his deep baritone voice with the precision of a musical instrument. Some thought him a caricature of a humbug politician, but he was a canny player at the art of politics and a man to be taken seriously. Moreover, he was one of Barry Goldwater's closest friends in the Senate.

It was the Vice President who first spotted the rough waters on the horizon. "It's starting to smell like a sheep pen when I pass by the offices of some of our Republican colleagues," he told us during the second week of June. Senator Goldwater had taken no public position himself on the Civil Rights Act, but few doubted what he would do when the roll was called, if for no other reason than there was too much at stake politically for him to do anything else. His campaign had become a safe haven for extremists and crackpots of the far right, the kind of people who thought Eisenhower was a Red, but also for plutocrat union busters, blacklisters, militaristic warmongers, Klansmen, Texas oilmen whose only God was money, and paranoids who thought the country needed to be run by a dictator.

John F. Kennedy's preoccupation with the international situation during the month of June did not help our cause. He flew to New Delhi for the summit just as debate on the Act was getting underway; it might have been a big step forward in his foreign policy when he shook hands with Khrushchev and Chou En Lai, but it was definitely a step back in our efforts to line up Republican support. Overnight, with cries of "appeasement" in the air, they had another reason not to make common cause with Kennedy.

The persistent rumor that the Vice President was only weeks from being dropped as the President's running mate didn't help; said rumors being linked back to the Irish Mafia and the Attorney General, a situation which made badly needed cooperation between the Vice President and Bobby Kennedy impossible. It didn't help matters that Senator Humphrey was often listed as the top choice to replace Johnson.

"The President told me that I have his full confidence," Johnson would say when the subject was broached, "and nothing has changed." The Vice President was a proud man and the whispers about him being replaced must have hurt deeply.

The Southern forces in the Senate opposed to us began their expected filibuster on the day floor debate began; their leader was the venerable Senator Richard Russell of Georgia, a master of the arcane rules of the body and a man who knew every trick needed to stop legislation in its tracks. He'd represented my home state in Washington since FDR's first term and if he was not a fire breather like his colleague Thurmond from next door in South Carolina, there was never any doubt that the preservation of white supremacy was the cornerstone of his public career. "Dick Russell is damned and determined to talk this thing to death," the Vice President commented, "and he knows how to do it." So did Senator Thurmond and Senator Byrd of West Virginia, both of whom could hold the floor for hours at a time.

The remedy to this situation was a closure vote, which took two-thirds of the Senate voting "aye" to cut off a filibuster and the votes to do it would have to come from the Republican camp. "I know Senator Dirksen is a man who puts his country above his party," Senator Humphrey said to the press at one point. "I know he'll do the right thing." I have to hand it to Hubert, he never lost his temper, he always had a smile for the Southerners who were fighting him with a tenacity that would have drawn the admiration of Stonewall Jackson, and he always kept communications open with everyone.

I spent a lot of hours during June talking to the staffs of Senators from the Old Confederacy,

over and over, I heard spirited defenses of state's rights and "our traditions;" during this time, a group of black college students tried to integrate a bowling alley in Atlanta, Georgia and two of them were beaten to death on the sidewalk out front by a mob wielding baseball bats. Then three young northerners who'd gone to rural Mississippi to participate in the "Freedom Summer" disappeared after being arrested by a local sheriff in Neshoba County, an area with which I was familiar. I was certain those three brave young men were dead as soon as I learned the facts of the case.

We were living in two different countries with a chasm between them and my faith that in America things always progressed ever upward was badly shaken.

On June 24th, Senator Dirksen requested a meeting with the Vice President, along with Senators Humphrey and Mansfield in Johnson's Senate office. Time was running out and if Dirksen had any deal to propose, this would be have be the moment. The 4th of July recess was coming up and beyond then, the Republican National Convention, which would kick the Presidential race into high gear, making any kind of compromise that much harder to achieve.

Joining Dirksen in the meeting was Senator Thomas Kuchel of California, the biggest supporter of the Civil Rights Act on the Republican side. I considered this a good sign that Dirksen just might be about to throw his weight behind the bill at last; as I sat in Hubert's office, waiting for the meeting to break up, I couldn't help but feel as if this was make or break for all our efforts since January.

The expression on Hubert Humphrey's face when he walked through the door told me the bad news; Dirksen would not be getting on the right side of history.

It came down to Title II of the act, the section dealing with discrimination in public accommodations, chiefly restaurants, diners, hotels and motels; as written, the Act outlawed all discrimination based on race in any and all of them, anywhere in the United States, with stiff civil penalties for violators. An "unconstitutional violation of individual and property rights by a dictatorial Federal government" according to Senator Russell, who hit the nail on the head as far as his side was concerned, or "putting an end to an unjust and fundamentally un-American system of laws directed against decent citizens for no other reason than the color of their skin" as Senator Humphrey put it on the opening day of debate, speaking for all of us untied in this holy cause.

For me and many others, it was a simple matter of right and wrong, no doubt and no compromise allowed, but the final decision rested with politicians, many of whom were in my own party, who did not see it my own stark terms.

It was the political necessity of Senator Everett Dirksen that prevailed, a necessity which demanded he and his fellow Republican Senators accommodate an insurgency in their own party which had delivered the Presidential nomination to the insurgency's leader and stood a chance of delivering the Presidency as well.

What none of us knew at the time was that Dirksen and Russell had met with the President the evening before in the family quarters of the White House, away from the press, where the President told them if an acceptable compromise could be worked out, he would sign it. Kennedy had decided that passage of the Civil Rights Act in any form would be a big plus in November.

In his meeting the Vice President, Senator Humphrey and the others, Dirksen told them there would be enough Republican votes to end the filibuster; whereupon Title II would be amended so there would no longer be Federal civil penalties for violations of discrimination in any public accommodation, but a criminal charge instead, punishable by a thousand dollar fine after a jury trial - an all-*white* jury trial in any jurisdiction south of the Mason-Dixon line. And that would happen only if the local District Attorney would file charges in the first place. In other words, Jim Crow would survive for another day in all its hateful glory, even though the Act would eliminate discrimination in hiring, abolish literacy tests for voting, and speed up school desegregation.

After all our hard work, we would have to accept compromise and a flawed result. It was a bitter pill to swallow after all the distance we'd traveled since January.

My disappointment with this turn of events must have palpable upon hearing the news, because Hubert threw his arm around me and said, "Johnny be proud, you hold your head high, you understand me?"

His words did me little good that day, I remember going back to my apartment and getting drunk on a bottle of Jim Beam.

It took a few days for everything to get put in place, but on June 29th, the vote for closure carried with nearly 25 Republicans voting for it; the South yielded the field and the amendment to Title II calling for jury trials was introduced - it was later learned that the amendment had been written in Senator Russell's office. It was passed by a coalition of Republican Senators and Southern Democrats despite a pro forma futile opposition by Senator Humphrey and the liberals. The full Civil Rights Act went before the Senate for a vote before the 4th of July recess and it passed overwhelmingly with a lot of liberals holding their noses when they said "yea." It then had to go back to the House to be reconciled, a fight which would have to wait until midsummer.

I think Dr. King summed it up best when he said, "We have come to the point where half measures are no different than inaction. Those who settle for half a loaf are cheating themselves of the justice they deserve and have more than earned." On the day the Senate voted for the full Act, a day which should have been one of great triumph, I couldn't help but think of the thousands of committed Americans who had marched and protested for weeks to get this law on the books; of the rabbis, of the priests and clergymen who had made this a holy and righteous cause, of the those in the Deep South who on that same day were risking their lives to be full American citizens and know there was no way I could look any of them in the eye.

If anybody took this turn of events worse than me, it was the Vice President; he was the very picture of dejection during the last week of June. And why shouldn't he have been after having fought his way back from the brink of political oblivion and making himself relevant again by devising and implementing a strategy that took the Civil Rights Act from the basement of the House Rules Committee to the triumph of a vote in the full Senate, only to have the President strike a deal which tarnished this legacy.

Then there were the raw politics of the matter, Johnson's work getting the Act passed had won him legions of new allies and supporters in the activist left of the Democratic Party, like Joseph Rauh and the Americans for a Democratic Society, who had so staunchly opposed him in 1960. A watered-down Civil Rights Act made him look exactly like the old LBJ who made deals and sold out ideals when he was running the Senate - the kind of man who ought to be dumped from the ticket. On July 1st, a syndicated column by Drew Pearson and Jack Anderson quoted unnamed sources in the Kennedy campaign as saying the dropping of Johnson had already been decided. "Too much stuff has yet to come out in the Bobby Baker case," one of them was quoted as saying, "and the President just can't take the risk of running in the fall with Johnson on the ticket." Nobody thought these unnamed sources were speaking without Bobby Kennedy's permission."

It was against this backdrop that I received a call from, of all people, Senator Russell's secretary on the day before the 4th of July adjournment, requesting that I come by. I had been in the Senator's presence a few times in my days on Capitol Hill, but we had never been formally introduced, and considering my background, I was hardly the type of person Dick Russell would ever want to associate with under any circumstance. Having no knowledge of why the senior Senator from my home state would want to see me, I traveled down to his office and was ushered by an aide into a back room where Senator Russell rose from behind his desk to shake my hand and offer me a drink. He then proceeded to ask about my home town of Newnan and of many mutual acquaintances we shared there. Not once did the man bring up the Civil Rights Act or anything else which would have been even remotely divisive, and I must say I was impressed despite his lifelong commitment to the preservation of segregation. When I remember my visit with Senator Russell now, I am filled with sadness with the knowledge this man might well have made a fine President of the United States if not for the place of his birth and its difficult history.

After a good half an hour of conversation, the Senator got to the reason I was called to his office: "Mr. Compton, I need you to take care of a small chore for me and do so without question, do you think you can do that? It concerns our dear friend, the Vice President." Since it involved Johnson, I didn't hesitate in answering in the affirmative. The chore, as Senator Russell described it, seemed like an odd one to me at the time: go immediately to a bar two blocks away from Capitol Hill and find a man sitting at a table in the back - I would know him by the black bow tie he would be wearing. The Senator then took out a business card for his Capitol Hill office and signed his name to the back of it before handing it to me. "Show this card to man, he will give you a package. Please take it back to Lyndon's office and hand the package directly to him. He'll be expecting it. Be sure to give him this business card as well. Thank you very much, Mr. Compton."

After shaking hands with the Senator, I left his office and did as he requested, walking the two blocks on a particularly pleasant day for the hottest part of the summer. I found the bar and the man at the back table; he was wearing a black bow tie, which went well with his white linen jacket, the kind found in the best DC menswear stores. After taking a look at the card with Senator Russell's signature, the bow tie wearing gentleman produced a large manila envelope from under the table and handed it to me; I distinctly remember the envelope bulging in the middle. "Sir, you are doing a great thing for your country and I hope one day you know just how much," was his parting words. Doing as instructed, I hurried back to the Capital and the Vice President's office.

I had no idea that by taking that plain manila envelope back to the Vice President's office, I was helping land the hardest blow in the nastiest political feud in modern American history.

Lt. Colonel Martin Maddox (VI)
June - August 1964

I spent the summer of 1964 working on Cuba every day, a place where things consistently refused to go according to plan. We no longer had an operations plan to guide us and thanks to the agreements made in New Delhi; we now had nine months to install a free government, get the economy up and running again, constitute new armed forces and get every American soldier off the island - except for Guantanamo; a tall order indeed.

What no one knew, not even Ralph Gillison and any of my other co-workers in the White House, was how I had been drawn into the back alley of American politics, a place of sleazy betrayals and big time double crosses; a battlefield for which I had no training or preparation. I had to talk face to face with Vance Harlow and get the low down on how things had come to such a state. I asked for a meeting at O'Donnell's and refused to take no for an answer.

I came right to the point as soon as he sat down across from me in the booth, demanding to know just who was peddling pictures of me at Marcello's place.

"Colonel, I could give you a name," was his weary reply, "and what would that accomplish? You are an officer in the United States Marine Corp who obeys orders and follows a time-tested code of honor. The person you are asking about knows no duty, no honor and no country; the only thing they are "always faithful" to is their own absolute self-interest. There is nothing you could personally do or say to them that would affect anything they might ever do in any conceivable way. You are a good soldier and a brave man, but this is not your kind of fight."

I knew this to be the truth, but I simply could not sit there and have my fate completely in the hands of others who had utterly no concern whatsoever for me or my family. What do I do, I asked Harlow, what do I need to know? With whom did I need to talk; the Attorney General or my own lawyer as soon as I hired one?

"You do nothing, you talk to no one," Harlow replied, "except to me. But especially do not approach the Attorney General, do that, and he'll decide you are a liability to him or his brother and orders will instantly be cut transferring you to the Aleutian Islands. Your story should be something like this, you hadn't been to New Orleans in years and just slipped down there for a day or so by taking advantage of free military transport - wouldn't be the first officer to do that. While in the Big Easy you made a stop at the Town and Country because the shrimp gumbo had been recommended to you by a number of fellow officers. I chauffeured you there because we share a mutual friend who worked on the Racket's Committee with the Kennedy brothers. During your meal at the Town and Country, its owner, Mr. Marcello, an honest businessman as far as you knew, refused your money and the drinks and meal were on the house as a gesture of admiration and respect for our brave fighting men who were about to hit the beaches in Cuba. Mr. Trafficante, a dear friend and business associate of Marcello's, was also there and shook your hand. Just a nice visit with nice people as far as you knew."

"Why would I desert my duties at the White House in the middle of a crisis to go and enjoy the charms of New Orleans?"

Harlow shrugged and said, "Say it was the stress of the job, you just had to get away for 24 hours and since you're a hard-core fan of both jazz and blues, the only place to be was The Big Easy on the Mississippi."

"Who the hell would believe such a bullshit story?"

"It doesn't have to a good story, it doesn't have to be a believable story, it just has the same story that you tell over and over if required. Be prepared just in case."

Harlow words were of little comfort; doing nothing is seldom a solution.

"Nobody will be able to prove otherwise," Harlow added. "This is politics, which, it has been said, is war by other means. A war I am much better prepared to fight in than you are, Colonel. Look, you've been a real Marine through all of this; you just need to go on being one."

The people in the know would keep their mouths shut, Harlow insisted, there was no real proof in danger of becoming public which would reveal that the Kennedy Administration had made common cause with the Mafia against Castro.

There was one more thing. "I'm saying this as a precaution, Colonel, but from here on out, if you feel the need to get in touch with me, don't use your home phone and sure as hell don't use the one in your office. They might be tapped."

I couldn't believe I was hearing this. "That's against the law," I replied, the memory of my naiveté at this moment almost makes me wince, after all, I had already shaken hands to seal a deal with Carlos Marcello.

I left O'Donnell's no more assured than when I'd entered, but I had no choice but to go back to the White House and do my job, but I did a lot of thinking over the next few days, rolling over in my head exactly what I would do and say when and if I was called to explain my presence in New Orleans back in April.

There was plenty to keep me occupied in my day job as we dealt with the aftermath of the New Delhi summit. Many now considered Cuba to be primarily a political problem where the setting up of a provisional government ahead of the pullout of our forces to be the task at hand. Despite continued armed opposition, General Abrams did a good job of getting the casualty rate down, but flag-draped coffins were still coming home every week.

"Colonel, are you familiar with the war against the Philippine insurgency?" Ralph Gillison asked me at one point.

I considered myself well versed in American military history, but I was only vaguely aware of what had happened in the former Spanish colony in the first decade of the century and confessed as much.

"It lasted over three years and cost us at least six thousand dead; Filipino dead could have been as high as a million. But what is most remembered about that war was how savage it got, how brutal both sides were at the end."

I didn't have to ask what point Ralph was making; mentally I began planning the inevitable briefing I might well have to give President Kennedy in the near future. It was not something I looked forward to doing, for the Administration had shifted gears after the summit and was stressing how "Cuba belonged to the Cubans and a freely elected, democratic and peace-loving government in place in nine months will be the final American victory." Those were the words of the President as he stood before the cameras at Andrews Air Force upon his return from New Delhi.

There simply was nothing with which to put together even a provisional government - the only people with experience running Cuba were former officials in Castro's regime or Batista's dictatorship, hardly the seeds with which to sow democracy on short notice. Secretary of State Rusk was laboring on the problem, and I wished him luck, he was certainly going to need it.

Then there was the Russian contingent at Camaguey, a good 25,000 strong, and still on the island at the end of June, for Moscow seemed in no hurry to pull them out. "It is going to look like a flat out defeat," the President observed in an Oval Office meeting, "when pictures of those Soviet troops boarding a transport bound for home are seen around the world. Khrushchev knows this, so does Brezhnev and the rest and they're going to stall as long as they possibly can."

"Maybe they're hoping all of them will defect en masse," Secretary McNamara said, "and end this trouble."

No such luck was the President's reply.

In any event, General Andreyev and this Russians were creating more than a few problems, not the least of them being the high number of Castro's men who had sought sanctuary inside the Russian enclave, some of whom were believed to be members of the Intelligence Directorate possessing critical information on the events in Dallas. General Abrams tentatively entered into negotiations with Andreyev to have these men turned over to us, but the Soviet commander refused to even discuss it; diplomats from the State Department took over the task with little success. What were so galling were the thousands of pounds of rations we were now delivering to Andreyev and his men, as per agreements made in New Delhi. I would have thought it would have given us some leverage, but evidently not.

The kid glove treatment became a domestic political problem for the President, as Senator Goldwater, the presumptive Republican Presidential nominee, began referring to the "coddling of Communist invaders in the Western Hemisphere" in his speeches, it was taken up by more than one speaker at their convention in mid-July and looked to be issue in the fall campaign.

On the other side of the political spectrum, there was a rally on the UC campus in

Berkeley California on the last day of June decrying the invasion of Cuba, along with the bombing of North Korea and Vietnam, and the holding of Fidel Castro at Guantanamo. It was highlighted by some old fellow travelers like Pete Seegar and Dave Dellinger, but what was significant was the large number of young people who attended and applauded wildly to denunciations of "American militarism and imperialism." If these malcontents didn't like it in this country, they were free to leave. It's how I saw it, but there was something about the images of those cheering kids, shown on the evening newscasts, that depressed me for days.

If Cuba was at the top of the list of foreign policy concerns post summit, then the situation in Iran was a close second as the Soviet incursion there ground to a final halt. Like the United States in Cuba, they had agreed to have their troops out at the end of nine months; unlike the United States in Cuba, they had to contend with a very active, organized and well armed opposition that wanted them out of their country immediately. If anything, the fighting in Iran had grown worse in the days after the New Delhi summit.

After the President came back from there, we assumed the Soviets would leave and the Shah would return and take his seat on the Peacock throne; there was just one problem with this conceit: the future of Iran was being decided on the battlefield by the Iranian people, who were doing the heavy lifting to throw the Russians off their soil.

It turned out that the opposition to the Soviets was not being led by officers of the Shah's military, but by the Ayatollah Khomeini, a fierce opponent of the Shah's who'd returned from exile in Iraq, who after seizing a radio station, began exhorting his countrymen to wage Jihad and show no mercy to the invaders. Hundreds of thousands of Iranians had heeded his call, many of them willingly sacrificing themselves in suicide attacks on the Soviets that would have made the Japanese kamikaze fighters blush. But this Ayatollah was no lover of western style democracy, a report from British intelligence stated that Khomeini considered the Shah nothing more than a puppet of infidel foreign powers and detested him more than the Soviets. Ominously, the British report detailed how dozens of the Shah's high officials and top officers had been summarily executed directly on this Khomeini's orders.

In an effort to mitigate the disaster, the Soviets had attempted to arrange a cease fire, something insisted upon by Khrushchev, but it had failed miserably and their casualties had continued to mount with more than 2,000 killed in the last week of June alone. When word reached the troops on the front lines that an agreement had been reached for a Soviet pullout at the end of eight months, morale collapsed. As an officer who has led men under fire day after day on a foreign battlefront, I can tell you nothing can be more calamitous than for your men to lose confidence in their mission. This is what happened to Soviet mechanized and infantry units who were taking fire round the clock in places like Qom, Istafhan, and Yazd. This resulted in junior officers being shot by their own men, soldiers self inflicting wounds in order to be sent to a hospital unit in the rear, while in some cases whole units refused to obey orders - not the kind of stuff that happened in the fearsome Red Army.

This is what finally cost Marshall Malinovsky his job as Defense Minister, but then his replacement, Marshall Andrei Grechko promptly requested five fresh divisions be sent to Iran to stabilize the situation and relieve the clearly fatigued forces in the field. On this, Khrushchev, Brezhnev and Gromyko were of one mind and that was not to throw good after bad.

"We cannot go forward and we cannot stand still," Khrushchev reportedly said in a Poltiburo meeting called to discuss Grechko's request for more troops on July 24th, "so the only thing to say is, the hell with it." It was a decision with devastating consequences.

Most of this information came for Vladimir Roykov, the man in charge of Kennedy's back ally channel to the Kremlin, who had failed miserably to predict the coup, but got the Iranian withdrawal right.

By September 1st, the Soviet forces on the ground had been reduced by half from their peak right after the invasion. It was a stunning reversal, spurred on no doubt by the continued seething unrest under the surface in Eastern Europe, primarily Poland and Czechoslovakia.

Behind the scenes in Washington, the mood had changed, for despite the fierce criticism, President Kennedy saw the New Delhi summit as an unmitigated triumph; in his eyes, we'd bagged Castro, forged an opening to Red China and weakened the Soviet Union, quite a feat. Much of the discussion in the Oval Office concerned the upcoming November summit with Khrushchev, where the President planned to discuss controls on the proliferation of nuclear weapons for the first time. He talked about that far more than the fall election, rapidly approaching. I would have thought different, even though the President saw the events of the last few months triumphantly, Senator Goldwater was coming on strong, at least that is how I saw it over the summer, then again, what did I know about politics.

But I was getting a hard lesson. On the afternoon of August 10th, I received a call at my desk in the White House basement from a gentleman with the hint of a Cajun accent who gave his name and said he was a reporter for the *New Orleans Times-Picayune* and wanted to ask me a few questions about my visit to the Big Easy in March, specifically a stop I made at the Town and Country Motel and Restaurant while there. A flat out denial that I had ever been in New Orleans, much less on the date in question, was almost out of my mouth when I simply slammed the phone back in the receiver, cutting the conversation off before it had begun. Better to say nothing than speak and risk anything. That's when I realized a reporter for the *Times-Picayune* could not possibly have access to the phone in my office.

Had somebody been trying to get me to confirm my presence at Marcello's back in March to make a recording of me incriminating myself? Somebody with enough pull to get the number of an office in the White House?

I sat there and felt a sense of anxiety not experienced since I was under fire in Korea.

That anxiousness was nothing compared to what I felt a few hours later when my phone rang a second time. "Colonel Maddox," said President John F. Kennedy when I picked up, "could you please come up here to my office right away."

Dorothy Jean Brennan (II)
June - July 1964

I dismissed the man who had the message for Wade Harbinson as a Loony Toon, a type of person who showed up daily on the campaign trail, they always presented themselves as quite professional and competent, and each and every one claimed to possess vital secret information about President Kennedy's personal life or something nefarious the American government was conducting secretly that our campaign needed to know about right away. In the course of a month, I heard about Kennedy's "secret first wife" or his "love affair with a known German spy during WWII," or the "100,000 Red Chinese soldiers just below the Rio Grande" who were about to attack with the collusion of the Pentagon or they had proof positive that "Martin Luther King had been educated in Moscow by the KGB" and received all his money from Communist Russia.

I promptly stuck the note in a file folder - because you never know when they might turn out to be valuable in some way - and went about my duties as assistant press secretary to Goldwater '64.

It was about a week or so later, a time when the convention was coming up on us fast, when I arrived back at my temporary office in Phoenix one morning to find a visitor waiting for me. He was a middle-aged gentleman who greeted me by name, introducing himself as Vance Harlow. By his bearing, I instantly tagged him as a former officer in a branch of the military, or maybe the FBI, a serious man who had spent his life during serious work. I was proven correct when Mr. Harlow informed me that he had worked with Senator Goldwater on the Senate Investigations Committee when they had gone after labor thugs like Jimmy Hoffa and Walter Ruether, and how he was now a private investigator in the employ of men who very much wanted the Senator to be the next President of the United States.

He then surprised me by repeating exactly what the man in New Orleans had said, including the claim he could give Harbinson a better deal on something than Harlow, and that he knew something which could bury the Kennedy's. "My I ask why you did not immediately inform Mr. Harbinson?" Harlow asked. I told him about the daily Loony Toons and explained why I did not waste either my or Mr. Harbinson's time. Harlow thanked me for doing so, saying the gentleman who spoke to was named Clay Shaw, an associate of some bad characters in New Orleans, the kind of people the campaign did not want to be connected with under any circumstances and who would create quite a problem for Goldwater '64 if it were to become public. Furthermore, Mr. Shaw himself was a sexual degenerate, reason enough alone not to have anything to do with him.

Then he said, "Miss Brennan, by not giving that note to Mr. Harbinson, you did the campaign, Senator Goldwater and certainly the United States of America a great service. I believe it's a service you should continue to give. If in the next few weeks, you should be approached a second time by Mr. Shaw or anyone else wishing to use you as a conduit to Mr. Harbinson, I would be much obliged if you would contact me first. A lovely young lady like you doesn't know it, but there are some very bad people indeed out there; people who want to use good and faithful patriots like Barry Goldwater to further their own ends, I think it's much better I deal with them than you." He handed me a business card. "I can be reached at that number, and I don't expect you to just do a favor out of the goodness of your heart or a sense of duty to our fine candidate. Anything you do for me will be properly compensated; I know those old money bags running Barry's campaign aren't about to pay a lovely young lady with a journalism degree from a great college like USC near what you're worth, so I'm sure you can use the money."

I thanked Mr. Harlow and put his card in the top drawer of the desk as soon as he left; quite sure I'd never have any use for it. Still, he was right about me needing the money, that's when it hit me that Vance Harlow had investigated me before coming to my office, how else would he have known I'd gone to USC. I didn't like it, and suddenly I didn't trust Mr. Vance Harlow so much.

Once Senator Goldwater nailed down the nomination with his victory in the California primary, the real campaign began, and one of the first orders of business was the endorsements by former opponents in the name of party unity. The leader of this cohort was Richard Nixon, who'd been sitting on the sidelines gleefully hoping for a deadlocked convention which would turn to him; with this hope dashed, he flew to Washington and endorsed the Senator in front of a room full of reporters. This was my first encounter with Eisenhower's former Vice President, the man whose loss in 1960 so disappointed my father. I was not impressed, the man was an opportunist and a modern day Uriah Heep; if there had still been an iota of a chance he could have snagged the nomination, the man would have been on the phones night and day to the heads of the delegations, reminding them that he was available for a draft.

Nevertheless, we saw a lot of Nixon over the next few weeks as he worked to bring on board a lot of party establishment figures who had not been keen on Goldwater from the start; many of them big movers and shakers from the East who had been behind Eisenhower in '52. Clif White spoke for many when he said, "We didn't come all this way and work this hard just to turn around and suck up to the Wall Street guys who sneered at us and then lost to us." Dean Burch smoothed things over and helped Nixon set up meetings with the Senator and some big money men from Lehman Brothers and E.F. Hutton; someone said it was quite the triumph when your defeated enemies joined your side - except those money bags didn't look defeated to me. What Nixon got for his trouble was a prime-time appearance at the convention where he would place Senator Goldwater's name in nomination.

While this was going on, the Goldwater campaign was being completely ignored by the press and the networks; their eyes were only for Kennedy and his shenanigans in New Delhi. A cartoon in the *Los Angeles Times* showed a dejected looking Barry Goldwater off to himself while a mob of reporters and camera crews surrounded Kennedy and Khrushchev as they shook hands. This might be what the elites in the big eastern newspapers and the nightly news saw, but there were plenty of real Americans who were paying attention to what was going on, and more importantly, listening to what Senator Goldwater had to say. We got plenty of outraged calls and pledges of support in the weeks after the New Delhi summit, where the leader of the free world extended his hand to a blood stained Red Chinese tyrant. Seventeen retired Admirals and Generals flew to Phoenix to announce their support for Goldwater in the face of this "tide of appeasement." The Senator was particularly incensed at the sellout of Chaing Kai-Chek, a man he called a "loyal ally and friend in time of war."

There was much more animating the Goldwater people: the agreement to just walk away from Cuba after American boys had spilled blood to liberate it; the way Kennedy had let the Soviets off the hook after their aggression in Iran when we had the means to deliver a crushing military defeat to them by air power; the way we had yet again turned a blind eye to the enslaved peoples behind the Iron Curtain, who at the height of the crisis, demonstrated their desire to be free only to be met with a stony silence from Kennedy, who issued an order to the commander in West Berlin not to resist if the Soviets made a move on them; the missed opportunity to finish off the North Koreans once and for all and the ignoring of Communist aggression in South Vietnam.

Then there was this so-called Civil Rights Act moving through Congress, millions of small businessmen and homeowners were terrified of what this act would do to the hard work of a lifetime. I had only to think of my own great-grandfather, who'd run a haberdashery in Sacramento, California for twenty-five years; he'd have burned it to the ground rather than let the government tell him who he could hire. A lot of good Americans felt the same way and were not about to stand by and let their country go to hell.

Neither was Barry Goldwater, who while John Kennedy was hobnobbing with Communist dictators, made speech after speech to ever increasing crowds, telling them, "we need a President committed to resisting with every ounce of strength and resolve at his command the aggression of our sworn enemies and one who will honor the hallowed tradition of individual liberty which has guided this country from its founding."

If the starry-eyed reporters and worshipful pundits had looked around in the early summer of 1964, they would have seen an energized movement of real patriots ready to take on the vaunted Kennedy machine.

The Republican National convention opened on July 13th in San Francisco with no doubt as whom the nominee would be; it was Senator Goldwater's party now and his people filled the delegations and called the shots. I spent four days shuttling between our hotel downtown and the Cow Palace, briefing the press and mostly enjoying the spectacle.

Again the eastern elite press and especially the networks devoted much time to looking down their noses at the assembled heartland patriots who had come together to take back their country. Over and over the network commentators used the terms "extremist," "radical," "right-wing," and "reactionary," in their commentary, Walter Cronkite being the worst for this, and I must say their contempt was thrown right back at them. I was proud to be in the hall when former President Eisenhower denounced "sensation-seeking columnists and commentators," and the delegates who then stood on their feet to shake their fists at the network booths above them were only expressing their righteous indignation at their misuse of the freedom of the press. Nelson Rockefeller got some well-deserved boos when he appeared before the convention to endorse a proposed plank in party platform on "extremism" which was designed to do nothing more than embarrass the Senator.

The only real drama I was privileged to witness happened in Senator Goldwater's hotel suite in the early hours of Thursday, July 16th, right after he had been formally nominated on the convention floor. It was time to pick a Vice Presidential running mate and to our astonishment, the Senator said he had not given it too much thought, and asked the room, which consisted of all the inner circle of the campaign, along with some heavy hitters like Nixon, whom they thought would make a good running mate.

One of the first names mentioned was General LeMay, whose opposition to the way Kennedy had been pulling his punches ever since the Missile Crisis was well known, but Senator Goldwater said LeMay would make the ticket too unbalanced by having a pair of Air Force officers on it. Wade Harbinson spoke up and said, "Why not put John Wayne up for Vice President; Goldwater-Wayne, that could be a winning ticket." This touched off a serious discussion of whether the movie star would actually accept the nomination; someone else brought up Paul Harvey, which led to Clif White to say why not consider Ronald Reagan, "he's been making great speeches on behalf of GE for years, and the camera loves him." A couple of genuine office holders, like Ohio Governor James Rhodes, were thrown into the discussion. Finally, Senator Goldwater said he liked Bill Miller, a Congressman from New York and the RNC chair who almost no one had heard of before, because he knows "how to needle Jack Kennedy."

Former Vice President Nixon took the floor and said emphatically that this was an opportunity which could not be treated lightly; how every national poll had us within striking distance of the President and in order to get serious consideration from serious voters, there had to be a man with real statue and substance on the ticket with the Senator. "Statue and substance," Senator Goldwater responded, "that sounds an awful lot like you, Dick. You want your old job back?" I thought Nixon's words were a thinly veiled pitch of himself for the second spot on the ticket, but the look on his face when the Senator actually offered it to him told me it was the last thing the man wanted. Nevertheless, a lot of those assembled thought a Goldwater-Nixon ticket to be a good idea, the perfect bridging of the past and the present. By that point, it was getting daylight and a decision had to be made very soon, so it really did look like the former Vice President was going on the ticket whether he liked it or not. Although I didn't speak up at all during the discussion and no one asked me for my opinion, the thought of Nixon running for Vice President again was an abhorrent idea. I doubted the man's sincerity and I think events have proven me right.

Thankfully, Senator Goldwater himself was not serious about putting Nixon on the ticket. "I know you don't want it, Dick," he said at last, "and I won't twist your arm, but you are right about getting someone with statue and substance. My old friend Ev Dirksen fits that bill, get him on the phone and let's see if he'll run with me." Senator Dirksen was 68 years old and had been mentioned as a possible running mate on a Republican ticket as far back as when FDR and Dewey ran against each other, but in that room and at that moment, he seemed like a wise and serious choice, much better than a movie star or some little-known Congressman. It took Senator Goldwater a half hour of cajoling before Dirksen would agree to run with him, the man was reluctant at the prospect of having to give up the United States Senate; no matter, when the announcement was made at 9:30 a.m. local time, it officially became the Goldwater-Dirksen ticket.

The final night of the convention, when Senator Goldwater made his acceptance speech and set the tone of his campaign, was one of supreme triumph for all of us who had worked so hard for so long. I was in the hall sitting behind the podium where first Senator Dirksen and then Senator Goldwater spoke. "It is a profound and distinct honor" the Vice Presidential nominee said in his speech, "to run with a man who is the modern embodiment of the virtues the Founding Fathers treasured: courage, honor and the dedication to principle over self-interest."

Everett Dirksen had a reputation as quite the orator, but nobody remembered what he said after Senator Goldwater spoke. "I would remind you that extremism in the defense of liberty is no vice. And let me remind you also that moderation in the pursuit of justice is no virtue!" It was the line everyone remembers, and the delegates cheered for nearly five minutes in response; it was the perfect repudiation to everything the pusillanimous Kennedy Administration stood for. He drew the line in the dirt clearly and unambiguously: Negotiate from a position of strength with the Soviets or no negotiating at all; no pull out from Cuba until real democracy had been restored, and Castro had faced justice; no more cozying up to Red Chinese tyrants and no backing down in Korea and Vietnam; no more coddling of the switchblade-wielding criminals who are taking over the streets of our great cities; respect for the rights of states and individuals to conduct their affairs as they see fit and reign in the tyranny of the Federal government.

When he began his campaign many months earlier, Senator Goldwater had promised us a choice, not an echo; it was a promise he had most certainly delivered on. The audience at the Cow Palace rose as one when the Senator speech was finished and cheered him for nearly a half hour. There was no doubt in my mind that we would beat John F. Kennedy decisively and thoroughly in November.

I was feeling the effects of sleep deprivation pretty good the next morning as I was checking out of the San Francisco Hilton; as I was making my way across the lobby after paying my bill at the front desk (and rifling through my purse for a pair of sun-glasses to hide my red eyes if memory serves me) when a figure appeared in front of me. "Little lady, could I please have a moment of your time," said Wade Harbinson.

Wade L. Harbinson (IV)
July 1964

I was not in San Francisco for the opening day of the 1964 Republican National Convention, a triumphant moment for all of us who had dedicated so much time and effort get the nomination for Barry Goldwater, but as much as I hated to not be at the Cow Palace, there was a far more important chore waiting to be done, one which could deliver to us and Senator Goldwater a far, far greater triumph. On that Monday, as the opening session of the convention was being gaveled to order, I was yet again at the Carousel Club in Dallas, Texas, on far more important business.

In the same back room in which we had met twice before, Vance Harlow and I sat down at the same table to talk. There were some complications, which did not surprise me, no truly risky venture is without them; it's what makes the reward ever so sweet.

Harlow informed me that I had competition, there was someone else out there willing to pay big bucks for the same merchandise. This was quite a turn, for it seemed the "sundry individuals," as Harlow referred to them, knew the value of what they possessed and had made inquiries to other interested parties who might be willing to pay well to get the dirt on JFK; bottom line: I was being outbid on my own deal. "It's no different than you letting it be known that you're in the market for a vintage 1939 Cadillac," Harlow said, "and the man down the street with one parked in his garage realizes what he has, and in turn, lets it be known that he's sitting on a treasure he'll only part with for the prettiest penny, no matter who pays it."

Now, you don't get as me rich in Texas by being stupid, and my first reaction was that I was being shaken down by a bunch of lowlifes, the kind of people who would put a tape recorder under a bed or break in and rifle through files. Then I realized the obvious; these new bidders had to be the Kennedy's themselves or maybe some of old Papa Joe's rich cronies who could always be counted on to open their wallets in return for God knows what kind of back scratching favors.

A lot of good people in this situation would have royally lost their tempers right then and there at the prospect of a crasher coming in and taking their own game away from them, but I've played my share of Five Card Stud, and nobody leaves the table a winner and mad at the same time. Instead, I asked Harlow what proof he could give me that it was worth my time to stay in the game. Always let them know you are willing to walk away, works when you're buying a Cadillac, works anywhere else.

Harlow reached in his jacket pocket and produced an envelope. "Thought I might need this," he said as he pushed it across the table. It contained a photograph, obviously taken at a distance and blown up, of two men standing in what appeared to be a lobby, engaged in conversation, and by the smiles on their faces, they seemed to be getting along quite amicably.

Harlow explained what it all meant. "The younger of these guys is Lt. Colonel Martin Maddox, USMC and who has lately been occupying an office in the White House basement where he reports directly to the President; much of the final work and planning for the invasion of Cuba was done by the very able Colonel Maddox. The other gentleman, who looks like he chews rusty nails as a hobby is Carlos Marcello and this picture was taken at the Town and Country Motel, an establishment outside of New Orleans owned by Mr. Marcello. I'm sure I don't have to tell you who Marcello is and how he makes his living, it is not exactly common knowledge, but he and a number of his associates had a large investment in hotels and casinos in Batista's Cuba; all lucrative businesses which were confiscated by Castro when he took over. Why is an honorable member of our armed forces enjoying the company of a Mafia Kingfish? Because they've just reached a deal of mutual convenience whereby in return for vital information about Cuba that will be of great help to the United States military in the upcoming invasion, Marcello and his partners will get all of their property back in a post-Castro Cuba. In effect, American boys will die liberating the island in part so that a bunch of Mafia crooks and murderers can go back to doing business as usual. That's it in a nutshell: Kennedy in bed with Mafia goons; that really ought to tarnish his glamorous image quite a bit if the American public learned of such conniving."

It was good enough to make me want to continue, but I asked about the other allegations Harlow had mentioned at our last meeting: the romps with the whore in the White House and the secret medical history, what proof could show me that they were legit. He had nothing in hand at the moment, Harlow told me, since the "sundry individuals" were not showing anything more until they saw the money; he only had the picture because it was a gesture to prove they were serious. But, he added, before I made any decisions, it might interest me to know that the woman Kennedy fornicated with at the White House could well be an East German spy, and he had it on good authority that inside the President's secret medical file was the diagnosis of a certain nasty "social disease."

There was no way I could walk away from proof that Kennedy was both a degenerate and a traitor; I would not rest until the confirmation was in my hands. I wanted it all and quoted a figure to Harlow, one which I will not reveal for obvious reasons, but suffice to say, it was a more than fair price and would have made all the "sundry individuals" wealthy men for the rest of their lives.

Harlow said the amount I had just quoted "might be a tad shy of the mark." The other potential bidders had fat wallets, and I would need one myself if I wanted to trump them.

I then informed him that I wanted to up my bid, but would need time to raise the money, hopefully a couple of weeks, but maybe a month or more.

"That sounds fair enough," Harlow said, "and I am on your side in this, after all, if you hadn't had the guts to put the money up in the first place, no one would be looking at the possibility of going home rich. But we're dealing with some real shithouse rats here; they have no loyalty except to what puts a buck in their pocket, and they're always looking for an angle. For this reason, some of them have been quite enterprising, so much so that they have discovered who is putting up the money and have tried to make personal contact with you in an attempt to eliminate the middle man and strike a deal on their own."

This was news to me. "I can assure you I have spoken to no one about our arrangement, no one at all."

"I know you did, Wade, but one of those shithouse rats approached the lovely Miss Brennan and tried to have her pass on a message to you. Lucky for you, I intervened and told her a lie with a ring of truth to it, and made sure things did not progress any further. But now Miss Brennan is a bystander who can link you and me, if only by a third party association. It's the kind of thing which under the right circumstances could put us at the same defendant's table.

My reply was succinct, "Doesn't matter, all I'm looking for is the equivalent of a bullet to Kennedy's head."

"Be careful who you say that in front of in this town," Harlow replied. I knew to what he was referring, but I didn't give a damn. A Texan should never have to apologize for speaking honestly.

We left it there, but if I was going to have to up the ante and compete with Kennedy money, then I needed to bring in some big artillery myself. On the flight out of Dallas, I was thinking of whom I could call with the kind of deep pockets needed and who hated the Kennedy brothers enough to empty them.

I made it to San Francisco on the third day of the convention, in time to be the hall when the roll of states was called and Barry Goldwater became our nominee for President, I got to participate in the Vice Presidential selection process and I was quite serious in suggesting John Wayne for the second spot on the ticket, the Duke is a true American and a great patriot, beloved by millions; the kind of man who would be a real asset in a tough race and great contrast to those slick Kennedy's. My council was not taken, politicians just naturally gravitate to other politicians, but I think Duke would have been a superb choice.

The day after the convention is when I took care of a dangerously dangling loose thread: I brought Dorothy Brennan aboard and gave her the lowdown lest she inadvertently do something which might put her and the whole campaign in jeopardy, since you never know what a blonde might do.

John Compton (IV)
July - August 1964

I'll admit to being quite in quite a foul mood over the 4th of July, 1964, mainly because I felt all the hard work, good faith and sacrifice of so many had been utterly betrayed when Kennedy agreed to compromise the Civil Rights Act just to get it passed by the Senate. I was not naïve; I knew how politics worked, and the President clearly wanted to run in the fall on a record which included getting the Act through Congress, something dear to the hearts of many liberals in the party.

Congress would not return to take up reconciliation until the second half of July, so I didn't have much to do during this time period, so I watched the gavel to gavel coverage of the Republican convention in San Francisco. What I saw put my head back in the right place. The convention proved to be a frightening spectacle as the party of Lincoln became the party of Jim Crow, John Birchers, McCarthyites, right to work fanatics, and everyone else who wanted to repeal the 20th Century. And the adoration showered on Barry Goldwater by his dewy-eyed acolytes reminded me of nothing so much as the rapt audiences who shrieked *Seig Heil* in those old newsreels from Nazi Germany. When Congress came back to town a week later, I was ready to do anything to save America from Goldwater and cohorts. If that meant the passage of a flawed Civil Rights Act, then so be it.

As soon as Congress was back in session, new potential problems with the Civil Rights Act emerged; House liberals were threatening to sink the whole thing rather than voting for it in its present form, while Senator Dirksen, the lower half of the Goldwater ticket, was running on a platform which explicitly rejected any version of the proposed law; would he still be there for us. The broad coalition of Civil Rights workers, starting with Dr. King himself right down to the brave citizens out there marching were none too happy about the compromise and were quite vocal about it; a lot of big corporate money men who wrote checks for the re-election campaigns of a lot of Republican Senators were making it plain they sided with Goldwater.

Into this thicket, John F. Kennedy stepped, which was only fair since the compromise was his doing. He had the leader of the House liberals, Emmanuel Cellar of New York, come to the White House for a meeting and somehow brought Cellar around to the "half a loaf is better than none" point of view; Cellar returned to the House and pulled the plug on any liberal rebellion against the bill. There was a similar meeting with Dirksen, who, in the end, didn't jump ship on us and neither did any of the other Republican Senators who had previously supported the bill. "The President didn't have to go to all that trouble," Senator Humphrey told me later, "Everett Dirksen is a man of his word and a true patriot; there was no way he was going to desert us once he was committed."

The people the bill was ostensibly supposed to help were less than happy with these developments, and why not, it was far from the first time Black America was told they had to accept less than what they deserved. Dr. King put his best face on in public, telling reporters in Atlanta on July 20th the Act would "go a long way toward paying down a bill that has been long overdue." In private, he was not so magnanimous we were told, something hinted at a few days later when Ralph Abernathy, King's right hand, stated publicly that "a bunch of white politicians in Washington D.C. are doing nothing more than what they always do: promising and then not delivering." Those words stung.

Nevertheless, the process proceeded, and an amended version of the Civil Rights Act passed both the House and Senate by the same margins as before on August 5th and the President scheduled a signing ceremony at the White House the next day. Senator Russell called it a "truly tragic day in the history of our great country and a terrible defeat for freedom," although he surely knew it could have gone much worse for his beloved South, while Senator Humphrey told the press, "this day would see millions of Negro Americans unshackled from the degradation of Jim Crow." He surely knew those words were not quite true.

Kennedy was well aware of how the compromises made him look, so he made a number of public gestures during the summer to counter this criticism, starting with his public call for a Federal investigation when those three Civil Rights workers went missing in late June. He appeared in the press room and made the announcement himself that J. Edgar Hoover was going to Mississippi to lead the effort to find Goodman, Schwerner, and Chaney. He also made public the transcripts of the telephone calls he made to local officials who were clearly dragging their feet, not just the one to Governor Paul Johnson, but also to Sheriff Lawrence Rainey of Neshoba County where the three went missing, who must have been mortified to pick up the phone in his office and then be verbally browbeaten by John Kennedy into promising to find those three brave young man no matter what it took. The good Sheriff could have told Kennedy they were buried in an earthen dam only a few miles from the jailhouse since he was in on the murders from the start, but that would have taken the kind of courage a coward is incapable of possessing. The story would not end well, and if JFK's was grandstanding and using a crime for his own good ends, then so be it.

I was in the back of the room at the White House ceremony on August 6th where John F. Kennedy signed the Civil Rights Act of 1964. It took a quick visit to Atlanta by Robert F. Kennedy, followed by a closed-door meeting, but whatever was said, it was enough to get Dr. King to the White House that day. He stood behind the President as he put his signature on the bill and smiled for the cameras. I guess he figured three steps forward and one step backward was still progress. Senator Humphrey was to one side of King, while the Vice President was on the other; both men looking quite pleased, Johnson especially so, for he had seized the opportunity and made himself politically relevant again.

My own feelings at the signing ceremony were mixed: I was proud of everything we had done to get the Civil Rights Act passed, and I could take some comfort in the knowledge that my fingerprints were nowhere to be found on the compromises which watered it down.

Among President Kennedy's remarks at the signing ceremony were words which touched on these feelings: "In the struggle to achieve a more perfect union, there will be more battles, more clashes between those who wish to see America live up to its promise of equality and dignity to every citizen and those who cling to the status quo of an unfair and unequal past. I have no doubt which side will ultimately prevail."

With the signing ceremony over, I considered my work in Washington done; I was looking forward to practicing law again in Georgia. But on my way out the door, I was waylaid by Lyndon Johnson. "I'm going to have a damn tough job this fall," Johnson explained, "the President expects me to hold Texas for him and maybe save a few other Southern states. It's going to be a bitch for Democrats in Dixie after today, but we've got to do it, I've got to do it, and you, Johnny, have got to help me."

I got the full Johnson treatment.

The Vice President was talking like a man who was absolutely sure he was going to be re-nominated in Atlantic City in three weeks. This ran counter to the rumors which had been blazing through Washington all spring and summer which had Johnson being dumped in favor of Humphrey, Scoop Jackson or Stuart Symington. Governor Terry Sanford of North Carolina was also on the list of possible replacements according to the latest gossip emanating from the Kennedy '64 headquarters on Connecticut Avenue. That Bobby Kennedy was determined to have Johnson dropped, ostensibly because of his links to the Baker scandal, was common knowledge, and Bobby was the de facto head of his brother's re-election campaign, which in the eyes of many, sealed the Vice President's fate.

Yet, here was Lyndon Johnson, three weeks before the convention, talking as if his re-nomination was a done deal. I said yes to him then and there despite my better judgment and what all my good common sense was telling me. At the time, I chalked it up to Johnson's legendary powers of persuasion and a momentary desire to tell him what he wanted to hear; I would be heading back to Georgia in a few weeks anyway, I told myself as I left the White House, as soon as Bobby Kennedy finally had his way.

Kevin McCluskey (II)
August - September 1964

As a reward for ferrying money across the country, I received a promotion to "Assistant Coordinator" for Kennedy '64, it was a meaningless title, but it reflected the esteem I was now held in by the top men in the campaign; I was no longer one of many troubleshooters, I was now the number one troubleshooter. The job was earned after I transported a quarter of a million dollars - mostly in twenty-five thousand or more increments from different donors from around the country to Washington. No questions were asked and no explanations were given; being part of the Kennedy campaign meant you had to be something like a modern day buccaneer.

I had just settled into my new duties the week before the Democratic Convention.

It was held the last week of August, and the orders came down that it was to be a smooth sailing ship, which turned out not an easy accomplishment. Although there had never been any doubt as to the President's re-nomination a few brush fires had broken out on the way to Atlantic City. The hottest one flared up from the South, where we faced the possibility of a mass walkout of on the convention floor of old Dixiecrats, who were traditionally chosen at white's only state conventions and were being challenged by local civil rights activists. There is nothing dirtier and nastier than when American politics meets the question of race. There would be no walk-out by Southern whites, those orders came straight down from the Oval Office; Kennedy did want to see the sight of lifelong Democrats denouncing him on TV and endorsing Goldwater.

I was tasked with telling Mississippi Freedom Democratic Party that it was the President's wishes that they withdraw their challenge from the credentials committee in the best interests of the country. "The country has just weathered a tough crisis, and we don't need to accentuate internal dissension and strife at this time." Those were the exact words I was told to say on the day before the convention opened to a group of black Mississippi citizens who had been beaten, threatened and jailed repeatedly for the crime of wanting to take part in the democratic process. Among this group was the formidable Fannie Lou Hamer, who replied, "I'll pray to Lord Jesus for the country, but there's been a tough crisis going on in Mississippi for a lot longer and we're not going anywhere, and the country will just have to be fine with it."

I learned later that one of the reasons I was selected to speak to this group of black civil rights activists was that someone high up in the campaign - whose exact identity has never been discovered - thought it would be a good idea if the speaker were "ethnic" in appearance since "those Negroes might relate to him better." This was a reference the olive skin and jet black hair I inherited from my mother and a very good indicator of how badly out of touch some people were in the Kennedy campaign. I didn't learn any of this until some years later, and I was more amused than insulted afterward.

The Mississippi Freedom Party pressed ahead with their challenge despite a personal appeal from Senator Hubert Humphrey, who got about the same answer as was given me. Mrs. Hamer gave a compelling address to the Credentials Committee, one which would have made quite an impression if it had been covered on live TV as the networks originally planned, but it was suddenly preempted when President Kennedy went on TV from the White House to announce he had received word from Khrushchev that the Soviet leader had formally agreed in writing to attend a summit in Stockholm a week after the Presidential election in November. What the President didn't say was that this note from Khrushchev arrived the day before and had been sitting on his desk since then. When the Mississippi Freedom Democratic Party threatened to occupy the seats reserved for the regular Mississippi on the floor, the Sergeant at Arms let it be known that they would be detained by the Secret Service as a security risk; in the end, there was no walkout of Southern white regular Democrats.

The Mississippi Freedom Democratic Party was a problem we could see coming, not so the arrival in Atlantic City of thousands of activists for the International Peace March on Wednesday, the 25th of August, the day Kennedy was officially nominated for a second term. It was led by professional agitator, David Dellinger and ivory tower academics from Harvard and Yale. Their beef was with everything the Kennedy Administration had done for the past six months starting with Cuba, specifically the invasion and overthrow of Castro. Their group was made up of college students, civil rights activists and fellow travelers; they numbered nearly five thousand when assembling just off the boardwalk at two in the afternoon. They were within three blocks of Boardwalk Hall before the street was hastily blocked by patrol cars of the Atlantic City PD, thus saving the Democratic Party from the debacle which would have occurred if the Peaceniks had crashed the hall just as Kennedy's name was put in nomination by Governor Pat Brown of California.

This nearly came to pass because Steve Smith and the Irish Mafia who were running things were caught with their pants down by a bunch of left-wing zealots, their bacon being saved only by the quick thinking of the local police chief. As it was, news footage of demonstrators waving placards calling JFK a murderer for his actions in Cuba, Vietnam and Korea made onto the evening newscasts. Almost every placard demanded the immediate release of Castro or a slogan which used some combination of "Imperialist," "Colonialism," and "Racism." The President, who was still in DC, did not like what he saw and made a number of tense telephone calls to Atlantic City; Steve Smith put out a statement deriding the demonstrators as "hard-line Communists." This was undermined when it was revealed that among those arrested was Dr. William Slone Coffin, the head of Yale, and Benjamin Spock, the renowned baby doctor.

The convention was designed to be the roll out of the Kennedy campaign for the American people, a showcase for the President's response to all the bullshit Barry Goldwater and his crew had been telling the country for months. Over the main entrance to

Boardwalk Hall was a huge placard bearing a headshot of a smiling JFK, looking slightly to the left, confidence beaming from his eyes; this despite the fact that JFK had never formally announced he was running for a second term. It was something I was not aware of until the opening day of the convention, when a public ceremony was scheduled at the White House where the President would stand in front of the microphones and declare himself.

The drama, of course, was not if the President would run, but who would be his running mate, for ever since my first day with Kennedy '64, there had been rumors that LBJ would not be on the ticket a second time. Back in the winter, when I first signed on, the Vice President's stock had been so low within the campaign that his being dropped in favor of someone else was considered a done deal.

Two weeks before the convention, I was in a D.C. bar with some of the other guys who were working right under Steve Smith in the campaign, and one of them - who will remain nameless - told me, "Bobby Kennedy hates Old Cornpone's guts like nobody else's with the possible exception of Jimmy Hoffa, he's going trump up all the shit from the Bobby Baker thing to send Johnson's ass back to Texas before the convention. Moreover, just to ice the cake, there will be a Federal indictment against LBJ for taking bribes sometime in the New Year just to make sure he remains a political corpse. Bobby plays rough." That was not all, according to my drinking buddy, it was down to Senators Humphrey and Jackson or Governor Sanford as who would be the new VP. It would all be decided just before the opening gavel in Atlantic City on August 23rd.

So imagine my surprise on opening day, when, in a televised ceremony in the Rose Garden, John F. Kennedy stepped forward and formally announced that he would be a candidate for a second term; this was hardly news, but the sight of a beaming Lyndon Johnson at the President's side was the photo which appeared above the fold on the front page of the *New York Times* the next day under a headline which proclaimed IT'S OFFICIAL: KENNEDY-JOHNSON AGAIN IN '64. "The Vice President was an invaluable asset four years ago," a self-assured sounding JFK declared to the assembled reporters, "he has been an invaluable asset for the past four years, and he will be an invaluable asset in the next four years." When asked by Helen Thomas about all the rumors concerning Johnson being dumped, the President replied, "It's been a boring race on the Democratic side this year, you reporters had to stir up something to make it interesting." Then he and Johnson walked back inside the White House, ignoring completely the fact that all of those rumors originated from Kennedy's own men.

"Everybody was talking about replacing Johnson," my drinking buddy explained later when I asked about his carved in stone prediction, "except for the President, and in the end, what he said was the only thing which counted."

One of my most vivid memories of the last night of the convention was being in a hallway when Jackie Kennedy passed by on her way to the VIP box; it was the closest I would ever get to her, and the beauty of the woman up close was stunning. The photos in the magazines did not begin to do her justice, the President was a supremely lucky man, and in light of later revelations, it was something he did not fully appreciate. My backstage vantage point proved to be the perfect spot from which view JFK and LBJ step back on the political stage for the '64 campaign; it was the first time either of them had taken part in a purely political event since that trip to Dallas the previous November which almost ended in an unspeakable tragedy, and setting off a crisis which kept the President out of the political spotlight thereafter.

Until the evening of August 27[th,] 1964, when John F. Kennedy strode onto the stage and took the podium, and in an acceptance speech clocking in at three quarters of an hour, offered up a spirited defense of his four years in office, a straight out rebuttal to Goldwater and the case for a second term. The President made the first point by paraphrasing his inaugural address, "We have paid the price, borne the burden, met the hardship, stood with our friends and turned back our foes to assure not only the survival of liberty, but its triumph." This brought the entire hall - including the all-white segregationist Mississippi delegation - to its feet with the biggest sustained roar of approval of the night. He needled the Goldwaterites with, "I would remind our opponents that history has taught us that the extremist, the demagogue, and the fanatic are no lovers of liberty. I would also remind them that the virtue of moderation is not one and the same with cowardice and faintness of heart." And he made the argument for his re-election with the statement, "We shall go forward as proud Americans in the 20th Century, with confidence gained through trials endured and challenges overcome, with the courage to face our enemies and look them in the eye; to not accept the notion that we are forever condemned to live in fear of a nuclear Armageddon, but to strive and reach the common ground where an enduring peace between all nations can be found; to not be forever bound by the hatreds and conflicts of our own past history, to instead commit ourselves to live in a nation where the dignity and worth of all citizens is recognized and respected by one and all."

Earlier, Vice President Johnson gave his own acceptance speech; nothing from it was memorable, except for one passage, "Four years ago, I put myself forward to be your nominee and asked you to go all the way with LBJ; you did not take me up on the offer, instead I had the high honor of becoming Vice President of the United States and serving under a great President. But I still have a fondness for my old campaign slogan and I think it's time to take it out of the garage and put it back on the road, only I'd make one little change. This year, I'm going around this great country of ours, from the Atlantic to the Pacific, and I'm going to tell every fine American within the hearing of my voice that it's time to go All the way with JFK!" The crowd knew its cue and immediately responded with a roaring chorus of "All the way with JFK!" It was even more spontaneous and thunderous when the President and Vice President along with their spouses stood before the convention with their hands raised high at the end of the evening. When they wrote their memoirs years later, some of the Kennedy men would claim the President was highly annoyed with Johnson for rephrasing and re-treading his old slogan and hated having to listen to it at every campaign event from then until November. It's what they said later, but standing before a packed Boardwalk Hall on the night he accepted re-nomination for a second term in the White House, the John F. Kennedy I saw was truly a man fully enjoying his moment of high triumph.

The convention ended on a high note with the fall campaign set to formally launch a little more than a week later with the President going up to Detroit and addressing a huge crowd of union members on Labor Day. I thought we had the election won easily, in no way could the millions of good Americans out there buy what Goldwater was selling; this optimistic notion took a beating when everyone with a paid position in the Kennedy '64 campaign got a call the day after we left Atlantic City informing them that there would be a meeting the next day, Saturday, at the National HQ a few blocks from the White House. At the meeting, we were addressed by Lawrence O'Brien, who told us he had quietly given up his Congressional duties and was now unofficially a co-campaign manager with Steve Smith. O'Brien's main concern would be day to day operations and making sure strategy was being implemented. "If any of you think this race is going to be a cake-walk," he told us, "then let me disabuse you of that notion right now." He then backed up his words by producing a bunch of mimeographed handouts which contained a detailed analysis of the polling by Gallup, Roper, and Harris since the beginning of the year.

The gist of it went like this: the President got consistently high approval ratings - 60% or better - during the winter and spring following the assassination attempt through the invasion of Cuba; the numbers started to decline with the first week of combat operations. "This was when the first flag-draped coffins started coming home," O'Brien pointed out. The President's support sagged further when the Soviets went into Iran, and the bombing operations were launched against Vietnam and Korea, but still the President's numbers were above 50%, and he was beating Goldwater by ten points in hypothetical matchups. Then at the end of June, his ratings dropped a sudden five points almost overnight - that was when the Civil Rights Act was being debated in the Senate and right after the President was in New Delhi shaking hands with Chou. The point was made; JFK's bold moves had cost him politically.

We were then treated to a rundown of Goldwater's numbers, which had steadily improved since March, edging up a point or two a month until he clinched the Republican nomination. O'Brien showed us where the race stood on the eve of the Democratic convention, with the President leading his opponent by 7 points in the Roper poll, 9 points according to Gallup, and 10 points according to Harris. This appeared to be a solid lead, but the state by state breakdowns painted a somewhat different picture in the Electoral College, which showed Kennedy-Johnson losing all of the Old Confederacy except for Florida, where they were tied; in all important Texas, LBJ's home state, they were losing by 5 points. Illinois was a dead heat because Dirksen was on the Republican ticket; California, which should have been a lock for Kennedy now that Nixon was not running for the first time in over a decade, was a dead heat. What was even more worrisome were surveys which showed Goldwater's fiery anti-Communism and his opposition to the Civil Rights Act were finding favor with ethnic blue collar Democrats in Michigan, Ohio and Pennsylvania.

The enthusiasm for George Wallace I'd witnessed among blue collar Democrats in Wisconsin back in the spring was now proving to be a possible harbinger of trouble for us in the fall as all those WWII veterans on the assembly lines or out in the fields began to take Goldwater seriously as the summer came to an end.

Then O'Brien outlined our response. "We are going to win back every wayward Democratic vote - every single one. How will this be accomplished? We will mobilize our unions and make sure every single household of a member is contacted and reminded of Senator Goldwater's labor record. Our message will be blunt: do they want a man who opposes the very concept of collective bargaining in the White House? Do they want a man opposed to the concept of a 40 hour work week and overtime pay proposing laws from the Oval Office? I think we know how that conversation will go?"

O'Brien then went on to say what the campaign's main argument for the re-election of John F. Kennedy would be: it comes down to a choice between whose finger could best be trusted with the nuclear button. The argument would go something like this: events had forced this President to the brink of a world war multiple times, but his leadership had prevented the world from going over the brink; he had stood up to the Communists in Cuba and turned them back, yet had journeyed to New Delhi to find a path to peace with our most committed rivals. That was true statesmanship, not the cravenness and appeasement charged by Senator Goldwater, a warmongering gunslinger who if given the opportunity, would fire off A-Bombs as if they were rounds in a revolver. On the issue of Civil Rights, our strategy would be simple and our message clear: if you elect Barry Goldwater President, he will then govern America the same as if he was Jefferson Davis. This we would say all day, every day, until Election Day.

Mr. O'Brien ended his talk with the announcement that the President and Goldwater had agreed to conduct three debates during the fall campaign, the first one being in San Francisco on September 17th. It was the second debate which caught everyone's attention for its choice of location: Dallas, Texas on October 1st. It would be Kennedy's first trip back to the scene of the attempted assassination since the crime had occurred.

My job did not change with the ending of the convention or the changes at the top of re-election committee; after the meeting, Mr. O'Brien sought me out and shook my hand, saying he'd heard great things about my work and for me to keep it up. "You'll have your hands more than full between now and November," he said.

I accompanied the President up to Boston on the Monday after we left Atlantic City for an "unofficial" campaign event in his home-town at Fenway Park. The stadium was packed to capacity as wildly enthusiastic crowd greeted the President and Mrs. Kennedy. "This may well be my last quest for elective office," the President told them, "and I'll always be grateful to you who made this all possible." There were not many dry eyes when the President was finished. Three days later, there was another "unofficial" event, this time in Florida, when the President flew down to Miami to greet one of the first Army units rotated out of Cuba, where fighting was still flaring up as Castro's fanatics refused to give up. While he was in town, the President made an appearance at a rally organized by his old friend, Florida Senator George Smathers. Everyone was concerned as to how it would go; Florida, after all, was still part of the South, and there had been a lot of fear and resentment stirred up by the influx of refugees from Cuba, though the torrent from the spring had slowed to a trickle by late summer.

Our fears proved to be groundless, for when the President took the stage before a crowd of Florida Democrats, they stood and cheered for five minutes. His remarks were brief and general, but when Kennedy said, "Let it be said we did not cower before tyrants, and we did not stand by while a free people were subjugated," the roar of approval was loud and clear.

Those first days of September, just before the Presidential campaign kicked into high gear, were the best, the polls coming out of the Democratic convention were good, showing the President up by two or three points and in a good position nationally to fend off the Republicans; we were told that John F. Kennedy would begin his quest for a second term by effectively rebutting Goldwater's appeal to blue collar voters when he spoke in Detroit on Labor Day.

I was told it was a great speech, one of the best Ted Sorenson ever wrote for the President; too bad he never got to give it before the audience for whom it was intended.

On a Friday evening marking the beginning of Labor Day weekend, 1964, a black motorist in the Watts neighborhood of South Los Angeles was pulled over for drunk driving by members of the LAPD. The driver resisted arrest and was struck upside the head with a nightstick by a zealous officer; by then a crowd from the neighborhood had gathered in the street and what began as heckling of the police quickly escalated to bottle and rock throwing. The arrival of backup units served to make things worse as long-standing resentment among black citizens of the predominately working class community over police brutality and discriminatory housing practices erupted into violence. Within minutes the streets were choked with rioters and the LAPD was forced to retreat.

What followed was an explosion of rage across a thirty block section of Los Angeles that worsened by the hour as stores were looted and fires burned out of control, while anything with any connection to white authority was attacked with a fury. This had happened in America before, more than once, but this was the first time it was broadcast to the whole country and the world beyond. On Saturday evening, every broadcast on every channel featured footage of black mobs smashing plate glass storefront windows and snatching whatever was in arm's reach, followed by scenes of looters brazenly walking down the street with newly stolen TV's, cases of liquor, and cartons of cigarettes clutched tightly. Even more shocking were the images of unfortunate white motorists, who because of a wrong turn, were in the wrong place at the wrong time, being surrounded by black mobs and dragged from their cars to be beaten and left for dead in the street.

By Sunday more than a thousand officers of the LAPD and LA Sheriff's Department were being deployed to restore order. Before the day was out, three thousand National Guardsman were ordered in to back up local law enforcement; by then there were more than fifty dead and four times that many injured. I was in my DC apartment on Saturday night packing for a morning flight to Detroit, where I was to be part of a troubleshooting team whose job it was to go in ahead to the President's Monday event in the city and take care of any local problems, when my phone rang right after 9:00 p.m.; it was Steve Smith's chief deputy informing me that it would be announced in the morning that the President's trip to Detroit had been postponed due to the events in Los Angeles. "The President made the call himself," I was told, "since there was no way possible for him to engage in partisan political activities while an American city burned." I was stunned in the moment, so engrossed was I in the campaign; everything depended on sticking to the plan, or so I thought, but by Monday, it was clear L.A. was going to be a big political problem for the Democrats. The riot in Watts was a potential boon for Goldwater, as it seemingly made his argument that lawlessness was out of control in the country for him. And coming less than a month after the compromised Civil Rights Act had been signed with much fanfare in the White House and on the eve of the Presidential campaign kickoff, the timing couldn't have been worse.

The mood inside Kennedy '64 headquarters on Labor Day was anxious, to say the least; the riot showed no sign of being suppressed and the airwaves were filled with accusations and recriminations as to the cause of the carnage. Depending on which side you were on, the Watts riot was a long overdue insurrectionary response to years of racism and oppression by the police department and city government in Los Angeles or a breakdown in social order led by the lazy, the ignorant and the criminal, and instigated by malcontents and agitators eager to do the bidding of Moscow.

Shortly after the noon hour, a group of us younger guys were sitting in a back room, all of us nursing beers and stewing in our disappointment that we were not in Detroit listening to the President make his speech before thousands in Cadillac Square when the call came down: we would be traveling, after all, only it would be a day late and not to the Motor City, instead President John F. Kennedy would be flying to Los Angeles on Air Force One the next day.

Lt. Colonel Martin Maddox (VII)
August - September, 1964

"Colonel, I understand you had quite a trip down to New Orleans last spring," said the President as I stood before his desk in the Oval Office on the afternoon of August 10th. Hearing those words, I was sure the trajectory of my military career was about to take a sharp turn into a dead end. "You don't have to answer that," he continued. "I called you in here today because at some time in the immediate future, you will hear an explanation for that trip and the events surrounding it which varies greatly with the facts as you know them. Very probably you will be in the room when said version of the truth will be spoken; in that case, I will not ask you to tell an untruth or even to nod an assent. All I ask from you is your silence, nothing more. After all the hard work you have done for the good of your country, do you think you can do that, Colonel Maddox, can you give me your silence?"

There were only the two if us in the Oval Office on this day, just myself and the President, and though he was not asking me to lie, to compromise my honor as a Marine officer, I knew damn well what my silence would mean. I knew it then, and I know it now.

Without hesitation, I told President Kennedy he could count on me.

What neither I nor anyone else in Washington knew on August 10, was that events were happening thousands of miles away which would have tremendous repercussions in the near future. The accelerated pullout of Soviet troops from Iran was proceeding at a steady pace, and so were the mass arrests of ranking officers from returning Soviet units, most of who were picked up by the KGB within hours of their setting foot back on Russian soil. Somebody had to take the blame for the failures of the Iran invasion, and the worst of it was reserved for the poor guys who'd done nothing but obey their orders from the men inside the Kremlin. It wasn't their fault the whole operation was doomed to failure because of improper planning and a rushed implementation, not to mention a complete underestimating of the enemy they would be facing. How many Colonels, Majors, and Lieutenants dropped to their knees in gratitude when they got back to Mother Russia, thankful they'd survived the meat grinder in Iran, only to find themselves whisked before a Kangaroo court martial on trumped up charges of "incompetence and betrayal" and then sentenced to a work camp in Siberia for Siberia. No mercy was spared for the KGB officers who accompanied the Red Army units into Iran either, their failure was even greater in the eyes of their superiors, for it was their job to ensure the success of the operation and maintain party discipline. Several hundred agents found themselves breaking rocks on the tundra along with the men they were supposed to have been watching.

These developments were meant to inspire fear and intimidation, but sometimes people just don't or won't get the message.

At about this same time, several dozen high-ranking members of the Shah's government, including Cabinet ministers, were released from confinement in Teheran by the KGB, given transportation and sent south to Qom, a holy city where the forces of Khomeini's resistance were in full control. These members of the Shah's government were given a cease-fire proposal by the Red Army commander on the ground in a bid to suspend the fighting until the withdrawal was complete. All but three of the Iranians sent to Qom were summarily executed by the Khomeini's irregulars, who did not even bother to listen to the Soviet's cease-fire proposal. The three who lived did so because once out of sight of the Russians, they high tailed it to the Iraqi border. I point this out because, at this time, Washington's policy was that the Shah would return as soon as the Soviets were out of his country and resume his rule; nobody here had bothered to ask the Iranian people what their thoughts might be on their future.

There were other simmering brush fires left over from the multiple crises of the spring: the bombing of North Vietnam appeared to have been effective in the short run; Viet Cong units in the South had gone on the defensive and dug in, it was left to the newly arrived US Marines to try and push them out.

Of course, the most smoke was coming from Cuba, where multiple problems for our now occupation forces were cropping up, the least of which was a population which did not see us as liberators. Organized resistance had melted back into the Sierra Maestra mountains, where units of Castro's army still held out, but it was small groups, some nothing more than a pair of snipers, who were giving General Abrams real trouble - eighteen US service men came home in coffins the third week of August, each of them taken out by an ambush on the streets of Havana and Santiago. On August 27th, the day President Kennedy accepted re-nomination at Atlantic City, General Abrams sent a memo to the Pentagon stating for the first time that there was significant resistance on the island from "guerrilla forces." This was not what the Administration wanted to hear since it wanted to start a significant drawdown of forces on the island before the summer was over and the Presidential campaign was in full swing.

There were also real complications in Cuba yet to be dealt with as the summer moved toward fall, the foremost of them still being the large Russian presence on the island. General Andreyev's command at Camaguey had grown by several thousand by August, as more Russian "advisors" and former Castro officials, now refugees in their own land. The Soviets dragged their feet in repatriating their troops out of spite, repeatedly claiming that they had been invited into Cuba by the "legitimate government" and could only remove them when so requested by the same authority. There being no government in Cuba at the time except for General Abrams's command, Khrushchev's standing on the strict letter of the law just to poke the United States in the eye despite agreements reached in New Delhi. The President was taking a lot of flak for "coddling" the Red Army in Cuba on the campaign trail, but worse, important Cubans who could have shed light on the events in Dallas were behind Russian lines in Camaguey, safe from American interrogators.

The other Cuban problem was Fidel himself, now recovered from his injuries and currently residing in a naval brig at Guantanamo Bay, while the State Department insisted his fate would be decided "by the free people of Cuba." In mid-August, a delegation made up of British Labor MP's and other members of various western European Socialist parties arrived in Havana demanding to visit the former Communist dictator, denouncing the imprisonment of Castro as an "outrageous breach of international law." This was quite the contrast with Senator Goldwater, who called for Castro to be extradited to the United States where he could promptly be charged with conspiracy to commit murder. Things were not helped in the least when 75 prominent law professors, including the Dean of Harvard's school, signed a petition calling the continued holding of Castro an illegal act and violation of Habeas Corpus.

With no central authority on the island other than the United States military, which had its hands full, the Cuban people took full advantage of the opportunity to even all the scores accumulated under Communist rule as anyone even remotely suspected of ratting out their neighbors for so-called "counter-revolutionary activities" was dealt with most harshly. On the first of September, every morning newspaper in the country featured a photo of five dead Cubans, face down in a Havana alley, gaping bullet holes in the backs of their heads from which streams of blood trickled into a nearby storm drain. The accompanying story explained how this was the fate of former block captains for the Communist Party, responsible for sending many Cuban citizens to Castro's work camps for "re-education."

For us, in the basement of the White House post invasion Cuba was turning out to be more of a headache than when Castro was in charge. Not the least of our problems was that Cuba was no longer the priority now that there were a hundred thousand American troops on the island and Fidel was locked away in Guantanamo. There were two top priorities for the Kennedy Administration at the end of the summer of '64: re-election and the summit with Khrushchev and the Soviet leadership in Stockholm a week after the election in November. The winning of a second term took up 75% of the President and his brother's attention from the week of the Democratic National Convention onward, and what consideration remained was given over to the upcoming summit, the achievement the President was most proud of coming out of New Delhi. "After this past year, there is no way the Cold War status quo can continue," the President told us in one NSC meeting, "I know this and Khrushchev knows it as well." He went on to explain that he was going for broke at Stockholm, not only a reduction of tensions over Berlin and the division of Germany, but a reduction of nuclear arms as well; maybe even a discussion of a joint USA-Soviet effort to reach the moon. "We have too long been living with the mistakes and miscalculations of World War II and the generation that blundered into it," he said as a way of summing up what he wanted his legacy to be. "It's up to us who fought on the front lines to find a path to a more peaceful world."

These were lofty sentiments, certainly words worthy of a statesman, but it was street level concerns which put me in a seat on Air Force One on the day after Labor Day when the President flew across the country to Los Angeles, a city engulfed by a race riot, now in its fourth day. I'd gotten the call at the last minute from the President's secretary, informing me that I would be accompanying the President on this trip because he "needed someone with my military expertise by his side when he got to L.A." This made me believe the President was planning some kind of dramatic federal intervention in the City of Angels; from the reports that had come into the White House and what I could follow on TV, it was the worst eruption of urban violence in an American city since the Civil War. When I inquired as to why I would be making the trip to California, the President's answer to me was, "Colonel, I need a man of your experience on this thing."

I learned what he was talking about when I found myself sitting behind the President in the Los Angeles city council meeting room as the council, the Mayor, the Police Chief, the commander of the National Guard, and Governor Brown, along with state legislators, businessmen, and community leaders. All of these Californians were doing their best to explain how they would get the situation under control very soon - we had seen plumes of smoke rising from the city as Air Force One flew in and was greeted at the airport with reports that more than a hundred were dead and three times as many wounded. There was a lot of hemming and hawing in answer to the President's question as to why such racial violence had broken out in this place at this time - giving the impression that Kennedy was calling them all on the carpet.

I was sitting right behind President Kennedy as he listened to all this, sticking out like a sore thumb in my Marine uniform as I sat among the civilian staff who had accompanied us to California. The President listened intently to their assurances, nodding his head and furrowing his brow at different times, and not breaking in to ask questions as was his usual style. When they finished, he told them that he hoped their assessment of the situation was the correct one, because if it was not, he, as President was not about to sit by and let an American city burn while its citizens and property were at the mercy of a lawless mob. President Kennedy went on the say that the federal government had many more capabilities at hand to deal with a situation like the one raging in Watts at the moment, and extremely capable men. That is when he turned around and singled me out, saying, "Like Colonel Maddox here, he did much of the planning for our successful invasion of Cuba back in the spring."

Those California politicians clearly got the message without any direct threats from the President: clean up this mess, or I'll put the men who cleaned Castro out of Cuba in charge and they'll get the job done. The fact that most of the office holders were fellow Democrats made the kid glove treatment necessary; President Kennedy would have to depend on them to carry the Golden State in November. And I now knew why he wanted me sitting on inches away when he made his point. One thing which sticks in my mind, more than anything the President said or did, happened after the meeting in the council room broke up and while President Kennedy was in a huddle with Governor Brown, the mayor and the police chief: an intense looking gentleman approached me as I waited for the President and identified himself as a member of the Los Angeles city council - he was wearing a white turtle neck, something seldom seen at the time. But it was not what the man was wearing that I remember most vividly; instead it was what he said. "The invasion of Cuba was a war crime and you, sir, are a war criminal, and if there is any justice, you will stand accused in a court of law one day."

My first inclination was to punch the guy in the face, even if it wouldn't have been a fair fight since the councilman appeared as if he barely tipped the scales at 120; but Marine officers do not hit civilians, no matter what the provocation.

The other vivid memory of the Los Angeles trip is of being with President Kennedy an hour later when he toured a neighborhood which had been the victim of rioters only a day previous. We walked past dozens of looted storefronts and burned husks of what had been thriving businesses only days before. It was a sight familiar to anyone who has ever been in a war zone; the shocking part was that this war zone was in an American city. That was how I got to be in an iconic photo, snapped by an alert press photographer when John F. Kennedy paused in his tour to listen to the plight of a dress shop owner whose business was picked clean by the looters. "They didn't even bother to break into the register," the shop owner told the President, "just carried the whole damn thing away with them." In the foreground of the picture is President Kennedy, in a white shirt and dress slacks, and a middle-aged black man, hands high in the air in a gesture of exasperation while the President appears to listen with a pensive look on his face. They are under a cloudless blue sky while smoking ruins are off to one side. I am among the many standing a respectful distance from the President, sticking out because I'm the only one in uniform.

This image would grace the covers of both *Life* and *Newsweek* magazines the next week.

One other thing sticks in my mind from the L.A. trip, it was catching a glimpse of the drop dead gorgeous Angie Dickinson in an elevator at the Ambassador Hotel, where the President was staying; years later, I would learn that seeing her there was no happy accident.

Wade L. Harbinson (V)
September 1964

If I were going to up the ante and compete with Kennedy money, then I would need to bring in some big artillery myself. My first call was to H.L. Hunt, a fellow Texas oilman, and someone truly after my own heart; he hated Kennedy almost as much as he hated Communism and he was most interested in what I had to say. The other was to a mutual associate who would pass a message along to the head of the United Brotherhood of the Teamsters, James R. Hoffa. I have no use for unions and the lowlifes who populate them, but if there was anybody in this great country who hated the Kennedys more than Jimmy Hoffa, I don't know who they would be.

Mr. Hunt was quite enthusiastic after I described the details of the material Harlow had presented me, but he wanted to see the real thing before he committed any dough. Mr. Jimmy Hoffa was quite cagey at first. I had to go back and forth with some underlings, but with Bobby Kennedy's justice department trying to send him to the Big House for a long, long stretch, he couldn't afford to let pass a chance to take down the Kennedy brothers. And after I finally got a face to face meeting in Nashville the week Kennedy got re-nominated, I got an assurance of generous support, no doubt from the Teamsters' pension fund. I never had a worry that I could get both Hunt and Hoffa to commit; you're not a success in the oil business in Texas without being a good salesman.

With both f them in my corner, I was able to assure Harlow at our next meeting that I would beat any price the other side might be offering; I gave him a substantial figure, one which he claimed the "sundry individuals" would find more than reasonable. The next problem would be the how and the where the transaction would take place. This was a real sticking point; because of the risks involved, the "sundry individuals" would only come to me in a place where they felt absolutely comfortable. "Otherwise," Harlow said, "they are willing to make a deal with the other party and take less, figuring it is preferable to be somewhat less rich, but very free."

Harlow had a solution. "If you want to get Kennedy, and get him good, you need to do it right before one of the debates, have all the shit break hours before he has to get on the stage and stand next to Senator Goldwater and look the American people in the eye. Something he cannot duck out of, not if he wants to survive politically." The thought of John F. Kennedy refusing to take the stage at a debate out of fear of questions about his criminal and immoral behavior truly put a smile on my face, and something well worth the risk to make it happen.

"You can do it right here in Dallas," Harlow continued, "just before the debate on the first of October. The Adolphus Hotel would be a perfect place; it's public - which makes it neutral ground - but affords the right measure of privacy." He went on to say I should rent out the entire top floor, it had easy access to the freight elevator; if any of the rooms were already rented, then offer the hotel double what they were getting, if it was still a problem, make it triple - no hotel manager would turn down that kind of money.

"Now," he added, "this is the most important thing: this must appear as if you are there conducting legitimate business; make it look like you are soliciting investors to drill on some land you own, I'll get a lawyer I know who'll go along and write up some phony contracts that will make it all appear nice and legal. Everyone's ass will be covered; that's the main part. But be sure to spend some money, put out a spread, buy the best whiskey, and hire the finest whores - whatever it is you do in Texas to loosen wallets. The reason you need to do this is that if any time in the future, you have to put your hand on a Bible and answer questions as to what transpired at the Adolphus Hotel on a certain date, you won't face a perjury charge when you tell the court it was nothing but you and some fellow investors going about the business of making your next million."

By the time I left the Carousel Club, I was certain that goal was within grasp. Once the documentation was in my hands, it would only be a matter of lining up friendly contacts in the press who could guarantee front page stories in some of the biggest morning and afternoon dailies in the country. The Goldwater campaign had few if any friends at the big networks run out of New York, but there were lots of editors, especially in the Hearst and Pulliam papers, along with the *Los Angeles Times*, who already had investigative reporters digging into Kennedy's dirty secrets. They were getting nowhere because they didn't have the deep pockets of my friends and me, but they were about to get the scoop of the year courtesy of us.

The mood in the Goldwater campaign was upbeat at the end of the summer, despite being 6 points behind Kennedy; money was pouring in, and Dirksen proved to be a big help in getting the party unified behind the Senator.

Then on Labor Day weekend, Kennedy's chickens came home to roost when a significant part of Los Angeles went up in flames thanks to a rampaging mob of blacks. That such a thing would occur not 30 days after that Communist-inspired Civil Rights Bill was signed by the President came as no surprise to me or anyone else who knows how this country works. The black man cannot handle the burden of legal and social equality with whites, and it does him no good to pass draconian laws which attempts to mandate such nonsense. The proof was evident in the newsreel footage of black mobs looting and burning - equality with such lawless cretins would be the utter and final ruin of America. To make matters worse, Kennedy actually flew to Los Angeles in a feeble attempt to appear "in charge" after he had signed blatantly unconstitutional legislation which had been the direct cause of the riot. The man actually got out and walked the streets, even talking with some of those looting and arsonist bastards. It was enough to make a true patriot puke. What Kennedy should have done was send in the National Guard, with orders to shoot on sight anyone caught looting. If any citizen refused a command to clear the street, they were to be encouraged to do so with the crack of a rifle butt upside the head, anyone refusing after that would get the sharp end of a bayonet. That's how we would have done it in Texas.

A lot of us in the campaign told Senator Goldwater he needed to take full advantage of the riots, tragedy though it was for many Americans, for they showed the country exactly what Kennedy's Civil Rights policy was leading us into. He had to hit Kennedy hard on the riots, tie him to the arson and looting, show Americans what their future would be if they re-elected this man. It was disrespect for authority, disrespect for the police, and a total undermining of essential order. The Senator was reluctant at first to see things our way, he thought he could win black votes by telling the story of how he integrated his family department store in Phoenix, but when the argument was put in those terms, he warmed up to the theme, the day after Labor Day, the same day Kennedy flew to Los Angeles, Karl Hess tore up the Senator's stump speech and wrote him a new one which ripped into Kennedy for giving aid and comfort to criminals. It went over like gangbusters before the surging crowds in mid-September.

Behind the scenes, I went about putting things in order, for what I was sure would be a most profitable evening at the Adolphus Hotel on the 30th of September. The required number of hotel rooms was snagged at the last moment without any extra expense. By a fortunate coincidence, I was planning to make a bid on Swift Drill and Dye, the largest maker of oil drilling equipment in the USA, and was able to arrange for a group of investors to be there earlier in the evening. If the question was ever to be raised, Mr. Hunt and Mr. Hoffa were simply looking to get in on a good deal.

I had another meeting with Harlow at that strip joint, one I sincerely hoped would be the last, on the 17th of September; he informed me that everything was a go on his end, that the "certain individuals" would be there at the hotel at the exact time agreed upon with the evidence I wanted and with every intention of making a deal.

It was just like Gypsy Rose Lee sang; everything was coming up roses. Before we were through with him, Kennedy was going to wish Oswald's bullet had blown his brains all over that Dallas Street.

Dorothy Jean Brennan (III)
September 1964

I will make no excuses, Senator Goldwater did not knock it out the park in those first days of the campaign, the man had to find his groove, so to speak, and it took some time. Looking back, he was simply trying too hard in his speeches, which were all over the place in his attacks on Kennedy for not being tough enough on the Communists, for wasting taxpayer's money, for enacting unconstitutional legislation, and for presiding over the moral decay of the nation. Before large crowds on his first campaign swing, his speeches were filled with references to Cuba, Castro, Khrushchev, Iran, the Red Chinese, the sellout at New Delhi, rights of property, his personal distaste for segregation, state's rights, the coddling of switchblade-wielding criminals - not necessarily in that order. There were plenty of stories in the press of how Goldwater was not "connecting" with voters.

It did not help that the Democrats flooded the airwaves with a barrage of anti-Goldwater adds, chiefly one that used a bunch of totally out of context quotes spoken over a black and white photo of the Senator with a particularly truculent expression that made him sound like he would begin bombing the Soviet Union on Inauguration Day. There were other ads that made it sound as if he would abolish the minimum wage and force the American worker to labor for a dollar a day while doing away with Social Security for good measure. It was all delivered by the best Madison Avenue minds the Kennedy's money could buy.

And we got a crash course in how rough the Kennedy's played hardball, which included having federal meat inspectors visit the St. Louis sausage factory owned by head of the Goldwater campaign in Missouri three times in the month of August; more than a dozen of the biggest contributors to Goldwater for President in Ohio, Indiana, and Pennsylvania had their tax returns audited for the past ten years; the co-chairman for Citizens for Goldwater in Florida had three serious complaints lodged against him with the state bar association. There were overtures made to certain Republican Governors and Senators whose lack of enthusiasm for Goldwater was well known with offers of favors in return for an endorsement across party lines.

We got a break, such as it was, when part of Los Angeles went up in flames over Labor Day weekend. I know it sounds opportunistic and cynical, but that event was a real opening Senator Goldwater, a real chance for him to draw a stark contrast with the America of Kennedy and the America of Barry Goldwater. There were some closed doors meetings to discuss strategy and afterward, the candidate was truly more focused with a clear line of attack. "I can promise you this," he said in a speech in Columbus, Ohio, on the 7th of September, "if I am your President, I will never drop everything and scurry across the country to hold the hands of rioters and looters, instead I'll leave them to the National Guard." The audience loved it, and he managed to work a variation of that line into every one of his speeches, always getting the same response, especially before crowds in the factory towns and cities of the Mid-West and North East. These were the voters that were crucial if we wanted to win, and those out of control criminals in Los Angeles had given us a way to reach them.

The polls began to reflect what we were seeing on the campaign trail; Kennedy dropped four points in the week after the riots, according to Gallup, while Goldwater gained three to pull within the margin of error. We were going to win and the road to victory was laid out in front of us.

Of course, it would not be that easy, at a rally at Wrigley Field for Kennedy in mid-September broke all records for a political event in that city according to people who were there at the time. "We're matching Kennedy with the crowds," Dean Burch explained to me, "that's good as far as it goes, but it does not mean we're winning, it just means we're not losing."

On account of our momentum, the first Presidential debate in San Francisco became even more crucial. The debate, held on the campus of Stanford University on September 17th, and to our disappointment, was called a draw in the popular press. This was cited as a victory for us by some because it meant that Senator Goldwater held his own against a supposedly popular and charismatic incumbent. The topic was to be domestic issues, but more than half the time was spent on the Los Angeles riots. I thought our candidate scored a direct hit on Kennedy when he said, "In America, public safety cannot be compromised anyplace, at any time; it is the number one job of all public officials, from the court house to the White House is to preserve law and order. In that job, Mr. President, you failed the citizens of Los Angeles, and you failed America." Kennedy's response to say something pompous about America still fighting the Civil War nearly a hundred years after Appomattox, it was widely quoted after the debate by many of the President's acolytes in the media. I thought the debate moderator, Eric Severed, was openly favoring Kennedy, which was only natural since he was a protégé of Edward R. Morrow, a well-known leftist.

If he didn't score a knockout at the San Francisco debate, Barry Goldwater at least proved he was Kennedy's equal.

That was the public face of my job during September of 1964, what was happening behind the scene is a story that has never been told in full. What I will say is this, I was approached by Wade Harbinson the day after the Republican National Convention adjourned and was told of the scheme to obtain the "lowdown dirty truth on John F. Kennedy" which once revealed to the public, would guarantee the election of Goldwater. What he was talking about was documented proof of "adultery, deliberate perjury, and criminal conspiracy" committed by the Chief Executive of the United States. This scheme was in Harbinson's own words, "deep undercover" and not involving anyone else in either Goldwater '64 or the Republican National Committee, it was a solo operation, but he was bringing me aboard because I had inadvertently learned some sensitive info.

I pressed Harbinson for details and was informed about the scheme to purchase evidence of Kennedy's misdeeds by working with Vance Harlow; I was thrilled at the thought of Kennedy going down in flames along with the prospect of Barry Goldwater being elected by a landslide. Despite some reservations and a serious dislike of both Harbinson and Harlow, I was in.

That was how I came to be at the Adolphus Hotel on the eve of the second televised debate in Dallas; Senator Goldwater suspended the campaign two days before so he could go back to Phoenix and prepare for the all-important second confrontation with the President where the subject would be foreign affairs. I was supposed to fly to Dallas with the Senator on the morning of the debate, but a few days before, Harbinson took me aside during a rally in Cleveland, Ohio and told me to be at the hotel the night before. "Think up a reason to be part of the advance team," he told me, "I need you to be at the Adolphus on Wednesday night, that's when we finally drive the nails in Jack Kennedy's political coffin."

When I asked why I needed to be there, he replied, "I need a witness who can back up my side of the story, just in case it ever becomes necessary - which it won't."

He was clearly implying there might be legal consequences down the road, something I had not truly considered; it was frightening.

Before I could voice my concerns, Harbinson said he did not expect me to do this solely out of devotion to Senator Goldwater and made a promise of ample compensation. Those were welcome words when all you have in your bank account is a thousand dollars and some change.

It was easy enough to find a reason to fly to Dallas a day ahead of everyone else; the networks and the big daily papers were already encamped at the Trade Mart, the site of the debate, and I could better brief them on the Senator's debate preparations in Phoenix (which included huddling with William F. Buckley and Brent Bozel) from there.

I was staying at the Sheraton, but Harbinson sent a taxi to bring me over to the Adolphus, and that is how I came to be present at one of the most fateful encounters in American history. This is the first time I've told what I saw and heard at the Hotel Adolphus in Dallas, Texas on the last day of September in 1964.

Wade L. Harbinson (VI)
September 1964

There was no damn way anyone would have mistaken my get together at the Adolphus as anything other than a gathering of men of means with the intention of acquiring even more means. I followed Harlow's plan to the letter and rented out the top floor of suites at the Adolphus, paying for it out of my own company's accounts - making sure there were receipts for everything, right down to the fine whiskey served to be stocked at the bar the main suite where it would all go down.

Despite all his hard work to make it come about, Vance Harlow himself was not in attendance at the Adolphus on that evening, as he explained to me, "I'm the designated middle man in all this, my fingerprints, figuratively and literally are all over this thing and I can tie you directly to some pretty unsavory dealings, so my presence there would put you in a dicey situation legally and make it hard to keep up the pretense this was just a meeting of rich Texans doing what rich Texans do best." Nevertheless, he hired a lawyer, whose discretion he vouched for, to be in attendance and give the proceedings a gloss of legality while hiring a pair of technicians to sweep the place to make sure it wasn't bugged.

I was joined in my suite at the right time by Mr. Hunt and Mr. Hoffa, who had brought along with them the cash they had promised; their money, along with mine, was in a room down the hall guarded by professionals who were being well paid to not remember anything they might see or hear. I would dare say that never before under one roof in Texas had there been so much cash.

The plan went like this: at different appointed times, the "sundry individuals" would be let in through the back service entrance and make their way to our floor by way of a freight elevator; they would then be directed to a suite where they would wait until summoned. Once everyone had arrived and was in place, they would be sent for and escorted to my suite where they would present the "smoking gun" evidence for my partners and me to examine up close to our satisfaction. We would hear them all out and if we liked what we saw and were convinced beyond a shadow of a doubt of its authenticity, an offer would be made, there would be back and forth until a price was agreed upon. Once that was arrived at, paperwork would be signed and money would change hands. This is where an all but defunct holding company I've owned for five years came in very handy, for the paperwork was for leases to drill for oil on parcels owned by Dallas Properties - my holding company - by the "sundry individuals," who to anyone looking at these contracts in the future, where now wild-cat oil drillers.

I brought Miss Brennan into the proceedings because I wanted to assure her full complicity and what's wrong with having a lovely blonde in the room when there is dickering between men of business.

Everyone was in place by eight in the evening and the thing got underway. The first prospective entered the suite, and produced from a briefcase a file filled with photos exposing Operation Mongoose, the secret three year effort to overthrow Castro, specifically by way of an alliance with certain Mafia goons who, in return for their cooperation, would get all their hotels, casinos and whorehouse back in Cuba once the Commies were kicked out. One picture showed Sam Giancana, the head of the Chicago Outfit sitting down with the CIA station chief in Miami, while others concerned Carlos Marcello and Santos Triafficante in similar situations. This was offered as proof the Administration was in bed with organized crime.

Personally, I considered Castro to a far worse menace to the United States than a bunch of greasy Italians and getting him out of Cuba was surely a case of the ends justifying the means. But Kennedy was a threat to America too in his own way, and the sight of him making illegal deals with known pimps and murderers would not set well with the millions of honest American.

Of course, I and my partners had the necessary skepticism and questioned the prospect extensively as to how this evidence came into his possession and to its authenticity; after all, photos can easily be faked and doctored in any camera shop these days. What we heard was the testimony of an inside man, one who had been involved with Mongoose from the beginning, and before that had a working relationship with a number of those Mafia bigwigs. When asked why he was doing this besides the ample financial reward, he replied with a list of names and then told us: "They were my brothers, one was killed on the beach at the Bay of Pigs, the other was put in front of a firing squad by Castro, they died while that son of a bitch Kennedy sat on his ass in the Oval Office and did nothing. The invasion came four years too late for me, and I'll never forgive him."

When it was pointed out that all the contacts between the President and the mobsters were through low-level officers, thus giving him the alibi of claiming they were "off the reservation" so to speak, our attention was directed to a particular photograph, which showed a clean cut young man shaking hands with a laughing Marcello. This young man, we were informed, was a colonel in the Marine Corp and worked out of a basement in the White House. "He talks to Kennedy every day." That was the cherry on top, so to speak and good enough proof for me.

But the plan was to hear out everyone and then talk money; the first prospect was excused, and Miss Brennan went down the hall to fetch the second one; though a familiar face to anyone familiar with Presidential politics, this man was a proxy for someone far more powerful who wished to remain behind in their suite rather than show their face, I will say they were someone with an understandable grudge against Kennedy.

This prospect also had a briefcase, from which he produced a medical file belonging one Dr. Max Jacobsen, a man referred to by many of his patients as "Dr. Feelgood." The patient this file belonged to was the President of the United States, and its contents were pure dynamite. It proved beyond a shadow of a doubt that Kennedy's image of vigor and good health was nothing but a lie and that his true condition had been covered up and hidden from the American people. This cover up had led the President to seek treatments from this Dr. Jacobsen that were dubious at best and a threat to his ability to carry out his duties as Commander in Chief. The short of it was that this "Dr. Feelgood" was jacking Kennedy up on amphetamines and injections of God knows what to combat his back pain; it was nothing but high class "speed," and I've known men in the oilfields who took too much of that stuff to keep going and then walked right out in front of a truck as though it wasn't there. Now we had a guy in the same condition with his finger on the nuclear button. In addition, Dr. Jacobsen's file revealed that Kennedy suffered from Addison's disease, a life-threatening thyroid condition which had also been hidden from the American voters. That, and the fact Kennedy was treated for gonorrhea in the past, as if he'd been a hard up sailor just off the boat and prowling the Yokohama docks for tail.

This was damning evidence indeed, yet it was obvious the good Dr. Jacobsen had not simply turned over this most sensitive file to men with more than a grudge against the President. This prompted some intense questions as to how the file was obtained. "I have no firsthand knowledge of how these papers left the office of Dr. Jacobsen," was the reply from the prospect, "and anything I might tell you would be conjecture and hearsay. All I know is that they were given to me by some concerned citizens who wanted the truth about the President to come out. That is my story, and I suggest it be your story if we conclude our business amicably and you are ever questioned in the future about how they to be in your hands."

True to form, the next prospect also had a briefcase in his hand when escorted into the suite by Miss Brennan; he could best be described as a lobbyist who traveled in the same social circles as the President. His evidence consisted of a top of the line recorder and the tape of a young woman who gave her name as Ellen Rometsch, who described in graphic detail a number of sexual encounters between herself and John F. Kennedy. Judging from the photograph accompanying the tape, Miss Rometsch bore a striking resemblance to Elizabeth Taylor; she was what could loosely be called a "party girl," one of the many such women who worked for the disgraced Bobby Baker at the notorious Quorum Club in the Carroll Arms Hotel, where they would entertain members of Congress after a long day. It had been the job of our third prospect to procure women for the President and bring them to the White House, where they often serviced Kennedy by the pool after he took a swim for his bad back, an affliction which limited his positions during sex according to Miss Rometsch.

But here was the real kicker to Miss Rometsch's story: the young lady was not an American citizen, but born on German soil, more importantly, that part of Germany overrun by the Red Army in the closing days of WWII and had grown up under Communist rule, something she embraced before escaping to West Germany and marrying a West German army officer who was ultimately posted to the embassy in Washington. It seems the fetching Miss Rometsch once belonged to a number of Communist youth groups during her time in East Germany and who knows what the hell else, possibly their intelligence services as well, which could have sent her to the West to act as a modern day Mata Hari. That is how it would look to a good many Americans when they discovered the truth.

This was the equivalent of a political H-Bomb, and we knew it, but my partners and I gave this third prospect a tough questioning as to how he came to possess such a tape and what his motives might be beside the obvious financial ones. He claimed it was out of pure patriotism and love of country along with disgust for the President's conduct; he had flown to West Germany and paid the destitute Miss Rometsch to reveal all after she and her husband were kicked out of the country at the behest of the President's brother. He also gave us the alias she had used when signing in on the White House visitor's log for her trysts with the President.

That alias, when revealed to the public, would be as good as a confession we were told.

We thanked the third prospect and had Miss Brennan escort him back to his suite, same as the others. Then my fellow investors and I got down to the business of deciding to whom we would make an offer and how much green with which we were willing to part.

"Load for bear," said Hoffa, "make all three an offer they can't afford to walk away from. This is a goddamn war, and we need every damn weapon we can get our hands on."

"I see it the same way," said Hunt, "those sons of bitch Kennedy's play rough and to beat them we'll need a mighty big dose of their own kind of medicine."

It turned out to be unanimous; we would make a good offer to all three prospects; the lawyer hired to make things appear nice and legal was instructed to get three drilling contracts ready to be signed. There wouldn't be much haggling for sure, and the suitcases containing the cash would be handed over to the prospects - no doubt the highest payments ever made for "drilling rights." Once all the business at the Adolphus was concluded, phone calls would be made to the proper members of the press - this was where the lawyer hired for the occasion would be most useful - and all of the "smoking guns" would be in the hands of reporters within hours. I estimated that before the day reached the noon hour, John F. Kennedy's presidency would effectively be history.

I opened a fine bottle of bourbon to celebrate and glanced at my watch, which said 9:05 p.m., the exact minute when the election of Barry Goldwater was assured.

I took a sip and distinctly remember how sweet it tasted. I often think back to that moment and savor it in my memory; the instant, when all good things were not only possible but inevitable.

I do so because the moment passed in the blink of an eye. There was a knock at the door, and Miss Brennan hurried to answer it; then everything changed.

John Compton (V)
September 1964

It turned out Lyndon Johnson knew exactly what he was talking about when he spoke as though his re-nomination for Vice President on the Kennedy ticket was assured. I thought otherwise that day in August at the White House when the ink of the President's signature on the Civil Rights Act was barely dry. I was proven quite wrong not three weeks later in Atlantic City when LBJ proclaimed it was time to go All the way with JFK and stood with arms held high on the podium the night Kennedy gave his acceptance speech to the delegates and the country.

I still didn't want to take the Vice President's offer to come work on the fall campaign having had quite enough of Washington DC for awhile. It was Senator Humphrey who convinced me to take Johnson's offer. "Johnny," he said, "you only think you'll be happy back home, but after a week of watching the campaign on the news and reading about in the paper, you'll jump on a plane, come back and beg Lyndon for a job. The work isn't finished, in your heart, you know it and won't be satisfied until it's done."

So I took the position with Johnson's campaign, and in doing so, ensured that I would have a role in one of the most unsavory chapters in the history of American politics.

My official title was Assistant Coordinator for Kennedy-Johnson '64, attached to the Vice President, in reality, my job was to keep track of Democratic fortunes in the Old Confederacy and make sure Lyndon Johnson was where he most needed to be to get him and JFK reelected.

In the fall of 1964 that seemed like a thankless job, because Dixie, including Texas, had fallen hard for Barry Goldwater. Before Labor Day, the official opening of the campaign, Goldwater-Dirksen yard signs were turning up by the scores in suburban neighborhoods from Houston to Austin to Dallas and even Lubbock. A Goldwater rally in San Antonio on September, 13th drew the largest crowd anyone could ever remember in the Lone Star state for a non-football event. "We need a Federal government," the Republican candidate thundered to the throng, "that neither steals your hard earned money or your sacred rights, guaranteed by the Constitution." The good people in the audience roared back their hearty approval. Every loyal Democratic county chairman had a story to tell about life long, Yellow Dog members of the party who were jumping to the GOP that year.

We were in trouble, and LBJ knew it, which meant there were plenty of flashes of the infamous Johnson temper behind the scenes, more than once I witnessed him tongue lash a loyal aide like Walter Jenkins to within an inch of his life. Yet he always treated me with respect, the worst I endured was a curt word after a long day. And there were a lot of long days as Johnson, grimly determined not to suffer the mortification of losing Texas in November, stumped across the state from Texarkana to El Paso as if he were running for Lieutenant Governor. The crowds which greeted the Vice President often had their enthusiasm well under control and his exhortations on behalf of Kennedy such as "We got a good man in the White House, a good friend to the farmer, the factory worker and the man who works the register at the Piggly Wiggly, and we are going to keep him there come November 3rd," was no match for Goldwater's fire and brimstone.

The lavish praise heaped on Johnson for his help in passing the Civil Rights Act only made his stock plummet in Texas and the rest of Dixie; one well-heeled Austin home builder blanketed the state with billboards denouncing "Judas Johnson."

If Texas was bad, the rest of the South was worse, as white Southerners reacted with fury against a President who dared to sign even a watered down bill favoring blacks, as poll after poll put the Republican ahead all across the Deep South and the Carolinas. There was virtually no Kennedy campaign to speak of at all in Mississippi and Wallace in Alabama was ominously silent on the race now that he was not a candidate himself. There was talk Strom Thurmond would break party ranks and endorse Goldwater, the same thing for a least a dozen Democratic members of the House from the South.

We were under the gun because a Goldwater sweep of the old Confederate states made the race extremely tight for Kennedy-Johnson in the Electoral College. Johnson's diminished state was noted in Washington D.C. where a Mary McGrory column in *The Washington Star* on September 17th summed up the thinking among the Kennedy men: "It now appears as if JFK's masterstroke in 1960 - the choice of LBJ as Vice President - threatens to come a cropper four years later as Johnson can no long guarantee Texas in the Democratic column or any other Southern state for that matter."

Then, just before Kennedy was set to return to Dallas for the first time since the assassination attempt, Johnson's dour mood suddenly brightened, for no apparent reason, for as far as everyone knew, the men running the Kennedy campaign were still perfectly content to let him twist in the dry Texas wind.

This was the state of things when, late on the evening of a hard day on the stump, the telephone rang in my Austin hotel room. The voice on the other side identified himself as Dave Powers, the assistant to the President, a man with whom I'd never spoken to before. Mr. Powers proceeded to ask me a number of questions about the day I visited Senator Russell's office and the subsequent events. The upshot of this call was me giving Powers an assurance that I could finger the man who'd given me the manila envelope if the opportunity presented itself. "Good enough, Mr. Compton," Powers said, "I shouldn't have to remind you not to discuss this call or anything we have talked about. I'll be back in touch with you in a few days." Then he hung up, leaving me more puzzled than ever.

But when the man who speaks to the President every day asks you to keep your mouth shut, you do as you are told. For the next three days, I went about the business of trying to get the ticket of Kennedy-Johnson re-elected. I even missed being there when Kennedy arrived at Love Field the day before the debate. I was a few miles away in the Dallas Hilton, trying to polish an upcoming speech for the Vice President to make him sound partisan and statesmanlike at the same time. I had just stepped out on the balcony to puff on a Marlboro when I was called to the phone. "Johnny, my boy," LBJ's voice boomed through the receiver, "I need you to do a great service for your country, for your party, and for me. I need for you to be outside the service entrance at the Hilton at eight o'clock tonight on the dot. Don't let me down. Be there." He did not give me time to respond before he hung up.

That is how I came to be at the Hotel Adolphus on the evening of September, 30th, 1964.

I did as I was told and was picked up at the Hilton by secret service agent in a black rental sedan who transported me to the rear of the Hotel Adolphus, where I was ushered inside by way of the loading dock and then up in a freight elevator to a high floor, where I was greeted by a contingent of agents, who tersely informed me to wait there.

I really did not get nervous standing there in the hallway, surrounded by unsmiling and silent Secret Service agents. Was I under investigation? My mind raced as I recalled the events of the summer afternoon that began with the visit to Senator Russell's office and ended with me handing the envelope over to Lyndon Johnson in the Vice President's office. I desperately tried to remember every action, every word spoken, during the hour and a half that began with me arriving at the Senator's office and ending with my exit from the Vice President's.

Then a man rounded a corner and stuck his hand out. "Good to meet you, John Compton," he said. "I'm Dave Powers; I believe we had a conversation on the phone a few days ago. Please come with me," I followed him back around a corner and down a long plush carpeted hallway, passing multiple doors with room numbers affixed to them. "As you might have surmised, Mr. Compton," Powers said as we walked. "Your presence here relates to our earlier conversation on the phone. I do apologize for the brusqueness with which you were compelled to be here, but I think you'll understand."

At first, I thought the place was empty, but through the dim lighting, I began to make out silhouettes amongst the shadows at the far end of the corridor. As we grew closer, I easily picked out a few more Secret Service agents among them, but there were others there as well, including a young man wearing a suit and tie quite a bit more fashionable than the attire of the government men. One door was cracked open slightly, through it I glimpsed an older man sitting on the end of a bed, smoking a cigar; through the half open door I could feel this man's gaze lock on me, and I had the distinct impression I was being "sized up."

Without saying a word to anyone milling around in the corridor, Mr. Powers stopped at a door and knocked; from inside the suite came the sound of voices, they were loud…and angry, but muffled just enough so as to keep me from understanding what was being said. They fell silent, and the door opened just wide enough for someone to step out into the hall. He was a younger man, and though he was wearing a business suit similar to the Secret Service, from his bearing, I pegged him for being military and not just any branch of the service, but Marine. This hunch proved to be correct when Powers addressed him as Colonel and said, "This is the guy who can clinch the case."

The Colonel nodded and crossed the corridor to another suite, opening the door and beckoning me to follow. "John Compton," the Colonel said, "do you recognize either of these gentlemen." I stood in the doorway looking at two men sitting on the edge of a bed, both looked as if they were about to be marched in front of a firing squad. The oldest of the pair I did not know, he had the features of a man who'd drunk too much Ancient Age, smoked too many unfiltered cigarettes and was starting to pay the price. I did recognize the other; he was wearing the same fine linen summer suit and still sporting a black bow tie. It was the man who had given me the manila envelope with the bulge in the bar on that day back in July. That is what I told the Colonel and Dave Powers, who were both standing in the room.

"Johnny my boy," said Lyndon Johnson, who stepped out of the bathroom as soon as I made my identification, "I'm so sorry you had to get caught up in this shit, but it just couldn't be helped."

Kevin McCluskey (III)
September 1964

The Los Angeles riots were a potential disaster for us; it is never good for any incumbent President when a major American city is turned into a war zone. By flying there at the height of the trouble, Kennedy earned some good press and more than a little credit for helping calm a deteriorating situation. The problem came with the footage of looting and burning by mobs of black Americans coming not a month after the President signed the Civil Rights Act; millions of nervous white suburban voters had no trouble making the connection; within days, Goldwater's speeches began sounding a most unsubtle theme: the Negroes are out of control, and it's all Kennedy's fault. "Over and over," the Arizona Senator proclaimed at the first debate in San Francisco, "this administration has given aid and comfort to those who excuse the robber, the looter, the mugger; over and over this administration has extended an open hand to those who have no respect for law and order, those who sow dissension and rancor, those who have no respect for property. And what do we have to show for it, an American city in flames."

I thought the President gave it back twice over when Goldwater basically said he'd bayonet demonstrators who engaged in sit-ins because they were a threat to public order. "The right to redress grievances is guaranteed by the Constitution to every citizen, no matter the color of their skin. More to point, it has fallen to this generation to take up the great unfinished business of American history, business that has been left unfinished since Appomattox; business that refuses to go unfinished any longer. The unfinished business of equality between the races will not go away; it will not be intimidated and silenced by the threat of a bayonet, a police dog or a fire hose. I have met this problem head on and dealt with it as the moral crisis it is: Senator Goldwater believes he can brutalize the righteous cause of aggrieved Negro Americans into submission. He is wrong."

The effect of the first debate was to harden the poll numbers in place with the President ahead by no more than 5 points at best; Kennedy had come off good enough to fire up Democrats, but Goldwater, whom I thought had come off as angry and hard-hearted, had told his fervid supporters exactly what they wanted to hear and they loved him for it. More to the point, the Senator's tactic of lumping Civil Rights protestors in with street criminals and looters scored points with a lot of blue collar Democrats in the North - again, I remembered the Wallace rally in Wisconsin during that long ago primary in the early spring.

The plan had been for the President to put Goldwater away in the first debate and pull into an insurmountable lead and ride it all the way to November. When things did not work out that way, Bobby Kennedy was furious; according to some accounts which trickled down to us on the lower rungs, there were some intense meetings behind closed doors at the headquarters down on Pennsylvania Avenue. If anyone thought the gloves were coming off, there was one problem, John and Bobby Kennedy never put on gloves in the first place. We just kept on doing what we'd been doing, only more so.

By more so, it meant sharpening up the adds we ran against Goldwater, a week after the first debate, the "Daisy" spot began running on TV - the one that starts with the little girl plucking the petals off a flower and ends with a countdown, a nuclear explosion and an excerpt from President Kennedy's speech at Andrews Air Force Base right after he got back from the New Delhi summit where he said, "If we do not see our opponents as human beings, then all of humanity is doomed." It was tough stuff, the Goldwater campaign cried foul, claiming the spot implied their candidate was a war monger; our response was basically "so what." The ad was damned effective, especially with the independents we were trying to reach, but in the years since, I've had many a staunch Democrat tell me they thought the spot was a low blow.

The plan was to put Goldwater on the defensive, paint him as a cowboy who'd reach for the nuclear button like it was a six-gun; Kennedy would run as the rational President who'd stood up to the Communists in Cuba, Vietnam and Korea, but who was not afraid to extend his hand to Khrushchev in the hour of maximum danger and avert World War III. It was a point the President made at every campaign appearance from coast to coast. Goldwater and his surrogates fired back: by attacking the planned withdraw from Cuba as a sellout; by questioning why there was still a large Soviet contingent on the island, functioning freely in the city of Camaguey and giving sanctuary to many of worst characters in Castro's regime; why was Castro still living like a king in a cell in Guantanamo Bay when he should have been marched before a Cuban firing squad months ago; how the Soviets had walked over two-thirds of Iran without a single American bomber being sent in to impede them; why was our staunch ally, the Shah, still in exile in Paris and not back on the Peacock throne; why had North Korea been allowed off the hook for the second time in a little more than a generation; why was South Vietnam being sold down the river after it was the victim of naked Communist aggression. After all these crimes and incompetence, how could the country trust Kennedy, the man who let an opportunity to win a decisive victory in the Cold War slip away because liberals are simply not tough enough to win.

After the first debate, the President hit the campaign trail hard, filling up stadiums and walking in parades in every city with a population over a hundred thousand from New England to the Great Plains, the part of the country where the most wavering independents could be found if the polls were to be believed. Because he had sat out the primary season and not made a partisan appearance until just before the convention at the end of August, Kennedy's campaigning skills should have been rusty, but if that was true, the man got back up to speed in no time. Day after day, the John F. Kennedy of 1964 strode to the podium before massive crowds of cheering Americans and had them hanging on his every word as he spoke of a United States secure and at peace, with prosperity shared by all; and by all, he made a point of stressing, that meant the black man too. "Do not listen to the naysayer, the fearful, the angry and the bitter," he told an audience in Akron, Ohio on the 20th of September, "America is not a nation in decline. Through this generation's hard work and sacrifice, there is a great future ahead of us…if we have the courage and grit to grasp it." I thought it was one of his best lines; a lot of credit is given to Ted Sorenson and his team of speechwriters, but it was the President who delivered them to such great effect.

If the President projected confidence before the American people, it was another story behind the scenes as Larry O'Brien and Bobby Kennedy pushed everyone like we were down by 10 points. No one was cut any slack, and as a designated troubleshooter, my reports to headquarters cost a lot of party hacks their cushy positions in a dozen states by mid-September - no one was allowed to just take up space and ride coat tails.

I heard an earful out on the road as well.

Most memorable was my trip to Austin, Texas, where I did not have the pleasure of meeting the Vice President, but I got more than an earful from the state senator who was the assistant to the Chairman of Re-Elect Kennedy-Johnson in the Lone Star state. "You Goddamn Yankees," he drawled to me in a conference room in the state capitol building, "always screwing it up. Kennedy could have at least waited until the second term to sign a Goddamn Civil Rights Act. And JFK wouldn't be in the White House in the first place if it wasn't for Lyndon and the votes he went out and got for Kennedy in Dixie four years ago. Now you're expecting him to do it again and it's damn near impossible because most Texans think Kennedy is siding with the niggers and Goldwater is the only one sticking up for white people."

In short, they were not happy with us in Texas as the date for the second debate between Kennedy and Goldwater, set for Dallas on the first day of October; as it turned out, that would not be my concern, for I was given specific other duties on the next to last day of September.

These are events I have never spoken of. Since for years I was told that if I did so, I would be investigated, hauled before a grand jury, forced to hire a lawyer and very likely be indicted for bribery and extortion. Over the years I have been asked many times about Dallas by investigative journalists, historians and crackpots of all kinds on what transpired the day before the second Kenney-Goldwater debate, and I always remained silent. I didn't care so much about myself, but there were family considerations.

While on the trip to Austin, I received a call from the national headquarters, ordering me to drop everything, book a flight, and be back in DC before first light the next day. It was eleven hours later, at a little past 3:30 a.m., when I walked into Steve Smith's office and was greeted by him and Dave Powers, who complimented me on the good job I was doing for the campaign, especially the discreet manner in which I had handled a number of sensitive chores on behalf of re-electing the President. "Kevin," Mr. Powers said, "the Attorney General has been most impressed by work you've been doing for us; especially with the degree of prudence you've brought to the job. He has a special chore for you, something which has to be done ahead of the debate on Tuesday, and one that's a hell of lot more important than anything you've done so far for the President. It's going to mean turning around and going right back to Texas on no sleep. Think you can do it?"

I did not hesitate to answer in the affirmative, and yes, I knew damn well that "prudence" and "special" where synonymous with unethical.

I listened carefully and intently, as the instructions were given to me verbally, nothing was put on paper. I asked a few pertinent questions and then did exactly as I was told; twenty-four hours later I was sitting inside a DC-3 on the tarmac at Love Field in Dallas Texas. Also inside the plane were a half dozen trunks - the kind travelers used when they booked passage on an ocean liner - and two men hired to guard them - my job was not to let those trunks out of my sight from the time we took off at National Airport until they reached their destination in Dallas by way of a stopover in Baton Rouge.

At the airport, I made some phone calls; then we sat in the DC-3 and waited a few hours until the sun had set. During the wait, I ordered take out and talked baseball and hockey with the two hired guards; all the while making sure the trunks never left my gaze.

We loaded the trunks into another rental just after sundown and drove them to the appointed destination - one I had been given by Mr. Powers back in DC. It was the service entrance of the Adolphus Hotel; by the looks of the place when we arrived, we were not the only ones expected. There were a number of cars parked in the back alley and out on the street, I could hardly maneuver the rental truck up to the loading dock. Mr. Powers was there to meet us and I distinctly remember how he complimented me for being punctual - it was just after 9:00 p.m., the exact time we were to arrive. We unloaded the trunks and stacked them aboard a flat-bed cart, the kind used at the hotel to haul luggage. The hire guards left in the rental, and I never saw either of them again. Accompanying Mr. Powers were a pair of Secret Service agents, who took over the duties of the hired guns, duties which did not include any type of manual labor, for I had to push the flat bed cart into the freight elevator that took us to an upper floor.

Once there, Mr. Powers directed me to push the cart down a long hall to a suite whose number I don't remember now. What I do remember is the loud voice coming from behind one door as we passed, I could not make out the words, but more than one somebody sounded like they were not happy.

As soon as we were inside the room, Mr. Powers produced a set of keys and proceeded to unlock the trunks and open them. Their contents did not surprise me, for I had figured it out back in DC: rows upon rows of neatly stacked twenty dollar bills. How much it added up to, I would not venture a guess, but well into the six figures by the look of it. One thing was plain - it was obvious a lot of people besides me had carried brief-cases filled with money back to Kennedy '64 headquarters.

"Kevin, I'm going to need you to sit tight," Mr. Powers informed as he shut and locked the trunks, "and be ready to be of use the minute you're needed. I don't have to tell you because you've proved yourself over and over to the campaign and the President, but the reason why you're here and what we're doing here requires ultimate discretion." I answered in the affirmative, ever mindful of what "discretion" truly meant.

That is what I thought in the moment I answered Mr. Powers, but I had no idea how much "ultimate discretion" this night would ultimately require from me. I was to learn and learn fast, starting minutes later when I followed Mr. Powers back into the hallway: an older man in a dark pinstripe was entering the room directly across from us; for an instant, the door was open, and I caught a glimpse of another man on the inside.

The other man was Richard M. Nixon.

Colonel Martin Maddox (VIII)
September 1964

If someone in the waning days of the summer of '64 had have told me that my next field of battle would be a Dallas hotel room, and that it would be as fierce and decisive as any frozen ground I'd trod in Korea, I'd have said they were full of shit.

A week before the second Kennedy-Goldwater debate, I was informed by way of a phone call from the President himself that I would be accompanying him to Dallas. I asked the President why it was necessary for me to leave my post in DC for a purely political event. His reply was a familiar one, "Colonel, I need a man with your experience with me."

As far as the press was concerned, I would be there in the Presidential party in an advisory capacity, and except for those few words from the President, I heard nothing more from the White House except for the departure time and when I needed to be at Andrews in order to be on Air Force One when it left for Big D on the morning of September 30th. I spent most of the trip sitting in the back of the plane while the President was huddled with closest aides and some of his most important advisors like Theodore Sorenson and Arthur Schlesinger, all of whom, I assumed, were prepping him for his second debate with Senator Goldwater. I was following the campaign with great interest and was well aware of how the first debate had been something of a success for the Republican candidate simply because of the perception that he'd held his own against charismatic Kennedy. So a lot was riding on this second encounter between Kennedy and Goldwater, and the President needed to do whatever he had to do to get back to his "fighting weight" so to speak.

We were 30 minutes from touching down in Dallas, and I was napping when an aide woke me up and relayed an order from the President that I come to his cabin immediately. I did as requested and found a tired looking John F. Kennedy, with his shirt sleeves rolled up and without a tie, doing his best to relax. Also in the cabin were David Powers and Kenneth O'Donnell, the two closest to the President after his brother.

President Kennedy beckoned me to take a seat. "Colonel," he said, "a short time back, I asked if you could remain silent while you heard events in which you took part described differently than you knew them to be. The events I am referring to is your trip last spring to New Orleans, and I'm asking you here and now what I asked you before: can you remain silent?"

Nothing had changed since our first discussion as far as I knew, so my answer was, "Yes sir."

"Do not take this lightly, Colonel," the President continued, "because your silence may open you to accusations that you are complicit in a lie and your honor will be impugned. Think you can deal with that?"

There are those who think I should have told the President that a United States Marine never simply stands there and let's mud or worse be thrown on his character. All I can say is that they were not on Air Force One minutes from Dallas with John F. Kennedy looking you in the eye; there was no way I was not going to give the President the answer he wanted to hear.

"Yes, sir," I said for the second time, "I can deal with it." Although I've questioned the wisdom of my answer over the years, I've never regretted it.

Describing the crowd at Love Field as enthusiastic hardly does them justice on the day John F. Kennedy returned to Dallas; they went wild when the President walked off the plane and across the tarmac. The people in Dallas knew they had been given a second chance and they turned out determined not to let so much as a discouraging word ruin the moment. What President Kennedy was thinking as he came down the steps and approached the roaring crowd, kept at a safe distance by a chain link fence, I would not venture a guess, but there was no way he could not remember how close he came to having it all end in a split second on a street only minutes away.

He shook the outstretched hands and acknowledged the many signs that said some variation of "Dallas Loves JFK," before moving on to a waiting limo. There would be no repeat of that fateful motorcade from 10 months earlier; the car sped away with a heavy police escort with the rest of us following in backup vehicles. Another parade was out of the question this time, if for no other reason than they would have to do the same thing for Senator Goldwater when he arrived the next day out of simple courtesy.

Our destination was a large ranch house, which had been donated by a prominent and well-connected Democrat for the President's use before the debate - lots of spacious rooms with high ceilings. For most of the afternoon, I simply stayed out of the way of the President's men, who were involved in debate prep sessions with him. Later in the day, another limo arrived and out popped Vice President Johnson, who had not been at the airport to greet the President because of a campaign event in San Antonio. President Kennedy came out to greet his Vice President, who looked tired and tense.

The two men stood in the drive for a few minutes, but instead of going inside, they strolled out into the yard, all the way to a far corner. There they stood for some time, engaged in an animated conversation: first Johnson gesticulating wildly with his hands, all but jabbing the President in the chest with his finger. At length, Johnson must have finished his say because JFK's hands went to his hips and he began to talk for another five minutes, occasionally wagging his finger in the air as if to underscore a point. Finally, the President offered his hand, and Johnson shook it vigorously as if some agreement had been reached. I was not the only one observing, as every window in the house was filled with the President's men, watching the drama.

The Vice President got himself a drink and was soon regaling some junior Kennedy men with political stories from years past, while the senior men barely acknowledged his presence and kept a noticeable distance. It was a couple of hours later when an aide came and found me with the message the President wanted to see me about some point that might come up in the debate. In an upstairs office, I found the President seated at a desk with Mr. Powers and Mr. O'Donnell sitting on a couch; a chair was offered to me.

"Colonel," the President said, coming right to the point, "there is a conspiracy at work in this city, a conspiracy whose purpose is to destroy this administration, to undermine all the hard work we have done in the last four years. It is a conspiracy that is about to come together and succeed because it is about to get possession of evidence which could expose our dealings with certain dubious individuals who were in a position to give us aid in our efforts the rid Cuba of Castro. To the public at large these dealings will make it appear as if this administration is morally compromised; if made known, there will be lengthy investigations, Congressional hearings, which will likely be televised, grand juries impaneled and indictments issued. This could all end in trials, convictions, huge legal bills, and reputations irrevocably ruined, not to mention a jail sentence."

Thanks to the message from Harlow, I knew all about it, some rat was selling us out, and if that happened, my future would be grim.

The President continued, "If this conspiracy does succeed, I will not be re-elected, there will be no summit with Khrushchev and a hard-won opportunity to change the direction of Cold War, and make the world a much safer place for our children will be lost for good. This cannot be allowed to happen, and we must do everything possible to make sure it does not happen. And to do that, Colonel Maddox, I will need your help. Earlier today, you assured me of your silence when it could be most critical; now I'm asking you to do whatever it will take to help me stop this conspiracy in its tracks before any damage is done. Can I count on you to do just that?"

Until right then, I had not seen the whole picture nor realized how deep in the mire I had sunk.

"Yes, sir, Mr. President, whatever it takes, you can count on me."

After the President left the room, Mr. Powers and Mr. O'Donnell enlightened me further. "To put it in blunt language the President won't use," Mr. O'Donnell said, "this is about dirty laundry being aired in public. Very dirty laundry."

Mr. Powers was even more succinct. "There are people in Dallas gunning for the President again. What we - with your help - are going to do is make sure they take their fingers off the triggers, put their weapons down and then walk away no worse for the wear. If that does not happen, if triggers are pulled, then by this time tomorrow, this President, this administration and everyone associated with it, will be finished."

They then filled me in on the details of what would be occurring in the next few hours and what my part would be; looking back, what they said didn't come close to preparing me for what really happened.

Later in the afternoon, while most of us were catching a bite to eat, four black 1963 Chevrolet Impalas, rented from a dealer in Fort Worth, were delivered to the ranch. They were vehicles much less conspicuous than the Presidential limos or any other autos in the

Presidential party, all of which were well known on sight to the press. Sometime late in the day, I was able to snag a quick shower and change into a civilian suit, something both Mr. Powers and Mr. O'Donnell had insisted I do.

This is what happened on the evening of September 30, 1964 as I remember it.

There was only a faint glow left in the western sky when those four rented Chevrolets left the ranch house, I was in the second car with part of the Secret Service detail, most of the others were in the first car, the President and his aides road in the third with the Vice President bringing up the rear. We drove back into Dallas, taking extra turns and slight detours to make sure no one was following.

The car I was traveling in parked a few blocks from the hotel and we walked the rest of the way as another precaution against being followed. The Secret Service had already secured the service area and dock at the rear of the hotel by the time I arrived. The agent in charge radioed that all was clear; moments later, the one carrying the President pulled up to the dock, and John F. Kennedy got out and walked confidently up the narrow back steps into the building as if he were going to a Cabinet meeting. The rest of us, including Mr. Powers and Mr. O'Donnell, followed him inside.

A few minutes later, the vehicle carrying the Vice President and the other agents arrived; everyone gathered just off the loading dock where we were met by the chief of the of the Secret Service, who was holding a freight elevator. This was where I got my first big surprise of the evening, for standing there in the middle of the dock was Carlos Marcello, puffing on a cigar and looking none too happy to be there, not only was the Mafia boss of New Orleans in the room, but Guy Bannister as well, along with the man with the painted on eyebrows, Neither of them appeared to be pleased to be there either, both Marcello and Bannister glowered at the President, while their companion stared at the concrete floor. When the President entered the room, two large agents placed themselves directly in front of Marcello, obviously making sure he didn't get anywhere close to Kennedy. Marcello responded by making sure an ample amount of cigar smoke drifted into the agent's faces.

There were was another man there too, older and well dressed - his suit was clearly not off the rack - wearing a pair of horn-rimmed glasses and obviously not part of the New Orleans group. He was clutching a brief case tight to his chest, as though it contained something precious.

"Is everything ready?" the President asked as he looked around the room. "Is everyone here?"

"The cargo from DC is on its way from the airport," Powers replied. "It'll be here in a few minutes."

"It had better be," President Kennedy said, "because if it doesn't, then we don't have any rounds in our chambers; anybody else we're missing?"

"My boy Johnny's on the way," I heard the Vice President say, "he'll be here in a few minutes."

"Can't wait on him," Kennedy said, impatience in his voice, "we got to get this show on the road."

The President, Johnson, O'Donnell, and a Secret Service contingent got on the freight elevator and rode up. It was a good long eight or nine minutes before it returned to the ground floor. During that time, I could feel more than one pair of eyes boring holes into my back; Marcello and Bannister had recognized me, but not a word was spoken while we waited. When the doors of the elevator finally rattled open, the rest of us crowded inside, leaving only a pair of agents and Dave Powers behind to guard the loading dock.

After a quick ride up, the doors opened on a high floor filled with executive suites, the carpet in the hallway seemed especially plush. The President and the Vice President were having a discussion with the chief of the Secret Service detail, who was refusing to let them proceed until they were sure no one in a certain room was armed. I remembered what Mr. Powers had told me about there being people in Dallas gunning for the President.

Then an agent gave us the all clear, and I followed the President down the hall to a room at the far end.

None of my speculation could have prepared me for what happened next.

The agent leading the way stopped and knocked at the door to Room 721, two agents went through first, then the President, followed by the Vice President; I was further back, still in the hall, but it was impossible not to hear the shout of "You Goddamn son of a bitch, you got your fuckin' nerve," come from within.

What was going on in the suite might have been a bachelor party, one cut short by the President's arrival; there was a bar with open whiskey bottles and ice buckets, trays of finger foods set around, even a most attractive blonde who might have been mistaken for the entertainment if she hadn't been dressed like a secretary.

But it is safe to say that no wild bachelor party had numbered among its revelers, guests like H. L. Hunt, the most infamous of all Texas oil millionaires and James R. "Jimmy" Hoffa himself, the President of the International Brotherhood of the Teamsters. There was another man with them, who was not familiar to me, but I put him in the same class as Mr. Hunt, if for no other reason than the dark suit and distinctive string tie he was wearing - the kind you saw a lot of among the well-heeled in this part of the country. There was a fourth man, rather heavyset and clearly not cut from the same cloth as the others; something made obvious by the plaid sports coat he wore, who retreated behind the bar. The young lady, who looked quite out of place in this company, found refuge in a corner as if she wanted no part of this confrontation.

If looks could have killed, Hoffa would have put John F. Kennedy in the ground right then and there; Mr. Hunt and his friend wore similar expressions. I soon learned the third man's name: Wade Harbinson, an oilman, who if not quite in the league of Mr. Hunt, still stood pretty tall in Texas. Two Secret Service agents placed themselves firmly between this trio and the President and the Vice President. Otherwise the situation resembled a showdown from a John Ford western, with Kennedy and company on one side and Hoffa and friends on the other, the only things missing were the six shooters strapped around their hips.

What followed was indeed a showdown, one where words proved to be as lethal as bullets. "Good evening, gentlemen, and Mr. Hoffa," the President said as if he were greeting them in the Oval Office, "I heard about the business you were conducting here tonight, so I thought I'd come over and put my own offer on the table."

As President Kennedy spoke these words, from outside in the hall, there came the sounds of fists hammering on doors and demands from agents to open up.

Earlier, when Mr. Powers and Mr. O'Donnell filled me in on the details of this evening, I'd learned there were three different parties peddling info which could destroy the President, one of them involving our dealings with the Mafia. The other two concerned allegations of lying and adultery, but it would be all or nothing, because if one saw the light of day, all three surely would.

Mr. Hunt attempted to deny the whole thing. "We are legitimate businessmen, Mr. President," he said when Kennedy was finished, "and we have every right to conduct our affairs in private. With all due respect, sir, we do not answer to you, and you have no right to be here. Please leave."

The President's reply, "I believe you gentlemen have three million dollars in cash in another room on this floor, that doesn't sound like legitimate business to me. Same for theft of confidential documents, attempted blackmail, the exposure of a top secret operation against a hostile foreign government. Or let me put it this way: extortion, conspiracy and treason, just some of the charges which could be levied against you in federal court."

Upon hearing these words, the young lady spoke up and said she was leaving. "Miss, you may leave the room, no one will stop you, but I do insist you stay on this floor, at least until your employers and I have finished our business. Thank you very much." The President's tone changed on a dime when speaking to the blonde; he was firm, but the charm was there as well. She hurried out the door; the Vice President, who had said nothing so far, followed behind her.

Mr. Harbinson spoke up next. "Mr. President, if anyone is guilty of conspiracy and treason in here, it is not my two friends or me."

President Kennedy found a seat on a couch and then replied, "Treason is often in the eye of the beholder, Mr. Harbinson, or may I call you Wade? I know Mr. Hoffa prefers to be called Jimmy, isn't that right, Jimmy?"

After being pretty much silent so far, Mr. Hoffa spoke up. "You can call me Fuck You for all I give a damn, Kennedy; you and your Goddamn brother both." An agent took a step closer, as if to block the Teamster boss in case he decided to let his actions match his words. The agent got the most ferocious glare I've ever seen in return.

The President merely smiled at this outburst and said, "That's no way for a businessman to talk, Jimmy. And since we're here to do business and time is of the essence, let me put my counter offer on the table."

Mr. Harbinson and his two associates responded in the most vociferous terms that it was none of anybody's business what they were doing in that room.

It did them no good. Minutes after the President and the Vice President arrived at the Adolphus, so did a large sum of cash money from DC - which was trucked up to our floor in traveling trunks, so did Johnson's "boy" the President referred to earlier. He was a man whose last name was Compton, and as soon as he arrived, John F. Kennedy had all the ammunition he needed to take on these three who were determined to bring him down.

Take them on is just what he did.

Three different parties came to the Adolphus with dirt on the President in hand and the expectation of profiting from it. Each one was safely tucked away in their own suites on the same floor all paid for by Mr. Harbinson after striking deals with him and his partners to destroy the President. Now they would have to come back into that same room and face the man they traveled far to ruin.

First up was a young man named Bentley Braden and his older partner; they possessed a tape recording of a young woman who described in detail an illicit sexual relationship with the President. Mr. Braden came from a prominent South Carolina family, and whose listed occupation was lobbyist for the textile industry. The older man, whose name I will not mention here, simply because he later had a distinguished career in public service and I do not wish to cause his family distress, had been quite close to the Kennedy family, raising lots of money for the '60 campaign. Once having been successful in the real estate game, he was now broke after years of lavish living, and it seemed he felt used and discarded by the Kennedy brothers during his hard time. Both of them were quite familiar with the Quorum Club where the woman in question had been employed.

Braden and his partner panicked when confronted in their suite by the Secret Service, and were more than willing to talk when Lyndon Johnson came in and insinuated he might be able to help them out. I was asked to be in the room when Compton identified Braden as the man who had given him a package in DC containing a copy of the damaging tape in an attempted blackmail plot.

Once they were marched down the hall to the room where the President was waiting, the older of the two broke down and sobbed. It was Mr. Powers who did the talking while the President gazed down at the floor, clearly unable to look at his former friend. It was explained to them that the warrants were already written charging them with extortion, the only thing between them and the Dallas County Jail was a phone call and a signature.

"There will be trials and scandal," Mr. Powers explained, "reputations will be ruined, and careers flushed down the toilet. That is how it will go if you take Mister Harbinson and his associates up on their offer. You might take down the President, but neither one of you will ever enjoy spending one dime of their money. On the other hand, you can enjoy spending our money."

That really got the two would be blackmailers attention.

The offer was simple, in return for all copies of the incriminating tape, Braden and his associate would walk out of the Hotel Adolphus with a million dollars in cash to split between them.

Mr. Harbinson shouted for them not to take the deal, that, "President Goldwater will make sure neither of you ever spent a day in jail."

They were then reminded that if it came to charges, the two of them would be tried in a Texas state court, and whoever was President would have no jurisdiction.

From the look on his face, I think Bentley Braden would have told Dave Powers to go pound sand; I later learned that like many Southerners, he had an inordinate reverence for the Old Confederacy and a distinct dislike for John and Robert Kennedy and their sympathy for the cause of equal rights. He had tried to short-circuit the debate on the Civil Rights Act by slipping a copy of the tape to a certain Georgia Senator who wanted no part of it. This was how a copy came into John Compton's hands, who delivered it to the Vice President.

It was Braden's associate who spoke up instead, saying they would gladly take the President's offer. He then spoke directly to the Kennedy, saying words could not express how sorry he was for what he'd done. President Kennedy never once responded directly to him, but he did call Harbinson's lawyer over and told him to give the man one of those phony lease agreements for him and Braden to sign. "That way they can tell the world they came by the money legally." That was the closest the President came to saying anything to his former friend. Braden tried to object, but his partner told him to shut his mouth in no uncertain terms; he did the fool a favor, since if I read him right, Bentley Braden, who weighed 120 pounds soaking wet, was, as they used to say, "a little light in the loafers," and I don't think he would have enjoyed a stretch in a Texas prison.

The lawyer, who was a local Dallas attorney named Dean Andrews, was more than happy to comply with the President's wishes, the man obviously knew he could be disbarred for what he was doing and just as obviously, wanted to curry some favor with the side most in a position to do him the most harm.

As the deal with Braden and his partners were being finalized, the next group of dirt dealers was ushered down the hall from their suite. These were the men who were peddling information on the Administration's dealings with the Mafia; the end of my career would be the least consequence if what they had became public. There was a half-dozen of them, all men who'd held positions of authority in Cuba under the old dictator; their leader was Ramon Zayas, a member of a prominent family which included one of Batista's puppet Prime Ministers. Zayas was a former police captain in the Cuban capital, where his chief duty was to ensure that Batista's nightly cut from the casinos made it to the President's office first thing in the morning; his other responsibilities included making sure

Trafficante's daily take from the same establishments got safely on the plane to Miami. After the Revolution, Zayas and his cronies ended up penniless in America where they had to go hat in hand to their old Mafia bosses and beg for work; somehow he wound up in the middle of Operation Mongoose, a good place to pick up inside information. Zayas proved to be a competent detective, uncovering knowledge some men would pay very dear to know. This Zayas and his retinue, all dressed like they were going out for a night at a Havana nightclub, had done while true patriots like Harry Williams and Manual Airtime were dying to free their homeland.

Be that as it may, Zayas strode into the room with his men behind him, all carrying satchels and cases which contained the proof positive that the administration of John F. Kennedy was involved in an ongoing conspiracy with racketeers and murderers for mutual gain. "I am not afraid of you, Mr. President," he said upon entering, "the truth will protect me."

"There is no need for anyone here to be afraid," replied Kennedy, "we're all going to leave here as good friends; I'm sure of it."

"You are no friend of the Cuban people," Zayas spat. "Because of you, they lived years under a Communist dictator; because of you, my brother died in a hopeless battle on a beach. You could have liberated Cuba anytime, but only when your own life was nearly cut short by a bullet through the head did you act. Only when a drop of your blood was nearly spilled, not before an ocean of Cuban blood had drenched the island. Threaten me all you want, Mr. Kennedy; I will not bend for you."

The President sat and nodded as Zayas spoke, appearing completely unperturbed.

"That man is telling the truth!" Harbinson shouted when the Cuban was finished. "He's got the goods on your whole crew, enough proof to convince the world that the great JFK is in bed with the Mafia, making deals with murderers and pimps and worse while good American boys are dying in Cuba just so some crooks can get their swanky hotels and casinos back."

"This man is hardly speaking the truth," said Kennedy. "To start with, he didn't have a brother die fighting against Castro, as of this date, both of Mr. Zayas's brothers are currently running a brothel in Panama. But just so some crooks can get their swanky hotels and casinos back?' I've arranged for some pertinent people to be here tonight and set the record straight."

At this point, the door was opened, and Marcello, Bannister and the guy with the painted on eyebrows, whose name I later learned was David Ferrie, were ushered inside. The sight of the Mafia Kingpin of New Orleans in their midst had an immediate impact on Zayas and his crew, from the expressions on their faces, the Grim Reaper himself might as well have walked through the door.

Marcello took in a seat in an empty sofa chair without asking permission and promptly lit up a cigar and started puffing away while Bannister and Ferrie flanked him. The Secret

Service agents did a quick shuffle to reposition themselves so that some of them were between President Kennedy and a man who seriously entertained the thought of having the President assassinated.

The President continued, "I have asked Mr. Marcello to be here to set some things straight and clear up some misunderstandings. I understand how some parties might come to believe there has been a quid pro quo between the government and men in Mr. Marcello's line of work, but that's not the case. Is it?"

This was evidently Bannister and Ferrie's cue to speak up; they began by introducing themselves as a retired FBI agent turned private investigator and a former airline pilot respectively. Taking turns, they went on to detail how they became involved in aiding Operation Mongoose to free Cuba from the grip of Castro, doing so out of a deep-seated hatred for everything Communism stood for and a proud love of America. They had worked over the past few years with a number of organizations dedicated to helping free Cuba; Bannister chief contribution being a purchaser of arms while Ferrie flew the weapons to rebel camps in Central America. In this good work, they had turned to a man who had often employed their services in the past, Carlos Marcello of New Orleans, a man who shared their desire to rid Cuba of Castro. More than once, Marcello had stepped in to provide needed financial assistance to help pay for fuel for boats and planes. Marcello had provided other assistance as well; because he was a heavy investor in Cuba before the Communists took over and a frequent visitor to the island, he had given the American government vital intelligence, also convincing his good friend, Santos Trafficante, whose knowledge of Cuba was vaster than his own, to help the government as well. At no time was there any compensation from Uncle Sam for their help in ousting Castro, nor was there any promise of compensation in the future. "Everything we did, we did out of hatred for Castro and love for our country," was how Bannister summed it up.

"I've never heard so much bullshit in my life," was how Harbinson immediately responded. "That man," he pointed at Marcello and said, "was nearly deported by the Kennedy Justice Department as an undesirable alien; less than a year ago he was in a Federal courtroom being tried on charges of extortion and racketeering before beating the rap. There is no way he or any of you would ever do anything simply out of love of country. You're not patriots, you are all mobsters and worse, and you don't get out of bed in the morning unless you're getting paid."

Carlos Marcello's response was to simply puff on his cigar and glower.

Harbinson then turned on me. "You are a Colonel in the Marines," he said, "and you were negotiating face to face with these gangsters. There are pictures of you with them, so don't deny it and or say they were doctored. That won't fly here. Tell the truth here and now; you represented this administration, you spoke for the President, and you shook hands on a deal to return to the Mafia all their hotels, and nightclubs and casinos in Havana after good American boys died liberating them from Castro. Tell the truth, Colonel!"

It was the moment the President warned me about, the moment when a lie was to be told, and I would be required to remain silent.

President Kennedy spoke up. "Colonel Maddox was involved in an intricate way in the planning for the invasion of Cuba, in that capacity, he spoke to many intelligence sources, among them Mr. Marcello here, and his associate Mr. Trafficante. Together, they gave us the names of many patriotic Cubans who would be most willing to aid the American military in its battle to free the island and the occupation afterward. For reasons I think you will understand, Mr. Harbinson, our contacts with these men had to be handled most delicately and confidentially. It was something which could not be done through regular channels or documented in any way. A lot of intelligence work is conducted this way, but at no time was any quid pro quo deal made with either Mr. Marcello here or Mr. Trafficante. You might have the pictures, but they tell you nothing about what was said."

"With all due respect, Mr. President," said Harbinson, "I asked the Colonel a question, and I would appreciate it if he would answer me."

I did not waver in my duty, not once, not on a battlefield in Korea or in a hotel room in Dallas, Texas.

"What the President said is true, no deals were made, and if Captain Zayas says otherwise, then he is lying." I'll let those words stand for themselves.

Harbinson looked at me like he was about to spit, he knew he'd lost.

Throughout all this, Zayas and his accomplices were sweating bullets because their little attempt at a big payday at Carlos Marcello's expense had been exposed with the man himself in the room.

The President wrapped it up by saying he had a deal to propose: in return for a specific and substantial sum of money, Ramon Zayas would surrender all evidence he had gathered on any purported collaboration between the Administration and the Mafia. This was not to taken as a confirmation of validity by the President, simply as a preventive matter in an election year. "We'll even dress it up as one of Mr. Harbinson's lease deals," he said, "just to make it all appear legal."

Zayas was more than happy to accept the offer; I think he would have agreed to anything that would have gotten him out of the presence of Carlos Marcello. It again fell to Mr. Powers to usher Zayas and his cohort to the other suite, where the co-opted Mr. Andrews would get the appropriate paperwork done to make it look like Mr. Zayas had just bought the leasing rights to some oil rich land.

Marcello, Bannister and Ferrie were escorted out a few minutes later by the Secret Service; the Mafia boss did not acknowledge anyone, except for a quick nod to the President and a hearty handshake which he gave me by reaching out and grasping my right hand as he passed. I think it was his way of saying the deal we had made over the phone was still on.

There remained only one more group to deal with, and in fact, it was not a group at all, but one man, whose name was Murray Chotiner, who had been cooling his heels in another suite the longest time. Mr. Chotiner was a man well known to the President and was greeted like an old friend when he entered the room, so much so that Chotiner was the only one whom the President stood up for and whose hands he shook. Chotiner, unlike the others, was a man used to being in the presence of the politically powerful, and if he was intimidated in any way by the President, he didn't show it. "Well, this is a surprise," was the way he greeted John F. Kennedy.

Chotiner and Kennedy were not friends or allies. They were the exact opposite. Chotiner was to another famous man what Mr. Powers and Mr. O'Donnell were to the President. Chotiner had been peddling private medical records, ones that painted a radically different picture of the President's health than the one shown to the public. This was what he was selling to Harbinson and partners, but his presence there told us all we needed to know as to who was really calling the shots.

Wade Harbinson made a last play in an attempt to salvage the situation. "This man cannot get away with deceiving the country like he has been," Harbinson said to Chotiner. "You can put an end to him right here and now, Mr. Chotiner, it's what you've spent years working for." He then quoted a substantial figure if he held firm.

President Kennedy's response was to bring in the other man who rode up in the elevator, Dr. Mark Jacobsen, the man from whose office the records had been stolen. The doctor was to present a completely different set of records; ones which would paint the President as a man in nearly perfect health other than the afflictions known to the public. These records would make the ones in Chotiner's possession appear to be forgeries fabricated to smear the President. Chotiner would be sent away like the rest, well compensated in return for surrendering all copies of the stolen and damaging records.

That was the plan, but it never got that far.

Murray Chotiner took one look at the good Dr. Jacobsen and said, "Mr. President, if you accompany me down the hall and give me at least five minutes of your time, I think it will be worth your while."

"Murray, you're worth more than five minutes," was the President's response and he left the room with Chotiner and two Secret Service agents in tow. They were gone a lot longer than five minutes, and I cannot speak to claims that a certain former Vice President was in the other room and met face to face with President Kennedy that night. If someone else was there, I did not see him.

What I did see was the current Vice President come into the room and sit down in the chair occupied by the President only moments before. His attention was on Harbinson, Hunt and Hoffa, all three of whom had just had the rug pulled out from under them. "You men came here tonight to make a deal," Johnson said, "and things did not go as planned, but you don't have to walk away empty-handed." He then told them it was in everyone's interest to pretend this evening did not happen. LBJ then promised complete silence from each and every participant from the Kennedy Administration and the campaign, and this could be guaranteed in return for the not inconsiderable amount of cash the three of them had brought to the hotel that night in hopes of buying information to use against the President. "Of course it was all false," Johnson said, "complete bullshit which could easily be refuted, but there are always good people who fall for a smear job, which is why it was a necessity for the President to come here tonight."

Both Harbinson and Hunt became irate at hearing this, accusing Johnson of shaking them down.

"I would think two old Texas oilmen would know an opportunity when it was laid out right in front of them," Johnson said. He went on to explain that in return for their silence and generosity, the Administration would be willing to sweeten the deal. "Might be that your dealings with the FTC, SEC, even the mighty IR Goddamn of S will suddenly go a lot smoother. Investigations and audits could disappear or not be launched in the first place; no nasty little Feds pawing through your confidential business and prying where they don't belong. I think you gentlemen should appreciate that."

Hoffa had been silence so far, but not now. "My problem is with someone named Kennedy," he said. "My problem is with the FBI, the Justice Department and their Federal Marshalls and their Federal grand juries, the Congress and their damn son-of-a-bitchin' investigative committees. You don't speak for them, Lyndon. Your word ain't any good with me."

"Ask the President when we're done," was Lyndon Johnson's reply. "He'll stand by every word I say."

"It ain't Jack," Hoffa retorted, "it's that little bastard Bobby who's the problem." Johnson pointed out that the Attorney General was not there and his absence should speak for its self. That seemed to give Hoffa pause. I could say the three men mulled over the offer the Vice President had laid before them, but it wouldn't be true, once they were convinced it was on the level, they simply agreed. I think they simply wanted to cut their losses and get out of there.

Once the three men were on board, the Vice President pulled out a piece of paper from a pocket and let them read it. "I think this will give us all the legal cover we'll need," he said. "Let your lawyer go over it; I'm sure he'll say the same thing."

The President was out of the room a good 45 minutes, when he returned, it was Harbinson who addressed him. "Mr. President," he said, "an offer has been put to us, do you stand by it."

"Yes I do," he answered without hesitation. "I say that because, even though we are bitter enemies, it is in my interest you leave here tonight with at least something in hand. Someone said politics is war by other means - I think that person ever heard a gun fired in anger - and what happened here was as close as we can come in this business to a nuclear exchange. Let's go home and fight another day."

Then, the President offered his hand to Harbinson, who took it after some hesitation, the same for Hunt, who grimaced but shook Kennedy's hand just the same. Jimmy Hoffa was standing with his arms folded when the President thrust his hand forward, the Teamster Boss just glared at first, but with the Justice Department spending hundreds of thousands of dollars to build a case against him, he could hardly afford an offer from the President himself to ease up on him. Hoffa took the President's hand in the end; it is history's loss that no photo exists to prove it ever happened.

As I watched John F. Kennedy and Jimmy Hoffa shake hands, it sunk in how deep in this thing I was now, there would be no illusion of simply moving on from the White House staff to my next command like just another Marine officer. Done was done, and I was chained to the Kennedy's fortunes from now on, with no key to the lock.

I made a mental note to get in touch with Vance Harlow as soon as I got back to Washington, to say I had a lot of questions for the man is an understatement, to say the least, but try as I might, there was no finding him. As of October 1964, he simply vanished.

Wade L. Harbinson (VII)
October 1964

There is nothing that would change the fact that Kennedy was a lying, immoral, Communist-coddling son of a bitch who was ruining America.

Still, I do admit to more than a little admiration for the way he faced us down at the Hotel Adolphus; JFK should have been a Texan. We had him politically dead and buried, and he walked into that hotel room and resurrected himself on the spot. I still marvel at the guts it took to bring in that old bastard Marcello and Dr. Feelgood to make his accusers looks like liars. He upped the ante, and we could not help but fold in response.

On top of that, he was magnanimous enough to let me and my fellow investors walk away with something for our trouble - some would call it a bribe to buy our silence, but threats and intimidation would have accomplished the same thing. It's what most men in his position would have done; it's what I would have done.

One thing I knew for sure as soon as I left the Adolphus, I'd been had by Vance Harlow; the only way Kennedy could have known what was happening was if Harlow had told him everything; I later came to understand how I'd been played all along. No one picked up when I called Harlow's number repeated times

I called the Carousel Club. The owner told me a tale about not being able to get in touch with Harlow either; I knew he was lying.

In the days ahead, I could only speculate as to the vast conspiracy it must have taken to pull off what happened in Dallas on the last day of September. In the years since I have made discreet inquiries, but my hands have been tied; to reveal too much would have resulted in the kind of unwanted attention which would have led to appearances in courtrooms and before Congressional investigations, instances which would have required me to take the 5th.

I had no choice but to fold my cards and leave the table, but like any real Texan, I sat down at another table and dealt myself into a different game.

Dorothy Jean Brennan (IV)

Octobers 1964

There are no words to describe the shock I felt when I opened the door to find John F. Kennedy standing there, not to mention the Vice President and a handful of Secret Service agents. I had enough wits about me to know that I was in something way too deep, that I had been manipulated by both Wade Harbinson and Vance Harlow and I now had to do whatever necessary to protect myself. So I got out of there as soon as it was possible, with the knowledge I could never be called to testify about what I didn't hear and didn't witness in the first place.

I would have fled the building, but a big Secret Service agent blocked my path and directed me to an empty room and shut the door; I sat on the bed and waited as the sound of scurrying footsteps was heard outside in the hall.

At last, when all the business had been concluded, Kennedy's two flunkies, Powers and O'Donnell, came and got me.

I was never so apprehensive in my life as when Dave Powers and Kenneth O'Donnell took me in a hotel room and explained to me how I was complicit in more than a half dozen Federal crimes. "Miss Brennan, you have absolutely no idea what a prosecutor could make of your actions tonight," said Powers.

"Extortion, blackmail," said O'Donnell, "and considering the President of the United States was involved, treason is not out of the question."

They went on to explain how just being in the room made me an accomplice, how even though I had done nothing more than pour drinks and serve snacks, I was still guilty in the eyes of the law. "You need to keep that in mind, Miss Brennan," I forget which one said it. Then when they thought I was sufficiently scared enough (and I was scared) they said things did not have to come that, there was no reason why I should ever fear appearing in a courtroom. All I had to do was remain silent, to never mention being at the Hotel Adolphus, much less mention anything or anybody I'd seen or heard there.

"The President and Mr. Harbinson, have reached an agreement, so have all the other parties," Powers said. "There is no reason why you shouldn't walk away with something for your trouble either, Miss Brennan."

That was it, first intimidate me and then buy me off, this after hearing evidence of the President's lying, infidelity, and malfeasance in office. I told them they could have my silence if Kennedy and Harbinson had made some self-serving, face-saving agreement, but I would not take their money. I would go along because they'd threatened me, not because they'd bought me. Both men tried their best to talk me into taking a sum of money I could have used a lot. It clearly frustrated them that I wouldn't take it and they obviously did not trust anyone who couldn't be bought - shame on them.

Once I was free to leave, I discovered that Mr. Harbinson had already left the hotel and

I no longer had a ride. Thanks, I get threatened with treason and then ditched. I went back to the empty suite to call a cab, and that is where the one good thing to come out of all this happened, I was asked out on a date by a guy who said he recognized me from TV and wanted to take me out to dinner; he had a Massachusetts accent thick enough to be cut with a knife which pegged him as one of Kennedy's minion. He was also nearly half a foot shorter - I never dated guys shorter than myself. I told him to call me after the election when he would have a lot of free time since his candidate was going to lose November. He took me up on it; I thought it would be the last I'd ever hear from him.

And that is what happened to me at the Hotel Adolphus on the night of September 30th of 1964.

I encountered Wade Harbinson the next morning at the Sheraton; I was groggy after only three hours sleep, but I remember every word he said after ushering me into an empty conference room. "Neither you nor I were ever at the Hotel Adolphus," he told me. "None of it happened, and if you ever say it did, you will be all alone, your name ruined and your life will never be the same in the worst possible way. Do I make myself clear, Miss Brennan?"

Not even an apology for leaving me behind.

I pulled myself together and did my job; the second Kennedy-Goldwater debate was to be held at the Dallas Trade Mart that night, and my hands would be full briefing the press. The Senator himself arrived in Dallas in fine spirits; both Clif White and Dick Kliendendst, who had been heavily involved with his debate prep in Arizona, were confident the Senator would not only hold his own against Kennedy, but really go on the offensive against the President's coddling of Communists.

The rally held in downtown Dallas on the afternoon before the debate was the biggest one ever for a Republican in Texas. Looking out over the sea of faces, it was hard not to believe we were going to steal Texas right out from under Kennedy and Johnson. When the Senator told them, "This is your country, you built it, you paid for it, you've shed blood for it, and no one is going to take it away from you," the roar in response nearly knocked us off the stage.

I was in the audience at the Trade Mart when the Senator and the President took the stage at 8:00 p.m. sharp for the debate. Looking at John F. Kennedy standing up there behind the podium, I couldn't help but remember what I'd learned about the man, not 24 hours before - liar and adulterer. It was enough to make me want to get up and shout the name Ellen Rometsch, just to see his reaction. I fantasized about slipping a question to Walter Cronkite, the debate moderator, asking the President if he'd ever been treated by Dr. Mark Jacobsen for gonorrhea. I was glad Mrs. Kennedy wasn't there, what that poor woman must have had to endure; the official story was said she had a conflicting campaign appearance in Portland, Maine that night. The unofficial story said she refused to set foot back in the city where her husband had nearly gotten his head blown off as he rode beside her down the street.

In the debate, I thought the Senator came out swinging and scored points right away. "Mr. President," he said in his opening remarks, "you have repeatedly let the Soviets off the hook, you have repeatedly snatched defeat from the jaws of victory, and the sons and daughters of this generation will pay the hard price in the far future for what you have done." Throughout the next hour, Senator Goldwater hammered Kennedy for his embrace of Khrushchev and Chou at the summit; for his decision to withdraw from Cuba after Americans boys died to liberate the country; his decision not to unleash American air power against Soviet aggression in Iran; his betrayal of a staunch ally, the Shah; for the continued presence of a Soviet division in Cuba; for not sending more troops to South Vietnam; and for agreeing to meet with Khrushchev after the election for what promised to be "a sequel to Yalta."

I'll hand it to Kennedy; the man did not rattle when his failures were thrown in his face; he stood there and defended the un-defendable with vigor. He kept talking about pulling back from the "brink" and making the "tough decisions." There was a lot of talk about "having borne the burden and paid the price" to keep America safe and hold the free world together. The man tried to portray himself as someone who had stood on the frontline of the Cold War and kept it from turning into World War III. What absolute crap from a man whom I now knew as a moral degenerate. Kennedy also tried to make something of Senator Goldwater's often repeated statement that extremism was no vice, claiming such views would inevitably lead to nuclear war. I loved the Senator's comeback, "The difference between you and me, Mr. President, is that you are afraid to lob one into the Men's room in Kremlin, while I am not."

After the debate, as I made my way to the stage to offer congratulations to the Senator for doing a such a good job, I inadvertently found myself only a few feet from the President, and to my chagrin, he clearly recognized me from the previous night and gave me a knowing wink and a smile in return.

Inside the Goldwater campaign, we were ecstatic about the Senator's performance in the debate, we felt he had given the country a clear alternative to Kennedy, one which most Americans couldn't help but choose on Election Day. It only made us angry when the rest of the media claimed Kennedy had gone into the debate and succeeded in making his case that Goldwater was a shoot from the hip cowboy.

"What this country needs is a cowboy in charge, no apologies, that is what we're going to tell the people," was how Cliff White put it the next day as we flew out of Dallas.

It seemed to be sure winner and the first polls after the debate appeared to back it up: we were within 5 points of the President in the Gallup Poll and neck and neck in the Electoral College with the big states of Ohio, Florida, Illinois, California, and especially Texas, in contention.

It was going to take a lot of hard work, but we were going to pull it off.

Kevin McCluskey (IV)
October 1964

At the end of the night, I got another lecture from Dave Powers on the necessity of "ultimate discretion," he didn't have to tell me a second time after what and who I'd seen at the Hotel Adolphus that evening. The President of the United States, the present and a former Vice President, a Mafia bigwig and the dictator of the Teamsters, big rich Texas oilmen and a celebrity doctor, all together in one place at one time - that is the truth of it, though no one would believe it. That's because none of them were about to talk and they made damn sure the rest us kept our mouths shut as well.

Oh, and there was one other person there that night: the most beautiful girl I ever laid eyes on. She was the former beauty queen who did press briefings for Goldwater, who'd been roped into the shenanigans, I later learned, by the campaign's treasurer. There was a moment when she was alone while using the telephone and I seized the opportunity to ask her for a date. She said she didn't date guys shorter than herself. My response was to ask for her number, telling her I'd call after the election and maybe I'd grow in the meantime. "You do that and call me after the 3rd of November; all you Kennedy men will have a lot of free time after he loses." Those were her exact words to me; I remember them after all this time. She thought she'd never hear from me again, but I'd gotten her number.

There are a few things which stick out from the end of the evening in my memory; one of them being a glimpse of John F. Kennedy relaxing by enjoying a cigar with his two close aides and LBJ after everyone left. They were in the suite where it had all gone down, and when I walked past, the door was open just enough for me to see inside. I was designated other chores, no puffing on a stogie for me, for I was loading money into a truck, and it was not the cash I'd shepherded into the Hotel Adolphus hours earlier. It seemed our side had not been the only ones who'd come there with a few dozen or so pieces of luggage crammed with packs of twenty dollar bills. They were secreted away in a room at the other end of the hall. The men hired to guard the stash having been paid for their trouble and dismissed. It fell to me and one of Johnson's men to haul the satchels down in the freight elevator and stuffed into the back of one of the limousines. This turn of events was not part of the plan, for only when the job was done did a pair of ex-Texas Rangers show up - both having been called on short notice by the Vice President. They were packing two of the biggest revolvers I'd ever seen, along with the sawed off shotguns they were toting. It fell to them to chauffer the money to a bank in downtown Dallas - whose name I will not disclose even after all this time - where a manager let them into the vault at 12:15 a.m. for an unscheduled deposit.

Though I would have loved to have stayed in Dallas for the big debate with Goldwater, I was on a flight back to DC two hours after sunrise, I slept all the way, I would have slept the day away in my apartment, but as soon as I opened the door, there was a call to come down to Kennedy '64 HQ on Pennsylvania Avenue. I headed there with the expectation being told of another brushfire somewhere threatening the President's re-election and needing my immediate attention. What I got was a chair in Lawrence O'Brien's office where he thanked me profusely for all my hard work in Dallas, how both Kennedy brothers really appreciated what I'd done. Then he said that if at any time in the future, I was asked about my whereabouts for the past 24 hours, I was to say I'd taken some R and R from the hectic pace of the campaign, driven to Ocean City, Maryland, and checked into the Holiday Inn. My name was already on the motel's register and the room I rented for the night was #27, where I spent a day and a night catching up on some much-needed rest. Mr. O'Brien said there was little chance I would ever need to use such a story, but it paid to have one just in case.

I asked him if there was anything I should be concerned about and was told no, but who knew what might happen down the road.

Down the road indeed, there would more than one occasion in the years ahead when I was glad my name was on an old register at the Ocean City Holiday Inn.

John Compton (VI)
October 1964

I have not divulged the name of Bentley Braden's accomplice; I will not do it here, simply because I was asked not to do so because the man was a friend of the President who found himself in desperate straits and was taken advantage of by Braden, who was nothing more than a conniving blackmailer. My presence there was necessary as I was one of the few, if only, persons who could place the incriminating tape in Braden's actual hands. It was part of some delusional plot to influence the debate on the Civil Rights Act; only the Senators would not play along.

For most of the rest of the evening, I stayed in an adjacent hotel suite, pretty oblivious to what else was going on around me, that is until I was summoned by the Vice President to the room where he and the President, along with Dave Powers, Kenneth O'Donnell and the Marine in civilian clothes, were enjoying a cigar and one for the road. Indeed their suite looked as if had been the scene of quite the party earlier with a bar crowded with open liquor bottles, empty trays where snacks had been served, not to mention the ashtrays filled to over-flowing with cigarette butts and accompanying smoke still lingering in the air. This was the only time in the night I was in the presence of John F. Kennedy, who did take the time to shake my hand and thank me for all I had done. "Good men like you, sir," he said, "are hard to find today, and I want you to know it won't go unappreciated."

Then the Vice President took me out in the hall and said there was a chore needed doing and since I was there, it fell to me. The next thing I knew, I was in another suite staring at more money than I could ever make in three lifetimes, all in packs of twenty dollar bills. They were stuffed inside carrying satchels; it was the kind of thing which made me think of the term bagman. "This is how you beat Goldwater in Texas," said Lyndon Johnson, "not by ballots, but by bucks." He told me who this money came from, and a story I still find hard to believe even though I know it to be true.

My chore, it turned out, was to transport this cash haul down to one of Dallas's finer banks where it would be locked away in the vault. This I did with the help of the young man I'd seen in the hall earlier, he was from Kennedy's national campaign and would not stop talking about the blonde girl, who worked for Goldwater, and how he'd asked for a date. "I'm going out with a beauty queen," I remember him saying at one point, "and my brothers are going to crap their pants when they find out." Good for him, but my older and wiser head was more than a little concerned about the finer points of the law, and just how many of them we might be breaking. Just following orders doesn't cut it at a disbarment hearing.

I slept little in the next 24 hours; there was a big Kennedy-Johnson rally at a minor league baseball park in the Dallas suburbs at mid-day; twice as many as planned for showed up. When his speech was done, Kennedy waded into the crowd of ordinary

Americans, shaking the outstretched hands with a most brilliant smile on his face. I'm sure the Secret Service had heart attacks, but it went a long way toward putting some bad recent history into the past, both for the city and the man.

At the debate that night, Kennedy stood toe to toe with Goldwater's best bellicose cowboy act and answered him point by point: we intentionally didn't fire on Soviet troops in Cuba because we were not at war with them; he never ordered the American Commander in West Berlin to surrender if Soviet forces attacked; we did not "finish the job" in North Korea and "bomb day and night" Soviet forces in Iran because those actions would have provoked a wider war. "Our objective was to remove the Castro dictatorship in Cuba," the President said at one point. "This we accomplished, our other objective was to prevent a catastrophic world war between us and the Soviets from breaking out. This too, we accomplished."

Senator Goldwater hit back hard with his contention that the very act of meeting with Khrushchev and Chou En Lai was nothing less than surrender. I thought the Republican candidate was scoring points until I heard Kennedy's reply. "We live in an age where it is possible to reduce all the work of human civilization to ashes in less than a day. That this horrendous fate might come about through miscalculation or mistake is unthinkable. It requires us to go the extra mile, to make the larger effort, to cross barriers and borders, to pull back curtains either Iron or Bamboo, if only for a day, or even a moment, to establish even the smallest measure of trust and make sure such a holocaust does not happen."

Goldwater accused the President of selling out our "loyal WWII ally, Chaing Kai-chek, but Kennedy had the perfect comeback. "Meeting with Chou En Lai does nothing to diminish Chaing Kai Chek's contributions to history and how we fought side by side against a common enemy. But the high risks of this dangerous age ultimately compel us to recognize the reality that Chaing does not rule China, now or in the future." It was a brave thing to say; Chaing had a lot of supporters in America, big and powerful ones like Henry Luce, the influential publisher of *Time* and *LIFE.*

I noticed the contrast between the John F. Kennedy I saw up on the stage and one I'd witnessed the night before at the Hotel Adolphus. One was a statesman, pure and simple; the other was a politician, ruthless and crafty.

We were euphoric after the debate; sure the President had scored a knockout over Goldwater. It was the Vice President who brought me back to earth. "Jack did well," he said backstage at the Trade Mart, "but Barry is still standing." The next day, most of the daily papers pronounced the second debate a draw.

The most immediate consequence of the debate was a sudden announcement that Kennedy would do a campaign swing across Texas with the Vice President and Governor Connolly over the next two days. It was a testament to the friendly reaction Kennedy received in Dallas, and it was the boost our efforts to carry the state needed.

At every stop, from Fort Worth to San Antonio to Austin to Houston, Kennedy defended his plan to meet with Khrushchev again right after the election. "We must take every step necessary on the path to a just and lasting peace; we must never let pass an opportunity to look our adversaries in the eye and let them know we are determined to achieve it." This was strong stuff in hawkish Texas, and at every stop there were signs in the crowd calling Kennedy a Red appeaser or worse, but only a few. At every rally, those words prompted applause and cheers from the audience.

Kennedy's swing through the Lone Star state coincided with a speech Goldwater gave to the country after buying a half hour of time on the networks. In it, he doubled down and boldly stated, "As your President, it will be my stated objective to seek a resolution of the Cold War on terms favorable to the United States and for all free people everywhere. Communism must give way if humanity is to have a future."

"So, old Barry is telling the American people he's not going to be satisfied with anything less than World War III," the Vice President commented as we were flying from a rally in Galveston to one in Texarkana. "That ought to guarantee us a few million votes right there."

Everyone agreed the Republican candidate had gone too far, and how he was pissing away what chance he had left of winning, little did we know that unseen events were about to force John F. Kennedy to eat his words.

Colonel Martin Maddox (IX)
October 1964

If I have given the impression that all the White House was concerned with in the fall of 1964 was political maneuvering, then it is a false one. There was unfinished business in Cuba and Iran to concern us every day, while preparations were going forward for the next summit with Khrushchev right after the November election. The upcoming summit became the focus of the President's foreign policy team, who, in hindsight, were operating under the assumption the Kremlin would be on their best behavior lest they do something which might scuttle the summit or endanger Kennedy's re-election. It quickly became apparent that a lot of concerned parties did not get the memo.

The continued ineffectiveness of the South Vietnamese Army meant the Marines in country had to shoulder the burden of the fight against the Viet Cong, who were being resupplied with Soviet weapons from the North; our casualties there increased every week during the month of September.

The events in Southeast Asia did not escape the notice of the press, which put them on the front-page of all the major dailies. That meant Vietnam became a topic on the campaign trail where the President had to take heat from Goldwater over it.

On September 15th, the *New York Times* published a front page interview with Che Guevara, who was in hiding somewhere in Latin America after escaping Cuba late in June. He claimed to be in touch with elements of the Cuban Army still resisting the American occupation on the island and was actively recruiting volunteers, "who are eager to go to Cuba and continue the fight the American Imperialist oppressors." Guevara promised tens of thousands of them would soon be taking to the sea in small boats to slip past the American navy and land on the beaches in a second invasion which, "would drive the Yankee bastards into the Caribbean."

Good luck in that I thought, because American forces on the island at the end of September included over 80,000 Army infantrymen and specialists, 25,000 Marines and another 20,000 Naval personal. There was still active resistance from Castro's dead-enders, but they were mostly in the country side and the mountains; our casualty rate had dropped from a hundred men a day at the height of the fighting in April to barely a trickle now, although flag-draped coffins were still coming home every week. Ominously, the casualty rate among the civilian population had skyrocketed, as the victims of Castro's dictatorship sought retribution against anyone who might have aided the former tyrant; roving bands of vigilantes dealt out summary justice in what had become a civil war at its most ugly. Making matters worse, there was not even the semblance of a provisional government; that part of the plan went up in smoke with the disappearance and presumed death of Harry Williams and Manual Artime.

The problem of General Andreyev and the Soviet troops at Camaguey had not resolved itself, mainly because the Soviet leadership was dragging their feet on sending transport to evacuate them from the island. The CIA speculated the Kremlin's strategy was to avoid the humiliation sure to occur at the sight of Russian troops marching past the victorious Americans on their way to the ships which would take them home; there were also concerns the Kremlin was stalling because it wanted to preserve some kind of presence in Cuba once American forces withdrew. To further complicate things, Andreyev made it plain, first to General Abrams and then to officials from the CIA that he would not even consider turning over any official from the Castro government who had sought asylum inside Soviet lines, including members of Cuban Intelligence wanted in questioning in the November '63 assassination attempt; this led some to question if Andreyev's real motivation was to cover up a Soviet connection to Oswald.

Another complication was the plan by the Kennedy campaign for the President to visit Cuba before Election Day. A touchdown at the airport followed by a big rally where grateful Cubans would show their appreciation to the man responsible for freeing them from Communism, a plan I'm sure originated in the Oval Office.

This was not a good idea. "It's like the Wild West down there," a fellow Marine officer told me, "half of Havana has guns, and they're pointing them at the other half and shaking them down. You can make a fortune running cans of soup, beans, and spam into the island. And you can make even bigger bucks running guns down there too; it's worse than when Fidel was in charge."

While all this was going on, the situation in Iran was not getting the attention it should have; we were forced to rely on British Intelligence tell us what was going on until late summer when Director McCone finally managed to insert multiple teams of agents into the country. They were real professionals who managed to get a network up and running in a matter of days, giving us accurate reports on a country in chaos as the Soviets rapidly pulled out. The Red Army in retreat lashed out at the Iranian civilian population, burning to the ground entire villages when a sniper killed a single Russian soldier, raising apartment buildings in Teheran to the ground if they were believed to house resistance fighters, while immediately executing any man or woman who impeded their withdrawal in any way.

The real news in these reports was the picture it painted of the Ayatollah Khomeini, who if anything was worse than the Russians. Khomeini believed in summary executions as well; there were no Soviet POWs held anywhere in Iran. Equally worse was the fate of any member of the Shah's regime who fell into Khomeini's hands; they joined the luckless Soviet soldiers in front of a firing squad. It was obvious from these reports that there was no way the Shah would simply return home and resume his place on the Peacock throne, even if it was still the policy of the American government that he do so.

What we had absolutely no intelligence on were the happenings a few hundred miles to the north on the other side of the border with the Soviets. The purge of officers suspected of failing to do their duty during the operation in Iran, both in the Red Army and among the

KGB, continued without letup, inching up the chain of command to district commanders, who were accused of insufficiently instilling the proper "Revolutionary Spirit" in their troops. In the last week of September, the Generals in charge of the Turkestan and Caucasus military districts were hauled before a pair of Kangaroo tribunals and the next thing they knew they were packing for Siberia. During the same week, a least forty East Germans managed to scale the Berlin Wall and make their way to freedom, this is notable because they did it within plain sight of their country's border guards who refused to obey orders and fire upon them. On the first day of October, five guards simply walked away from their posts and into the West. An infantry squad was prevented from hijacking a half dozen trucks and ramming one of the Wall's gates by a Soviet tank which blocked their way at the last minute. Hours later, Walter Ulbricht sent a message to Moscow warning that a general uprising among the East German people was imminent.

These actions lit a fuse under another far-flung group of conspirators inside the Soviet government, powerful men in the Red Army and the KGB who were, as one later put it, "not going to simply fall in line while we were nailed to cross for the sins of Iran while the men inside the Kremlin escaped all blame."

These were members of the Communist Party and the military who were more than alarmed at the possibility of an East German disintegration and collapse of the Warsaw Pact. And they believed the first appropriate action to remedy the situation was the removal from power of Nikita Khrushchev and Leonid Brezhnev, whose rash policies since the second coup were responsible for this crisis.

That the two leaders in question didn't move swiftly to confront an impending crisis in East Germany nor understand how there would inevitably be a backlash in the middle ranks over their harsh punishments for the failures in Iran can be blamed on fatigue after months of crisis, and hubris on the part of Brezhnev, who believed he was untouchable once all his rivals on the Politburo were gone. A terse note was sent to Ulbricht to take "whatever matters necessary to resolve his countries problems;" Brezhnev then promptly flew to Leningrad, ostensibly to meet with the Mayor and other city officials, but really to look over some of the latest models from Chevrolet, which had been smuggled across the border from Finland. Khrushchev on the other hand badly needed to get away and take a true vacation ahead of the Stockholm summit with Kennedy in November; the events of the past year were making the man feel his age. Khrushchev and Brezhnev's departure from Moscow on the 9th of October was the opening their enemies needed.

Sometime in the early hours of the next morning, elements of the 8th Rifle Division, a unit which had gotten the hell shot out it in Iran, along with a squad of handpicked KGB officers, infiltrated the Kremlin, before sun up they were in complete control of the palace, while orders were being dispatched by Marshall Grechko to commanders in all Soviet military districts and the Warsaw Pact. Before the morning was out, three agents walked into the Lubyanka, requested access to the acting KGB Director's office by claiming they had knowledge of an imminent coup. As soon as they were standing across the desk from the Director, they pulled out their guns and shot him to death, then killed his secretary and four deputies. That effectively brought the KGB on board and the success of the third Moscow coup in less than a year was guaranteed.

The first hint of the doings in Moscow came when Vladimir Roykov arrived at the gate of the American Embassy requesting asylum. Within the hour a cable was in the hand of Secretary Rusk, who called the President in Kansas City, Missouri, where he was looking forward to a day of hard campaigning, with news of yet another crisis breaking. The President would spend the day getting updates every time he walked off a stage after a speech, with the eagle-eyed press core, who'd vowed never to let the wool be pulled over their eyes again like it was during the early days of the Missile Crisis, quickly catching on that something was up.

"The shit just won't stop hitting the fan," was Vice President Johnson's take on this turn of events.

This was why the Attorney General and I were back at that fine French restaurant in Georgetown two nights later, meeting with Colonel Sergei Ivanov. He had little actual intelligence to tell us, but of those now in charge, he would say, "These men have learned the hard lessons," Ivanov told us, "and they're not going to leave anyone in a position to turn the tables on them. It's how Stalin did things."

Robert Kennedy pressed him on who was in charge, he wanted a name and a face, and he wanted to know who his brother would have to sit across the table from now. "You will need to have a little patience," was Ivanov's answer. "I'm sure a first among equals will rise in due time." The Attorney General inquired about the Colonel's own position and if he was safe in light of this new regime. He also let Ivanov know there was a standing offer of asylum if he felt the need of it. The Colonel thanked the Attorney General but said he was a true Russian patriot at heart and could never leave behind the homeland where his wife and children dwelt. We never saw him again after that meeting; he was recalled to Moscow a month later with orders to personally brief the new head of the KGB on all his dealings with the Kennedy Administration. We later learned he was accused of passing state secrets in his meetings with the Attorney General and me, and subjected to lengthy interrogation and torture. Sergei Ivanov died in a Soviet work camp; I never found out what happened to his wife and children.

MOSCOW COUP; KHRUSHCHEV OUT was the *New York Times* headline on October 12, 1964; the NSC had been meeting virtually round the clock since the first news reached Washington and we still had little or no idea whose finger was on the nuclear button. All attempts to establish contact with the men inside the Kremlin had come to naught. There was footage of troops on the move in the Soviet capital in the early hours of the coup before total blackout was ordered by the new government and any foreign correspondent caught on the streets would make the acquaintance of the Red Army.

It wasn't until the 14th that we got our first real look at who was in charge when a Moscow television station broadcast what was purported to be a meeting of the "State Committee of the National Emergency" in the Kremlin. It consisted of nearly a dozen men, seemingly headed by the notorious hard-liner Mikhail Suzlov, a man who had been out of sight for nearly three and a half months. That was because he had been in a cell after his arrest was ordered by Brezhnev in June, a fact which precluded him from being the mastermind of this latest coup. Who we should have been paying attention to at the time was the man who sat at Suzlov's side at the meeting, Yuri Andropov.

This "Committee" declared a state of emergency as the Ministry of State Security ordered 300,000 pairs of handcuffs and emptied Lefortovo Prison in preparation for what came to be called the Third Great Purge.

One thing abundantly clear was that the Stockholm Summit with Khrushchev scheduled for the week after the November election was now dead. This was a deep personal blow to the President; only his closest aides knew how hard he took it at the time. In his memoirs, John F. Kennedy wrote of "a golden opportunity to halt the nuclear arms race with the Soviets and permanently thaw the Cold War," which slipped away in October of 1964. There was no chance the new men in charge in Moscow were going to enter into the kind of hard negotiations and agree to the tough sacrifices that an end to the Cold War would have entailed; only an old Stalin hand like Khrushchev or even a veteran Kremlin infighter like Brezhnev could have managed such a feat. Both of them were lucky to have made it through October alive. The President himself gave the order for American fighters from one of our bases in Turkey to give air cover to the plane which flew Khrushchev and his family out of the Soviet Union on October 14th; the man had to be forcibly put aboard the Russian version of our DC-10 at an air base in the Crimea where he was vacationing. In fact, the plane had trouble taking off because all of Khrushchev's security detail jumped in the plane with him; they were directly disobeying orders to hold him in custody until a KGB execution squad arrived from Moscow. Our jets shadowed the Russian plane all the way until it touched down in Egypt, protecting it from any Migs which might have been scrambled to shoot it down. Khrushchev didn't mention that little detail in his own memoirs, which portrays his daring escape and flight in an exceedingly different light.

Leonid Brezhnev simply road across the border to Finland in one of those Chevys he'd gone to Leningrad to look over and made a deal on the spot with British Intelligence to tell them everything he knew about the men who ousted him for the equivalent of five million dollars in British currency. Despite monetary inducements from MI5 and the CIA, he never gave up any state secrets, in those matters, Brezhnev remained a Soviet patriot.

No account of October 1964 can leave out the other major foreign policy crisis's that erupted simultaneously, when only days after the coup in Moscow, a human wave assault was launched against the headquarters of the 1st Marine Battalion outside Kontum in the Central Highlands of South Vietnam; the resulting battle cost 25 Marines their lives with three times as many wounded. The following day a report from General Westmorland revealed that at least two full divisions of the North Vietnamese Army had moved into the South in the previous weeks; clearly, the North was preparing to wage all-out war.

The NSC meeting on the situation was short, and the decision was unanimous; because we were now dealing with a new and hard-line leadership in Moscow, America could not afford to appear weak and indecisive, not within days of the Moscow coup. Those were the expressed views of Secretaries Rusk and McNamera, along with McGeorge Bundy, the NSC head. It was also the view of Attorney General Robert Kennedy, who said, "We can't afford to let Vietnam become our Achilles Heel." At no time did the current domestic political situation come up in the meeting, there was no mention of any possible fallout at the polls for the President as a consequence for any action taken.

At 9:00 p.m., President Kennedy gave the necessary authorization for Admiral Sharp, the CINC in the Pacific, to order the F-8's to resume bombing on North Vietnamese military targets. Those orders were issued from Honolulu to the *Bon Homme Richard*, an aircraft carrier patrolling off the coast of South Vietnam, within the within the hour. Before the sun rose on Washington DC the next day, the bombs were falling.

"I want to know what happens next," the President said after he read the first report on the success of the bombing raids. "The last thing I want to do is to go into Vietnam without a plan."

There was another event that week which did not receive near the attention it should have in Washington: on October 17th, the Ayatollah Khomeini entered Teheran, proclaimed Iran freed from "the infidel and the Zionist puppet" since it was now an Islamic Republic and promptly put a bounty on the head of the Shah.

Dorothy Jean Brennan (V)
October 1964

On the flight out of Dallas, I seriously considered resigning my position with the Goldwater campaign; the events at the Adolphus Hotel had revealed to me a side of political life in America, which in my youthful naiveté, I had no idea existed. I also understood that I had allowed myself to become involved in things which could have a negative impact on my future if even a whiff of it ever became public; my mind was filled with images of me being chased by mobs of reporters. I was only one newspaper story away from becoming a house-hold name…and not in a good way. These thoughts made me want to move to Alaska and get a job waitressing under an assumed name.

But running away was not an option, done was done. Besides, the reason I became involved in politics in the first place was still very valid: I still believed Barry Goldwater was undoubtedly the best man to lead America in these trying times and none of the disgrace of that evening at the Adolphus tarnished him in any way.

When we got back to Phoenix, I went about my duties as if nothing had ever happened. I made a point to steer clear of Wade Harbinson, which turned out the be not a problem as the man seemed bent on avoiding me as much as I wanted to avoid him. He flew out to the West Coast two days after the Dallas debate, ostensibly to coordinate fundraising with some of Senator Goldwater's biggest and most wealthy backers for the final days of the campaign, which were now upon us.

We knew damn well it was going to be a tough fight against the Kennedy machine, but we all took inspiration from what the Senator himself told us in one meeting three weeks before election day, "Taking Omaha Beach was an uphill battle all the way, but they took it and kept it, no damn reasons why we can't do the same thing to the White House."

The Kennedy campaign hit us hard on TV and the radio with ads where decorated veterans put on their combat medals and denounced Goldwater as a warmonger who would start WWIII; senior citizens claimed President Goldwater would abolish Social Security; factory workers outside of an auto assembly plant warned that a Goldwater Administration would abolish the 40 hour work week along with the minimum wage.

Those ads were effective, no one could deny it, but we had ammunition of our own with which to return fire. It was just a matter of finding the most effective way to use it. This is where the genius of Clif White showed itself again. He saw the real potential of drawing a stark contrast between the present day reality in America and the possible future depending on who was elected on November 3rd and commissioned the "What kind of country do you want?" ads, which were the product of some guys at the marketing department at Warner Brothers who had been recommended by Jack Warner himself.

We hit Kennedy back with a one-minute ad contrasting footage of the lawlessness the whole country saw on their TV sets during the Los Angeles riots with footage of the peaceful and orderly neighborhoods that all real Americans aspired to live in. At the end, the voter is presented with a simple statement, "Which country do you want? The choice is yours November 3rd: Vote Goldwater-Dirksen."

Clif White made sure that ad ran in every major market across the country, especially in the big Northeastern and Midwestern cities where the Democrats were supposed to have an advantage. Some of the Arizona Mafia were not too keen on this approach at first; Dean Burch made a point of saying it was "crude." Mr. White replied that this was simply taking the battle right to the heart of the Kennedy constituency, "We are showing the people in Chicago, Kansas City, Cleveland, Pittsburgh, and Jersey City just what life is going to be like if they vote this man back in for another four years." There were others where we took on the leniency in criminal justice system, the loss of property rights, and the lack of respect for basic American tradition by making the same stark contrast.

My favorite was the one with John Wayne where he looked the viewer straight in the eye at the end of the ad and said, "It was men with guts who made America great, the kind of men who settled the West, built our great cities, and answered the call to keep this country free for nearly 200 years. I'm proud to say I consider my good friend, Barry Goldwater, to be one of them."

Our poll numbers edged upward, especially in the industrial Mid-West with a lot of blue collar households.

Kennedy was probably in bed with some prostitute when they had to roust him out with news of Khrushchev's fall; then, only days after the Moscow coup, came news that the bombing of North Vietnam was being resumed on a limited basis - another weak response to Communist aggression sure to grab the notice of the new thugs in charge in the Kremlin.

The Russian coup and Vietnam were top of the agenda when Goldwater and Kennedy met for the third and final Presidential debate in Cleveland on the 20th of October. I was in the theater throughout the entire debate, seated only a few feet away from both candidates, and despite what the pundits and the Eastern liberal press wrote, it most definitely was not a "debacle" for Senator Goldwater. Speaking from behind a podium for more than an hour, I saw and heard a man who stood up for patriots, promised to make Communism retreat, and refused to put up with the current coddling of criminals and the general disrespect for law and order. The Senator had every right to get angry when one of the journalists present, Tom Wicker, a card-carrying leftist, asked him about a supposed endorsement he'd received from the Alabama Ku Klux Klan. There never was any such endorsement, and it was nothing but a *New York Times* reporter trying link the Republican candidate to the worst elements in American society. There was clear bias from the debate moderator, Chet Huntley, from the beginning, and never more so than when he admonished the Senator about his "intemperate" tone.

Huntley and Wicker and the rest of them were not nearly so hard on Kennedy, all the more galling to me after what I'd learned about the man back in Texas. I received another knowing wink from the President as I was making my way to the stage after the debate to congratulate Senator Goldwater for a fine performance. Talk about no shame.

We now had two weeks until Election Day, Goldwater was still behind, but far from out according to the polls; we were within striking distance of the President in 10 states. All we needed to do was carry half of them, and when added to the states we had already locked up, it was more than enough to give the Senator a majority in the Electoral College.

It was just a matter of finding a way to move the right amount of voters, and this set off a contentious argument inside the campaign, Dean Burch wanted the Senator to hit Kennedy hard for not "finishing the job" against the Communists when we had the upper hand, and for doing to South Vietnam what Truman had done to China, abandoning an Asian ally to Red insurgents. Cliff White, on the other hand, wanted the Senator to focus on crime and disorder here at home, and draw a straight line between the Los Angeles riots and the results of Kennedy's big government liberalism.

Senator Goldwater heard both sides out, and then said, "win or lose, I've got to do it my way." He never did make a choice and stick to one theme, and as a result his speeches in the final weeks often jumped from back and forth from one point to another; if it was a problem, the crowds didn't seem to mind as the candidate received wildly enthusiastic responses in such varied places as Indianapolis, Houston, Milwaukee, and Denver.

The one piece of advice the Senator did listen was from some of his wealthy California backers to have Ronald Reagan come to Arizona and give him some valuable tips on how to deliver his speeches. Reagan was a skilled speaker who'd honed his talents giving patriotic talks to GE employees; he is the reason why more detailed anecdotes and examples were in Goldwater's speeches at the end of the campaign, something which did not come naturally to the Senator. That is why Goldwater would invoke a plumber or secretary when talking about the burden of high taxes or a GI who had fallen in Cuba when criticizing Kennedy's outstretched hand to Khrushchev. It was wise council, and it really paid off before the crowds. Reagan is justifiably lauded for his "Time to Choose" TV speech late in the campaign, it was perfect articulation of conservative principles and launched his political career, but the work Reagan did behind the scenes was just as important

The biggest event of the campaign was at the Rose Bowl in Pasadena, California during the last week before Election Day and it is the one all of us who worked so hard to elect Goldwater remember with the most fondness. The crowd was enormous and pumped; we learned later they had to turn away thousands at the gate. The few Hollywood stars willing to come out for the Republican ticket were there: James Stewart, Ginger Rogers, Mary Pickford, Alice Faye, Irene Dunne, Robert Taylor, and of course, John Wayne. Nixon was there as well; he managed to introduce the candidate as the "next President of the United States" with conviction.

The crowd hung on Senator Goldwater's every word, proof positive of how much he had improved as a candidate since he had first stomped through the snows of New Hampshire back in the February. He answered the attacks the Kennedy campaign had been hurling at him night and day for weeks when he stood before the throng in the Rose Bowl and stated, "Moderation will not keep America free; Moderation will not keep America safe from enemies bent upon its ultimate destruction; Moderation will not deliver to our children the precious heritage of liberty, duty, and God-given individual rights which previous generations handed down to us." I still get chills at the memory of his final words. "America has always been a bright light in an often dark world, a beckon of hope to those under tyranny's heel. I've always believed that was God's destiny for this country. I now fear that light has dimmed and that this great land is in danger of falling short of its grand and divine destiny, that the tyranny so many have fled to our shores to escape has now taken root in our own precious soil. It is our job, here and now, my fellow Americans, to restore the full glow to the torch of liberty, to banish even the hint of despotism from our land, to extend a hand not to the foreign dictator, but to the men and women he has enslaved. In this great crusade, I ask for your vote, and I ask for your help. God bless America!"

I saw tears in the eyes of a couple of the movie's greatest tough guys when the Senator was finished, and the crowd in the Rose Bowl was on its feet, giving him an ovation which lasted for nearly ten minutes. There were tears in my eyes as well, not because of the Senator's words, but because if not for a deal struck at the Adolphus Hotel, the American people would have learned the truth about Kennedy and this great man, Barry Goldwater, would be looking at a landslide victory in a matter of days.

In that moment, I felt history would never forgive me, if I didn't do something.

John Compton (VII)
October 1964

In the history of the Kennedy-Johnson re-election effort in 1964, there is before Dallas on October 1ˢᵗ, and then there is after Dallas; or, for those of us in the know, there was before the Adolphus Hotel, and then there was after the Adolphus. The official historians write about the genuine joy and enthusiasm from the citizens of the Lone Star state that Kennedy received upon his return to Texas for the first time since the assassination attempt the year before and the clear spirit of forgiveness and generosity with which he welcomed it. It is true, Kennedy and Johnson toured the state for the next two days and were met with huge crowds wherever they went - Fort Worth, Austin, San Antonio, Houston - while the surge to Goldwater, plainly visible to any observer for the past few weeks, appeared to have crested and receded. But appearances were misleading, Kennedy's tour brought only a momentary lift to the campaign, and it is doubtful any of his speeches changed the minds of those already hell bent on voting Republican in November.

No, what truly made the difference was the cold hard cash we had deposited in a Dallas bank in the early hours of October 2ⁿᵈ after the events at the Adolphus; money which was then liberally spent all over Texas, the rest of the South, and even points far North and West in the remaining days of the campaign. There are no ledgers and receipts to document this windfall, no withdrawal slips to show the daily flow of funds into campaign coffers, but its presence is there for all to see, it is only a matter of perspective.

The first place this sudden infusion of cash made itself felt was on the airwaves in every radio market in Texas, where they were deluged with 10- and 30- second spots extolling the President's decisiveness and thoughtfulness in a time of crisis, always describing him as "a man who will keep the peace." At the same time, there was a multitude of ads going after Goldwater on his opposition to Social Security, Federal aid to farmers, old age medical insurance and just about everything else enacted in the 20ᵗʰ Century to make life better for the working man in America.

"If we can get Texans and even a few more Southerners to forget where Barry stands on Civil Rights," the Vice President said at one point, "even for a little while, they'll see that he's never lifted a finger to do a damn thing for them. In fact he's worked hard to make their lives worse."

By the second week of October, we had good reason to believe this tact was working: even though the polls did not reflect it yet, you could feel the pendulum in Texas swinging back toward the Democratic ticket. It was out there on the campaign trail, an energy among the crowds which were growing, and in the large number of volunteers who were flocking to party headquarters across the state. The national Kennedy-Johnson headquarters liked what they were hearing so well, that they authorized spending money to make anti-Goldwater ad buys in selected radio markets in the rest of the South; which meant more money packed in suitcases inside the bank's vault and hand carried to Nashville, Memphis, New Orleans and Atlanta.

Then, just as we were feeling awfully good about our chances, every TV in the country was interrupted by one of those Special Bulletin logos; a coup in Moscow, Khrushchev was out, and God only knew whose hand was on the nuclear button. There was a new sheriff in the Kremlin, and he wasted no time in ordering mass arrests behind the Iron Curtain and letting us know he wasn't about to abide any agreement old Nikita had made at New Delhi.

This event made it appear as if the Kennedy Administration had been completely blindsided and his claims of steady leadership in the preceding months ring hollow, along with putting into doubt all his lofty goals in foreign policy for the second term. Suddenly, it made having a tough guy like Goldwater, a man who said he would have no problem lobbing one into the Men's Room at the Kremlin, as President, make a lot of sense to voters. It did not help when South Vietnam heated up again within days; to anyone following events, it appeared as if the new bosses in Moscow were wasting no time in challenging the American President. Newspaper editorials across the country unanimously pronounced the President's policy of reaching out to Russia a failure, his plans for negotiations to lessen tensions and reduce nuclear arms so much dust in the wind. The papers in Texas really gave the President hell, calling him a fool for not pressing the advantage over the Reds when he had the chance.

Kennedy had no choice but to pivot politically in the face of changing events; there couldn't anymore talk of summits. Overnight, there needed to be more speeches along the lines of "pay any price, bear any burden."

The third and final debate was set for October 20th, in the wake of the Moscow coup. For the President, it was both a challenge and an opportunity; the challenge would be fending off the inevitable "I told you so" attack from Goldwater while taking advantage of this opportunity to retake the offensive against him.

I remember watching the debate on a TV set in a Baton Rouge motel room, and having my heart sink when the Republican candidate came out swinging in his opening remarks, attacking Kennedy's foreign policy as hopelessly naïve and feckless against an aggressive and intractable enemy. Then there was the first question of the night to the Arizona Senator from a *New York Times* reporter asking him if he was willing to repudiate an endorsement from the United Klans of America. My motel TV was black and white, but I could still see Goldwater's face redden, and the fire come out his ears; later he would claim to know it was a question designed to embarrass him and to be determined not to take the bait. "The Klan, the Communist Party, the Socialists, or the Know-Nothing Party are free to do whatever they want. I don't have anything to do with it." What the millions watching saw was a man who refused to renounce the Ku Klux Klan; if you watch a tape of the moment now, you can see John F. Kennedy fighting hard to hide a smile as his opponent steps in it on national TV. Goldwater lost his temper and never quite got it back for the rest of the debate; his Klan answer was front page news across the country the next day, not his slashing attacks on Kennedy's foreign policy. Two days later, follow up reporting would reveal there had never been any such endorsement of Goldwater by Robert Shelton, the Grand Dragon of the UKA, but the damage was done.

Kennedy, on the other hand, seized the moment when asked his inevitable question on a "foreign policy seemingly in shambles after the events in Moscow." He said, "I have not given up, nor will I ever give up on my quest for a more peaceful and secure world for all of our children. If the new men in the Kremlin feel the same, they will find no more willing partner in such an endeavor than me. However, if they wish to rule their Communist empire in the manner of a latter-day Stalin, they will find me to be a relentless foe. If they doubt my words, then I suggest they go and ask Fidel Castro."

I knew a great line when I heard one and "Go ask Castro" would be heard many times at Democratic rallies in the remaining days of the campaign. Our fears that the Republicans would make hay out of the Moscow coup were allayed.

The reason I was in Baton Rouge was to see a gentleman named Howard Prentiss, who had a plan which would put some of the money in that Dallas vault to good use. We met in the kitchen of a barbecue and ribs joint during the lunch hour since we mutually decided his home or a too public a place might entail too much risk of future exposure. Mr. Prentiss walked with a limp he got at Leyte Gulf while serving as a cook in the segregated Navy in the Pacific. After the war, he came back to his home in Louisiana and vowed he'd never let fear and intimidation rule his life; somehow he got a small loan with a high interest rate from a bank, bought a little grocery store in the black section of Baton Rouge and proceeded to work hard. Now twenty years later, he owned half dozen small stores in similar neighborhoods, along with two funeral parlors; pretty good for a black man in the Deep South. And during those twenty years, Howard Prentiss had paid a lot of taxes and the more taxes he paid, the more determined he was to vote despite poll taxes, grandfather clauses and literacy tests. Through sheer guts and will, he had gotten his name on the voting rolls in his parish and stayed there despite having the barrel of a pistol put to his head by a deputy sheriff who ordered him to get his ass back to the courthouse and have his name removed by the registrar.

Now in the fall of 1964, Howard Prentiss was showing the same fortitude, only it was now a plan to organize and transport every black registered voter in the state of Louisiana to the polls on Election Day. Mr. Prentiss assured me he had the people; he just needed the money for transportation drivers and protection for the citizens to and from the polls. The risky part of his plan concerned hiring black men with guns for security. Secrecy was the key, because if news of his plan got out before November 3rd, it was a cinch that a few of the black men and women on the voting rolls would get a bullet in the back as they were going to and from work.

What was needed was cash, something in the mid five figures, to make Prentiss's plan work. I was sitting across from him because an officer on the ship on which he served at Leyte Gulf went on to become a successful shoe manufacturer in Massachusetts and a big contributor to the political campaigns of fellow Navy veteran from the Bay State, and Prentiss had reached out to him. There were many reasons for not giving Howard Prentiss the money he wanted; the least of them being a potential charge of vote buying; accessory to murder if any of the security men were forced to use deadly force on Election Day. The political blowback could be devastating.

I didn't give any of it a second thought; I shook Howard Prentiss's hand and made arrangements for him to get every penny he needed. "My good friend, Doctor King," Mr. Prentiss said as we parted, "would not approve of my hiring men with guns to protect our people. I'm afraid the good Doctor will just have to be disappointed." I asked him why he was so willing to take such a risk to vote in a state where all the polls said Goldwater would take it in a landslide. He replied, "The President of the First Bank and Trust of Baton Rouge, where I pay my mortgage every month, says Goldwater will protect state's rights, and every good son and daughter of Louisiana should vote for him. What he's really saying is Goldwater will protect to right of the good white sons and daughters of Louisiana to deny me my rights. I say to hell with them and to hell with that. Besides, don't count us out down here in Louisiana just yet, you have friends you don't know you have."

I would contrast my meeting with Howard Prentiss with the one Bobby Kennedy had with Martin Luther King the same week, when he quietly slipped down to Atlanta to try and persuade Dr. King to publicly endorse JFK for re-election. The Attorney General got a polite, but very firm no, and then sat there while Dr. King explained his problems with the President's willingness to compromise with Southern Senators on civil rights, his refusal to commit during the Presidential campaign to a new Civil Rights Act which would guarantee the right to vote to Black Americans, his promise to consider an outright segregationist for the Supreme Court, his decision to invade Cuba, bomb North Korea and South Vietnam, all of which resulted in the deaths of many defenseless men, women and children. Bobby Kennedy was not a happy man when he left Atlanta, and calls were made as soon as he got back to his office in the Justice Department. There was much cursing and shouting as he wanted to know who had leaked the fact that Harold Cox was at the top of the President's list for the next Supreme Court vacancy because of a deal made with James Eastland. It was the reason why I received a call from Senator Humphrey in the middle of the night, wanting to know if I had breathed a word about what I'd seen and heard in the Vice President's office that day. I could honestly deny it, I knew who I was dealing with and was not about to do something which would burn every bridge I'd built in Washington. They never did discover who let it slip out about Cox, but my best guess, considering how things turned out down the road, would be LBJ himself.

On the last weekend before Election Day, the Vice President made a swing across the Old Confederacy. According to all the polls and analysis, it was sure to be Goldwater country when the voting was done, but it was important to fly the Democratic flag nevertheless. Kennedy had made a foray into several Southern states the week before and had received a surprisingly warm welcome in Dixie, so it was decided a visit by Johnson might payoff in some upsets. So between Friday and Sunday, we flew to New Orleans to Nashville to Atlanta to Miami to Charleston to Raleigh to Richmond. What I remember mainly was the absence of any and all Democratic elected officials, most of whom didn't want to get on the bad side of their constituents who were going to vote overwhelmingly Republican the following Tuesday. Surprisingly, the major exception was Senator Russell in Georgia, who though he did not come and sit on the stage with the Vice President at the Democratic rally in Atlanta, did greet Johnson's plane at the airport and was photographed shaking his hand.

There were plenty of Confederate flags and Goldwater signs waived from the back rows at those rallies, but otherwise, those crowds were the picture of Southern hospitality, even in Charleston, where it was rumored Strom Thurmond was marking his ballot for Goldwater.

We had just boarded the plane in South Carolina on the last Saturday afternoon of this long campaign when I was informed that the Vice President wanted to see me back in his compartment. Three minutes later I was in the room alone with Johnson, who turned to me and said, "Well, it looks like we're going to have to spend every Goddamn penny sitting in the bank vault, Howard Hughes arranged for Goldwater's treasurer to tap into a $500,000 secret account set up in a bank in the Bahamas."

I asked the Vice President how he came by such confidential knowledge.

I'll never forget LBJ's answer. "That should be Goddamn obvious; one of Barry's top guys is really working for us."

Kevin McCluskey (V)
October - November 1964

The re-election campaign of John F. Kennedy has never been written about with the same fervor the down to the wire battle with Nixon in '60 has. That first crusade, with the built-in drama of two World War II veterans fighting it out as the torch is passed, was an epic which told itself. Not so in 1964, for some reason, the battle with Goldwater against the backdrop of a near third World War just has not captured the imagination of historians in the same way.

I don't know why, I had a ring-side seat during the last month, and what I witnessed from the front lines was a battle royal. Kennedy came out of the Dallas debate in good shape, and the game plan was for the President to begin pulling away in the polls over the next two weeks, then putting it away in the final debate on the 20th of October. After that, it would be a cruise to victory.

If only it could have been so easy.

One speed bump were the polls coming out of Michigan, Illinois and Ohio the first week of October, after leading by more than 5 points in all three states since Labor Day, Kennedy had fallen to within the margin of error in the first two states, while Goldwater had edged ahead in Ohio. Those hard hat voters were responding to the Republican's "What kind of country do you want?" appeal; another unpleasant echo from that Wallace rally in the Wisconsin VFW Hall in April.

To the great credit of Lawrence O'Brien, Steve Smith, and the Kennedy brothers themselves, they realized they had a potential problem and got on top of it in record time. By the second week of October, every UAW man in Flint and Detroit, every steel-worker in Gary and Youngstown, and every meatpacker working the line is a Chicago slaughterhouse, knew exactly what Barry Goldwater thought of unions, the minimum wage, overtime pay, the 40 hour work week and Social Security.

Those tight poll numbers were the reason why I spent the first two weeks of October in the heartland, traveling from one party headquarters to another, with more than one detour to a union hall. It was my fault the state chairman in Michigan was quietly eased out of his job with three weeks to go before the election because he couldn't stay sober after the lunch hour.

There was one other job I was asked to do that October, three times I journeyed back to Dallas and to a certain bank vault, where each time I left with a satchel full of cash. How much? I made a point of not counting, but somewhere north of six figures would be my guess. One trip was to Chicago, where I handed over the money to a gentleman who worked out of Mayor Richard Daley's office, even though he was on the payroll of the Sanitation Department. The other was to Nashville, where I put the money in the hands of a high-ranking official of the Teamsters, which told me the politics of necessity had forged some strange bedfellows. My final trip was out to the West Coast, where I left a suitcase filled with packs of twenty dollar bills in the company of a well-dressed man of Latin heritage who wore the coolest pair of sunglasses I have ever seen anywhere on anyone. I have no idea who he was or what he was going to do with the money. I was just the delivery boy.

While all this was going on, the Soviets kicked out Khrushchev, the North Vietnamese went to war with the Marines, and some old fanatic in a turban took over Iran. You would have thought the country would have become used to foreign policy crisis by this point, by my count it was at least the sixth one in less than a year, but you could feel the country suck in its breath yet again. On the inside at Kennedy '64, there was a fear the country would say "enough," and decide it was time for a change. For a week, the Washington headquarters took panicky calls from Governors, Senators and Congressmen who were up for re-election, claiming they could feel a shift toward Goldwater in their states, though in most cases it was a slight one. They were worried that we were at a point in the race where even a slight shift could turn into a tidal wave under the right conditions. The big worry was that the new guys in the Kremlin would seek to regain the initiative and do something catastrophic like try to snatch West Berlin as payback for Cuba.

I watched the third Kennedy-Goldwater debate from a hotel room in Los Angeles, and when it was over, I breathed a sigh of relief; Goldwater had been aggressive in his attacks on the Kennedy foreign policy, but had completely tripped himself up over the Klan, while everyone remembered Kennedy's retort, "Go ask Castro."

As soon as I arrived back in Washington, there was a call to come to Steve Smith's office, where I was praised for the exemplary work I had done so far; so exemplary they felt, that I deserved some "lighter" duty; in other words I was to take over the advance detail for the President in the remaining days of the race. This meant I would fly into any city where Kennedy was to make an appearance 24 hours ahead of his arrival and make sure everything was running smoothly and that expectations were being met. "And if they are not," I distinctly remember Steve Smith saying, "it will be your job to kick ass until things are running smoothly." It would be my fault if the President were embarrassed in any way, at any time, during these waning days of the campaign. And woe to anyone found at fault, we'd heard stories about the verbal ass-kicking administered by the President's brother to even the most senior men who did not fulfill their duty to John F. Kennedy in his eyes.

I didn't ask about the guy who'd had the gig before me; I later learned he'd been exiled to Boston to oversee mass mailings. Like a good soldier, I saluted and did the job handed me and flew to Seattle where the President was scheduled to speak before thousands the next day. Being the Pacific Northwest, the organizers wanted to move the event inside because they feared small crowds, I overruled them and kept the event outside; I gambled the voters would turn out no matter what, and the downpours held off long enough for John

F. Kennedy to speak before a record gathering for that city. I immediately decided this job was going to be a piece of cake.

I lost any such notion over the next few days when I was called on to deal with snafus over food, marching bands, permits and potential security threats, and worst of all, who would sit next to the President and get their photo on the front page of the local paper. It was almost enough to make me want to quit, but not quite, because I was making myself useful to powerful men who could open any door in the country for me in the future, and because I grew to like the work, any and all of it.

My worst moment came on a West Coast campaign swing which took the President to San Francisco in late October; forty-five minutes before Air Force One touched down at San Francisco International airport, I was informed that thousands of demonstrators had gathered downtown with the intention of crashing the President's motorcade on the way to a rally. With memories of what happened in Dallas the previous year fresh in everyone's mind, the Secret Service talked of canceling the event, which would have been a huge embarrassment, but Mayor John Shelley insisted we stay with the plan and got the extra manpower in place to prevent what could have been an ugly scene. Nevertheless, both sides got bloodied in the process as the demonstrators were kept well away from the President's motorcade.

This was my first brush with the growing opposition to the Kennedy foreign policy on the far left since the Atlantic City convention; it had found a home on college campuses, especially at Berkeley. In San Francisco, I got a good look at them, a mostly young crowd, mixed black and white and carrying signs which said things like, KENNEDY: GET OUT OF CUBA AND VIETNAM or STOP BOMBING PEOPLE WHO ARE NOT WHITE. This incident in the City by the Bay sparked this left wing movement, their presence began turning up in every stop for the President in the days ahead and they just weren't confined to left wing college towns, but in places like Santa Fe and Denver. They were not always thousands in numbers, sometimes only a bare hundred, but the passion for their cause was fierce. They wanted America out of Cuba and out of Vietnam, first and foremost, but their signs also proclaimed opposition to nuclear weapons, the Cold War and racial injustice. It was easy to dismiss them as malcontents and agitators, which is what the campaign press office did, but it didn't mean their message was falling on deaf ears. At Thanksgiving dinner that year, my younger brother called Kennedy's policy in Cuba criminal, my father had to physically separate us before we were done.

Nevertheless, my position in the campaign gave me a ringside seat to history and a great view of one the finest politicians in American history at the top of his game. In the last weeks of the Presidential race, John F. Kennedy was on fire, striding onto the stage at open air rallies or taking command of the podium in auditorium after auditorium, his voice firm, his finger jabbing the air to make a point, and giving speech after speech after speech on where he wanted to take the country in the next four years, somehow making it sound new and original before each audience. Ted Sorenson and the other writers really earned their pay because the President had to adjust his tone more than once during the month as events beyond his control forced him to do so.

The coup in Moscow and the escalation of fighting in Vietnam ended any and all talk of the Stockholm Summit; speeches on the subject of reducing tensions with the Soviets and ending the nuclear arms race were thrown in the trash. Overnight, everything had to be rewritten; a politician of lesser talents could not have pulled it off, but JFK did not miss a beat, going from dove to hawk without so much as getting his hair ruffled. "We have been sorely tested," he said in Denver on the 25th of October, "and have not been found wanting; we have been gravely challenged, and have risen to meet it, we have looked into the eyes of the tyrant, and not blinked. Let Moscow, Peking, and Hanoi remember; we have not retreated one step, we have not faltered once in our resolve, we have not let the flag of freedom touch the ground." The audience stood and applauded for five minutes when the President was done.

Yet he never completely gave up on his original cause, the one which most clearly engaged him. In a New York speech before a room filled with supporters that was taped and aired on the networks days later, he hit on all his hawkish themes, but he ended with these remarks, "Yet we in America do not seek a state of perpetual conflict, with its endless stockpiling of weapons, both conventional and nuclear, until both us and the Soviets are crushed under the weight of our own enormous arsenals. We do not seek to live in a world of never ending fear and suspicion, where enemies eternally connive against one another. We are not satisfied to forever live on a planet with half the world walled off from the other half. What I will never stop working for is a world free from strife, fear and despotism. What I hope to one day see is a world at peace, not just for my own children, but all the children of this earth." I do remember those words very well.

The other thing Kennedy never failed to mention was the cause of equal rights, even when it might have cost him votes in some quarters, and I don't mean just the South. Maybe it was the stinging criticism he'd received from the far left of the party for compromising on the Civil Rights Act, but in nearly every speech there were at least a few lines about "making America a better nation by making it a more equal nation for all of its citizens." When he went up to Michigan or in the steel towns of Pennsylvania and Ohio and stood before blue-collar audiences filled with men and women who feared integration would mean blacks competing for their jobs or moving into their neighborhoods, Kennedy looked them in the eyes and said that "making sure the doors of opportunity would be open wide to both black and white" would be his top domestic priority in a second term. These were not exactly welcome words with some local Democrats. I was asked by more than one Mayor or Congressional candidate during the campaign's final swing through the industrial Midwest if I would pass on to the President that it would be most appreciated if he would not say anything overtly about civil rights during meetings ahead of a

Presidential visit.

The only time I felt anything like outright fear while doing this job was when I learned the President would be making a foray into the Deep South, specifically having Montgomery, Alabama and Jackson, Mississippi added to the itinerary after a visit to Florida. What I remember most vividly was the Whites Only signs on the public restrooms in the state capitol buildings in both towns, seemingly shining with defiance. Then there were the Colored signs over the water fountains. They were freshly painted as if to remind everyone that the men running these states planned on keeping segregation around for a long time. How could the President who had just signed the Civil Rights Act be welcome in such a town, much less his advance man? Luckily for me, the campaign had sent in a big gun ahead of my arrival, Lawrence O'Brien himself had paid quiet visits to both Montgomery and Jackson and worked out a plan which somehow satisfied both the President and the segregationist local politicians.

The press called Kennedy's venture into enemy country a token gesture. In truth, it was an attempt to blunt Goldwater's surge in the region, to depress his vote totals by even a few points with very conservative white voters, which could pay-off in Texas and Florida. Moreover, it was an attempt by the President to make sure all of his bridges to the Southern Democrats hadn't been burned yet; there would be many political battles in the second term where he would need all the good will he could get.

Larry O'Brien made it clear the President would be speaking to an integrated rally in Montgomery, and all the state's Democratic elected officials made it plain they would not attend; in the end, it was arranged for Kennedy to speak at a ballpark once used by a Negro League team. I arrived in Montgomery late in the day before Air Force One was to touch down, filled with dread at having to deal with one of the most notorious Southern demagogues in recent American history. To my surprise, everything was moving smoothly, and everyone was cooperating, although publicly, Governor Wallace was making it appear as if he was having nothing to do with the "mixed race" rally for the President. Behind the scenes, he instructed the State Police to give the Secret Service everything it asked for and to make sure some of the city's more vocal and active racist elements were elsewhere during the President's visit. "Son, we're not going to have a repeat of Dallas here," the Governor told me in his office in the Capitol building. "No, sir, John F. Kennedy is going to get a welcome worthy of the good people of Alabama." He fixed with a most steely gaze as he spoke these words, and I wondered if they were really a threat. The unsmiling Superintendent of the Alabama State Police standing beside him made me think as much.

In the end, the President spoke before a "mixed race" crowd that had far more white faces in it than would have been expected; they were also quite respectful. A prayer was said by a local black minister, but he was followed by John Patterson, a former Governor who was reputed to be more pro-segregation than Wallace, but Patterson had also served in the Pacific and was a friend of Kennedy's, proudly introduced "a fellow veteran and our nation's President." The national press openly speculated if Kennedy would deliver a pointedly pro-civil rights speech in the Cradle of the Confederacy. What he did say on that unusually warm day - he'd taken off his dark jacket and rolled up the sleeves of his white shirt - was an attempt to find some common ground on which both races could stand on in this deeply divided part of America. "The chains of a long dead past," Kennedy said to the upturned faces, "must no longer bind us. We are all Americans, whether we are Black or White, North or South, and we all want the same things for our children: For them to live in peace, to enjoy the fruits of their labors, to have a glorious future in this great nation."

After the rally, there was a "private" reception at the Governor's mansion with Wallace and a gaggle of Alabama politicians. Along the streets of Montgomery, the reception was decidedly "mixed" in every way; here there could be found white men and women waving Stars and Bars with signs calling the President a Yankee Communist and suggesting he go back to Massachusetts or somewhere with a much warmer climate. On the other side, I remember seeing a middle-aged black woman in her Sunday best, standing on a corner enthusiastically waving Old Glory as the President's limo passed. A block away there stood a group of white men, some in cotton shirts and sporting terminal flat top haircuts while others wore bib overalls, their faces as stony as the figure atop a nearby Confederate monument.

I was not on the inside when Kennedy met with Wallace, but from all accounts, then and later, the Governor put on his best Southern hospitality for the President. The two men spent most of the time talking about their mutual service in World War II and deliberately avoiding their differences. The President made a point of saying "he knew he could count on all their support on November 3rd" when he spoke to a room filled with some of the most diehard segregationist politicians in the country; reportedly everyone, including the President, smiled broadly when he spoke.

When the President's party arrived in Jackson, Mississippi, it was greeted effusively by none other than Senator James Eastland, the man who had fought the Civil Rights Act tooth and nail in his Judiciary Committee and then all the way to the bitter end on the Senate floor. Yet there he was, acting as if he and John F. Kennedy had never had a difference between them, just two men who'd served in the Senate together. There would be much criticism and suspicion from the Civil Rights community over Kennedy's campaign swing through Deep South; not without justification, they were fearful another compromise might have been struck behind closed doors just like the one which had gotten the Civil Rights Act through Congress, but had nevertheless, preserved Jim Crow.

One reason Wallace and the others put their best foot forward for the President was all the federal dollars flowing into their states through defense appropriations, which a lot of Alabama paychecks depended upon. I couldn't help but remember the Wallace speaking at the VFW Hall in Wisconsin and the man who greeted the President at the Governor's

Mansion and not be struck by his hypocrisy.

I caught a lucky break when I was not needed for the President's controversial visit to Havana that was run completely by the Southern Command and was grateful for it. While the President was in Cuba on the last weekend of the campaign, I received a message in Philadelphia, where I was looking over the plans for a Sunday rally, and ordered back to DC immediately. Two hours later, I walked into Steve Smith's office, where I was met by Kenny O'Donnell, who informed me that the *Washington Star* was working on a story about attempted blackmail and a cover-up concerning the President and a visit to the Hotel Adolphus the night before the Dallas debate.

I opened my mouth to say something, but nothing came out, my mouth felt as though filled with cotton and my knees went weak.

Colonel Martin Maddox (X)
October-November 1964

The ripple effect from the Moscow coup continued to spread in the final days of the Presidential campaign, as with each succeeding day, it became ever more apparent that we were no longer dealing with a Kremlin interested in negotiation with the West. Reports flooded in from every embassy behind the Iron Curtain detailing mass arrests occurring there, especially among those East German and Czech military units which had balked at the rumor they might be deployed to Iran a few months earlier. Everything pointed to a mass purge which was only just beginning. The Kremlin sent the world a clear message when they rehabilitated such old Stalin-era figures as V. M. Molotov and Marshall Zhukov, rivals who had been ousted by Khrushchev nearly ten years before, who were now given seats at the table.

The new regime made itself clear on October 25th when Ambassador Dobrynin went to the State Department and handed Secretary Rusk a note informing the President that the Soviet Union was no longer interested in attending the summit in Stockholm unless the United States immediately agreed to pull all of its troops out of Cuba and restore the "legitimate government of the people," end all military operations in South Vietnam, pay respirations to the "victims of aggression of in the People's Republic of Korea," and agree that Iran belonged within the Soviet sphere of influence. Each and every one of those preconditions was a non-starter - to say the least. It was noticed with some amusement that the note was signed by Andrei Gromyko, who evidently had survived yet another change in the wind inside the Kremlin.

President Kennedy took this reversal of fortune in stride. "We tried to meet Khrushchev half way; it was worth the effort, and it still is, despite what's happened. Sooner or later, these new men in the Kremlin will get to the same place old Nikita was and realize there is no future in an unending stalemate. We just have to hold the line until they get there or more enlightened leaders take their place." One thing the President was emphatic about, Barry Goldwater was not the man to deal with this new situation.

Our immediate concern was the Soviet military and whether it would be used to provoke a new confrontation with the United States, either by going back into Iran or by pouring gas on a brush fire somewhere in the third world. On the 26th of the month, a formal request for at least one regular army division and two more Marine battalions from General Westmorland arrived on McNamara's desk, this based on an assessment of the situation on the ground in South Vietnam, and was prompted by a CIA report on an abrupt increase in Soviet military aid to the North following a secret visit by an unnamed "top Soviet official" only days after Khrushchev's removal. It appeared the Kremlin had shown its hand.

The decision to throttle up in South Vietnam was made by the President as he flew back from a campaign stop in Jackson, Mississippi. The NSC had been meeting in the White House for hours going over options and not arriving at any which didn't risk the imminent collapse of the South unless we acted decisively. I was on Air Force One when the President made the call, and despite what some have claimed long after the fact, the fear of being called soft on Communism by Senator Goldwater was never mentioned.

The iron hand of the new bosses in the Kremlin did solve one lingering problem. About ten days after the changing of the guard on Moscow, General Andreyev quietly let it be known that he was willing to discuss the subject of defection with General Abrams himself - one soldier to another. The negotiations took less than a day before an agreement was ready for the President to sign off on; all Russian nationals would be given the chance to stay in Cuba or travel to any country of their choice. An Indian trawler and a Hungarian transport would be made ready in the port of Santiago for any Soviet who wished to return to the Motherland by way of the Gdansk in Poland. The sticking point was the large number of former officials of the Castro regime who had found sanctuary inside Camaguey. Most would be allowed to leave, the exceptions being a list of names prepared by the Administration who would be turned over to the occupation forces. There would be a lot of criticism that the President bargained away a number of outright criminals, who had committed atrocities in Cuba, but it was a quick and final resolution to a thorny problem; the President took no more than fifteen minutes before he gave Abrams the okay. Within 24 hours, Andreyev and most of his officers laid down their arms; Andreyev chose to stay on the island of Cuba, while the American government began the difficult business of getting his family out of the Soviet Union - another condition of his defection. Sadly, most of the Red Army soldiers who returned home from Cuba spent many years in Siberian work camps.

With the Stockholm summit off, there was no longer any need to be bound by certain agreements made in New Delhi; the President quietly reversed his decision to withdraw all American troops from Cuba, we were there to stay for the foreseeable future.

The reason I was on Air Force One when the President made the call on Vietnam was because my presence had been requested at the President's side during the remainder of the campaign, my chief duty was to brief the President three times daily on the ongoing crisis's in Vietnam, Iran, Cuba, the Soviet Union and anywhere else trouble reared its head. John F. Kennedy did not want to be blindsided by any last minute blow-ups like the coup in Moscow, which had very nearly derailed his campaign.

During those last days before the election, the public saw a confident man on the stump, firm in his vision for a second term and eloquent in his reasoning as to why he deserved one, what the voters did not see were the hurried meetings on Air Force One, calls to Secretaries Rusk and McNamara and CIA chief McCone, and the President, his face often in a frown from back pain, although more likely from the intelligence reports I'd brought him.

While much of the press was fixated on the rest of the world, a lot was happening in Iran. The picture painted by both CIA and British MI5 operatives for us was grim; it seemed the Soviet invasion had stripped away hundreds of years of civilization, and now with this Khomeini in charge, the whole country had reverted to the Middle Ages. The reports that got out detailed mass executions of those suspected of collaborating with the Soviets, of serving in the Shah's government, or working too closely with the Americans. This last group included Iranians employed by U.S. corporations, especially the oil companies. Far worse were those who ran afoul of Islamic law, which had been made the rule of the land by the Ayatollah; I remember a gruesome picture of a man beheaded in the middle of a street in Teheran for the crime of "usury." Things went from bad to worse when one of the CIA teams went missing; we later learned they were being tortured inside one of the Shah's former prisons. Outwardly, the Administration's position was that the Shah would return to Iran when events in the country "stabilized." In private, the President made no secret of his disdain for the Shah, "a man who ran away at the first sound of gunfire." In public, the President repeatedly said that he was not worried about Khomeini, who we "would work with to resolve the situation in Iran." Through third parties, an attempt was made to open a back channel to Khomeini himself, this did result in a note from the Ayatollah himself; it was not encouraging as it opened with a demand for an apology from the President for American involvement in the 1953 restoration of the Shah after a coup had ousted him, along with an insistence that all those in the CIA who had been involved in this action be punished. "This Khomeini is just Goddamn nuts," was President Kennedy's response.

The one event which sticks in my mind the most during the last week of the campaign was the President's visit to Havana, even if it was for only a few hours. The visit took place on October 30th, and the original plan had been for the President to ride through the streets of the Cuban capital while receiving the cheers and accolades of a grateful and liberated people. Southern Command nixed the idea as soon as it was proposed; Bobby Kennedy tried repeatedly to overrule them as he wanted the visual of his brother being enthusiastically received in Havana to dominate the network news during the last weekend before Election Day. The truth of the matter was that there were no grateful crowds willing to surge in the streets to greet an American President, instead there were armed groups of Cuban vigilantes, determined to exact revenge on their former oppressors, and the organized resistance, made up of Castroites who had vowed to fight back against the Yankee Imperialists to the bitter end. In the end, the President stepped in and said he would do whatever the Secret Service and General Abrams requested. There was a ceremony at the airport and then a fast dash through the streets to the Presidential palace so that the next day, every daily paper in the country had a photo of a smiling John F. Kennedy standing behind the desk in Fidel Castro's office. All in all, the President was on the island barely three hours.

It was a short visit by any measure, but the President took in a lot while he was on the ground: the lack of even the semblance of a provisional government to greet him; the armed American GI's who lined the streets on the way to the Presidential Palace; the plumes of smoke rising over the city against a gorgeous blue sky, even though hostilities supposedly ceased months before; the crack of gunfire echoing in the far distance at the airport; the boarded up buildings everywhere; the desperate condition of the few Cubans the President glimpsed. Instead of being elated on the flight back to Washington, President Kennedy was pensive after a trip which was designed to highlight a political and military triumph. "The job isn't done," he said to a group of us while in the air. "I was a fool to have agreed to pull the troops out next year; there's no way this island could be ready to govern itself in that time. I wanted the summit in Stockholm so much that I made a bad deal with Khrushchev on Cuba to get it, but we're not bound by it anymore, and we're going to do right by all those people who have lost so much." They were noble sentiments; making them a reality would prove to be most difficult.

While on the ground in Havana, I did get a brief look at the badly damaged remains of the Tropicana and some of the other hotels, the once and future property of Santos Trafficante and Carlos Marcello; their tough luck, I thought to myself.

We arrived back in Washington from the Havana trip on Halloween's Eve for a day's layover, just enough for me to get time at home with my long-suffering wife and extraordinarily patient kids. While coaching my son on his Little League swing, a call came from Dave Powers at the White House. I picked up the receiver fearing the Soviets had created yet another crisis and quickly discovered the problem was much closer to home. Mr. Powers informed me that a reporter from the *Washington Star* was asking questions about the President, the Hotel Adolphus, and the night before the debate in Dallas. I will be honest, the first thing that popped into my mind was an image of me taking the Fifth before a Congressional Investigating Committee - it was so vivid I actually saw the TV news cameras recording my public humiliation.

Then Powers told me that if I was to receive a call from any reporter from either a newspaper or one of the networks concerning the evening in question: I was to say I had spent those hours at the ranch house outside Dallas where the President prepared for his second debate with Senator Goldwater. I knew nothing about the Hotel Adolphus or any purported visit there by the President or anyone else for that matter. "Can you do that, Colonel," Mr. Powers asked me. "If asked, can you deny you were ever at the Hotel Adolphus and state that you have no knowledge of anything which might have occurred there."

I did not hesitate; I told Dave Powers I could do just that and then some, whatever it took to get the job done. I was a Marine, and I would hold the line.

That is what I have done through all the years until now, I've held the line long after the war was over and there was no longer an enemy to make a stand against. And in all these years, I've often wondered whom it was who tipped off the papers in the first place because somebody there that night had to have talked.

Dorothy Jean Brennan (VI)
November 1964

This is what I did, once back in my hotel room at the Roosevelt on the night of the Rose Bowl rally, I first wrote out in long hand everything I remembered from the evening at the Hotel Adolphus - names, dates and everything else I heard, especially concerning John F. Kennedy - liar, adulterer and extortionist. What I didn't do was state my own name or mention anything I personally did that night, the last thing I wanted was a reporter calling me, instead of the guilty parties involved. When it was all down on a legal pad, I borrowed a portable typewriter from the press room and typed it all up, multiple times, until a had half a dozen copies, each six pages long and single spaced. The next step was to stuff all six copies into envelopes and address them, each one to a different political reporter at a different major newspaper, including *The Washington Star*, the *Los Angeles Times*, the *Dallas Morning News* and the *New York Times*. The sun was coming up when I dropped them into a mailbox on a corner located a block from the Roosevelt. I had worked straight through the night, not stopping until I was done lest I lose my nerve. I knew what I was doing in that moment, and I didn't care, it was better than lying down and taking it.

Only later in the day, when I had time to think about it, did the recklessness of my act sink in and the possible unintended consequences begin to dawn on me; namely the harm to my own personal safety or my parents, because, after all, in mailing those envelopes, I had threatened more than one Mafia boss. I realized I had been very foolish, and looking back, quite naïve in believing the press would just take the word of an anonymous tip and go after the President. In the end, my tip produced only one phone call to me, and that came from Wade Harbinson, it was the first time we'd spoken since Dallas. He said he'd just received a call from his old friend, the editor of the *Dallas Morning News*, warning him that some unknown tipster was peddling a story full of smears against not only President Kennedy, but also against some fine citizens of the Lone Star state. He then asked me if I knew anything about it, which I, of course, denied vehemently.

Harbinson said that was a good thing, but, "If you ever breathe a word to anybody about the Hotel Adolphus, if you so much as ever have that place and my name on your lips, I will make damn sure you are implicated up to your neck in the whole fucking mess. Think about that, little lady, not only will the Kennedy brothers move heaven and earth to bury you in a deep hole; I will be right beside them with a bulldozer. You have no friends. Remember that, girl!"

I spent the night in my hotel room, sobbing into a pillow, determined to quit the campaign in the morning and go back home to Idaho.

That did not happen, and nothing came of my anonymous letter writing. I went back to work: I am not a quitter, not then and not now. I would not talk about the Adolphus Hotel, and I would not let them run me off, but nobody was ever going call me "girl" in such a snarling tone ever again.

By now the campaign had only a few days to go, and we sensed a changing dynamic: we could feel the country making up its mind and rapidly moving ahead with the rest of us trying to catch up. The Senator flew from California to Ohio for a final swing through the Midwest; the last appearance was in East St. Louis, Illinois with Senator Dirksen, whose folksy style had been a big hit with the voters. I would like to say Senator Goldwater hit the ball out of the park, but he was dead on his feet and basically sleep-walked through his last appeal to the voters; Dirksen, who was on his own home turf, received the loudest cheers from the crowd.

On the plane back to Phoenix, a memo from Clif White was distributed to us, in it he gave a detailed analysis of how Senator Goldwater was going to win the Presidency the next day by sweeping the Old Confederacy, including Texas, taking Ohio and Illinois in the Midwest, carrying the normally Republican states of the Great Plains and the Rocky Mountains and then California on the West Coast. He made a point of saying that in all probability, Kennedy would win the popular vote by carrying the big cities on the East Coast, but Goldwater would pull it out in the Electoral College. Understandably, I had not been in the best of moods during those last days, but White's memo, which spelled out how we would march to victory on paper, reminded me why I had signed on in the first place.

We were going to kick those corrupt Kennedys out of the White House and make America the country it used to be again.

John Compton (VIII)
November 1964

The last polls came out in Texas the weekend before Election Day, and the news was not as good as we would have wished. The *Dallas Morning News* had Kennedy and Goldwater tied in the Lone Star state, while the Houston paper put the Republican candidate up by three points. A Gallup poll said about the same thing. It was clear the bump we'd gotten early in the month after the Dallas debate had leveled off, while the undecided voters were breaking late for Goldwater.

The Vice President's mood was dark on the last day, the worst thing that could happen, would be for Kennedy-Johnson to lose outright, the second worse thing would be for the ticket to win, but not carry Texas, a brutally humiliating prospect for Johnson. His last campaign appearance was in San Antonio, I would like to say Johnson hit a home run, but it wouldn't be true. Instead, he gave a rote speech hitting upon the same reasons to vote for Kennedy he'd made in every other speech for the past six weeks. Afterward, I went to Austin, where the Johnson victory celebration was supposed to be held in a little over 24 hours, the Vice President went back to his ranch, or so the press was told, only later did I learn he spent the wee small hours of Election Day down in the Rio Grande Valley.

The prospect of losing Texas hung over us all on November 3rd, we'd worked so hard and more to the point, risked so much, that losing, in the end, was something too bitter to contemplate. I was in my hotel room in the Austin Hilton watching TV, resisting the urge to get on the phone and talk to well-connected friends in Washington because I was scared at what they might tell me. In the afternoon, I went down-stairs and found a bar, so I had some liquid courage in me when the first returns started to come in at 6:00 p.m. local time. Kennedy jumped to a lead in the popular vote, but it was the state by state breakdown to which I paid attention, and as the Republican ticket swept across the South, my heart sank.

The Vice President arrived a half hour after the polls closed in Texas and we expected him to be in one of his rankest moods because of the close race in his home state, but the man who greeted me was anything but. "It's going to be a great night, Johnny," he said as he threw an arm around my shoulder, "A great night indeed." That is when I remembered how upbeat Johnson had been the previous summer when everyone was predicting how he would be dropped from the ticket and writing his political obituary. My spirits rose instantly, even though the early returns put Goldwater up by 50,000 votes in Texas and David Brinkley on NBC was talking about "an historic sweep of Dixie" by the Republicans. LBJ knew something and that was enough for me.

At 11:00 p.m. the margin for Goldwater was still the same with more than half the state reporting, that is when the Vice President, who was holed up in the room next to mine, got on the phone and made a series of calls behind a closed door; within 45 minutes, most of the remaining counties in the state reported. The upshot: at midnight, Kennedy pulled ahead of Goldwater by a half a percentage point. That's when Johnson announced he was going down to the ball-room and claim victory. When it was pointed out that none of the networks had called Texas for the Democrats yet, he replied, "It's in the bag, and I'm not waiting on any damn network to call anything. We've won."

A lot of news coverage the next day would talk about LBJ's brass and nerve in claiming victory prematurely on election night, in effect stealing some of the spotlight from the President. But his claim would prove to be true, Kennedy-Johnson would carry Texas by a little more than 24,000 votes, a margin too close for comfort by any reckoning, but it was a win, and that's what counted. It would not come out for decades, but a good chunk of those winning votes came courtesy of some veteran ballot box stuffers in South Texas who'd gotten their marching orders from Johnson himself the day before. It was his ace in the hole, one he'd played many times in the past.

There was one other thing which caught my notice as I sat in front of the TV; it was the neighboring state of Louisiana. Kennedy was behind there most of the night, but not by nearly the margin as the other Deep South states, at midnight he pulled even and by the time the sun was coming up on Wednesday morning, the President pulled ahead ever so much. It would take a couple of weeks, and no small amount of contention, before the final numbers were certified and John F. Kennedy was awarded Louisiana's electors by only 1,562 votes. Later, I would learn Louisiana had the highest percentage of registered blacks voting of any Southern state. It looked like Howard Prentiss's plan had worked out to perfection; I remembered his remark about us having "friends we didn't know we had." It turned out a lot of Catholics in Louisiana were not about to vote out the first Roman Catholic President no matter what his views on civil rights.

I was standing behind LBJ in the ballroom when he jumped the gun on the victory call in Texas; if you look at the old footage of it now, I can be seen standing in the background looking especially animated, which I attribute to all the liquid courage consumed in the hours before. I don't recall exactly what Johnson said in his speech to a packed room filled with enthusiastic supporters, but I do remember what he said to me as he left the podium, "Well Johnny boy, you ready to sign on for '68, because it's going to be All the way with LBJ next time."

Kevin McCluskey (VI)
November 1964

The last swing of the Kennedy campaign was a two-day sprint through the Midwest, which took the President to Cleveland, Cincinnati, Indianapolis, Detroit, Flint, Milwaukee, Saint Paul, Springfield, Saint Louis, and then back to Boston late on Election Eve so he could vote in his home-town before heading back to Washington on Election Day. Everyone was dead tired, except JFK, who seemed energized on what he knew to be his last campaign for elective office. The crowds were enormous, in Ohio, people waited six hours to just get a glimpse of him; they started showing up at three in the morning in Springfield, Illinois for a rally scheduled for three in the afternoon. There was an energy in the air like electricity, coming off the throngs of people that literally crackled.

I think Kennedy's best moment of this final swing came in Saint Louis, where he barely missed Goldwater, who made an appearance on the other side of the Mississippi the same day. "This generation," he told the crowd, "has seen the world torn apart by a World War; this generation has seen our country brought to its knees by an economic depression. This generation has paid the price and restored the peace; this generation has done the hard work and restored prosperity. But this generation will not be satisfied with that; this generation will not be satisfied until peace reigns over every corner of the earth and every one of its people is free from want. Our work will not be finished until that is done."

It was the kind of pie in the sky oratory the President's critics would take him task for in the future, but on this day, these farmers and factory workers and teachers and clerks standing under a late afternoon sun applauded every word. They were the people who'd grown up on county relief during the Depression and then gone on to storm the beaches on D-Day, the people who had raised families and put in long hours to put food on the table, and had asked for nothing more than to have a good life, a better life. And on this day, the last day of the 1964 Presidential election, these people truly belonged to John F. Kennedy, who despite being born to wealth and privilege, was truly one of them.

After the final rally in Boston, which went off without a hitch, my job was done. The last rally, late at night, was the only one during the whole re-election effort where Kennedy was actually seen to tear up during a speech. He usually never got sentimental in that way on the stump, but it was his last speech ever as a candidate, and these were the people who had started it all by electing him to Congress back in 1946. "To you, I will always be grateful," he said with Mrs. Kennedy at his side. "Your faith in me made it all possible." That was when he had to pause, clear his throat and wipe his eyes before continuing, it only lasted a split second, but everyone there had at least a lump in their throats as well.

I slept in my old bed in my parent's house, got up early and voted, then caught a flight and was back Kennedy '64 headquarters by late afternoon. The final Gallup poll had the President up by four points over Goldwater; the final Harris poll had him ahead by five points; the last Roper poll gave us the best numbers with Kennedy up by seven, while *U.S. News and World Report* had the worst figures with Kennedy ahead by only two points. Ohio, Illinois, Texas, Florida, and California were considered too close to call, which meant neither Kennedy nor Goldwater could be said to have the necessary electoral votes locked up to win.

With all of this in mind, the mood at the headquarters was cautiously confident when I got there; turnout was either at the same levels from 1960 or higher - a good sign, except for the South, where voters were flocking to the polls in numbers not seen in decades. The big worries were Texas and California, the former because Goldwater had shown consistent strength there all throughout the fall, and the latter because of a feared backlash from the riots in Los Angeles over the Labor Day weekend. If both of those states went Republican, Goldwater would have an excellent chance of winning the needed electoral votes while losing the popular vote.

An hour before the polls closed in the East, Bobby Kennedy made an appearance at the headquarters and told us, "It's not going to be close, there is no way Goldwater will win this in the Electoral College, my brother is going to win it going away."

Those were welcome words and our mood brightened considerably when the first returns started coming in right after 7:00 p.m. The President jumped into an early lead in the popular vote as Maine and Vermont went Democratic for the first time since FDR; New York and New Jersey fell into our column in short order. But Indiana went for Goldwater right off the bat; then we watched as one state of the old Confederacy after another go Republican. "Old Dixie has shown us exactly what it thinks of John Kennedy's policy on Civil Rights," was Walter Cronkite's comment when Mississippi was called for Goldwater. By then the President had won Pennsylvania, but was uncomfortably behind in the Buckeye state. Everyone was holding their breath when the first returns from the central Midwest came in, especially Illinois, because of Senator Dirksen's presence on the GOP ticket. When key precincts in the Land of Lincoln and Michigan reported heavily for Kennedy; I knew for sure we would win. The President was well ahead in the popular vote at 9:00 p.m., but there was still a long way to go. I remember nodding off in a chair as the long hours I had been putting in caught up with me, I didn't wake up until the room erupted in cheers when LBJ went on TV and claimed victory in Texas. There was some consternation because the state hadn't been officially called yet, but as someone observed it was Johnson's state and if he said we'd won it, then we'd won it.

The returns from Texas remained incredibly tight with the President ahead by a mere handful of votes; and as the hours moved toward midnight, the Great Plains and Rocky Mountain states fell into the Republican column one by one. Meanwhile the polls had not yet closed on the West Coast. By then, we were pulling ahead in Illinois, but the big worry increasingly was California, Kennedy's last poll numbers were good, but I remember Lawrence O'Brien saying if Goldwater could carry Texas and California even at this late hour, he would still have a chance at winning the necessary electoral votes to deny Kennedy a second term.

Then late returns from Tennessee put the President ahead narrowly there, and Louisiana tightened until it was too close to call, and out of nowhere, Arkansas went for Kennedy and suddenly, Goldwater's sweep of Dixie was no more. "That's it," I remember O'Brien saying, "it's all over." It didn't register at first, but of course, it was true, there was no way Goldwater was going to get the Electoral votes he needed without all of the Old Confederacy in his pocket. But who would have thought it would come down to Arkansas? As far as I knew, neither major candidate had set foot in the state; because of the President's record on Civil Rights and how Orval Faubus was still in the Governor's mansion in Little Rock, we'd written the state off as a hopeless Dogpatch for Goldwater. Yet ultimately the state would go for Kennedy by just over 60,000 votes. Go figure.

In the end, Kennedy-Johnson was re-elected by a vote of 353 to 185 in the Electoral College and split the popular vote roughly 55% to 45% with Goldwater-Dirksen.

Sometime after the first returns from California came in, a wave of drowsiness came over me, and I found a couch for a catnap. I woke in the early hours of Wednesday morning having missed the networks making the call for Kennedy at 1:00 a.m. I missed being there when the newly re-elected John F. Kennedy came over to the HQ to make a victory speech with Mrs. Kennedy at his side in the press room. There was just enough time for me to crash the line as JFK was leaving to return to the White House. All of my disappointment vanished the instant he grasped my hand, and with a look of recognition, said, "Mr. McCluskey, couldn't have gotten it done without your help." Anyone who overheard it might have thought the President was talking about all that time on the road I'd put in making sure all those rallies came off without a hitch, but I knew better.

A couple of hours later, I was back in my Washington apartment for the first time in weeks, watching a replay of Senator Goldwater's concession speech where he thanked all the volunteers who were wiping away tears in the Phoenix auditorium as he spoke. He'd said something about holding their heads high despite losing when the camera caught a familiar blonde lovely standing in the background, dabbing her eyes.

I immediately got up and went in search of a phone number I'd written down almost a month to the day earlier.

Colonel Martin Maddox (XI)
November 1964 - January 1965

The first week of November proved to be a quiet one, but the calm didn't last, on Veteran's Day, the Viet Cong staged an attack on Ton Son Nhut Air Base outside Saigon, killing two dozen USAF personal there in an advisory capacity. Over the next few days, similar attacks were launched all up and down South Vietnam, as it became obvious the VC and the North Vietnamese were operating freely out of bases in Cambodia and Laos, two supposedly "neutral" countries. Every evening news-cast of Huntley-Brinkley and Cronkite during the holiday season opened with video-tape from South Vietnam of burning villages, bombed out towns and fleeing ARVN troops.

But as bad as the news from South Vietnam was, the main focus of the White House right after Election Day was Cuba. "Maybe Khrushchev getting canned was a blessing in disguise," said the President at the first meeting of the NSC after the election. "If we had left Cuba in the shape it is in today, somebody who'd make Batista look like Thomas Jefferson would have ended up in charge down there."

With the withdrawal canceled, we now had to come up with a plan for how to proceed in Cuba. Not that there wasn't plenty of advice being freely given, especially from certain members of Congress and elements of academia who called what we did to liberate the island from Communism "aggression."

There was no provisional authority to work with in Havana; no functioning law enforcement or courts anywhere on the island; resistance by Castro supporters was still active in the countryside; armed groups of vigilantes controlled large parts of the cities and most towns; food distribution systems were barely functioning; the only the thing resembling authority on the island was General Abrams and the 100,000 troops doing occupation duty. Then there was the reason why we were in Cuba in the first place: Oswald's assassination attempt, exactly twelve months ago.

As of November, no investigation had yet to start on the ground in Cuba.

The Administration had put all of its chips on the table and bet on Harry Williams, Manual Airtime and Commander Juan Almeida to take up the reigns after Castro was ousted; but they were dead, and all that remained to take their place were discredited flunkies of Batista and turncoat Communists.

I sat in on the meetings where many of these problems were hashed out between Secretary Rusk, Secretary McNamara, CIA Director McCone, my old boss, Mr. Bundy, and of course, the Attorney General. To further complicate matters, Senator Fulbright, had announced plans to hold hearings on the future of Cuba by his Foreign Relations Committee, while at the same time, a bipartisan group in the House let it be known that they would introduce legislation in the new Congress requiring all American military personal to be off the island by the end of 1965. The *New York Times*, the *Boston Herald*, and the *Washington Star* ran editorials calling the continued military occupation an untenable situation and demanded the installation of a provisional "government of national unity" which would include Communists.

The general consensus among the President's advisors was that a governing authority had to be established and soon, but the devil was in the details.

A week before Christmas, I was called to the Oval Office by the President and his brother. "Colonel," said Robert Kennedy, "what do you think will be the end result if we were to set up a provisional government in Havana and then hold free elections? My brother and I would really like your honest opinion."

I gave the Kennedy brothers my honest answer: "Sir, I firmly believe anyone you would appoint to any provisional government at this point will be seen by the Cuban people as traitors and puppets of the Yankee Imperialists, and if you hold free elections, they will elect the most rabidly anti-American bastards they can find. I personally believe it will be many years before Cuba will be in a position to govern itself and live in peace with us. We lost our best chance for an easy resolution in Cuba when we lost Commander Almeida. It's just going to take a lot of hard work now. That is my honest opinion, Sir,"

"You are not alone in your thinking, Colonel," was how President Kennedy answered. "Not alone at all."

There were no more meetings about Cuba and a few calls to the right people in Congress got the Foreign Relations Committee hearings and any House resolution temporarily postponed until after the President's State of the Union address, which would come after the inauguration.

That was where things stood when on the morning of January 17th, 1965, the President stepped into the press room at the White House; accompanying him was the former Vice President of the United States and his opponent in 1960, Richard M. Nixon. The President read a statement announcing the formation of a "Provisional Administration" in Cuba, headed by Nixon, who would have the title of Governor General. President Kennedy said this was to be an interim authority until such time as a "government chosen by the Cuban people in a free election" could take over. When this would come about and how long it would take to get there was not specified, only that, in the President's words, "it would happen when Cuba is ready." Nixon said he was taking the job with gratitude and humility, happy for the chance to help a country which had been "the victim of a Communist tyrant return to the family of free nations."

The sight of Kennedy and Nixon, standing side by side, smiling and shaking hands, came as a shock to the political establishment in Washington, but not to me. I knew exactly who Murray Chotiner had been representing that evening at the Hotel Adolphus, someone who had been in a room just down the hall with all of Dr. Jacobsen's' medical records in his possession; records which ended up in the President's hands after a face to face meeting.

Later in the day, I was delegated to giving the former Vice President a full briefing on the Cuban invasion and the aftermath; I'm sure Nixon recognized me from that evening in Dallas, but he never let on; he as much as anyone knew the value of silence. "This job is going to be a bitch," he said when I was finished. "But it will get done, and when I'm finished, the stain of Castro will be wiped completely clean from one end of the island to the other. And I'm going to make sure that son of bitch pays for every crime he committed." He had his work cut out for him, the next day, an Army convoy was ambushed on a highway in Oriente province by militia units still loyal to the Communists, killing over 50 GI's before they faded back into the countryside. On the same day, a Communist-run newspaper in Paris printed a communiqué from Che Guevara calling for a worldwide revolution against the "forces of Imperialism" and vengeance for the "murdered innocents in Cuba." The CIA speculated he was in the Congo.

The consequences of our actions in Cuba were just beginning.

I spent Inauguration Day, 1965, in my basement office of the White House, monitoring cables from Europe; two days before, the Soviets began moving more troops and armor in Poland and East Germany, in the coming days, the military forces of both countries would be ruthlessly purged of all "undesirable elements." The new men in the Kremlin were making their presence felt.

In the days after the election, President Kennedy had been determined to open some line of communication with the men on the "State Committee on the National Emergency," specifically Mikhail Suzlov, who seemed to first among equals on that body, but to no success. The American Ambassador had been rebuffed multiple times since October when he requested a meeting, while at least twice; personal notes from the President himself had gone undelivered. A sad loss presented an opportunity when five days after President Kennedy was sworn in for a second term, Winston Churchill died; it went without saying that the President would attend the state funeral and he vowed to meet face to face with whomever the Kremlin sent to represent the Soviet Union at the last rites for the greatest statesman of the 20th Century.

The men heading the Soviet delegation were the recently rehabilitated V.M. Molotov and Marshall Georgi Zhukov, Churchill's World War II contemporaries, along with the great survivor, Foreign Minister Gromyko. The President got what he wanted, a meeting with the Soviets on the evening of January 30th in a reception room at the British Admiralty in London. There the President learned what it was really like to deal with one of Joseph Stalin's right-hand men. Molotov, though a much older man than the one who once sat at the Dictator's side, still proved himself to be quite a formidable presence. He made it clear that the Soviet Union and the United States represented two economic systems which would always be in opposition with each other, and that, "sentimental appeals to a common brotherhood of mankind, were the fantasies of bourgeois milksops." There was no amount of charm the President could muster that would melt the wall of ice he received from the old Stalinist. "You can't imagine how much I miss Khrushchev," the President told us when he arrived back in Washington the next day. He made several appeals for the deposed Soviet leader to come to America and meet with him, but Khrushchev, who had found temporary exile in India, turned him down. Only later, when some lucrative offers came in and with his health beginning to fail and in need of medical treatment did Old Nikita decide America might not be such a bad place to live after all. I always figured he was pretty jealous of the way Brezhnev was living high on the hog in Scotland on the dime of the British government.

"We are in a new Cold War," the President told the NSC a week after his fruitless face off with Molotov, "one which threatens to turn hot a lot faster than the old one we were fighting." He paused for a moment, and then said, "But we're not going to let that happen."

Despite such noble sentiments, South Vietnam was literally going up in flames as the second term was getting under way. At the end of the rainy season, the North Vietnamese began sending men and material south in a big way, by the end of January, General Westmorland estimated there were more than 100,000 Communist irregulars in the South, along with two divisions of the North Vietnamese army, a huge escalation in a matter of months and a force which would easily overwhelm the pitifully weak South Vietnamese armed forces and the American contingent already there. It was the view of Secretaries Rusk and McNamara and Mr. Bundy, this was a direct challenge by the new Soviet leadership, and it could not go unanswered. This is why in an address to the nation on February 1st, the President announced that America would be sending the equivalent of two Infantry divisions and one Marine Combat Division to South Vietnam. "We must heed the warnings of history," he said to the country, "and not let aggressions by a ruthless dictatorship go unchallenged."

I went into the Oval Office on the day after the President's speech and asked for a transfer to a field command, specifically in Vietnam. When asked why I was making such a request, I replied, "Sir, I've sat in an office and taken actions in the past year which have created a lot of veterans, in the years to come, I'd like to be able to look them in the face." The President nodded and said he understood.

My orders came through the next day; I was to report to MAACV in Saigon in ten day's time.

While I was at home packing to go on my last Friday in Washington, the phone rang. On the other end was a familiar voice, one I had not heard for some time. "You are one crazy son of a bitch, Colonel," said Vance Harlow. "You got it made with a nice office in the White House, the confidence of the President and his brother, and here you are throwing it away to go to a shit hole like South Vietnam. You know they shoot at you there." I had a million questions to ask Harlow, starting with where the hell was he and why couldn't anyone get in touch with him. "You got to know when it's time to close down the act," he said, "and get out of town ahead of the sheriff." That was all he would say about himself, the reason he called was to wish me well and that he would get in touch when I got back. "You're one of the good guys, Colonel, and I've met damn few of them in my life." The last thing he said was not to tell anyone we'd talked, life would be much easier for both of us, he said.

On my last day at the White House, the President called me into the Oval Office after a farewell party down in the basement, a party where Ralph Gillison had a little too much to drink and had to be chauffeured home.

The Attorney General was with his brother when I arrived. "Martin," the President said, calling me by name for the only time since I'd known him. "I just want you to know that the day you get back from South Vietnam, I will personally add your name to the promotion list and make sure you get your star." This was quite a surprise; it's rare for a President to jump over the recommendations of the promotions board and the service chiefs to put up a name of his own.

"It's our way of thanking you for all you've done for your country, Colonel." That was how the Attorney General put it.

In the light of what I've revealed, it can honestly be said the offer of an extra star could be considered a payoff. And it also might ensure my silence concerning certain things when I was out of earshot of Washington.

I'd prefer not to see it that way. I'd prefer to say that I earned everything I've got.

I thanked President Kennedy and his brother for the opportunity to serve, for the chance to make a difference and that it was an honor to work with them both.

And with that, my tour of duty at the White House came to an end; I saluted and left the Oval Office; it was the last time I ever saw the two Kennedy brothers together.

John Compton (IX)
November 1964 - September 1996

It was my intention to go back to Georgia after the first of the year and resume my practice there, during my time in Washington and on the campaign trail, I had grown quite lonesome for the tall pines of home. Three days after Christmas, I received a call from the newly re-elected Vice President Lyndon Johnson, who offered me the number two spot in the President's Congressional liaison office, a job which would pay me twice what I'd earned in my best year as a lawyer. "Johnny," the Vice President said, "you will have a chance to put your mark on every piece of civil rights legislation that will come before Congress in the next four years. History will literally be in your hands to be made. You won't be able to make near as much of a difference back in Cherokee County, Georgia, arguing a case before a jury of rednecks." I thanked the Vice President and said I'd consider it.

The next day I got a call from the President himself, asking me to take the job, telling me, "I know you want to help, I need your help, and your country needs your help. Can I count on you?" I gave the President the same answer I gave the Vice President.

I was genuinely torn because my heart really was back in those old courtrooms of Alabama, Georgia and Mississippi, with their big overhead fans, brass spittoons and the faint scent of furniture polish rubbed deep into the hardwood benches. It was my old hero, Hubert Humphrey, who helped make up my mind when I asked for his advice. "Johnny," he said, "there are hundreds of lawyers who can go down South and do what you do; very few are being asked to lead the fight right here in Washington."

I decided to stay, motivated in no small part by guilt over the compromises made to get the Civil Rights Act of 1964 passed; maybe I could accomplish more in the second term. Maybe I was naïve.

But the prospects for progress in the next four years were undermined from the start by the aftermath of the '64 election. There was no small amount of antagonism still festering between Bobby Kennedy and LBJ, made even worse by Johnson's premature declaration of victory in Texas on election night. According to Bobby, the Vice President had "made a Goddamn fool of himself in front of the whole country." There was much more to it. Thanks to my role as a go-between in Bentley Braden's little scheme, I knew Lyndon Johnson had used the tape of Ellen Rometsch to guarantee his retention on the ticket at Atlantic City. Johnson supposedly delivered the tape himself to the Oval Office in a gesture that said, "You know that I know that if you don't want anyone else to know, then..." JFK thought the whole thing funny and admired Johnson's nerve, but Bobby couldn't stand the idea of LBJ having pulled a fast one on them after he was all but booted out the door. I suspect JFK intended to keep Johnson on the ticket all along and just indulged Bobby, but the bad blood would stain all the good intentions of the second four years.

The other shadow was the rift between the Kennedy brothers and Dr. King after 1964, it was something none of the parties involved ever talked about openly; from my vantage point, I believe it was a matter of trust, and bad faith, starting with the ease with which the Kennedy Administration was willing to cut compromises to get the Civil Rights Act passed and the never publicly acknowledged deal with Senator Eastland to nominate Judge Cox to the Supreme Court. What none of us knew was the undercover harassment Dr. King was receiving at this time from Hoover's FBI; that, and the strong differences Dr. King had with Kennedy's policies in Cuba led to an almost complete breakdown in communication between both camps which did no one any good. Nobody in the White House was happy when King declared the continued American occupation to be, "a crime against a free people," and called for Fidel Castro to be freed from his cell at Guantanamo Bay.

We went into the second term intent on passing a federal voting rights act to end discrimination at the ballot box, it was the first legislation introduced in January 1965, but instead of taking six months to pass, it took a torturous eighteen, as Southern Democrats fought us tooth and nail, while Republicans offered little help because Goldwater's appeal to white fears had proven there were votes to be had by going down that road and many GOP Congressmen saw future electoral success in making sure barriers remained between blacks and the voting booth.

While we were fighting the good fight in Congress, Dr. King, SCLC and SNCC were fighting a real fight by confronting the segregationist voting system head on; week after week, there were well-organized marches and confrontations at courthouse after courthouse as hundreds of long-disenfranchised black citizens showed up and demanded they be registered to vote. Emboldened by the fact they had somehow saved Jim Crow, white segregationists went all out to stop the push for voting rights in its tracks. It really tried my patience to watch Walter Cronkite on the evening news reporting on the violence which erupted all across the South that spring and summer - beatings, fire hoses and dogs set on peaceful demonstrators and then having to sit down at the table the next day with Senators and Representatives who said they couldn't do anything to help us because their constituents thought, "the Negroes were being too pushy." What really hurt us was when the violence spread to the north in the summer of '65, as clashes between blacks and the police erupted into more full scale riots in Detroit, Philadelphia and Newark.

After an exhausting battle in both houses of Congress, we got a Voting Rights Act passed, but again, there was bitter compromise after President Kennedy negotiated behind closed doors with Richard Russell and Sam Ervin, the Senator from North Carolina who led the floor fight against the bill. We had hoped to consign the literacy test to the dust-bin of history, but it survived in a provision which allowed states to bar people who could not read or write from voting. JFK has been excoriated in many recent history books for his willingness to compromise on civil rights and his lack of boldness for the cause. What those of a later generation do not understand is the hardening of attitudes in that second term; the sight of black mobs burning down city blocks ignited the white backlash like a match to gasoline.

Since I was there on Capitol Hill and sat in on many meetings, I can honestly say JFK was a far more able politician in his second term than his first. The man would talk to anyone, even his most committed opponent, and always made sure the lines of communication remained open. Yes, he talked to Richard Russell while the Georgia Senator was planning a filibuster of the Voting Rights Act, making sure to remind the Senator it was nothing personal and that he still had the highest esteem for those who took a stand on principle. But he always turned around and had the Attorney General call someone close to Dr. King and tell them what to expect from Washington when they went into Mississippi to register thousands of disenfranchised blacks to vote.

If the President could be criticized for being too evenhanded, his brother was a different story. From the beginning of the second term, Bobby Kennedy embraced the cause of racial equality and made it his own, not afraid to order Federal Marshalls into even the smallest hamlet in the Mississippi Delta if a Deputy Sheriff so much as gave a dirty look to a civil rights worker there to register blacks. I was among the millions of Americans who applauded in September 1966, when he sent the Marshalls to Montgomery with a warrant to arrest Governor Wallace after he refused to turn over Alabama's voter lists to the Justice Department. Wallace would later claim he'd worked the whole thing ahead of time with Kennedy so he could look like a martyr to the white South. A judge would dismiss the charges the next day, but not before the whole country got to see the Governor taken away in hand-cuffs, just like many a black man who'd run afoul of the authority Wallace represented.

When Justice Tom Clark retired from the Supreme Court in 1967, the President proved himself to be as good as his word, personally calling Senator Eastland to tell him that Judge William Harold Cox was at the top of the list of replacements. Then the President made sure the list was leaked to the press, and the predictable uproar exploded over the possibility that a staunch defender of segregation might be named to the high court. Democratic and Republican Senators lined up to denounce Judge Cox as a racist and a reactionary who would never get their vote for confirmation. This drama went on for a few days, during which time President Kennedy had Judge Cox to the White House, ostensibly to discuss his taking the spot on the Court - it only fanned the flames of opposition even more. In the end, Senator Eastland got the message and called Kennedy to ask that his old friend and college roommate's name be withdrawn because he did not want to see him "dragged through the mud by a bunch of Northern Communist sympathizers." President Kennedy told Eastland he understood; two days later he named another man named Cox to the Supreme Court - Archibald Cox, former Solicitor General and Dean of the Harvard School of Law, and a Kennedy man from back in 1960 as well. I had spent years worrying about being an accomplice to putting Judge Cox on the Court, so glad it all turned out to be for nothing.

If in the end, the job of finally ending Jim Crow fell to Kennedy's successors, he at least had done the hard work of digging the grave so that when the time came, that rotten system could be buried deep.

I left Washington for good after the tragic events of April, 1968; afterward partisan politics no longer had any appeal for me. I pulled some strings and called in some chits, and got myself appointed a United States Attorney for the Southern District of Mississippi. To get this job, I had to go over a lot of heads, and it wasn't secured until I wrangled an Oval Office meeting with President Kennedy; out of consideration for the circumstances, I won't repeat anything from our conversation, except to say that I got the job I wanted. Over the next seven years, I racked up 28 convictions for violations of the Civil and Voting Rights Acts, including two Klansmen who got life for first-degree murder. They were the best years of my life.

In 1975, President Humphrey offered to put my name up for a Federal Judgeship, but Senator Eastland shot it down, he was still chairman of the Judiciary Committee and the man had a long memory. I'd put a few friends of his behind bars when I was a US Attorney, and I believe he still had it in for me for bad mouthing Judge Cox to his face all those years ago. On that matter I have no regrets, I'd do it again.

Over the years, the events at the Hotel Adolphus on the evening of October 1st, 1964, have taken on the trappings of a political urban legend. I believe the wall of silence held up because we all had too much to lose, and I'm not just talking about the principles involved, the rest of us involved did well for ourselves. I'll use myself as an example; the job in the Administration which came my way right after the election was not just in appreciation for all I had done for the Kennedy-Johnson ticket - although my hard work was deserving of it. The job paid for my children's education - something which was the least a far too absent father could do.

Around the mid 70's, I started getting calls from so-called journalists inquiring about the place and the date and if I had anything to say about it. I would always tell them I had no idea what they were talking about and hang up. The most persistent were activists like Mark Lane, who just wouldn't let it alone, but he could be dismissed as a crank - at least for a while. It was not so easy to blow off Bob Woodward, Joe McGinniss and others when they came a calling, but I can honestly say they never got anything useful out of me. But I had some sleepless nights when the Inouye Committee was looking into malfeasance by the CIA and the FBI; a lot of dirty laundry from the 1960's got dumped out for all the world to see and when they started subpoenaing the secret files from the Bureau, I couldn't help but wonder what might be locked away in some folder with my name on it in a file cabinet in the director's office. I had no trust in the discretion of J. Edgar Hoover or his successor, Cartha DeLoach. The best thing President Hubert Humphrey ever did was to clean out that nest of vipers at the Bureau.

So I guess no one talked on the record about the Hotel Adolphus…until now, when all the principles are dead, and the statute of limitations has long run out on any possible crimes committed. In the end, the people deserve to know the truth and make up their own minds.

I was never directly involved in another political campaign after 1964, except for one. In the spring of 1976, I left my practice in Washington D.C. to go down to Louisiana and help a candidate win a special election to the State Senate. I spent six weeks down there, stuffing envelopes and knocking on doors, the fun stuff of campaigning I'd never gotten involved in before. When my candidate was behind in the polls by a few points, and there was less than a week until the election, I got on the phone to Hyannis Port and recounted a story from the '64 election; two days later former President John F. Kennedy flew down to appear at a rally and personally endorse Howard Prentiss, who went on to win by 20,000 votes. When asked why he had come all this way to support a candidate for such a minor office, JFK, who was permanently on crutches by then because of his declining physical condition, replied, "I just wanted to return the favor for a fellow veteran of the Pacific."

I think about that now and smile.

Kevin McCluskey (VII)
November 1964 – August 2014

I called Dorothy Brennan three times before she would agree to go out with me, the first time she hung up when I identified myself; the second time she calmly explained why she would not go out with a Democrat under any circumstances, but on the third try, I impressed upon her how the two of us actually had a lot in common, not the least of which being our common close proximity to the two men who had just battled it out for highest office in the land. She said I could buy her dinner; I was on a plane to Los Angeles the next day, the reservations already made at Giorgio's in Beverly Hills for that evening. That first date led to a second one a week later, this time for dinner and a movie. She hadn't seen *Dr. Strangelove* yet, even though it had been out for nearly a year. We had a real spirited discussion afterward; I considered it a brilliant satire, and while Dorothy conceded it was funny, she still considered its basic theme to be borderline treasonous in the way it portrayed Americans as being no better than the Russians. I was quite pleased when *Strangelove*, Peter Sellers, Sterling Hayden and Stanley Kubrick won Oscars the next year, while Dorothy was thoroughly disappointed *My Fair Lady* didn't take the golden statue.

That's how I met my wife, and we are proof positive opposites attract.

One thing we did have in common was the Hotel Adolphus, and though we had many conversations on that subject, none of them within hearing of another person.

After Kennedy's re-election and finding a new girlfriend, the biggest thing that happened to me in November of 1964 was getting a job at the White House. My official title was Special Assistant to the President's Council, although it had nothing to do with what my actual duties would be. It was Dave Powers who laid it out for me, saying that while President Kennedy had won re-election by a solid margin, they had no illusions about the breadth and depth of the opposition to his plans for the next four years. My job would be to help gauge the strength of the forces fighting the Kennedy Administration. "We're not going to end up like Harry Truman in the last years of his second term," Mr. Powers said, "on the defensive while Senator McCarthy and his Red Baiters made every Democrat on Capitol Hill hide under their desks. If there is to be a Joe McCarthy in the 1960's, we want to see him coming." That was all I needed to hear, and the best part was once this plum gig was done, I'd be able to use John F. Kennedy as a job reference.

I was in the crowd in front of the Capital on Inauguration Day, 1965, having snagged a good seat near the front, I tried to talk Dorothy into coming with me, but she begged off, saying she was willing to date a Kennedy man, but not willing to watch the man himself put his hand on the Bible. I wished she could have seen what I witnessed, as first LBJ, and then Kennedy were sworn in for a second term, the goal for which so many had worked so hard and so long to achieve. Mrs. Kennedy, who had been such an asset on the campaign trail, looked especially radiant despite it being cloudy. The man who stood before us that day looked markedly older than the one who'd been there only four years prior; his temples were gray now and his face showed the wear by the pronounced crow's feet around the eyes - all made plain in the cover photo in *Life* magazine later in the week. However, there was nothing aged or worn about John F. Kennedy's voice. While his second inaugural address is not as memorable as the first - the critics said he spent too much time patting himself on the back for avoiding World War III - one line does stand out in my memory: "As arduous as the challenges have been in the last four years, they pale compared to what may confront us in the next four, but I have no doubt whatsoever that America will end the 1960's a far more prosperous and more peaceful nation than it is today. When we land a man on the moon, let that be seen as the crowning achievement of a generation that answered its nation's call the day after Pearl Harbor."

I moved into my office across from the White House the next day and started on what would come to be known as "opposition research," and "opposition" was not necessarily defined as Republican, but anyone who might be an impediment to the President's agenda. My work often required me to "think outside the box."

It went something like this: in the summer of '65, I pretended to be a freelance journalist and traveled through the South in order to find out what the foot soldiers of Dr. King's SCLC were thinking and saying as they prepared to challenge segregation once again; I was a truck driver looking for work at union halls in the Midwest to find out what steel and auto workers really thought about the civil rights movement as opposed to what the union chiefs were telling the President; I feigned being a student at more than a dozen colleges from coast to coast to gauge the mood of higher education, a hotbed of antagonism toward the Administration's policies in Vietnam and Cuba. When 75,000 more troops were sent to South Vietnam in August of 1965, the White House was not caught in the dark when demonstrations erupted on college campuses the next month. President Kennedy anticipated the blowback, and when he went to the University of Wisconsin in October, he was able to tell a hostile young audience that, "Your voices are being heard in the corridors of power, but there are other voices as well, the voices of those who are being crushed under the heels of tyranny, and we hear those voices too." Those words did not mollify the college kids opposed to the war, but the President did earn respect for at least being willing to come and speak.

My reports made the President aware of just apprehensive many white Americans were toward legislation which guaranteed black Americans the right to vote, get a job, or own a house. These were the people who labored long on assembly lines to keep a roof over their families' heads, and there was nothing they feared more than declining home values; I learned in no uncertain terms that nobody valued property rights more than the American Middle Class. "We're not going to give up the white working class to the Republicans without a fight," the President said at one point. That was why he never failed to mention hard work when he spoke places like Youngstown, Gary, and Flint during '65 and '66. It was also one of the reasons why universal health care came about under Kennedy, and if critics want to say it was just a payoff to keep whites from jumping from the Democratic Party while it pushed civil rights through Congress, then so be it.

There have been many books written heaping much praise upon John F. Kennedy's nimble political maneuvering in his second term; I would like to think all my hard work played some small part.

It was a strategy which worked well for a while, but as those of us who walked in "the corridors of power," came to realize, events moved fast in the 1960's and staying ahead of them ultimately became a losing proposition. President Kennedy's appeals to the white working class only went so far, especially when they increasingly saw themselves not as workers struggling to get ahead, but as taxpayers who were footing the bill. When the racial violence we'd seen in Los Angeles broke out again in Detroit, Newark, and Philadelphia in the summer of 1966, not even the President's prompt ordering in of Federal troops could soothe the fears of white Americans who now thought Goldwater's law and order rhetoric was right on the mark.

This truth was driven home when I went out to the West Coast in September of '66 and posed as property assessor for a week. I came back and told the men in the White House how their good friend Pat Brown was going to lose to the Hollywood actor, Ronald Reagan, in a landslide. When they recovered from their shock, I repeated what I'd heard from the good suburbanites of the Golden State, who were tired seeing students at their state colleges carrying signs which said GET OUT OF CUBA NOW and comparing the American military to the Nazi war machine; while black militants threatened to start another riot in Los Angeles unless their demands were met. Not only that, but the long hair the kids were now sporting and the marijuana cigarettes in their back pockets - a sight seen everywhere in California while I was out there - had convinced them their country had taken a wrong turn.

It did not help when Dr. King led the Second March on Washington at the end of the summer; there were 50,000 protesters, most of them black, descending on the capital demanding an end to the war in Vietnam, the occupation of Cuba, direct intervention to end Jim Crow; a billion dollars in government spending to end poverty; and the adoption of an Equality Amendment to the Constitution. This time the speakers did not stand at the Lincoln Memorial, but upon the backs of flatbed trucks at the foot of Capitol Hill (in violation of their permits) instead, giving the deliberate impression they were there to demand action from a bastion of authority. After the march, it was not the President who met with the march's organizers, instead, the job was delegated to Vice President Johnson, a man with no power.

Discontent with the war in Vietnam, the occupation of Cuba, and the split over the pace of the civil rights revolution had its effect on the Democratic Party in the November midterms when scores of Republicans mouthing sentiments identical to Goldwater two years earlier were swept into Congress and the state houses.

The last two years of the second term are the toughest; it was true for Wilson, for Truman, for Eisenhower. The same would be true for John F. Kennedy.

It was during 1967, the toughest days of the Kennedy Administration, when my "undercover" work was cut back, so I spent a lot of time in the office writing reports for the President concerning the level of antagonism toward him and his policies. In this capacity, I was given transcripts of telephone and private conversations of a number of individuals, including Martin Luther King and the leadership of the Southern Christian Leadership Conference; assorted radicals who'd spoken out at protests against American foreign policy like David Dellinger Abbie Hoffman and Pete Seeger; outspoken right-wingers like the head of the John Birch Society and the big wigs who'd funded it. There were also transcripts of meetings between Senator J. William Fulbright, the Chairman of the Foreign Relations Committee and opponents of the war in Vietnam. I had no knowledge of how this information was gathered or of any laws broken by Federal Agents in obtaining it; all I was asked to do was use it in compiling a report to be read by the President's men and in some cases, by the President himself. I was as shocked as anyone when the truth about Hoover and his FBI came out, along with the Kennedy brother's complicity. If anyone wants to call me naïve, I'll plead guilty.

There is one memory that stands out: on a beautiful day in the summer of '67, I received a call at my desk to come across to the White House. There to my surprise, I was ushered into the Oval Office, where I stood before President Kennedy and was questioned about certain points in a report I'd just compiled on the activities of Tom Hayden during his recent surreptitious visit to Cuba. The founder of the Students for a Democratic Society was believed to have smuggled guns to pro-Communist guerrillas, or at least that is what one of Hayden's associates claimed in a phone call to his girlfriend. For ten minutes, I stood there and answered questions put to me by the President and his brother, the Attorney General who was also in the room, along with J. Edgar Hoover himself, who sat unsmiling in a chair and glaring at me, clearly not amused at the sight of the President of the United States getting info from what to him was the office boy. The questions concerned whether anyone actually had seen Hayden and company handing weapons over to any Castroistas, and if my memory is correct, my conclusion in the report was in the negative as to that assertion. When the President was satisfied, I was thanked and dismissed; I remember how he called me by name and that Mr. Hoover never spoke once while I was there. That was my only encounter with the director of the FBI, and afterward, my shirt was wringing wet from the sweat, not all of it from the heat. I never learned the particulars of that meeting in the Oval Office that day, but two weeks later the Justice Department filed charges against Hayden on three counts of smuggling; he ended up doing three years in prison. Lest nobody forget, the Kennedy brothers played rough right to the end.

In August of 1967, Dave Powers invited me to join the Robert F. Kennedy campaign to succeed his brother as President, which came as something of a surprise as I, and the rest of the country, was unaware he was planning to run. "Bobby is going to run because he is the only one who can continue the President's work," Mr. Powers explained. "Can you imagine Lyndon Johnson in the Oval Office? What a disaster that would be for the country, I know you don't want that and we know you are a guy who can be depended upon. Don't worry about the dynasty issue; there's a plan to take care of it." I thought it over for a day and then said yes, it was tiring being tied to a desk in Washington and politics was in my blood now. I wanted to get back into the thick of it.

The plan to get around the "dynasty" issue was to make it appear as if there was a spontaneous yearning in the Democratic Party for the President's brother to succeed him. This meant having some discreet talks with assorted state party chairmen and selected power brokers. My first job for the RFK campaign was to fly out to Indiana to talk with the owner of the largest slaughter house in the state and prevail upon him in his capacity as chairman of the state central committee of the Indiana Democratic Party to introduce a resolution calling on Robert Kennedy to run at the committee's October meeting. He politely heard me out and then said no thank you because he was leaning toward Senator Humphrey in the upcoming campaign. I thanked him for his time and called Washington as soon as I got back to my motel room. An hour or so later, the state party chairman got an anonymous call informing him that a surprise inspection of his slaughter house's killing floor was coming in two days, and if he wanted to repay the favor, he should introduce that RFK resolution at the central committee meeting on October 2nd.

A similar scene was acted out over and over during the fall of 1967, so much so that by Thanksgiving more than a dozen state Democratic Parties had passed resolutions calling on Attorney General Robert Kennedy to run for President in 1968; by December there was a fully-fledged campaign operation on the ground in New Hampshire even though RFK had yet to resign and make an announcement. *Time* and *Newsweek* put him on their covers the same week and talked about the unprecedented possibility of one family occupying the Presidency for multiple terms. What both articles made clear was the difficulty Robert Kennedy would have running with his brother's "baggage," chief among them being the war in Vietnam, now raging in its third year after losing over 30,000 men there with no apparent end in sight. The Soviets were pouring men and material into the North at a level matching ours, while the South hung on for its life and the country's patience for the war was waning by the day as the election year loomed. This attitude reflected what I heard from good Democrats when I was out in the country, where over and over they'd tell me a variation on, "We love Jack Kennedy, but our people are really starting to hate that damn war."

Lyndon Johnson, knowing it was now or never, announced he was running for President the first week of January of 1968; Senator Humphrey, no doubt feeling similar sentiments, threw his hat in the ring a week later. Governor Wallace, saying there had to be "one candidate who'll stand up for the little guy," stood in front of the Governor's mansion in Montgomery on the 30th and entered the race. Despite all this competition and the war, Bobby Kennedy topped the polls of Democrats nationwide and in New Hampshire. But it was a narrow lead, and people who should have been the first to flock to his campaign held back because of Vietnam and the occupation of Cuba, now entering its fourth year. To my mind, it was going to be a fight all the way to the convention in Chicago to get RFK the nomination, with an even bigger battle in the fall.

Then on February 5th, out of nowhere, the President went on air at 8:00 p.m. EST to announce to the country that after a series of secret negotiations in Paris, a cease-fire agreement in Vietnam had been reached. It had been pulled off with the covert assistance of the Red Chinese, something which started with Kennedy's handshake with Chou back in New Delhi. The *New York Times* headline the next day told the story: VIETNAM CEASE FIRE! TROOPS COMING HOME! Right below the fold was this story: Attorney General Resigns to run for President.

I have been involved in many Presidential campaigns in the years since, made a good living at it, but none of the ones in subsequent years was anything like Kennedy '68. With the Vietnam War no longer a drag on the Kennedy name, Bobby surged in New Hampshire, winning the primary by 12 points over Humphrey on the 12th of March and bested the Vice President by 6 points in Wisconsin three weeks later. The nomination was now within our grasp, despite a still determined and vocal opposition to the occupation of Cuba among many Democrats, but after the sudden end to the war in Vietnam, everyone believed a similar resolution would be forthcoming for that sticky issue as well. I was given the names of 50 prominent state Democratic Committeemen and told to nail down as many endorsements for Bobby as possible; it was really a homecoming as many of the faces I'd seen four years before, returned to help put another Kennedy in the White House. Every day when I checked back in with headquarters in Washington, there was news of another major endorsement by a Governor, Senator or mayor - even Daley in Chicago was reported ready to jump on the bandwagon. The only other candidate making any progress was Wallace, who was clearly going to have the support of his Southern back yard, but nothing else.

On the day Bobby won the Wisconsin primary, we got the word that at the end of the week, he would be journeying to Memphis, Tennessee, to mend the rift with Martin Luther King, who would be in the city to support black sanitary workers who were striking for better pay and working conditions. This raised the possibility of putting together the kind of coalition between blacks and working class whites which would be unbeatable in November; I remember daydreaming about what position I would be offered in the Robert F. Kennedy Administration and whether I would rate an office in the West Wing.

I had just arrived at a motel in Kansas City on that fateful Friday afternoon when I learned the tragic news. It was on the black and white TV playing in the manager's office;

the image was unforgettable: John F. Kennedy, standing in the press room of the White House with a tearful Jackie at his side, his voice shaking as he read a statement reacting to the death of his brother and Dr. King, gunned down in the streets of Memphis by two snipers who put a round each right through their heads. I still have the issue of *Life* magazine with the iconic cover photo of two bright red smears of blood on black asphalt taken at the crime scene.

I learned some things over the following days and weeks, as two good men were buried after two very different funerals on two very different days, while cities in America burned and the people who were paid to do so told us what it all meant. I learned you can be knocked flat and still get back up in the face of unbearable tragedy. I also learned that I wasn't done with politics, despite what had happened; I knew a lot of guys who walked away from it all after Memphis, and never looked back; I was not one of them.

I helped shut down the Kennedy '68 headquarters and after declining an offer to come back and work in the Administration during its final months, took the Humphrey campaign up on a request to join them. The Minnesota Senator was not a Kennedy, but he was a good man and worth getting behind. I spent the summer of '68 hunting delegates for Humphrey and believe I did a good job; we were only a few hundred votes behind the Vice President by the time we got to Chicago at the end of August. But Larry O'Brien had gone to work for Johnson after Memphis and he ran a tough, disciplined campaign while using his ties to party big wigs like Daley to maximum advantage; O'Brien was able to deliver all the big mid-western states, except Michigan, to his man. We had hoped to get an endorsement from President Kennedy, but in an appearance on *Meet the Press* in June, Humphrey said he had "some real differences" with Kennedy's policy in Cuba, which nixed that possibility. Johnson said he'd stay in Cuba "as long as it takes," but didn't get any lying on of hands either; in truth, after his loss, I don't think John F. Kennedy cared who succeeded him. With the South lining up behind Wallace, the Chicago convention went all the way to the third ballot before nominating Johnson, who then picked Humphrey for Vice President. The President came to the convention only long enough to make a speech honoring his brother on the second night. I stayed on for the fall campaign as an advance man for Humphrey, all good experience which paid off well later. It was an easy victory on Election Day, as the great Republican "Dark Horse" proved to have not been such a good choice for a deadlocked GOP convention. Johnson and Humphrey took it by an even bigger margin than JFK did four years earlier; a fact which rankled many a diehard Kennedy loyalist.

Dorothy and I got married in December of 1965 at the home of her family in Idaho; we'd come back to DC and lived quietly while I worked at the Kennedy White House; now at the end of 1968, I turned down an offer to work in the new Administration and the two of us, along with some other veterans of the Goldwater and Kennedy campaigns struck out on our own as campaign consultants, or "hired guns" as we liked to think of ourselves. It was a decision to put what we'd learned to good use and make some big bucks along the way.

Many doubted our marriage would last, but not only did it flourish, but we also managed to raise two boys and a little girl in the process. Right from the start, we made one rule: I never bash Goldwater in front of her, and she never disparages John F. Kennedy in front of me. You don't have to make up if you don't have the fight in the first place.

I "made my bones" in the 1970 midterm election by helping save the careers of many Southern Democrats after Johnson rammed the toughest civil rights bill through Congress since Reconstruction. At the 1972 Democratic convention, when the choice for Vice President came down to Governor Carter of Georgia or Senator Harris of Oklahoma, my voice was one of the deciding ones when President Humphrey picked Fred Roy Harris to be Vice President. In October, when the race was tight, I was the first one to say that the Humphrey-Harris campaign had to put more effort into Illinois in the closing days, in the end, those 26 Electoral votes made all the difference.

A few years later, I journeyed out to Sacramento to urge the young Governor of California to run for President, explaining how the final years of the Humphrey Administration too much resembled the last years of Truman's, when after nearly two decades of Democratic rule, the country wanted change. The party would need a fresh face and a break with the past if it wanted to retain the White House. "If I'm the new Adlai Stevenson," Jerry Brown said, "then this doesn't end well, because Stevenson lost by a landslide." I answered that he wasn't Stevenson and the Republicans didn't have an Eisenhower. In the end, Edmund G. Brown Jr. did run for President in 1976, and at the age of 39, was a true break with the past. I was also instrumental in getting Senator Dale Bumpers of Arkansas, one of those Democrats I'd helped save back in '70, to run as his Vice President. Unfortunately, history did repeat itself, Jerry Brown lost, although not by the same margin as Stevenson did in 1952.

Over the years to come, I managed to get used to losing Presidential races as the Democrats spent as many years in the wilderness as the Republicans had in the previous decades; among those losing efforts were the campaigns of John Glenn, Hugh Carey, Walter Mondale and Lloyd Bentsen, all good men who got into the ring and gave it their best shot. I never lost my love of the game and figured we couldn't lose them all. I take great pride in being one of the earliest to see the potential in Bill Clinton, whom I met when I was helping Bumpers win his first Senate campaign in Arkansas. He was a natural politician and decorated veteran of Cuba, running him for President was a joy; I take credit for getting Mario Cuomo to take the Vice Presidency on the ticket with the Arkansas Governor after losing a tough nomination fight to him at the convention.

Besides three children and a love of politics, my wife and I have one other thing in common, the Hotel Adolphus. We did what we agreed to do, keep our silence, even when the investigators of the Inouye Committee got uncomfortably close to the facts in 1975, we actually thought about getting a lawyer at one point because we were so afraid a subpoena was imminent. But the other people from that night in Dallas who found themselves in the witness chair never talked either, although God knows some of them spilled their guts about plenty of other things. We were more than lucky to have been left alone, and neither of us is under the illusion that more than one door was opened for us over the years by unseen hands who had a vested interest in our continued well-being. We both know we might have ended up like Daniel Ellsberg.

Why are we talking now? Because of the passage of time and the passing of prominent individuals; the Kennedy years are ancient history now, and if I have any doubts, all I have to do is ask my kids. And I want my children to know what happened, what their parents once did in a long gone America when a man named Kennedy was President.

Dorothy Jean Brennan (VII)
November 1964-September 2014

There was one shining moment on election night, 1964, right after Ohio went in the Goldwater column when I actually thought the Senator had it won, then two of our must carry states, Arkansas and Tennessee, went for Kennedy and the next thing I knew, I was standing behind the Senator on the podium as he conceded the race, wiping the tears from my eyes. The next few days were spent in a state of deep mourning as I helped close up the Goldwater '64 headquarters in Phoenix; what really hurt was that I knew how different things might have been.

While closing down the campaign, I got two phone calls; the first was an offer to come and work on Capitol Hill, right in the center of the action and for good money. The second call was from the short guy who'd asked me out that night at the Adolphus, reminding me that I'd said call him after the election. The last person I wanted to spend any time with was a Kennedy man, I turned him down twice, but he was persistent and finally I agreed to go out with him on the condition we talk about anything but politics.

And that is how I got to together with Kevin McCluskey, the love of my life.

We were married in December 1965, in Idaho with just our immediate families present; my parents were polite, it took them awhile to get used to having an Irish-Italian Catholic in the family. Kevin's folks took it all in stride, and no one was allowed to mention anything more controversial than the weather, before, during, and especially after the ceremony. We went back to Washington where, if we didn't keep our marriage a secret, we did not advertise it either; Kevin worked at the Kennedy White House, while I accepted the job on the Hill, which meant we were working in enemy camps.

From my vantage point, I watched as the Republicans in Congress barely put up a fight against Kennedy's second term agenda, compromising over and over again as they negotiated with the White House to pass a so-called Voting Rights Act that decimated states' rights; a government takeover of the medical profession, which was nothing more than a liberal vote buying scheme using health insurance; a Fair Housing Act which stripped honest Americans of their Constitutionally guaranteed property rights; a so-called Anti-Poverty Act which was nothing more than a tax payer funded subsidy to the lazy and shiftless.

After a few years of this, I was ready to get back to doing something I loved - the give and take of political combat. It's the one great thing Kevin and I share, besides our three wonderful kids, so after Kennedy left the White House, the two of us caught the wave of the future and put our political talents out there for hire. In the ensuing years, we were quite successful, Kevin more so on the national level, while my best success has come on the marketing side - the writing and producing of political ads for Republican candidates. In 1970, I produced the spots which helped William Ruckelhaus win an upset in an Indiana

Senate race, if not for me, he would not have been on the ticket with Ronald Reagan two years later. That helped make my reputation and brought in a lot of work, in 1974, I earned a high six figures for designing the ads which helped defeat referendums to legalize abortion in six states, including California. I've been called a hack for the right wing many times. My answer has been to produce the hate mail I got for the full length newspaper ads I wrote in 1978 which were instrumental in swaying enough Illinois state legislators to pass the Equal Rights Amendment and make it part of the Constitution. Often my husband and I have ended up working on opposite sides in the same campaign; we learned very early not to talk shop at home.

I probably missed my chance for a seat at the table of power when, in 1972, I turned down a job offer from Roger Ailes who wanted me to come and be a producer on a show he was putting together called *American Perspective*, a daily half-hour of news and commentary. I was all ready to say yes until I found out the program was to be built around Richard Nixon, who was trying to repackage his image as a statesman after his years of running Cuba. But I knew some things about Mr. Nixon that Roger Ailes did not know, like how he'd stabbed Goldwater in the back in '64, and it was not even a decision I had to consider. I wished Mr. Ailes luck when I passed on the job. He didn't need it; with his slashing takedowns on President Humphrey's policies, *American Perspective with Richard Nixon* was a smash hit and turned out to be the perfect platform for a political comeback.

Of course, Kevin and I have the Hotel Adolphus in common, the place where we first got together. We have remained silent while the story of that night has been chased by many an investigative reporter, we've stayed way clear of them. Neither of us has been so naïve as to believe that all our good fortune has been solely because of our own hard work, as there were powerful people who had a vested interest we never got into dire straits and might need to sell a particularly juicy political story.

There were times when investigative journalist and the just plain nosy came awfully close to finding out about the Adolphus, especially during the wave of enquires into the CIA and the FBI during the Humphrey years, and it gave us a few sleepless nights. At one point, Kevin and I talked about what we would say in a statement when we went public if our presence at the Adolphus was exposed. It was much harder deciding what we would tell our children, to whom we had always stressed the value of honesty.

Why talk now? We both agree that since all of the principles involved are gone, and many of the scandals JFK paid to have covered up have since become known, there is little harm in coming clean at this late date. We wrote one book about how political polar opposites managed to stay married for 30 years and it made good money, no need to write another one.

Because of Kevin's role in the Kennedy campaign, he would get invites to reunions of their campaign staff in the years after JFK left office. I refused to go with him for many years, but with time came a sense of our place in history, and as the partisan battles of the

1960's receded, I relented and accompanied him to one of these gatherings in 1984. They were always held in Boston, even though the former President was living in Florida by then, not so Mrs. Kennedy, who had settled in Manhattan, although the two of them were always together at these reunions as if he wasn't secretly living with that actress. He was walking with the help of two canes by then as well, and every step he took was obviously causing pain, Kennedy's sons were there to help him if needed.

Like many of my fellow conservatives, I'd mellowed somewhat on John F. Kennedy by then, and had found positive things in his legacy. The hard line he took with the Soviets in his second term surely helped keep the peace and his deliberate pace on civil rights gave white America more time to accept some needed changes. So when our turn came, I had no problem with accompanying Kevin over to the former President's table for a few minutes of small talk. Up close, John F. Kennedy was clearly not the man he'd been in 1964; his hair had long ago gone completely gray, and he was a good thirty pounds heavier, in many ways he looked every bit a man of 67 years. All except his eyes, for John Kennedy still had the eyes of a much younger man. "Dorothy Jean Brennan," he said in that unmistakable accent, "you look just the same as you did 20 years ago." Moreover, he gave me exactly the same knowing wink he'd given me in an October long gone to history.

Wade L. Harbinson (VIII)
November 1964 - August 1999

John F. Kennedy beat me at my own game, so I made the best of it. After the events at the Adolphus, I had a vested interest in a Democratic victory, which made me a Kennedy man whether I liked it or not. During the last month of the campaign, I routinely informed Kennedy's inner circle of everything happening in the Goldwater camp, especially the confidential stuff. In the end, Kennedy won and Goldwater lost, and all the dirty laundry stayed hidden, and everyone's mouth stayed shut.

And John Kennedy was as good as his word, over the next four years, the Houston-based construction company I owned had all the government contracts it could handle from the building of a new Federal Courthouse in Austin to the widening of Interstate 10; my crews were busy day and night, so much so that I went out and bought two of my competitors just to keep up with all the projects falling into my lap.

But Texas was small change compared to what I made in Cuba - that country was a regular cash register during the reconstruction if you were connected. All it took was the right word spoken in Richard Nixon's ear; all those rumors about him were true, he ran the place like a gangster's fiefdom. I had the pleasure of making my first trip down to Havana in the fall of 1965; it was still a dangerous place even then, despite the presence of American soldiers, guns at the ready everywhere. I saw four bodies in the streets during the day and a half I spent there and the crack of gunfire was heard all night long.

I met with Nixon at his HQ, a big plantation house outside the city, it must have been 90 degrees in the shade, but there was the former Vice President, wearing a dark suit like he was still presiding over the Senate, sitting behind a desk in an office with the air conditioning cranked up on high. Somehow, sweat still beaded up on his upper lip like he was back debating Kennedy in '60.

The Adolphus never came up, since neither one of us were in each other's presence, the fiction was easily maintained. Nixon and I exchanged pleasantries, and he was effusive on the future of Cuba, which he clearly thought was his ticket back to the big time of Presidential politics. The real business was conducted later when Mr. Bebe Rebozo visited my hotel room at the rebuilt Flamingo. When he left, all the details were worked out, and I knew the exact figure which would guarantee my bid was accepted. This was the same Rebozo who was indicted two years later for taking kickbacks and would have done a long stretch in the pen if Edward Bennett Williams hadn't been such a good lawyer. Everybody thought Bobby Kennedy was behind it, making sure Nixon didn't run for President in '68; every single contractor who did business in Cuba during the rebuilding was subpoenaed and deposed except me. It didn't do Bobby any good; he wasn't elected the next year either.

I was active in the Republican nomination battle in 1968; I signed onto the Curtis

LeMay campaign early, LeMay was no politician, but a lot of patriots thought he was the man on horseback who could save the country. Reagan ran as well; he was a good man and a better politician than LeMay, but a lot of good conservatives wanted a man who would put the hammer down on our enemies and put it down hard. Both Reagan and LeMay were preferable to the other main candidate, Governor George Romney of Michigan, who, as far as many of us were concerned, was nothing more than a warmed-over Nelson Rockefeller. Either LeMay or Reagan could have won on the first ballot in Miami if the other had dropped out, but they stayed in and battled it out for four ballots before the delegates threw up their hands and turned to a "Dark Horse."

I'll admit to being impressed with the Governor of Maryland, when back in April, he had gone on TV and issued orders to the National Guard to shoot looters on sight while Baltimore was being burned to the ground by rioting blacks. This was the kind of leadership many Americans were looking for in a President and overnight, Spiro Agnew became a household name. He went to the convention as Maryland's favorite son and held tight through the first few ballots, putting him in the right spot at the right time. It was my home state of Texas who switched to Agnew on the fifth ballot, setting off a stampede in the early hours of Thursday morning. Most Republicans didn't mind when the new nominee picked Romney for Vice President in an effort to unify the party; they thought they had a sure winner against an over the hill hack like Lyndon Johnson in the fall.

Or so they thought; the day after the convention adjourned, I made a call to a contact in Lawrence O'Brien's office, reporting to him some interesting rumors I'd heard during the past 36 hours, rumors concerning lavish spending in the Governor's Mansion in Annapolis out of a secret account. Six weeks later there were front-page stories in the *New York Times* and the *Washington Post* detailing how Agnew had accepted $30,000 in bribes while in office and any chance he had of being elected President went up in smoke. It was an LBJ landslide, which was just what I wanted; he was just as involved in what went down at the Adolphus as anyone of us, so the good thing I had going continued for another four years. Only four years turned out to be a little more than two when Johnson died of heart failure in April of 1971 and Humphrey took over.

All bets were off in '72, and you can believe I worked my ass off to elect Reagan-Ruckelshaus that year. They would have made it if George Wallace hadn't made good on his threat to run as a third party candidate and took most of the South out of play. A lot of good Americans were sick of all that civil rights crap after Johnson and Humphrey had gone further than JFK would ever have dared, if all of them could have united behind Reagan he would have won in a landslide; as it is, he polled 500,000 more popular votes than Humphrey, but the damn Democrats stole Texas and Illinois and won it in the Electoral College.

I'll hand it to Dick Nixon in '76. He found a way to make a comeback even after all the dirt he got on himself with Rebozo's antics in Cuba. And who would have thought he would do it by becoming a TV star. The country was more than ready for a change after sixteen years of Democratic misrule at home and victories by our enemies abroad. Look at that Goddamn Hubert Humphrey, who let the Communists take over Vietnam and forced gas rationing on the country for six months when he should have gone over there and just took the damn oil from the Ayatollah. I was instrumental in making sure Nixon won the Texas primary over our native son, Congressman George H. W. Bush, who called in a lot of IOU's accrued over his years on the Ways and Means Committee. It was worth burning a few political bridges to get somebody back in the Oval Office who had been at the Adolphus. One of the reasons why John Connally jumped parties that year and ran as Nixon's Vice President was because of men like me who floated the idea early. As far as I was concerned, the Brown kid was still in short pants; it must have brought Nixon sweet satisfaction to defeat the son of the man who beaten him in the race for Governor of California fourteen years earlier. I would like to say that Nixon's election meant a return to business as usual, but he never did a damn thing for me after he was sworn in; I put a bid in to upgrade to docks at the naval base at Mobile Bay in April of 1977 and never heard anything back. I think once Nixon got to the Oval Office, he just said screw the rest of us; we couldn't pull him down into the mud without drowning ourselves in it as well.

The only real honest gentleman I ever met in politics was Barry Goldwater, and when I get to Heaven, which won't be long now, I will profusely apologize to the man for ruining his chance to be President.

I only saw John Kennedy one other time after the Adolphus, and that was in Palm Beach in July of 1969. I was in Florida to meet with some friends who were putting together a deal to invest in commercial real estate. It was at the West Palm restaurant in the afternoon when Kennedy came in for lunch; I was seated across the room with some associates when an excited buzz went through the place. It was the former President, out of office for six months and down there for the Moon launch. The former President and his party were led to a secluded table in a private room to spare him from being mobbed by admirers; everywhere he went in Florida there was some damn fool Cuban who would fall on his knees and thank Kennedy for saving his country. I barely caught a glimpse of the man when he came in, but a few minutes later, a waiter brought me a note requesting I come to the back, it was signed by JFK. I seriously considered ignoring the note, because - money notwithstanding - I still thought the 35th President of the United States to be the most morally reprehensible man ever to occupy that sacred office, but then thought the better of it. Maybe it was simple curiosity which made decide to go. After excusing myself to my lunch guests, I made my way to the back room, and after being checked by the ever-present secret service detail, was ushered inside. To my surprise, John F. Kennedy got up from his chair to greet me like an old classmate from Harvard. I caught an unmistakable wince as he rose from his seat, evidence of the bad back we'd all heard so much about. Mrs. Kennedy was with him and their youngest son, who was a toddler, along with Dave Powers and some other people I didn't recognize, one of which had to be the little boy's nanny.

There had been a lot of stories in the press asserting that Kennedy was nearly a broken man after his brother was killed; how he somehow felt responsible for what happened in Memphis. But the man who greeted me, who actually threw his arm around my shoulder, was the same confident politician who'd shaken my hand years before. Maybe it was seeing his vow to put a man on the moon before the end of the decade come true which put him in such a magnanimous mood, but as John F. Kennedy pumped my hand, he turned to his wife and friends and said, "This is Wade Harbinson, a man of his word and a true Texan. He and Bobby would have really hit it off."

John F. Kennedy was everything I considered wrong with America: a man of no fixed beliefs except personal expediency and who lacked the guts to really do what was needed to be done to fight Communism, a man with no respect for bedrock American principles and the people who lived by them. As for his brother, when Bobby Kennedy was killed, I said, "Good riddance." But right then and there, I did not hate this man despite all I believed he had done to the country I loved. In truth, I would have done anything for him after a compliment like the one he had just paid me in front of his family. In the years to come, I would separate the sin from the sinner; I never spoke ill of John Kennedy, the man, ever again and on the day he died, I actually shed a tear.

General Martin Maddox, USMC (Ret) (XII)
February 1965 - March 2005

The next time I spoke to President Kennedy was in December of 1965. It was during his ten hour visit to South Vietnam; he was on a tour of the Pacific and while in flight between Japan and Australia, made a detour. I came in from directing operations in the Mekong Delta after my presence was directly requested by the President. I ended up cooling my heels in the dim light of an air conditioned Quonset hut for a couple of hours while the President reviewed a line of awestruck troops and got a bunch of optimistic reports from Westmorland and his boys.

I jumped to my feet after being caught cat napping when the door flung open, and the President was escorted in by his Secret Service detail. He returned my salute and insisted we take a seat in a couple of fold up chairs usually reserved for company clerks. After about fifteen minutes of catching up, the President came to the point. "General Westmorland has just spent five hours explaining in great detail how this war is as good as won. How the Viet Cong and Ho Chi Minh are ready to throw in the towel if we just deploy another infantry division and expand our list of bombing targets into Laos. Colonel, I want your honest opinion, is that a prescription for victory?"

I did not hesitate in giving my honest answer. "No, sir," I replied. "You will need to send four more infantry divisions and expand your targets not only to Laos but Cambodia as well. I would also recommend sinking Soviet trawlers in the Gulf of Tonkien before they can off-load the estimated 2,000 tons of armaments and personal they are slipping into North Vietnam per month. You do that, and you will achieve victory - in five years."

The President nodded and thanked me for being honest; we shook hands and he got back on Air Force One and flew out of South Vietnam - the press was not allowed to report he was there until he left lest the Communists try to shoot the plane down. In his memoirs, John Kennedy stated that he came back from his visit to South Vietnam utterly convinced that an outright military victory would take too long and cost too many lives. He began making discreet inquiries through the Red Chinese embassy in Paris, recruited Henry Kissinger from Harvard to be a secret negotiator and opened one of his back channels to the North Vietnamese. It would be more than two years of on again and off again negotiations before a settlement was reached and the legacy of that agreement is a debacle - there is no South Vietnam today-but it got us out of that quagmire with our dignity intact.

I was in Iraq in the spring of '68, as part of Operation Jaguar - the covert war against Khomeini's Iran. At the time I was one of 5,000 active duty military personal and more 200 intelligence operatives deployed in the Persian Gulf to keep the Ayatollah boxed in. I ran into Al Haig there, it was a smaller world than I imagined. He was the one who passed on the bad news to me about Bobby and Dr. King just after I got back from a night time reconnaissance mission into Iranian territory; had to excuse myself and walk out into the desert for awhile, and as I watched the sunrise, my thoughts were elsewhere. I did wonder where Vance Harlow was right then; the man had become a ghost.

But there was little time to sort out the past; I had a busy few years ahead of me.

I was brought back to Washington briefly to work on Lyndon Johnson's NSC: I was there with LBJ when he met with Chairman Mao on a French warship anchored at Hong Kong in February of 1970. I am visible in the iconic photo of the two of them shaking hands on the deck, the tall Texan President towering over the short Chinese dictator. I helped wrap up the occupation of Cuba and was there as the last American troops pulled out and a popularly elected government took over - a goal we reached before the end of Johnson's first year in office. Do I feel bitter that the Cuban people freed Fidel Castro from prison as soon as they could? Not really, it was just their way of poking us Yankees in the eye after the occupation; in the end, Fidel got to go live in exile under Communist rule in Russia rather than ramming it down the throats of his countrymen. I was tapped to go to Saigon and plan the evacuation when the South went down the tubes. There have been some tough times in my life, but February 1972 was one of the worst as I had to make lists of those who were to be given preference for admittance to the United States while telling others they had to get in line with everyone else for a visa. I was not on the last helicopter out, but close to it.

During the September War in 1973, I helped oversee military aid to Israel after it was invaded by Egypt and Syria along with the airlifting of American troops into the Middle East when the Soviets sent a Red Army division to Egypt to stave off total defeat after the Israeli counterattack routed the Arabs. I was at the Pentagon when the first word came that Iran was exploiting the super-power confrontation by launching an invasion of Iraq; later I was in the Situation Room when President Humphrey made the call on the hot line to Andropov to diffuse the potential conflict in the Suez where American and Russian soldiers faced each other across the canal, fingers on their triggers. We owe the Ayatollah a debt of thanks for giving both sides a reason to pull back before it escalated into Armageddon, but at the time, all anyone remembers was the disruption to the flow of oil out of the Persian Gulf and the recession it caused.

Afterward, things got seriously screwed up for awhile in the wake of the "Secret War" revelations; I personally have no knowledge of who might have helped pass classified documents to Daniel Ellsberg or his subsequent murder. I do know that I was very lucky, a lot of good men were dragged before the Senate investigating committee and had their lives ruined after giving testimony that earned them jail time and bankruptcy.

The buildup to the invasion of Cuba came under great scrutiny with accusations that the evidence linking Castro to Dallas was faked; I testified as to my role in developing Operations Plan 365, and though the inquisitors on the Senate investigating committee came awfully close to the subject of my meetings with Marcello and Trafficante, I was never asked a question which would have forced me to take the 5th. During this same time,

I heard rumors that both CBS and the *New York Times* were looking into stories concerning a secret meeting between President Kennedy and a cabal of blackmailers during the 1964 campaign. Both news organizations supposedly spiked the story after being contacted by the former President himself, who offered evidence that debunked their "leads."

Nevertheless, I was on pins and needles for more than a year, fearing a headline which would have put me at the center of a scandal; a lot of guys believed Hubert Humphrey could have done a better job of invoking national security to contain the damage done to lives and reputations. I thought Ellsberg's leaks had already done enough injury, no use looking for another scapegoat, but for years afterward, if you wanted anybody to say something nasty at staff reunions, all you had to do was mention Humphrey's name.

I breathed a sigh of relief when Nixon beat Brown in '76, because whatever his faults, Richard Nixon had a real interest in keeping the lid on secrets like the Hotel Adolphus. Many people were curious as to why John F. Kennedy was so quick to offer advice and support to his bitterest political rival during Nixon's eight years in office; it was no mystery to me.

Some would say the general's star I earned after President Kennedy personally added my name to the promotion's list just before he left office was a payoff. And I don't care what some would say. I got my second star two months after Nixon was sworn in and a new job offer to be deputy director of the CIA; I accepted and after thirty years of active duty, exchanged my uniform for a suit and tie. I served under Director Vernon Walters during some challenging and rewarding times. These were the years of the thaw in relations with the Soviets when there finally was a summit in Stockholm between Nixon and Andropov, which came in the aftermath of the Polish uprising where the Soviet leader had ordered 50,000 Poles massacred in retaliation. It was Iran's continued aggression that forced the two super power rivals to work together; during the joint American-Soviet military actions in the Persian Gulf, I helped coordinate intelligence between Marshall Grechko and my old friend, General Haig. My long years of public service came to an end shortly after Nixon defeated Senator John Glenn and won a second term in 1980; thus I avoided the scandals of Nixon's second four years. President-elect Dole tried to lure me back with an offer of the director's job at the Agency in 1984, but once retired, I made a vow to stay retired, and I kept it.

After he left office, I saw former President Kennedy about twice a year, usually when he'd stop in Washington on his way from Hyannis Port down to Palm Beach and get together with people from his administration for drinks and cigars. The talk would seldom be about the past; President Kennedy was always focused on the now and what lay ahead in the future. He never spoke of his brother and what might have been. During the Johnson years, he never said anything disparaging about his successor despite what I'd heard about how the last thing he wanted was for LBJ to succeed him; I think the long shadow of the Adolphus had something to do with it. He was less kind toward Humphrey, saying at one point, "Hubert was perfectly happy to sit on his Goddamn ass and let South Vietnam go down the fucking toilet, all of it could have been avoided if he'd just sent the bombers back in to stop the North before they got rolling." Kenny O'Donnell later told me he wouldn't have been surprised if the former President hadn't marked Reagan's name in 1972.

During the investigations of the mid 70's, former President Kennedy let it be known that if anyone who had served in his administration were having trouble finding a lawyer or paying legal expenses, he would cover them. His legacy took a real hit in the wake of the Ellsberg revelations, it seemed like all at once, all the skeletons of the 1960's came tumbling out of the closet, including some unsavory stories of extra marital affairs as some of his many women began to talk. *Newsweek* ran a cover with the image of an old Kennedy campaign poster now splattered with mud and grime. A lot of those who had been critical of the invasion of Cuba, the firebombing of North Korea or the escalation in Vietnam came out of the woodwork to even old scores and slander reputations. At one point it got so bad that the former President was actually booed and called a war criminal during an appearance at Princeton, while some other so-called institutions of higher learning canceled their invitations for him to come and speak altogether. I'd contrast the way the former President was treated with the way the faculty at Berkeley practically fell at the feet of Che Guevara when he spoke there a few months later while on his book tour of the United States. If any of this bothered John Kennedy, he never let it show.

At some point, Mrs. Kennedy stopped accompanying him on his trips, by 1980, she and the two boys were living full time in New York while the former President spent the bulk of his time in Florida, and not without female company. There was never an actual separation, nothing on paper or an announcement and all comments were left to the tabloids. I read all twelve books John Kennedy wrote after leaving the White House, including his two-part memoirs, his authoritative history of the U.S. Navy in World War II, for which he won his second Pulitzer Prize, and those two spy novels. If the man had put his mind to it, he could have been another Ian Fleming.

I had a chance to get in on the ground floor when former President Kennedy put together a group of investors to buy up a half dozen failing daily newspapers, but passed on what I thought was a risky venture because I had kids to put through college at the time. Later, I could have kicked myself when even a thousand dollar original investment would have been worth ten times as much in return.

As the former President's health began to decline, our get-togethers became less frequent. His deteriorating back forced him to use crutches in private even before he left the White House; ten years later, a bad day would put him in a wheel-chair, although never in public where he always put his best foot forward. As the years went by, there was intestinal surgery for the removal of a malignant tumor, a severe bout with a respiratory infection, and an attack of angina which led to a diagnosis of coronary artery disease. It was tough for a man who had worked so hard as President to project an image of physical vigor.

He barely got through his speech at the 1988 Democratic Convention in Atlanta; the tape clearly shows his sons and a secret service agent hurrying over to help him off the stage. What no one saw was the oxygen he had to take as soon as they were backstage.

There was a big gathering of former Kennedy Administration officials in Palm Beach in the fall of 1991; there hadn't been such a reunion in nearly two years. When President Kennedy arrived it was obvious he'd lost some weight and was moving noticeably slower; his hair was snow white, and the lines around the eyes were deeper, for the first time, John F. Kennedy could actually be called elderly. But there was nothing wrong with his mind, there were lively discussions about the Soviet Union, which was in the process of brutally trying to keep its Eastern European Empire together, not to mention the ongoing problems in their Asian republics, where the spread of Islamic fundamentalism from Iran threatened to set off a civil war. "Well, if LeMay was here," I remember the former President saying, "he'd blame it all on me for not letting him bomb them back to the Stone Age in '64."

One other remark by President Kennedy stands out in my mind. After a lively take-down of the recent best-selling critical book, *False Promises, False Starts: A History of the Kennedy Years* by Paul Johnson, he said, "You know, if things had worked out a little differently in Dallas, who would they have had to blame for ruining the 1960's?" It was the only time I remember him directly referring to the events of November 22, 1963.

President Kennedy next made news in May of the following the year when he endorsed Arkansas Governor Bill Clinton for the Democratic Presidential nomination right before the critical California primary. It was no surprise JFK came out for Clinton; the Governor had served with the army in Cuba and in every speech, he made mention of his service there and his admiration for Kennedy. What was notable was that the endorsement came in the form of a written statement, read to the assembled press by his sons, John Jr. and Joseph Francis. A few weeks later, there was a brief story in the papers about his being admitted to Bethesda Naval Hospital suffering from "mild pneumonia."

John F. Kennedy died at 9:30 p.m. on the evening of July 4th, 1992 with his wife and children at his bedside. I was watching the fireworks on the Mall at my home in Virginia when the special report logo flashed across the screen followed by the announcement. I sat there for minutes on end, feeling as if I'd been slapped across the face, snapping out of it only when my wife handed me a cloth to wipe away the tears running down my face.

His flag-draped coffin lay in the Capitol Rotunda for two days while Americans lined up down Pennsylvania Avenue for a chance to file past and pay their respects, then there was a funeral mass and burial at Arlington, near where Bobby rested.

A week to the day later, the phone rang in my home office in Virginia and the voice on the other end greeted me with, "Hello, Colonel, sorry to be so damn long getting back to you." Despite the years, I recognized Vance Harlow's voice.

He wanted to see me in person right away and gave directions, along with a request to bring along a tape recorder and plenty of blank tapes. That is what brought me to a modest ranch style home in New Port Richie, Florida, the next day, having taken a cab from the Tampa airport; inside my duffle bag were the latest model Sony recorder and a dozen cassettes.

It was quite the modest home for a man who I suspected of pocketing some big bucks in his day. I was greeted at the door by a woman who might have been in her 50's at the most; she introduced herself as Helen and led me through the house to the backyard. "Vance could hardly sleep last night," she said, "he's so excited to see you." There were pictures of children and young adults displayed prominently on a table in the living room: first day at school, birthdays and sitting on Santa's knee, graduations; not unlike similar pictures back at my home in Virginia.

"It been too long, Colonel," said Harlow as he stood to greet me in the back yard, "and there's damn little time left." He'd been sitting at a picnic table under a shade tree and beckoned me to take the seat across from him. He was an elderly man now, far older than myself, his days of nimbly working in the shadows long in the past. Helen left us, saying she would bring back some ice tea.

He asked me about my family and how I was doing in retirement; the conversation turned to my time in Vietnam, and somehow we got onto what was the best movie made about that conflict; I fiercely defended my personal favorite, *Steel Rain*, the one which won Sam Peckinpah an Oscar. Then he asked me about President Kennedy and the last time I saw him.

"Bobby's gone and now Jack's at Arlington too," Harlow said when I was finished. "And they knew how to keep secrets; so did Powers and O'Donnell and the rest, always doing the dirty work and cleaning up messes out of a sense of fanatical loyalty to all things Kennedy. But there were jobs too dirty even for them. That's where I came in. Colonel, I got a story to tell if you'll sit here and listen, think you can do that for me?"

I knew anything Harlow would tell me would be a burden and that maybe I should just excuse myself and leave, but I stayed and if you ask me why, I would say out of a sense of duty. Helen brought us our glasses of ice tea and then excused herself. When she was back in the house, I produced the Sony recorder at Harlow's request and popped in a tape, then hit record. "Anytime you're ready," I told him.

"I made my living off my reputation," Harlow said, "and my reputation was that of a guy who could get things done - no matter what. I got such a rep through years of hard work, first at the Bureau and then on the Rackets Committee, where I first met both Kennedy brothers. I was the guy who could always locate a witness or get the necessary evidence to close a case and guarantee a conviction. Moreover, I was dependable and knew how to keep my mouth shut no matter what. When I went into business for myself in 1959, an awful lot of well-connected people lined up to pay me good money to use my skills on their behalf. If some of these people were criminals, no matter, their money was green, and it says something that they had no problem with my past in law enforcement, including a stint in as head of the FBI field office in Miami.

"My Miami connections brought me to the attention of Edward Lansdale, who was running Operation Mongoose in the early 60's; a man handpicked for the chore by JFK himself. Since I was not on the payroll of the CIA or part of the military, my name does not appear on any of the thousands of documents in the Mongoose file. This meant I was able to perform certain…what the Bureau called Black Bag Jobs, mainly having to do with the breaking and entering of the domiciles of members of the Free Cuba Committee who were suspected of having false loyalties and spying for Fidel. I was uncovered of a dozen double agents in 1961 alone. I was also hired by several anti-Castro groups in New Orleans, mainly to facilitate the purchase of guns to be smuggled into Cuba. Through this work, I met and won the confidence of a number of persons involved in the underground effort to oust Castro. Some were motivated by patriotism, some by less noble sentiments, both equally useful when it came to getting the job done.

"I'd impressed the Kennedy brothers while we worked together on the Rackets Committee in '57 and they hired me in '60 to discover if the Nixon people had any knowledge of certain indiscretions, which if revealed, would prove mighty embarrassing to Jack; I put their fears to rest after successfully infiltrating the Nixon inner circle. This cemented my working relationship with the White House after the election; they always had some small chore for me to take care of for them. It was during a November 1962 meeting with the Attorney General that the opportunity of a lifetime fell into my lap. I was giving Bobby evidence I'd uncovered proving there was an informant for the Chicago Outfit in the Federal Prosecutor's office in Springfield, and somehow our conversation turned to the just concluded Missile Crisis. I had congratulated Bobby on successfully making the Reds back down, but quickly learned neither he nor his brother saw it that way; both of them were furious at how Castro had wriggled off the hook yet again and to make matters worse, had been forced to swallow the poison pill of agreeing not to invade Cuba in the future as part of the settlement with the Russians. They'd thrown everything at him, and somehow Castro was still down there in Havana, thumbing his nose; Jack and Bobby really took it personally, they did not like to lose and their hate for that bearded bastard knew no bounds. But they were now stuck with a bad deal to keep their hands off lest it destroy any chance to improve relations with the Soviets and ease Cold War tensions.

"The words were out of my mouth almost before the thought was formed in my head: what if, I asked Bobby Kennedy, Castro would be foolhardy enough to try and assassinate the President - an act of war on American soil? It would be the 20th Century equivalent of the sinking of the Maine, a complete and utter provocation which renders null and void all previous agreements to leave that Commie son of a bitch alone. Think about it, I told Bobby, the end of Castro and the restoration of democracy in Cuba before November of 1964. That was the proposal I put on the table before him, all I would need was a hundred thousand dollars plus expenses, a free hand and no questions asked.

"Bobby didn't bat an eye, he took my proposal straight to his brother, and he got back to me a few hours later. They would go for it, Bobby told me, but on one condition of their own: he reserved the right to pull the plug on this 'act of war' at any time, including right up the last moment. I readily agreed, and the deal was sealed, the Kennedys loved doing things outside the box, and this was just about a far out of the box as you could get.

"To pull it off would really require the threading of a needle, but I never doubted it could be done. I hit the ground running the next day, putting together an intricate conspiracy from scratch with only myself being able to view all the moving parts in their entirety. I started with the Mafia, who were getting a lot of grief from the Kennedy Justice Department and had a lot to gain or lose, depending. I sat down with Marcello and Trafficante convinced them to go along because I was on a first name basis with the Attorney General who was trying to put them in Federal prison. I hand it to old Carlos, he was a tougher sell than Bobby, but in the end, the old son of a bitch had too much to lose by not pitching in, and too much to gain by not going along. Through Marcello, I was able to recruit, Bannister, Ferrie, Sergio Aracha Smith, among others, all men I already knew and who could be counted on to do what they were told and keep quiet. They were real patriots and men who hated Castro with a passion; some, like Bannister, were no fans of John Kennedy, but still thought what we were doing was for the good of the country.

"My plan was to con the Directorate of Cuban Intelligence into paying for a hit on the President, no easy task since they had thoroughly infiltrated the anti-Castro forces in the United States and Central America and knew all about Operation Mongoose and the plots to kill Castro. We did it through third parties in Mexico City, where I had Sergio Smith pose as a double agent and meet with a trusted associate of Manuel Piniero, the head of the Directorate, and got the Cubans to agree to put out a contract on JFK, with the killing blamed on disgruntled anti-Castro Cuban exiles. The killer would receive sanctuary in Cuba once the deed was done. None of this would have come about if Castro himself had not signed off on it. I made it easy for him by making it appear as if there was enough space between his government and the shooter without guilt falling on Havana, especially if the assassin ended up on the bottom of the Gulf long before he reached the sunny beaches of the island. Anyway, a solid Cuban connection had been achieved.

"I found my trigger man through George de Mohrenschildt, a Russian immigrant who'd done well in the Texas oil industry, who, because of his connections to the Russian community, was a secret asset to both the Bureau and the CIA. I brought him aboard because he was an ardent anti-Communist and detested Castro and he gave me Lee Harvey Oswald, a Goddamn nut with the heart of a true Marine. De Mohrenschildt's wife had befriended Marina, the woman he'd married in the Soviet Union during his supposed defection, and that was how he became friendly with Lee, whom he grew to suspect at having taken a shot at General Edwin Walker in April of '63. When I found out this guy had Communist sympathies and had no problems shooting a man from ambush, I knew he was a keeper.

"Oswald was convinced he was capable of great things and when the opportunity to strike down a great and powerful leader was presented to him, he could not refuse. We persuaded the son of a bitch we were working with Cuban Intelligence; determined to take out Kennedy in an act of self-defense against an American leader hell bent on overthrowing Castro and invading the island. Oswald was the willing participant in a con, completely unaware he was the mark. The biggest risk came when Oswald journeyed to Mexico City to meet with Piniero himself before the Cubans would sign off on the contract to kill Kennedy. It says something that they enthusiastically approved of the plan after meeting with Oswald, and promised that transport to Cuba would be ready and waiting on the day Kennedy bit the dust.

"When Kennedy, Johnson, and Governor Connally decided in early June on a Presidential visit to Texas in the fall, I knew before anyone else; same for the itinerary, which included the when and the where of the President's visit. This gave me plenty of time to get Oswald in place with a job at the Texas School Book Depository in Dealy Plaza, right along the route of the Presidential motorcade.

"Although he did not want to know any of the details in advance, I talked to the Attorney General on a regular basis; he was always emphatic that it needed to be something dramatic, something which would grab the headlines and the public's attention. Both Jack and Bobby were of one mind on this point, they understood, and there was no disagreement. They knew it would happen when the President went to Texas, but nothing more.

"But there was one side deal I made that the Kennedy brothers knew nothing about, it was with Marcello and Trafficante. They were willing to cooperate with me with the full expectation that their present and future problems with the Justice Department would go away, but just in case the Kennedy's pulled the plug on this scheme at the last moment and left them empty handed, Carlos and Santos wanted the trigger pulled anyway, only this would not be an attempt on the President's life - Marcello made it clear the round would go right through Jack Kennedy's head. As he put it, 'If the snake don't want to work with me, then I'll damn well cut its head off and make that Bobby just another lawyer. One way or another, the stone is removed from my shoe.' I didn't think twice before agreeing to go along, but with one stipulation: if it came down to an actual assassination, I wanted the hundred thousand Bobby would have paid me, plus another fifty grand for the extra trouble. Marcello and Trafficante hemmed and hawed, but in the end, agreed to my terms.

"Oswald was the perfect patsy, happily doing whatever was asked of him, including mail ordering a Manlicher-Cararno Italian Army rifle from Kline's in Chicago, one of the few methods available in 1963 which would guarantee a paper trail for investigators to link the gun right to him. I usually dealt with Oswald in the same manner as I had with informants in the FBI and on the Rackets Committee: we would meet late at night, usually in a car parked around the corner to make sure there were no accidental witnesses to our meetings. The man thoroughly knew his mission: to kill the President from ambush, make his escape from Dallas with the help of his fellow conspirators and travel south to Mexico, where active agents of Cuban Intelligence would get him to the island, where he would be treated like a true hero and live comfortably for the rest of his life. His wife and child would join him shortly thereafter; that was the one thing he was adamant about: Marina would know nothing of this business ahead of the assassination and that she and the kids would be with him when all was said and done and he had gotten away to his new life. I guess I should feel bad about that, but the man was a cold blooded killer, willing to make Mrs. Kennedy a widow and leave his children to grow up without a father. So in the end, screw him.

"And in the end, it all went like clockwork; it still amazes me considering everything that could have gone wrong. Air Force One touched down at Love Field at 11:30 a.m. local time on the morning of November 22nd, 1963, the exact time I placed a call to Bobby Kennedy's home in McLean, Virginia, so he could give me a yea or nay on the whole thing. After giving him a brief and succinct account of what was about to happen in Dallas, the Attorney General asked if I could give him a one hundred percent guarantee that his brother, the First Lady or no other innocent person would get hurt. I told him I could lie and give him the guarantee he was asking for, or tell him the truth, that there is always a risk, and how in the end, it comes down to just how badly you want the reward. After a moment of silence on Bobby's end, he told me, 'Just do it, but Goddamn it, Jack and Jackie had better be okay, they'd better be okay.' I don't think he truly got what was about to happen until right then.

"By the time I got off the phone to the Attorney General, the Presidential motorcade was underway in Dallas, traveling up Main Street at a slow enough speed that it would take 45 minutes to reach its destination, the Trade Mart. Dealy Plaza was at the far end of the route, only 5 minutes from the Trade Mart, giving us plenty of time to pull it off. It was simple enough, as soon as I hung up from my call to Bobby, I placed another call to David Ferrie, who was monitoring the progress of the motorcade and gave him the go ahead. When the President's limo was approximately 12 minutes from Dealy Plaza, Ferrie made a call to an office in an empty warehouse in New Orleans, which was answered by Guy Bannister. He was the one who made the calls to the police, the Texas Rangers, the FBI, and the *Dallas Morning News* alerting them all to the presence of a sniper on the 6th floor of Texas School Book Depository, who at the same moment was planning to shoot President Kennedy with a high-powered rifle as he passed by. I figured it would take the police and the Bureau guys 5 minutes to scramble and get the word to the Secret Service. They did it with seconds to spare; Oswald shot out the tail light of the limo instead of blowing off the back of Jack Kennedy's head off."

At this point I stopped Harlow and asked what to me were a few obvious questions, such as what would have happened if something, say along the line of an overly enthusiastic supporter of the President's rushing into the street just before it made the turn into Dealy Plaza, throwing the motorcade off schedule and allowing the police and secret service to get to Oswald before he could get off a shot.

Harlow shook his head with amusement at my question. "The mere fact we had a shooter on the scene, a shooter with connections to Cuban Intelligence would be an "act of war" in and of itself. Jack and Bobby could have made do with just that, but a bullet fired at the President and a smoking gun were the icing on the cake. But I knew my man Oswald would get the shot no matter what, just as I knew that if he were to be cornered in the School Book Depository with gun in hand, he'd never be taken alive. Of course, I had a contingency plan, there was a Mafia hitman with a high-powered rifle of his own across the street, hidden by a railroad yard fence and could have been signaled to take out Oswald just as he was sighting on the President. It would have been messy and would have required the concocting of a whole new story to cover up the truth, but it could have been done. But even if Oswald had been captured, there was a plan in place to silence him in police custody.

"In the end, it all went off flawlessly, the President's life was saved by a matter of seconds, and Oswald was riddled with bullets at the scene, and the investigations were off and running, following a carefully laid trail back to Havana. That is where you came in Colonel, carefully connecting the dots to Castro way ahead of anyone else on the NSC and putting a big feather in your own hat. The three suspected Cuban operatives - Vargas, Hernandez, and Lopez - really were that, hired by Piniero to pick up Oswald at the bus station, but their mere presence in Dallas was enough to point the finger in the right direction. The "smoking gun" evidence was planted at the bus terminal by Ferrie and Smith and discovered at the right time to close the case in the court of public opinion, allowing the White House to take the ball and run with it all the way to the first bomb falling on Havana.

"Of course my job was not finished by a long shot; I had a good thing going, and cash was still to be made. Plus somebody had to take care of all the loose threads and make sure none of them got pulled. This meant paying Ferrie, Bannister, Smith, and De Mohrenschildt, among others, for a job well done; there was Jack Ruby, the owner of the strip club where a lot of the planning was done with Oswald in attendance. All of them well compensated. The only one I had trouble with was Clay Shaw, who helped tie Oswald to the Fair Play for Cuba Committee; Clay thought he should have been paid better for his small contribution. A word in the right ear took care of Mr. Shaw - no one likes a malcontent.

"Then there was Marcello and Trafficante, with an invasion of Cuba now certain, they were more than willing to be helpful for a price - something I don't have to explain to you, Colonel. You better believe I made some good coin setting up that deal. I also had a vested interest in making sure John F. Kennedy got his second term he wanted so badly; it wouldn't do to have Barry Goldwater's Attorney General drag us all in front of a grand jury in order to discredit the previous Democratic Administration. It was most fortuitous when Wade Harbinson called me with his scheme to dig up dirt on JFK, if I hadn't handled it, he might have been the first President to resign before he was impeached. I made good money off of Harbinson to lure the skeletons out of the closet, and even better money to waltz them right into Kennedy's hands at the Hotel Adolphus.

"Everyone walked away a winner, that was the genius of John F. Kennedy; Harbinson had millions in government contracts steered his way; H.L. Hunt made hundreds of millions off of dubious mergers which somehow got SEC approval; Jimmy Hoffa never again had to worry about going to jail while a Kennedy was in the White House. He got to go on being President of the Teamsters until 1980; that bomb wired to the ignition of his Cadillac blew pieces of Hoffa all over a Detroit street, so maybe things didn't work out all that great for him. But they certainly did for LBJ and Nixon, who both went on to be President and Dr. Max Jocobsen's problems with the New York State Board of Regents all went away before they could revoke his medical license. Murray Chotiner was elected to the House from a district in California two years later after an incumbent Democrat unexpectedly decided not to run for re-election. Your name, Colonel, got added to the promotions list at the President's insistence, so I really should be calling you, General.

"You know, John Kennedy had a reputation for being for pushy and aggressive, for going for victory at all costs, but not in 1964; he was smart enough to know that being magnanimous would get him more. LBJ blackmailed his way into staying on the Democratic ticket because a recording of Ellen Rometsch fell into his hands thanks to Bentley Braden's addle-brained attempt to derail the passage of the Civil Rights Act. Bentley got to spend the next 20 years penning a thrice-weekly column denouncing liberals who were determined to punish the deserving rich by confiscating their money and giving it to lazy people with dark skin, while extolling the virtues of the Confederacy. He wouldn't have had such success if calls hadn't been made to some of Jack's friends in the newspaper business. That was John Kennedy's doing all the way, making sure everyone got something for their trouble and had something to lose if they talked.

"Not everyone was happy, though, not Bobby Kennedy, and because Bobby wasn't happy, ultimately Carlos Marcello got real pissed off. The President's brother didn't like what went down at the Adolphus because he didn't like being in debt to people he felt were morally beneath him and his brother. That sounds strange considering some of the shit he and Jack got away with, but it's how he saw things, and there was no arguing with him. During the invasion and the fighting afterward, Marcello and Trafficante's valuable hotels and casinos sustained considerable damage when they were suspected of harboring Castro's high command. That particular intelligence came right from Bobby, all it took was a call to Joe Califano at the Pentagon, and he took it from there. It was pure spite on Bobby's part, Marcello and the others got their property back as part of the deal to help with the invasion, only not in the same shape as when Castro stole them; fortunes of war, anyone would say, just bad luck for the Mafia. But dignity and respect meant a lot to an old son of a bitch like Carlos, not to mention honoring a deal, and violators were not forgotten - ever."

This prompted me to ask the obvious questions about Memphis and April of 1968.

"My association with the Kennedy brothers was a thing of the past by then," Harlow replied. "I quit right after the Adolphus, which pretty much guaranteed Kennedy a second term, pocketing all the money the Kennedy's owed me and walked away while there was still a door to go through. You can't do what I'd been doing and not eventually get a bullet in the back because somebody decides they can't take the risk that you might talk down the road. Look at it: assassinations, faking evidence, brokering deals with Mafia kingpins, swindling Texas oil millionaires; I was lucky to still be alive as it was, it was time to get while the getting was good. I had more than enough money to be set for life, and I had another good reason. I'd married Helen two years before, she'd been my secretary ever since I'd gone into business for myself, and she was pregnant with the first of our four children in the fall of '64. You can't be in this kind of business and have a family, for me it was no choice. So I put everything in her name, bought a nice house here in Florida, got a job as a private investigator for a big law firm and settled into the good life as a middle-aged suburban husband and father, doing 4th of July barbecues, Little League, and all the rest. It has been a nice life, and I don't miss the old one.

But as for Memphis in '68, I put that squarely on Marcello; Bobby never did give him the pardon as per the deal you arranged, that was just Bobby being stubborn, so Carlos felt he was due some payback because he'd come through on his end and the Kennedys hadn't on theirs. And more to the point, he and his fellow bosses had survived eight years under JFK, they weren't about to risk another eight under a treacherous RFK; so they paid a pair of shooters to nip the problem in the bud. They probably used the same guy I had for backup in Dallas. As for King, there'd been a fifty thousand dollar contract on his head for years, put up by some Georgia businessmen who thought segregation was God's will. J.B. Stoner was their contact man, and I figure Marcello took him up on it and killed two birds with one stone. Bobby and King were dead before they hit the pavement in Memphis and two fall guys were dead a day later when they were cornered by the police. There was a nice trail of evidence linking them to white supremacist groups, which leads me to believe somebody was following my playbook. It was just plain hubris that led Bobby to try and succeed his brother, convinced he had to finish Jack's work, along with the fact that Bobby couldn't stand the thought of LBJ succeeding JFK.

It had taken Vance Harlow more than an hour to tell his story, and it was more than I could process at the moment, too many names, dates and allegations to keep straight. But one detail did stick in my mind during the telling, one little thing he'd left out, either intentionally or by simply forgetting. "Where were you on November 22nd, 1963?" I asked.

"Where were you when you called Robert Kennedy at his home in Virginia? Those calls can be traced pretty easily, and I don't believe you would make that kind of mistake, so you'd have to use a safe phone, one which couldn't be found just anywhere."

Harlow smiled and nodded. "That's why you are such a success, Colonel. You see what others don't; you hear what others miss. On the morning in question, I was inside the Dallas, Texas, field office of the FBI, sitting at a desk in a small side office all to myself, with a phone at my disposal. Why was an ex-agent long gone from active service afforded such privileges? Because Cartha DeLoach had called the agent in charge and told him to give me whatever I asked for within reason. Why would the deputy director of the FBI make such a call? Because for 30 years, J. Edgar Hoover had vacationed annually in Florida, where he regularly indulged his passion for betting on the horses and won not a small sum of money. This was a problem since the track he frequented was secretly owned by a Mafia front, and most of the races were fixed, something which would have been mighty embarrassing to the Director if had become public knowledge. There was a reason why Hoover never went after organized crime and that's because the Mafia had the goods on him. I was able to get my hands on a transcript from a wiretap of Santos Trafficante telling Johnny Rosselli he doesn't have a thing to worry about from the FBI because they have proof Hoover won over ten grand on fixed races. The original recording was destroyed on J. Edgar's orders, but not before I transcribed it. No door in the Bureau was closed to me, but I do want to apologize for something you never knew Colonel, for months after the get together at the Adolphus, you were kept under surveillance by some of Hoover's best. I needed to know who among those there that night might be talk and the Director was happy to oblige after I told him all about what happened Hotel Adolphus, the man did love a secret so, and he needed all the leverage possible if and when Kennedy attempted to force him to retire. I couldn't have that. I was happy to learn that not a one of you let slip a single word of what went on, not the lawyer who worked for LBJ, the kid who couriered the money down from Washington, not the blonde chick who came with Harbinson, and most certainly not you, Colonel. You all knew you had a good thing going, although I had a worrisome moment when the kid who brought the money went out to California after the election to visit the blonde. I was worried they might be in cahoots in some scheme to shake down some of the involved parties, especially when she spent the night in his hotel room after their second date. But it turns out they were just crazy in love, a happy ending for one and all.

"What is really amazing is how everyone kept their mouths shut all these years, especially back in the 70's when everything else that went on in the shadows during the Kennedy years was being investigated. And if you ask me who killed Daniel Ellsberg for leaking all the secrets, I would give you a list of fifty names and say 'pick one.' My name was on one list to be subpoenaed, but no one knew where to find me, and I still had more than a few friends in high places to protect me. Not that I would have told them a damn thing anyway; when Nixon came in, the lid got screwed back on tight, he had as much to lose as anyone if his fellow Republicans ever found out how he'd screwed over Goldwater when their man was literally a scandal away from the White House. Then again, Jack Kennedy was ten times the politician Goldwater was, so you can say he never really had a chance. Anyway, it's all done now."

Harlow's tale left me at a loss for words at the audacity of its revelations and implications…almost. I asked him why; why the deceiving, the lying and the double crossing?

"It's simple," he answered, "for the money. It's why anyone does anything. Look, I was the best there ever was at doing dirty work - nobody before or since has ever been able to touch me when it comes to doing the kind of shit work men in tailor-made suits who sit in high offices behind cherry wood desks need to have done but don't have the guts to do themselves. And I had the right to be well paid for doing it. I liked Jack and Bobby Kennedy, actually think they did some good things for the country, some things which needed to get done as opposed to Goldwater and my old boss, J. Edgar, who would have taken the country back to the 1890's if they'd had their way. But that doesn't mean I wouldn't have let Oswald put a bullet through Jack's head in Dallas if it had meant more money in my pocket. My father spent a lifetime walking behind a mule's ass in Oklahoma, three of my children graduated college with degrees in law and engineering, while the fourth one joined your blessed Marine Corp and was just promoted to Captain last year. I look at them and have not one damn regret for anything I've done to make their lives better."

The afternoon was growing long while the day was getting short, but I had one more question.

"Why talk now, and why tell me?"

"Because they're all gone," he answered. "Most of them or the ones who would be hurt the most, like Jack and Bobby, if what I know became public. And I'll be joining them soon enough, got some bad news back in the winter - happens to all of us if we live long enough. So I came to a decision that somebody needed to be told, somebody who would understand and who I trusted; there weren't many who fit both bills but you, Colonel. I'm approaching the end of my days, and have come to doubt the wisdom of taking my secrets to the grave; it's the kind of thing only a dying man thinks about. I apologize if this is a burden, Colonel, I truly do, but I've got no doubt you can handle it. You can stop recording now, I've said it all."

We were done.

The two of us chatted for a little while longer, catching up on some mutual acquaintances from back in the day, the few still with us. He mentioned Carlos Marcello had recently suffered a stroke and was forced to give up being the big boss in New Orleans at long last. After awhile, Mrs. Harlow came out and asked if I'd stay for dinner, I politely declined and packed away the tapes, saying it was time for me to leave. Vance Harlow walked with me to the waiting cab when it arrived and shook my hand before I got in. "I trust you, Colonel," he said before shutting the door. "Always did." They were the last words he spoke to me, four months later Harlow was dead, leaving me with the burden of his story.

I put the tapes in a safety deposit box and tried to forget about them without much success. At times I tried to convince myself they might be the fantasy of an aged mind in a dying body. At one point, I tried to track down Harlow's co-conspirators to try and get some corroboration. I discovered Ferrie and Bannister had not survived the 60's, but learned that George de Mohrenschildt was in an assisted living facility in Houston, sadly, when I visited him in the spring of 1993, he could no longer remember what he had for breakfast much less if he'd known a man named Vance Harlow thirty years before. I even made a discreet inquiry at the guarded New Orleans mansion where Carlos Marcello had lived for decades, giving the man who answered the door my name and telling them I was an old associate of Mr. Marcello's whom he hadn't seen in many, many years. I made a point to drop a few names, but it got me nowhere, I was told Mr. Marcello no longer received visitors.

So I gave up on finding any validation for Harlow's claims. Then in July and August of 1994 came the 38-day conflict which became known as the Third World War, when an uprising against an aging Communist autocracy in East Germany escalated into an attack by the Warsaw Pact on West Germany, which prompted a response by NATO. The subsequent breakup of the Soviet Union and the collapse of the Communist empire in the wake of a limited nuclear exchange brought immediate comparisons to how Kennedy handled the crisis of 1964, when he kept a super-power confrontation from going from bad to worse to the point where Leeds, England and Kazan, Russia were reduced to flaming ruins by a pair of 20 megaton warheads. After that, it did not feel right to sully the legacy of a President being hailed as a visionary leader right when it appeared history was giving him a full vindication.

To be honest, I let those tapes sit so long because I didn't know how I truly felt about their revelations. The 1964 invasion of Cuba has never stopped being controversial, on the far left, it has continually been denounced as an act of criminal aggression; it's the reason why many liberals running for office will not mention the name of John F. Kennedy to this very day. It's also the reason why he is now venerated by the heirs of Goldwater on the right; to them, he is the liberator of Cuba, the President who stood firm for eight years against Stalin's heirs in the Kremlin. I've read *Kennedy's Crimes* by Howard Zinn, which excoriates the President for his imperialistic foreign policy, and *Man on the Wall* by Pat Buchanan, who credits JFK with winning the Cold War. In neither book does the President John F. Kennedy I knew appear, not the shrewd politician or the cautious commander in chief. In both books, the events of November 22nd, 1963 are merely a footnote.

I went back to Havana earlier this year; I saw the statue of JFK in the harbor and walked down the avenue named for him. It was a testament to his popularity with a majority of the Cuban people that when Raul Castro came back after years in exile in Africa and was elected President of Cuba in a democratic election, he made no attempt to remove the statue or change the name honoring the man who destroyed his brother's revolution. It says something about the way things worked out that while Castro was President, the largest Wal-Mart outside of the United States opened in Havana.

I finally came to a decision on what to do with the tapes on the day I got back from Cuba. I would tell the story of the Kennedy years exactly as I experienced them and how I came to understand it all in later years. Did the Kennedy brothers conspire and then fake an assassination attempt to create a justification for starting a war? There are only the words of a dying man saying so much was true. So, I'll tell the story in the same manner I came to it; and I'll trust we'll be a mature enough people to decide what is true and what really matters.

Both Kennedy brothers are buried at Arlington Cemetery, not far from the tomb of the Unknown Soldier. That they were warriors, there can be no doubt, but the cause for which they battled the fiercest, either for the nation they swore an oath to protect or their own naked political ambitions, is the question.

As for the answer, I will leave that up to others.

The End

About the Author

F.C. Schaefer is an avid reader who put down the book he was reading one day and picked up a pen and paper to try his hand at writing one and found he liked doing it. He is the indie author of BEATING PLOWSHARES INTO SWORDS: AN ALTERNATE HISTORY OF THE VIETNAM WAR along with the horror novels CADEN IS COMING and BIG CRIMSON.

Made in the USA
Lexington, KY
02 February 2018